Praise for *The Heart of the Hunter*

"Out of post-apartheid South Africa comes a thriller good enough to nip at the heels of Le Carré . . . Wonderful setting, rich, colorful cast, headed by a valiant/vulnerable protagonist . . . Fans of the genre won't want to miss Meyer's U.S. debut."
—*Kirkus Reviews* (starred review)

"An exciting and oddly hopeful look into what feels, smells, and sounds very much like life in today's South Africa . . . *Heart of the Hunter* is the dark, explosive side of Alexander McCall Smith's Botswana books, as full of love for the vast beauty of the country but also riddled by the anger of South Africa's recent racial and political struggles."
—*Chicago Tribune*

"Brilliant . . . Meyer uses political intrigue as the fuel for a fast-paced crime thriller."—*The Times-Picayune*

"If you haven't read Deon Meyer you need to start—now! Deon Meyer is someone who deserves a greater audience."
—George Easter, *Deadly Pleasures*

Heart

OF THE

Hunter

A NOVEL

Deon Meyer

Translated by K. L. Seegers

Grove Press
New York

Originally published in English in 2003 by Hodder Headline
and in Afrikaans in South Africa in 2002.

Printed in the United States of America

ISBN: 978-0-8021-4578-9

Grove Press
an imprint of Grove/Atlantic, Inc.
841 Broadway
New York, NY 10003

Distributed by Publishers Group West

www.groveatlantic.com

12 13 14 15 16   10 9 8 7 6 5 4 3 2 1

FOR ANITA

1984

He stood behind the American. Almost pressed against him by the crush of Le Metro. His soul was far away at a place on the Transkei coast where giant waves broke in thunder.

He thought of the rocky point where he could sit and watch the swells approaching in lines over the Indian Ocean, in awe at their journey over the long, lonely distance to hurl and break themselves against the rocks of the Dark Continent.

Between the sets of waves there is a time of perfect silence, seconds of absolute calm. So quiet he can hear the voices of his ancestors—Phalo and Rharhabe, Nquika and Maqoma, the great Xhosa chiefs, his bloodline, source, and refuge. He knew that is where he would go when his time came, when he felt the long blade and the life run out of him. He would return to those moments between the explosions of sound.

He came back to himself slowly, almost carefully. He saw they were only minutes from the St. Michel Metro station. He leaned down, only half a head, to the ear of the American. His lips were close like a lover.

"Do you know where you are going when you die?" he asked in a voice as deep as a cello, the English heavy with an accent of Africa.

The tendons in the back of the enemy's neck pulled taut, big shoulders tilted forward.

He waited calmly for the man to turn in the overfilled crush of the train. He waited to see the eyes. This is the moment he thirsted for. Confrontation, throwing down the gauntlet. This was his calling, instinctive, fulfilling him. He was a warrior from the plains of Africa, every sinew and muscle knit and woven for this moment. His heart began to race, the sap of war coursed through his blood, he was possessed by the divine madness of battle.

The body turned first, unhurried, then the head, then the eyes. He saw a hawk there, a predator without fear, self-assured, amused even, the corners of the thin lips lifting. Centimeters apart, it was a strange intimacy.

"Do you know?"

Just the eyes staring back.

"Because soon you will be there, Dorffling." He used the name contemptuously, the final declaration of war that said he knew his enemy, the assignment accepted, the dossier studied and committed to memory.

He saw no reaction in the lazy eyes. The train slowed and stopped at St. Michel. "This is our station," he said. The American nodded and went, with him just a step behind, up the stairs into the summer night bustle of the Latin Quarter. Then Dorffling took off. Along the Boulevard San Michel toward the Sorbonne. He knew prey chooses familiar territory. Dorffling's den was there, just around the corner from the Place du Pantheon, his arsenal of blades and garottes and firearms. But he hadn't expected flight, thought the ego would be too big. His respect deepened for the ex-Marine, now CIA assassin.

His body had reacted instinctively: the dammed-up adrenaline exploding, long legs powering the big body forward rhythmically, ten, twelve strides behind the fugitive. Parisian heads turned. White man pursued by black man. An atavistic fear flared in their eyes.

The American spun off into the Rue des Écoles, right into the Rue St. Jacques, and now they were in the alleys of the university, barren in the August of student holidays, the age-old buildings somber onlookers, the night shadows deep. With long, sure strides he caught up with Dorffling, shouldered him. The American fell silently to the pavement, rolled forward, and stood up in one sinuous movement, ready.

He reached over his shoulder for the assegai in the scabbard that lay snug against his back. Short handle, long blade.

"Mayibuye," he said softly.

"What fucking language is that, nigger?" Hoarse voice without inflection.

"Xhosa," he said, the click of his tongue echoing sharply off the alley walls. Dorffling moved with confidence, a lifetime of practice in every shift of the feet. Watching, measuring, testing, round and round, the diminishing circles of a rhythmic death dance. Attack, immeasurably fast and before the knee could drive into his belly, his arm was around the American's neck and the long thin blade through the breastbone. He held him close against his own body as the light blue eyes stared into his.

"Uhm-sing-gelli," said the Marine.

"Umzingeli." He nodded, correcting the pronunciation softly, politely. With respect for the process, for the absence of pleading, for the quiet acceptance of death. He saw the life fade from the eyes, the heartbeat slowing, the breaths jerky, then still.

He lowered the body, felt the big, hard muscles of the back soften, laid him gently down.

"Where are you going? Do you know?"

He wiped the assegai on the man's T-shirt. Slid it slowly back into the scabbard.

Then he turned away.

MARCH

I.

Transcript of interview with Ismail Mohammed by
A. J. M. Williams, 17 March, 17:52, South African
Police Services offices, Gardens, Cape Town

w: You wanted to talk to someone from Intelligence?

m: Are you?

w: I am, Mr. Mohammed.

m: How do I know that?

w: You take my word for it.

m: That's not good enough.

w: What would be good enough for you, Mr.
   Mohammed?

m: Have you got identification?

w: You can check this out if you want to.

m: Department of Defence?

w: Mr. Mohammed, I represent the State Intelligence Service.

m: NIA?

w: No.

m: Secret Service?

w: No.

m: What then?

w: The one that matters.

m: Military Intelligence?

w: There seems to be some misunderstanding, Mr. Mohammed. The message I got was that you are in trouble and you want to improve your position by providing certain information. Is that correct?

[Inaudible]

w: Mr. Mohammed?

m: Yes?

w: Is that correct?

m: Yes.

w: You told the police you would give the information only to someone from the intelligence services?

m: Yes.

w: Well, this is your chance.

m: How do I know they are not listening to us?

w: According to the Criminal Procedures Act, the police must advise you before they may make a recording of an interview.

m: Ha!

w: Mr. Mohammed, do you have something to tell me?

m: I want immunity.

w: Oh?

m: And guaranteed confidentiality.

w: You don't want Pagad to know you've been talking?

M: I am not a member of Pagad.

W: Are you a member of Muslims Against Illegiti-mate Leaders?

M: Illegal Leaders.

W: Are you a member of MAIL?

M: I want immunity.

W: Are you a member of Qibla?

[Inaudible]

W: I can try to negotiate on your behalf, Mr. Mo-hammed, but there can be no guarantees. I un-derstand the case against you is airtight. If your information is worth anything, I can't promise you more than that I do my best. . . .

M: I want a guarantee.

W: Then we must say good-bye, Mr. Mohammed. Good luck in court.

M: Just give me—

W: I'm calling the detectives.

M: Wait . . .

W: Good-bye, Mr. Mohammed.

M: Inkululeko.

W: Sorry?

M: Inkululeko.

W: Inkululeko?

M: He exists.

W: I don't know what you're talking about.

M: Then why are you sitting down again?

OCTOBER

2.

A young man stuck his head out of a minibus taxi, wagging a mocking finger and laughing with wide white teeth at Thobela Mpayipheli.

He knew why. Often enough he had seen his reflection in the big shop windows—a great black man, tall and broad, on the tiny Honda Benly, the 200 cc ineffectively but bravely putt-putting under his weight. His knees almost touching the handlebars, long arms at sharp angles, the full-face crash helmet incongruously top-heavy.

Something of a spectacle. A caricature.

He was self-conscious those first weeks when to add to it all he had to learn to ride the thing. Going to work or home, every morning and afternoon in the rush-hour traffic of the N2, he was awkward and unsure. But once he learned the skills, learned to dodge the vans and 4x4s and buses, learned to slip between the gaps in the cars, learned to turn the pitiful horsepower to his advantage, the pointing mocking fingers ceased to trouble him.

And later he began to revel in it: while they sat trapped and frustrated in the gridlocked traffic, he and his Benly buzzed between them, down the long valleys that opened up between the rows of cars.

On the road, from Cape Town, east to Guguletu. And Miriam Nzululwazi.

And Pakamile, who would wait for him on the street corner, then run alongside the last thirty meters to the driveway. Silent, six-year-old solemnity on the wide-eyed face, serious like his mother, patiently waiting till Thobela took off the helmet and the tin work box, swept his big hand over the boy's head, and said, "Good afternoon, Pakamile." The child would overwhelm him with his smile and throw his arms around him, a magic moment in every day, and he would walk in to Miriam, who would be busy already with cooking or washing or cleaning. The tall, lean, strong, and beautiful woman would kiss him and ask about his day.

The child would wait patiently for him to finish talking and change his clothes. Then the magic words: "Let's go farm."

He and Pakamile would stroll down the yard to inspect and discuss the growth of the past twenty-four hours. The sweet corn that was making cobs, the runner beans ("Lazy housewife, what are you hinting at?" asked Miriam), the carrots, the squashes and butternuts and watermelons trailing along the beds. They would pull an experimental carrot. "Too small." Pakamile would rinse it off later to show his mother and then crunch the raw and glowing orange root. They would check for insects, study the leaves for fungus or disease. He would do the talking and Pakamile would nod seriously and absorb the knowledge with big eyes.

"The child is mad about you," she had said on more than one occasion.

He knew. And he was mad about the child. About her. About them.

But first he had to navigate the obstacle course of the rush hour, the kamikaze taxis, the pushy 4x4s, the buses belching diesel exhaust, the darting Audis of the yuppies switching lanes without checking their rearview mirrors, the wounded rusty *bakkies,* pickup trucks of the townships.

First to Pick 'n' Pay to buy the fungicide for the butternuts.

Then home.

The director smiled. Janina Mentz had never seen him without a smile.

"What kind of trouble?"

"Johnny Kleintjes, Mr. Director, but you need to hear this yourself." She placed the laptop on the director's desk.

"Sit, Janina." Still he smiled his hearty, charming smile, eyes soft as if gazing on a favorite child. *He is so small,* she thought, *small for a Zulu, small for such a great responsibility.* But impeccably dressed, the white shirt a shout in contrast to the dark skin, the dark gray suit an expression of good taste, somehow just right. When he sat like that, the hump, the small deformity of back and neck, could barely be seen. Mentz maneuvered the cursor on the screen to activate the replay.

"Johnny Kleintjes," said the director. "That old rogue."

He tapped on the computer keyboard. The sound came tinnily through the small speakers.

"Is this Monica?" Unaccented. Dark voice.

"Yes?"

"Johnny Kleintjes's daughter?"

"Yes."

"Then I need you to listen very carefully. Your daddy is in a bit of trouble."

"What kind of trouble?" Immediate worry.

"Let's just say he promised, but he couldn't deliver."

"Who are you?"

"That I am not going to tell you. But I do have a message for you. Are you listening?"

"Yes."

"It is very important that you get this right, Monica. Are you calm?"

"Yes."

Silence, for a moment. Mentz looked up at the director. His eyes were still soft, his body still relaxed behind the wide, tidy desk.

"Daddy says there is a hard drive in the safe in his study."

Silence.

"Are you getting this, Monica?"

"Yes."

"He says you know the combination?"

"Yes."

"Good."

"Where is my father?"

"He is here. With me. And if you don't work with us, we will kill him."

A catch of breath. *"I . . . please . . ."*

"Stay calm, Monica. If you stay calm, you can save him."

"Please . . . Who are you?"

"A businessman, Monica. Your daddy tried to trick me. Now you have to put things right."

The director shook his head ruefully. "Ai, Johnny," he said.

"You will kill him anyway."

"Not if you cooperate."

"How can I believe you?"

"Do you have a choice?"

"No."

"Good. We are making progress. Now go to the safe and get the drive."

"Please stay on the line."

"I'll be right here."

The hiss of the electronics. Some static interference on the line.

"When did this conversation take place, Janina?"

"An hour ago, Mr. Director."

"You were quick, Janina. That is good."

"Thank you, sir, but it was the surveillance team. They're on the ball."

"The call was to Monica's house?"

"Yes, sir."

"What data do you think they are referring to here, Janina?"

"Sir, there are many possibilities."

The director smiled sympathetically. There were wrinkles around his eyes, regular, dignified. "But we must assume the worst?"

"Yes, sir. We must assume the worst." She saw no panic. Only calmness.

"*I . . . I have the hard drive.*"

"*Wonderful. Now we have just one more problem, Monica.*"

"*What?*"

"*You are in Cape Town, and I am not.*"

"*I will bring it.*"

"*You will?*" A laugh, muffled.

"*Yes. Just tell me where.*"

"*I will, my dear, but I want you to know, I cannot wait forever.*"

"*I understand.*"

"*I don't think so. You have seventy-two hours, Monica. And it is a long way.*"

"*Where must I take it?*"

"*Are you very sure about this?*"

"Yes."

Another pause: long, drawn out.

"Meet me in the Republican Hotel, Monica. In the foyer. In seventy-two hours."

"The Republican Hotel?"

"In Lusaka, Monica. Lusaka in Zambia."

They could hear the indrawn breath.

"Have you got that?"

"Yes."

"Don't be late, Monica. And don't be stupid. He is not a young man, you know. Old men die easily."

The line went dead.

The director nodded. "That's not all." He knew.

"Yes, sir."

She tapped again. The sound of dialing. It rang.

"Yes?"

"Could I talk to Tiny?"

"Who's speaking?"

"Monica."

"Hold on." Muffled, as though someone were holding a hand over the receiver. *"One of Tiny's girl-friends looking for him."*

Then a new voice. *"Who's this?"*

"Monica."

"Tiny doesn't work here anymore. Nearly two years now."

"Where is he now?"

"Try Mother City Motorrad. In the city."

"Thank you."

"Tiny?" asked the director.

"Sir, we're working on that one. There's nothing on the priority list, sir. The number she phoned belongs to one Orlando Arendse. Also unknown. But we're following it up."

"There's more."

Mentz nodded. She set the program running again.

"Motorrad."

"Could I speak to Tiny, please?"

"Tiny?"

"Yes."

"I think you have the wrong number."

"Tiny Mpayipheli?"

"Oh. Thobela. He's gone home already."

"I need to get hold of him urgently."

"Hold on." Papers rustled, soft cursing.

"Here's a number. Just try it. 555-7970."

"Thank you so much." The line was already dead.

New call.

"Hullo."

"Could I speak to Tiny Mpayipheli, please?"

"Tiny?"

"Thobela?"

"He is not home yet."

"When do you expect him?"

"Who is calling?"

"My name is Monica Kleintjes. I . . . he knows my father."

"Thobela is usually home by a quarter to six."

"I must speak to him. It's very urgent. Can you give me your address? I must see him."

"We're in Guguletu. Twenty-one Govan Mbeki."

"Thank you."

"There is a team following her and we've dispatched another team to Guguletu, sir. The house belongs to a Mrs. Miriam Nzululwazi and I expect that was her on the phone. We will find out what her relationship with Mpayipheli is."

"Thobela Mpayipheli, also known as Tiny. And what are you going to do, Janina?"

"The tail reports that she is traveling in the direction of the airport. She could be on her way to Guguletu. As soon as we're sure, sir, we'll bring her in."

The director folded his delicate hands on the shiny desktop.

"I want you to hang back a bit."

"Yes, sir."

"Let's see how this unfolds."

She nodded.

"And I think you had better call Mazibuko."

"Sir?"

"Get the RU on a plane, Mentz. A fast one."

"But, sir . . . I've got this under control."

"I know. I have absolute confidence in you, but when you buy a Rolls-Royce, sometime or other you must take it for a test drive. See if it is worth all the expense."

"Sir, the Reaction Unit . . ."

He raised a small, fine-boned hand. "Even should they do nothing, I think Mazibuko needs to get out a bit. And you never know."

"Yes, sir."

"And we know where the data is going. The destination is known. This creates a safe test environment. A controllable environment."

"Yes, sir."

"They can be here in"—the director examined his stainless-steel watch—"a hundred and forty minutes."

"I'll do as you say, sir."

"And I assume the Ops Room will get up and running?"

"That was next on my agenda."

"You're in charge, Janina. And I want to be kept up-to-date, but I'm leaving it entirely in your hands."

"Thank you, sir." She was being put to the test. She and her team and Mazibuko and the RU. She had been waiting a long time for this.

3.

The boy was not waiting on the street corner, and unease crept over Thobela Mpayipheli. Then he saw the taxi in front of Miriam's house. Not a minibus, a sedan, a Toyota Cressida with the yellow light on the roof—PENINSULA TAXIS—hopelessly out of place there. He turned up the dirt driveway and dismounted, more a case of careful extraction of his limbs from the motorbike, loosened the ties that held his tin box and the packet with the fungicide on the seat behind him, rolled the cords carefully in his hand, and walked in. The front door was standing open.

Miriam rose from the armchair as he entered; he kissed her cheek, but there was tension in her. He saw the other woman in the small room, still seated.

"Miss Kleintjes is here to see you," said Miriam.

He put down his parcel, turned to her, put out his hand. "Monica Kleintjes," she said.

"Pleased to meet you." He could wait no longer, looked to Miriam. "Where is Pakamile?"

"In his room. I told him to wait there."

"I'm sorry," said Monica Kleintjes.

"What can I do for you?" He looked at her, slightly plump in her loose, expensive clothes: blouse, skirt, stockings, and low-heeled shoes. He struggled to keep the irritation out of his voice.

"I am Johnny Kleintjes's daughter. I need to talk to you privately."

His heart sank. *Johnny Kleintjes.* After all these years.

Miriam's back straightened. "I will be in the kitchen."

"No," he said. "I have no secrets from Miriam." But she walked out anyway.

"I really am sorry," said Monica again.

"What does Johnny Kleintjes want?"

"He's in trouble."

"Johnny Kleintjes," he said mechanically as the memories returned. Johnny Kleintjes would choose him. It made sense.

"Please," she said.

He jerked back to the present. "First, I must say hello to Pakamile," he said. "Back in a minute."

He went through to the kitchen. Miriam stood by the stove, her eyes outside. He touched her shoulder but got no reaction. He walked down the short passage, pushed open the child's door. Pakamile lay on the little bed with a schoolbook, looked up. "Aren't we going to farm today?"

"Afternoon, Pakamile."

"Afternoon, Thobela."

"We will go farming today. After I have talked to our visitor."

The boy nodded solemnly.

"Have you had a nice day?"

"It was okay. At break we played soccer."

"Did you score a goal?"

"No. Only the big boys kick goals."

"But you are a big boy."

Pakamile just smiled.

"I'm going to talk to our guest. Then we'll go farm." He rubbed his hand over the boy's hair and went out, his unease now multiplying. Johnny Kleintjes—this meant trouble, and he had brought it to this house.

They strode in time across the parade ground of First Parachute Battalion, also known as the Parabats, or simply the Bats. Captain Tiger Mazibuko was one step ahead of Little Joe Moroka.

"Is it him?" asked Mazibuko, and pointed to the small group. Four Parabats sat in the shade under the wide umbrella of the thorn tree. A German shepherd lay at the feet of the stocky lieutenant, its tongue lolling, panting in the Bloemfontein heat. It was a big, confident animal.

"That's him, Captain."

Mazibuko nodded and picked up the pace. Red dust puffed up at each footfall. The Bats, three whites and one colored, were talking rugby, the lieutenant holding forth with authority. Mazibuko was there, stepped between them and kicked the dog hard on the side of the head with his steel-capped combat boot. It gave one yelp and staggered into the sergeant's legs.

"Fuck," said the Bat lieutenant, dumbfounded.

"Is this your dog?" asked Mazibuko. The faces of the soldiers expressed total disbelief.

"What the hell did you do that for?" A trickle of blood ran out of the dog's nose. It leaned dazedly against the sergeant's leg. Mazibuko lashed out again, this time in the side. The sound of breaking ribs was overlaid by the cries of all four Parabats.

"You fucker . . . ," screamed the lieutenant, and hit out, a wild swing that caught the back of Mazibuko's neck. He took one step back. He smiled.

"You are all my witnesses. The lieutenant hit first."

Then he moved in, free and easy, unhurried. A straight right to the face to draw attention upward. A kick surely and agonizingly to the kneecap. As the Parabat toppled forward, Mazibuko brought up his knee into the face. The white man flipped over backward, blood streaming from a broken nose.

Mazibuko stepped back, hands hanging relaxed at his sides. "This morning you messed with one of my men, Lieutenant." He jabbed his thumb over his shoulder at Little Joe Moroka. "You set your fucking little dog on him."

The man had a hand over his bloody nose, the other on the ground trying to prop himself up. Two Bats came closer, the sergeant kneeling by the dog, which lay still. "Uh . . . ," said the lieutenant, looking down at the blood on his hand.

"*Nobody* fucks with my people," said Mazibuko.

"He wouldn't salute," said the lieutenant reproachfully, and stood up, shaky on his feet, the brown shirt stained darkly with his blood.

"So you set the dog on him?" Mazibuko strode forward. The Parabat raised his hands reflexively. Mazibuko grabbed him by the collar, jerked him forward, and smashed his forehead into the broken nose. The man fell backward again. Red dust billowed in the midday sun.

The cell phone in Mazibuko's breast pocket began to chirp.

"Jissis," said the sergeant, "you're gonna kill him," and knelt beside his mate.

"Not today . . ."

The ringing got louder, a penetrating noise.

"Nobody fucks with my people." He unbuttoned the pocket and activated the phone.

"Captain Mazibuko."

It was the voice of Janina Mentz.

"Activation call, Captain. At eighteen-fifteen there will be a Falcon 900 from Twenty-first Squadron standing by at Bloemspruit. Please confirm."

"Confirmed," he said, his eyes on the two Parabats

still standing, but there was no fight in them, only bewilderment.

"Eighteen-fifteen. Bloemspruit," Mentz said.

"Confirmed," he said once more.

The connection was cut. He folded the phone and returned it to his pocket. "Joe. Come," he said. "We've got things to do." He walked past the sergeant, treading on the hind leg of the German shepherd. There was no reaction.

"My father said . . . more than once . . . if anything ever happened to him, I should get you, because you are the only man that he trusts."

Thobela Mpayipheli only nodded. She spoke hesitantly; he could see that she was extremely uncomfortable, deeply aware of her invasion of his life, of the atmosphere that she had created here.

"And now he's done a stupid thing. I . . . we . . ."

She searched for the right words. He recognized her tension but didn't want to know. Didn't want it to affect the life he had here.

"Did you know what he was involved with after 'ninety-two?"

"I last saw your father in 'eighty-six."

"They . . . He had to . . . Everything was so mixed up then, after the elections. They brought him back to help. . . . The integration of the intelligence services was difficult. We had two, three branches, and the apartheid regime had even more.

The people wouldn't work together. They covered up and lied and competed with one another. It was costing a lot more money than they made provision for. They had to consolidate. Create some order. The only way was to split everything up into projects, to compartmentalize. So they put him in charge of the project to combine all the computer records. It was almost impossible, there was so much: the stuff at Infoplan in Pretoria alone would take years to process, not to mention the regime's weapons manufacturers like Denel and the Security Police and the Secret Service, Military Intelligence, and the ANC's systems in Lusaka and London, four hundred, five hundred gigabytes of information, anything from personal information on the public to weapons systems to informants and double agents. He had to handle it all, erase the stuff that could cause trouble and save the useful material, create a central, uniform, single-platform database. He . . . I kept house for him during that time, my mother was sick. He said it upset him so much, the information on the systems. . . ."

She was quiet for a while, then opened her big black leather handbag and took out a tissue as if to prepare herself.

"He said there were some strange orders, things that Mandela and Defence Minister Nzo would not approve, and he was worried. He didn't know what to do, at first. Then he decided to make backups of some of the material. He was scared, Mr. Mpayipheli, those were such chaotic times, you understand. There was so much insecurity and people trying to block him and some trying to save their careers and others trying to make theirs. ANCs and whites, both sides of the fence. So he brought some stuff home, data, on hard drives. Sometimes he worked through the night on it. I kept out of it. I suspect he . . ."

She dabbed at her nose with the tissue.

"I don't know what was on the drives and I don't know what he meant to do with it. But it looks as if he never handed it in. It looks as if he is trying to sell the data. And then they phoned me and I lied because—"

"Selling it?"

"I . . ."

"To whom?"

"I don't know." There was despair in her voice, whether for the deed or her father, he couldn't say.

"Why?"

"Why did he try to sell it? I don't know."

He raised his eyebrows.

"They pushed him out. After the project. Said he should go on pension. I don't think he wanted that. He wasn't ready for that."

He shook his head. There had to be more to it.

"Mr. Mpayipheli, I don't know why he did it. Since my mother died . . . I was living with him but I had my own life, I think he got lonely. I don't know what goes on in an old man's head when he sits at home all day and reads the white men's newspapers. This man who played such a major role in the Struggle, pushed aside now. This man who was once a player. He was respected, in Europe. He was somebody and now he is nothing. Maybe he wanted, just one more time, to be a player again. I was aware of his bitterness. And weariness. But I didn't think . . . Perhaps . . . to be noticed? I don't know. I just don't know."

"The information. Did he say what was so upsetting?"

She shifted uneasily in the chair; her eyes slid away from his. "No. Just that there were terrible things. . . ."

"How terrible?"

She just looked at him.

"Now what?" he asked.

"They phoned. From Lusaka, I think. They have some hard drives, but that is not what they want. I had to get another drive from my father's safe."

He looked her in the eye. This was it.

"In seventy-two hours I must deliver another hard drive in Lusaka. That's all the time they gave me."

"Not a lot of time."

"No."

"Why are you wasting time sitting here?"

"I need your help. To deliver the data. To save my father because they will kill him anyway. And I"—she raised the hem of her long, wide skirt—"am a little slow." He saw the wood and metal, the artificial legs. "And not very effective."

Tiger Mazibuko stood under the wing of the Falcon 900 in his camouflage uniform and black beret, feet planted wide, hands behind his back, his eyes on the twelve men loading ammunition boxes.

He had waited thirty-eight months for this. More than three years since Janina Mentz, dossier in hand, had come to fetch him, a one-pip lieutenant, out of the Recces.

"You're a hard man, Mazibuko. But are you hard enough?"

Fuck, it was hard to take her seriously. A chick. A white woman who marched into the Recces and sent everyone back and forth with that soft voice and way too much self-assurance. And a way of playing with his head. "Isn't it time to move out from your father's shadow?" Mazibuko had been ready to go from the first question. The follow-up was just Mentz showing that she could read between the lines in those official files.

"Why me?" he had asked anyway, on the plane to Cape Town.

Mentz had looked at him with those piercing eyes and said, "Mazibuko, you know."

He hadn't answered, but still he had wondered. Was it because of his . . . talents? Or because of his father? He found the answer progressively in the stack of files (forty-four of them) he had to go through to choose the twenty-four members of the Reaction Unit. He began to see what Mentz must have known from the start. When he read the reports and interviewed the guys, looked into their eyes and saw the ruthlessness. And the hunger.

The ties that bound them.

The self-hatred that was always there had found a form, become a *thing*.

"We're ready, Captain," said Da Costa.

Mazibuko came out from under the wing. "Get up. Let's go to work."

Yes, they were ready. As ready as nearly three years of tempering could make them. Four months to put the team together, to handpick them one by one. Winnowing the chaff from the grain, over and over, till there were only twenty-four, two teams of a dozen each, the perfect number for "my RU," as the director referred to them possessively, *Aar-you,* the hunchback's English abbreviation for Reaction Unit. Only then did the real honing begin.

Now he pulled the door of the Falcon shut behind this half of the Dirty Double Dozen. The Twenty-Four Blackbirds, the Ama-killa-killa, and other names they had made up for themselves in the twenty-six months since the best instructors that money and diplomatic goodwill could buy had taken them in hand and remodeled them. Driven them to extremes that they physically and psychologically were not supposed to withstand. Half of them, because of the two teams of twelve, were continuously on standby for two weeks as Team Alpha, while the other as Team Bravo worked on refining their skills. Then Team Alpha would become Team Bravo, the members shuffled around, but they were a unit. A un-it. The ties that bind. The blood and sweat, the intensity of physical hardship. And that extra dimension—a psychological itch, a communal psychosis, that shared curse.

They sat in the plane, watching him—their faces bright with expectation, absolute trust, and total admiration.

"Time to kick butt!" he said.

In unison, they roared.

4.

CIA

SITUATION BRIEF

FOR ATTENTION: Assistant Deputy Director (Middle East and Africa) CIA HQ, Langley, Virginia

PREPARED BY: Luke John Powell (Senior Agent in Charge—Southern Africa), Cape Town, South Africa

SUBJECT: South Africa—ten years after

I. INTRODUCTION

It has been ten years since the then president of South Africa, F. W. de Klerk, made his famous February speech in which he unbanned the black resistance movement the African National Congress (ANC), released Nelson Mandela from jail, and negotiated a transition to black majority rule.

After a landslide victory at the polls in the country's first-ever truly democratic elections eight years ago, the ANC, with Mandela as president, became the ruling party.

Mandela (or Madiba, as he is affectionately called) served a five-year term until 1999 and was succeeded by current president Thabo Mbeki, after another huge election victory for the ANC.

Despite the major problems of high unemployment and crime rates and a fluctuating local currency (the rand), South Africa is politically and economically stable—extremely so, if viewed in the African context. This, despite the eleven official languages and culture groups (including Xhosa, Zulu, Tswana, Sotho, Ndebele, and Afrikaners), the nine provinces and separate capitals for the judiciary, the legislative, and the executive government.

2. **INTELLIGENCE AGENCIES**

After the 1994 elections, the ANC government faced the mammoth task of integrating three major military and intelligence forces:

- *Military structures:* The following military structures were forged into the new South African National Defence Force during a prolonged, often difficult, but ultimately reasonably successful process: the white regime's South African Defence Force (SADF); the ANC's own military wing, Umkhonto we Sizwe (translated from Xhosa, it means "the spear of the nation"); and the military wing of the Pan-Africanist Congress (PAC—the other, more extreme black faction that opposed the apartheid regime), the Azanian People's Liberation Army (APLA).

- *Intelligence structures:* The far less public and much speedier integration was between the former white government's National Intelligence Service (NIS) and both the separate ANC and PAC intelligence arms into the new National Intelligence Agency (NIA)—often simply referred to as "the Agency" and responsible for homeland security.

    The old Secret Intelligence Service (SIS), a.k.a. State Security Service, was transformed into the SA Secret Service and takes responsibility for foreign intelligence.

    In addition, the former South African Police was transformed into the SA Police Service, integrating the old Security Police.

    Internal bickering and old loyalties forced the ANC government to create a new service, the Presidential Intelligence Unit (PIU), in the late nineties. The main aim of the PIU is to keep an eye on other intelligence structures, in addition to both internal and external intelligence gathering.

Through the kitchen window they could see the child standing in the vegetable garden. "I never told him that men go away. Now he will learn for himself."

"I am coming back," Mpayipheli said.

She just shook her head.

"Miriam, I swear . . ."

"Don't," she said.

"I . . . it's . . . I owe Johnny Kleintjes, Miriam. . . ."

Her voice was soft. It always was when she was angry. "Remember what you said?" "I remember." "What did you say, Thobela?" "I said I am not a deserter."

"And now?"

"It's only for one or two days. Then I'll be back."

She shook her head again, filled with foreboding.

"I have to do this."

"You have to do this? You don't have to. Just say no. Let them sort out their own trouble. You owe them nothing."

"I owe Johnny Kleintjes."

"You told me you can't live that life anymore. You said you had finished with it."

He sighed deeply. He turned around in the kitchen, turned back to her, his hands and voice pleading. "It's true. I did say that. And I meant it. Nothing has changed. You're right—I can say no. It's a choice, my choice. I have to choose the right way. I must do the right thing, Miriam, the thing that makes me an honorable man. Those are the difficult choices. They are always the most difficult choices."

He saw she was listening and he hoped for understanding. "My debt to Johnny Kleintjes is a man's debt; a debt of honor. Honor is not only caring for you and Pakamile, coming home every afternoon, doing a job that is within the law and nonviolent. Honor also means that I must pay my debts."

She said nothing.

"Can you understand?"

"I don't want to lose you." Almost too soft to hear. "And I don't think he can afford to lose you." Her gaze indicated the boy outdoors.

"You won't lose me. I promise you. I will come back. Sooner than you think."

She turned to him, her arms around his waist, and held him with a fierce desperation.

"Sooner than you think," he said.

3. "OLD LOYALTIES"

To understand the intelligence situation in South Africa today, one has to keep in mind which alliances existed before the creation of the "New South Africa" in 1992–94:

- The white minority National Party government of the eighties was closely aligned with both the British MI5 and MI6 and American intelligence services, specifically the CIA.

    The latter was involved in a number of joint anticommunist African operations with the former Military Intelligence forces of the SADF in Angola, Namibia, Zimbabwe, Tanzania, and Mozambique. The CIA also furnished Pretoria with intelligence during the white regime's war against

Cuba and USSR-sponsored communist forces in Angola in the late seventies.

The ANC, as a banned and suppressed anti-government movement in exile, had very close ties with, and received strong monetary and military support from, the former USSR, East Germany (specifically the KGB and Stasi), Cuba, Libya, the Palestine Liberation Organization (PLO), and, to a lesser extent, Iraq and other Muslim countries.

- The PAC has stronger ties with Muslim extremists (such as Iran) and the PLO.

4. MUSLIM EXTREMISTS IN SOUTH AFRICA

Khalfan Khamis Mohammed, the al Qaeda agent hunted by the FBI and CIA after the bombing of the U.S. embassy in Tanzania, was found hiding in plain sight in Cape Town, South Africa, in 1999.

South Africa is not a Muslim country by any means, but among the followers of Mohammed in the Western Cape province is a small minority of extremists, divided into several splinter groups, all sympathetic to al Qaeda:

- Muslims Against Illegal Leaders (MAIL).
- Qibla (the word means "the direction in which the believer orients himself or herself for salat, the prayer of Islam"), far left, aggressive, and secretive.
- People Against Drugs and Gangsterism (Pagad): a vigilante group known for violent action against

drug lords on the Cape Flats, perhaps the most public of these groups and the least of a threat.

The biggest room on the sixth floor of Wale Street Chambers was known as the Ops Room and had been used only eight times in twenty-four months— for "readiness testing," the term Mentz used for the quarterly trials to test the systems and the standard of her team. The bank of twelve television screens against the east wall was connected to digital and analog satellite TV, closed-circuit TV, and videoconferencing equipment. The six desktop PCs against the north wall were connected by optic fiber to the local network and the Internet backbone. Next to the double doors on the west side were the digital tuner and receiver for the radio network and the cellular and landline exchange with eighteen secure lines and teleconferencing facilities. On the south wall was the big white screen for the video projector, which was suspended from the ceiling. The oval table with seating for twenty people occupied the center of the room.

The sixteen now seated around the table had a strong feeling that this late-afternoon call to the Ops Room was not a practice run. The atmosphere in the room was electric when Janina Mentz walked in; their eyes followed her with restrained anticipation. There would have been rumors already. The phone tappers would have hinted at superior knowledge, acceding with vague nods that something was developing, while their envious colleagues could only make guesses and use old favors as leverage to try and get information.

That is why the sixteen pairs of eyes rested on her. In the past there had been different kinds of unspoken questions. At first, when she was assembling the team for the director, they were gauging her skills, her ability to wield authority, because they were predominantly male and came from positions where their gender reigned supreme. They put her to the test and they learned that crude language and boorish behavior wouldn't put her off her stride; aggression left her calm and cold, thinly disguised antifeminism would not provoke her. Piece by piece they reconstructed her history so they could know their new master: the rural upbringing, the brilliant academic career, the political activity, the slow climb through the party ranks, because she was white and Afrikaans and somewhere along the way married and divorced. Until the director had sought her out.

Really they respected her for what she had accomplished and the way in which she had done it.

That is why she could enter the room with muted confidence. She checked her watch before she said, "Evening, everyone."

"Good evening, Mrs. Mentz." It was a jovial

chorus obedient to the director's wishes for formal address. She was relaxed, unobtrusively in control.

She tucked the gray skirt under her with deft hands as she took the seat at the head of the long table, next to the laptop plugged into the port of the video projector. She switched it on.

"Let us begin with one sure thing: from this moment the Ops Room is officially operational. This is not a test." There was a tingling in the room.

"Let there be no doubt that this is the real thing. We have worked hard to get here, and now our skills and abilities will be put to the test. I am depending on you."

Heads nodded eagerly.

She turned on the laptop and opened Microsoft PowerPoint. "This photo was taken nineteen days ago at the entrance to the American embassy as part of our routine surveillance. The man exiting the door is Johnny Kleintjes, a former leader in the intelligence services of the Struggle. He studied mathematics and applied mathematics at the University of the Western Cape, but due to political activity, restrictions, and extreme pressure from the Security Police of the previous regime, he never obtained his degree. He was an exile from 1972, too late to be one of the trailblazers, the *mgwenya* of the sixties. He quickly made a name for himself at the ANC and MK offices in London. Married in 1973. He was East German–trained at Odessa from 1976 and specialized in intelligence, where he earned the nickname *Umthakathi,* meaning 'wizard,' thanks to his skill with computers. Kleintjes was responsible for establishing the ANC's computer systems in London, Lusaka, and Quibaxe in Angola in the eighties, and, more important, was the project leader for the integration of Struggle and regime computer systems and databases since 1995. He retired at age sixty-two in 1997, after his wife died of cancer, and shares a house with their only daughter, Monica."

She looked up. She had their attention still.

"The question is: What was Johnny Kleintjes doing at the American embassy? And the answer is that we don't know. Telephone monitoring of the Kleintjes household was initiated the same evening."

She clicked the mouse. Another photo, black-and-white, of a woman, slightly plump, at the open door of a car, the coarse grain of the photo indicating that it had been taken at a distance with a telephoto lens.

"This is Monica Kleintjes, daughter of Johnny Kleintjes. A typical child of exiles. Born in London 1974, went to school there, and stayed on to complete her studies in computer science in 1995. In 1980 she was the victim of a car accident outside Manchester that cost her both legs. She gets around with prosthetic limbs and refuses to use crutches or any other aids. She is any personnel manager's affirmative action dream and currently works for the technology division of Sanlam as senior manager."

Mentz manipulated the keys on the keyboard. "These are the major players that we have pictures of. The following conversations were recorded by our voice-monitoring team this afternoon."

He sat with Pakamile at the kitchen table with the big blue atlas and the *National Geographic,* just as they did every evening. Miriam's chair as always a little farther back, her needlework on her lap. Tonight they were reading about Chile, about an island on the west coast of South America where wind and rain had eroded fantastical shapes out of the rock, where unique plants had created a false paradise and animal life was almost nonexistent. He read in English as it was written, for the child would learn the language better, but translated paragraph by paragraph into Xhosa. Then they would open the atlas and look for Chile on the world map before turning the pages to a smaller-scale map of the country itself.

They never read more than two pages, because Pakamile's attention faded quickly, unless the article dealt with a terrifying snake or other predator. But tonight it was more difficult than usual to keep his attention. The boy's eyes kept darting to the blue sports bag resting by the door. Eventually Mpay-ipheli gave up.

"I've got to go away for a day or two, Pakamile. I have some work to do. I have to help an old friend."

"Where are you going?"

"First, you must promise to tell nobody."

"Why?"

"Because I want to give my friend a surprise."

"Is it his birthday?"

"Something like that."

"Can't I even tell Johnson?"

"Johnson might tell his father, and his father might phone my old friend. It must be a secret between us three."

"I won't tell anyone."

"Do you know where Zambia is on the map?"

"Is it in . . . eee . . . Mpumalanga?"

Miriam would have smiled, under normal circumstances, at her son's wild guess. Not tonight.

"Zambia is a country, Pakamile. Let me show you." Mpayipheli paged to a map of southern Africa. "Here we are," he said, pointing with his finger.

"Cape Town."

"Yes. And up here is Zambia."

"How are you going to get there, Thobela?"

"I am going to fly on an airplane to here, in Johannesburg. Then I will get on another plane that is going to fly here over Zimbabwe or maybe here over Botswana to this place. It's called Lusaka. It's a city, like Cape Town. That's where my old friend is."

"How far is that, Thobela?"

"Oh, about twenty-five hundred kilometers."

"That is very far."

"It is."

"Will there be cake? And cool drink?"

"I hope so."

"I want to come, too."

He laughed and looked at Miriam. She just shook her head.

"One day, Pakamile, I will take you. I promise."

"Bedtime," said Miriam.

"When are you going to fly?"

"Just now, when you are sleeping."

"And when are you coming back?"

"Only about two sleeps. Look after your mother, Pakamile. And the vegetable garden."

"I will. Will you bring me back some cake?"

"The wild card is Thobela Mpayipheli," said Janina Mentz. "We don't know why Monica Kleintjes went to him. You heard the conversations—he is also known as Tiny, works at Mother City Motorrad, a BMW motorbike dealership, lives with Miriam Nzululwazi in Guguletu. We know she is the registered owner of the house, nothing else. Kleintjes went by taxi to the house, stayed just over forty minutes, and went straight home. Since then neither Mpayipheli nor Kleintjes has moved.

"There are two surveillance teams with her and one in Guguletu, with him. The Reaction Unit is on its way from Bloemfontein and should land at Ysterplaat any minute now. They will stay there until we have more information. That, people, is how things stand."

She turned off the video.

"Now we must jump to it. Radebe, we have only one man in Lusaka. I want four more. With experience. The Gauteng office is closest and they have enough of the right kind of people. Preferably two men and two women who can book into the Republican Hotel as couples. Discreetly and certainly not at the same time, but I'll leave that to you. Get your phone systems running. Quinn, we need to intercept the calls to the Nzululwazi home in Guguletu. Urgently. Rajkumar, bring in your team. I want to know who Thobela Mpayipheli is. I don't care what database you fish in; this is absolute priority. Right, people, go, go, go. Twenty minutes, please, then we are rolling."

Tiger Mazibuko was last one off the Falcon. He let the members of Team Alpha go first, watching them, white, black, brown, each with his own story. Da Costa, sinewy descendant of Angolan refugees with the knife scar on his cheek and a five o'clock shadow on his jaw. Weyers, the Afrikaner from Germiston with bodybuilder's arms. Little Joe Moroka, a Tswana raised on a maize farm at Bothaville, spoke seven of the country's eleven official languages. Cupido, the shortest, the most talkative, a colored town boy from Ashton with a Technikon diploma in electronic engineering. Even a "token Royal," as Zwelitini, the tall, lean Zulu, liked to call himself, although he was not a member of the king's family.

They stood in line on the runway. The Cape summer breeze blew softly against Mazibuko's cheek as he dropped to the tar.

"Off-load now. Hurry up and wait. You know the drill."

At the front door he put his arms around her, pressed her thin body against him, smelled the woman smell, the faint remains of shampoo and scent after a long day, the aromas of the kitchen and that unique warmth that was special to her.

"I will have to stay over in Johannesburg," he said softly in her ear. "I can only catch a plane to Lusaka tomorrow."

"How much money did she give you?"

"Plenty."

Miriam did not comment, just held him tight.

"I'll phone as soon as I get to the hotel."

Still she stood with her face in his neck and her hands around him. At last she stepped back and kissed him quickly on the mouth. "Come back, Thobela."

Janina phoned home from the privacy of her office. Lien, the eldest, picked up. "Hello, Mamma."

"I have to work late, sweetie."

"Maaa . . . You promised to help me with biology."

"Lien, you're fifteen. You know when you know your work well enough."

"I'll wait up."

"Let me talk to Suthu. She must sleep over, because I won't get home tonight."

"Ma-aa. My hair tomorrow morning."

"I'm sorry, Lien. It's an emergency. I need you to help out there. You're my big girl. Did Lizette do her homework?"

"She was on the phone the whole afternoon, Ma, and you know how those grade sevens are. 'Did Kosie say anything about me? Do you think Pietie likes me?' It's so childish. It's *gross.*"

She laughed. "You were also in grade seven."

"I can't bear to think of it. Was I ever like that?"

"You were. Let me talk to Lizette. You must get some sleep, sweetie. You need to be fresh for the exam. I'll phone tomorrow, I promise."

5.

The taxi dropped him off outside Departures; he paid, took his bag, and got out. How long since he had last flown? Things had changed; everything was new and shiny, to make a good impression on the overseas tourists.

At Comair he bought a ticket with the cash Monica Kleintjes had handed him in a stack of new hundred-rand notes. "That's too much," he had said. "You can bring me the change" was her response. Now he wondered where the money had come from. Did she have time to go and withdraw the cash? Or did the Kleintjeses keep that much in the house?

He sent the bag through the X-ray machine. Two pairs of trousers, two shirts, two pairs of socks, his black shoes, a jersey, his toilet bag, the remaining cash. And the hard drive, small and flat, technology that was beyond him. And somewhere in the electronic innards were unmentionable facts about this country's past.

He didn't want to think about it, didn't want to be involved; he wanted to give the stuff to Johnny

Kleintjes, see him safe, come home and get on with his life. So many plans for himself and Miriam and Pakamile, and then he became aware of the two gray suits behind him, the instinct a relic from another life, a muted warning in the back of his mind. He looked back, but it was just his imagination. He took his bag and checked his watch. Thirty-three minutes to boarding.

"What should we do?" asked Quinn, looking expectantly at Janina with his headphones pulled down.

"First I want to know where he's headed."

"They're finding out. He bought a ticket with Comair."

"Keep me informed."

Quinn nodded, shifted the earphones back, and spoke quietly into the mike at his mouth.

"Rahjev, anything?" she asked the extremely fat Indian seated behind his computer.

"National Population Register lists nine Thobela Mpayiphelis. I'm checking birth dates. Give me ten."

She nodded.

Why had Monica Kleintjes chosen Mpayipheli? Who was he?

She stepped over to Radebe, who was on the phone talking to the Gauteng office. Someone had brought coffee and sandwiches. She didn't want coffee yet and she wasn't hungry. She went back to Quinn. He was just listening, glanced up at her, calm and competent.

An unbelievable team, she thought. *This thing will be over before it has begun.*

"He's flying to Johannesburg," said Quinn.

"He has only one bag with him?"

"Just the one."

"And we are absolutely sure Monica Kleintjes is at her house?"

"She's sitting in front of the TV in the sitting room. They can see her through the lace curtain."

She considered the possibilities, ran through all the implications and scenarios. Mpayipheli must have the data. They could take it now and send their own team to Lusaka. Better control, with the RU as backup. Perhaps. Because it would be difficult to get Mazibuko and company into Zambia. Too many diplomatic favors. Too much exposure. The director might have to test his Reaction Unit some other time. The main issue: Keep it in the family. Keep it safe and under control.

"How good is the team at the airport?"

"Good enough. Experienced," said Quinn.

She nodded. "I want them to bring Mpayipheli in, Quinn. Low-profile, I don't want a confrontation at the airport. Discreet and fast. Get him and his bag in a car and bring them here."

He sat with his bag on his lap, and the awareness of isolation crept over him. He had been living with Miriam for more than a year now, more than a year of family evenings, and suddenly here he was alone again, as he had been in the old days.

He searched for a reaction in himself. Did he miss it? The answer surprised him, as he found no satisfaction in this privacy. After a lifetime of depending on himself, in twelve months they had changed his life. He wanted to be there, not here.

But he had to complete this task.

Johnny Kleintjes. The Johnny Kleintjes he knew would never have sold out. Something must have happened to change the old man. Who knew what was happening in the inner circles and walkways of the new government and the new intelligence services? It wasn't impossible, just improbable. Johnny Kleintjes was a man of integrity. And loyalty. A strong man with character. He would ask him when he saw him, when the data was handed over and Johnny got his money. If everything went off okay. It had to. He didn't feel like trouble, not anymore.

And then they were next to him, two gray suits. He hadn't seen them coming, and as they appeared beside him he started at the depth of his thoughts, the blunting of old skills.

"Mr. Mpayipheli," said one.

"Yes." Surprised they knew his name. They were right against him, preventing him from getting up.

"We want you to come with us."

"What for?"

"We represent the state," said the second, holding a plastic ID up to his eyes, photo and national coat of arms.

"I have to catch a plane," he said. His head was clear now, his body reacting.

"Not tonight," said Number One.

"I don't want to hurt anybody," said Thobela Mpayipheli.

Two laughed, hee-hee, amused. "Is that so?"

"Please."

"I am afraid you don't have a choice, Mr. Mpayipheli." He tapped the blue bag. "The contents . . ."

What did they know? "Please listen," he said. "I don't want trouble."

The agent heard the note of pleading in the big Xhosa's voice. *He's afraid,* he thought. *Use it.* "We could give you more trouble than you would ever imagine, big fellow," he said, and pushed back the tail of his jacket to display the pistol, steel butt in a black shoulder holster. He stretched out his hand for the sports bag. "Come," he said.

"Ai, ai," said Thobela Mpayipheli. In the time it took for the hand to reach the sports bag he had to make a decision. He had gleaned something from their behavior: They didn't want to cause a scene. They wanted to get him out of there quietly. He must use that. He saw One's jacket gaping as his arm reached for the bag. He saw the pistol butt, reached up and took it, turned, stood up. One had the bag in his hand, his eyes wide with shock. Mpayipheli leaned into him with the pistol barrel at his heart. Two was behind Number One. Other passengers here and there had not seen anything amiss.

"I don't want trouble. Just give me my bag."

"What are you doing?" asked Two.

"He's got my pistol," hissed One.

"You take the bag," Mpayipheli told Two.

"What?"

"Take the bag from him and put your pistol in it." He shoved the pistol in his own hand hard against One's chest, keeping him between himself and Two.

"Do what he says," said One softly.

Two was uncertain, eyes darting from them to the passengers waiting in the departure lounge, trying to decide. He made up his mind.

"No," he said, drawing his pistol and keeping it under his jacket.

"Do what he says," One whispered urgently, with authority.

"Fuck, Willem."

Mpayipheli kept his voice reasonable, calm. "I just want my bag. I am not good with revolvers. There are lots of people here. Someone might get hurt."

Stalemate. Mpayipheli and Willem intimately close, Two a meter away.

"Jissis, Alfred, do what the fucker says. Where can he go?"

At last: "You can explain to the boss." He took the bag slowly from Willem's grip, zipped it open and slipped his pistol inside, zipped it up and deposited it carefully on the floor as if the contents were breakable.

"Now both of you sit down."

The agents moved slowly and sat.

Mpayipheli took the bag, pistol in his trouser pocket with his hand still on it, and walked, jogged, to the passenger exit, turning to check. One and Two, Willem and Alfred, one white, one brown, staring at him with unreadable faces.

"Sir, you can't—," said the woman at the exit, but he was past her, outside, onto the runway. A security man shouted something, waving, but he ran out of the ring of light from the building into the dark.

A bellow from the fat Indian—"I've got him"—and Mentz strode over to his computer monitor.

"Thobela Mpayipheli, born ten October 1962 in Alice in the Eastern Cape, father is Lawrence Mpayipheli, mother is Catherine Zongu, his ID number is 621010 5122 004. Registered address is 45 Seventeenth Avenue, Mitchell's Plain." Rajkumar leaned back triumphantly and took another sandwich off the tray.

Mentz stood behind his chair, reading off the screen.

"We know he was born, Rahjev. We need more than that."

"Well, I had to start somewhere." Wounded at the dearth of praise.

"I hope his birthday isn't an omen," she said.

Rajkumar glanced from the screen to her. "I don't get it."

"Heroes Day, Raj. In the old days the tenth of October was Heroes Day. When the Afrikaners celebrated their pioneers. That address is old. Find out who lived there. He's forty years old. Too old to be Monica's contemporary. Old enough to have been involved with Johnny Kleintjes—"

"Ma'am," called Quinn, but she would not be interrupted.

"I want to know what that connection with Kleintjes is, Rahjev.

I want to know if he served and how. I need to know why Monica Kleintjes went to *him* with her little problem."

"Ma'am," called Quinn with great urgency. She looked up.

"We have a fugitive."

He aimed for the darkest area of the airport and kept running. His ears expected sirens and shouts and shots. He was angry, with Monica and Johnny Kleintjes and himself. How did the authorities suddenly know about Johnny Kleintjes's little deal?

They had known his name, the two gray suits. Had tapped a finger on the blue bag. They knew what was in there. Were watching him since he walked into the airport, knew about him; must have followed Monica to his house, so they knew about her, about Johnny Kleintjes, bloody Johnny Kleintjes. They knew everything. He ran, looking over his shoulder. No one was behind him. He had sworn to himself: no more violence. Two years he had been true. Had not shot, beaten, or even threatened anyone. He had promised Miriam those days were gone, and within thirty seconds after the gray suits had reached him it was as if all the promises were in the water, and he knew how these things worked—they just got worse. Once the cycle began, it couldn't be stopped. What he should do now was take the bag back to the woman and tell her Johnny Kleintjes could sort out his own mess. Stop the cycle before it went any further. Stop it now.

He pulled up at the wire boundary fence. Beyond it was Borchards Quarry Road. He was breathing hard, his body no longer used to the exertion. Sweat ran down his cheek. He checked behind again; the building was too far to distinguish people, but all was quiet, no big fuss.

Which meant that it wasn't a police or customs operation. The place would have been crawling.

That meant . . .

Spooks.

It made sense, if you took into account what was on the hard drive.

Fuck them. He was not afraid of spooks. He jumped for the fence.

"Put them on speaker," said Janina Mentz, and Quinn pressed the button.

". . . he was just lucky, Control, that's all."

"You're on speaker, Willem."

"Oh."

"I want to know what happened," said Janina Mentz.

"He got away, ma'am, but—"

"I know he got away. How did it happen?"

"We had everything under control, ma'am," said the voice in awe. "We waited until he sat down in the departure lounge. We identified ourselves and asked the target to accompany us. Control said we must keep it low-profile. He's only a motorbike mechanic; he sat there with the bag on his lap like a farm boy, he looked so shy and lonely. He said he didn't want any trouble. It was obvious he was scared. It's my fault, ma'am. I wanted to take the bag and he got hold of my firearm—"

"He got hold of it?"

"Yes, ma'am. He grabbed it. I . . . um . . . his actions were . . . I didn't expect it."

"And then?"

"Then he took the bag, with Alfred's firearm in it, and ran away."

Silence.

"So now he has two firearms?"

"I don't think he knows what to do with them, ma'am. He called my pistol a revolver."

"Well, *that's* a relief."

Willem did not respond.

Quinn sighed despondently and said in a quiet aside to Mentz: "I thought they could handle it."

"Ma'am, he just got lucky. Judging by his reaction, we'll get him easily," said Willem over the ether.

She did not answer.

"He even said 'please.'"

"Please?"

"Yes, ma'am. And we know he's not on a plane."

Mentz pondered the information. The room was very quiet.

"Ma'am?" said the voice on the radio.

"Yes."

"What do we do now?"

6.

There comes a time to show anger, controlled but with purpose, rejection not of your people but of their actions.

Mentz turned off the speakerphone angrily and walked over to her computer. "We were in control of this thing. We knew where she was, where he was, where he was going, how he was going to get there. Absolute control."

Her voice carried across the room, the anger barely submerged. Everyone was looking at her, but no one made eye contact.

"So why did we lose control? Lack of information. Lack of intelligence. Lack of judgment. Here and at the airport. Now we are at a disadvantage. We have no idea where he is. At least we know where he is going and we know the quickest way to get there. But that is not enough. I want to know who Thobela Mpayipheli is and I want to know now. I want to know why Monica Kleintjes went to him. And I want to know where he is. I want to know where the hard drive is. Everything. And I don't care what you must do to get that information."

She looked for eyes, but they were looking at the floor.

"And those two clowns, Quinn."

"Yes, ma'am?"

"Let them write a report. And when that's done . . ."

"Yes, ma'am?"

"Let them go. They don't belong on this team."

She walked out of the room, wishing there was a door to slam, down the passage, into her office—there was a door to slam—and dropped into her black leather chair.

Let the fools sweat.

Let them understand in the first place that if you can't take the heat, Janina Mentz will remove you from the kitchen. Because, Lord knows, this was no place for failure. She would live up to her promises.

The director knew. He sat there in his office in his snow-white shirt and he knew because he was listening. He heard every word spoken in the Ops Room—and judged it: her actions and reactions, her leadership.

It seemed a lifetime ago that he had asked her at their first interview for the job: "Do you want it, Janina?"

And she had said yes, because as a white woman in a black administration, there were only so many opportunities, never mind that your IQ was 147 and your record one faultless minor success after another, with the emphasis on minor, because the big chance had not yet come. Until the director had taken her to lunch at Bukhara's in the Church Street Mall and laid out his vision to her: "An intelligence service that is outstanding, Janina, that is what the vice president wants. A new intelligence service without a past. Next year he will be president and he knows he doesn't have the Madiba magic, the charisma of Nelson Mandela. He knows it will be hard work against every form of resistance and undermining that you can think of, nationally and internationally. I have carte blanche and I have a budget, Janina, and I believe I have the architect here before me this afternoon. You have the profile, the brainpower, you have no baggage, you have the loyalty, and you have the persistence. But the question is: Do you want it?"

Oh yes, she wanted it, more than he realized. Because it had been eleven months since her husband developed an itch for young things and told her, "The marriage is not working for me," as if it was her fault, as if she and the children were not enough fulfillment for him anymore, whereas the only fulfillment in question was the space between Cindy's legs. Cindy. The pseudo-artist with dirty feet who peddled her fabrics to German tourists from her stall at Greenmarket Square and fluttered her big brown eyes at married men until she caught one in the snare of her firm, free, braless breasts. And then the happy couple moved to Pilgrim's Rest to "open a studio for Cindy."

So, Mr. Director, she wanted it. She hungered for it. Because she was consumed by an anger that was fed by the rejection—oh yes, let there be no doubt. Fed by ambition, too, make no mistake; the only child of poor Afrikaners, she would pay any price to rise above the soul-destroying, pointless existence of her parents. Fed by frustration of a decade in the Struggle, and all she had to show for it despite her talents was a deputy directorship when she could do so much more; she could fly, she knew the landscape of her psyche, knew where the valleys were and where the peaks were, she was impartial in her self-awareness. She could fly—what did it matter where they came from, the winds that blew beneath her wings?

She did not say that. She had listened and spoken coolly and calmly at lunch and answered with quiet assurance, "Yes, I want it," and then began the very next week to work out their vision: a First World intelligence unit in a country trying to drag itself up by its Third World bootstraps, a new independent unit with a clean slate.

And she still wanted it. No matter what price must be paid.

Her phone rang with the single ring of an internal call.

"Mentz."

"Pop in for a moment, Janina, would you," said the director.

He took a minibus to Bellville—the first opportunity that came up. He was driven to put distance between himself and the airport, regardless of the direction; ramifications were coming through to him one after another. He could not go back to Monica Kleintjes; they were surely watching her. He couldn't phone her. He could not go home. He could not go back to the airport—by now there would be swarms of them. And if they were at all awake, they would be watching the station—bus or train travel was also out of the question.

Which left him with the big question. How to get to Lusaka?

He sat in the dark between the other passengers, domestics and security guards and factory workers on their way home, talking about the rise in the price of bread and the soccer results and politics, and he longed to be one of them. He wanted to leave the hard drive on Monica's lap and say, "There is one thing that you didn't take into account," and then he would go to Miriam and Pakamile and tomorrow he would ride to work on his Honda Benly and during lunch he would walk up St. George's to Immanuel the shoeshine man and play a game of chess with him between his cell-phone-talking, wealth-chasing clients and all the while they would good-naturedly mock the whites in Xhosa.

But right now he had two Z88 pistols and a flat hard drive in a blue sports bag standing between him and that life.

"And what do you do for a living?" asked the woman next to him.

He sighed. "At the moment, I'm traveling," he said.

How was he to get to Lusaka?

You wouldn't say that he was in the office by six every morning—here it was nearly half past eight in the evening and the director, in his early fifties, looked fresh, rested, and alert.

"I had an interesting call, Janina. This afternoon our Tiger assaulted a Parabat at Tempe."

"Assaulted?"

"Landed him in the hospital, and the commanding officer started phoning higher up. He wants justice."

"I am sure there was reason for the fight, sir."

"I am, too, Janina. I just want to keep you informed."

"I appreciate that, sir."

"Ask him about it when you see him."

"I will."

"Is that all, Mr. Director?"

"That is all, Janina. I know you are busy." And he smiled in a fatherly way. She hesitated a moment before turning away; she willed him to say something about the happenings in the Ops Room, he must bring it up so that she could assure him that everything was under control, but he just sat there with his smile.

She took the stairs, stopped halfway.

I know you are busy.

He was weighing her, testing her; she knew it as an absolute truth.

She laughed softly. If only he knew. She took a deep breath and took the last steps one by one, measuring, as if enumerating a strategic plan.

Radebe began reporting the minute she walked into the Ops Room, his voice softly apologetic, explaining the redeployment of the teams—six of the best at the airport, six at the Cape Town station, in two teams of three each to watch the trains and the bus terminal. His three teammates beside him were busy contacting every car-rental business in the city, with instructions to let them know if someone of Mpayipheli's description tried to hire a vehicle. They would also contact every private plane charter service. Three more teams of two each were in their cars, awaiting instructions, down below on Wale Street. There was no activity at Monica Kleintjes's or at Miriam Nzululwazi's.

She nodded. Quinn confirmed monitoring of the Nzululwazi phone. There had been no calls yet.

Rajkumar, ever sensitive, had a bearing of injured pride as he gave his report: "No record of Thobela Mpayipheli in the Umkhonto we Sizwe files. Mpayipheli's registered home address is Mitchell's Plain—the property belongs to one Orlando Arendse. Probably the same Arendse that Monica phoned this afternoon, looking for Mpayipheli. But Arendse's registered home address is in Milnerton Ridge." The obese body shifted subtly, self-confidence returning. "The interesting thing is Arendse's criminal record—twice served time for dealing in stolen goods, in 1975 and 1982 to 1984, once charged and found not guilty of dealing in unlicensed weapons in 1989, twice arrested for dealing in drugs, in 1992 and 1995, but the cases were never brought to trial. One thing is certain: Orlando Arendse is organized crime. Drugs. Big-time. Prostitution, gambling, stolen property. The usual protection racket. And if I read the signs correctly, the Scorpions are looking very closely at his dealings. That Mitchell's Plain address could be a drug house, seems to me." Rahjev Rajkumar leaned back in satisfaction.

"Good work," she said. She paced up and down the wall behind the Indian, her arms folded.

Organized crime? She grasped at possibilities, but it wouldn't make sense.

"Organized crime?" she spoke aloud. "I don't see it."

"Money makes strange bedfellows," said Rajkumar. "And if it's drugs, it's money. Big money."

"Mpayipheli could be a dealer," said Quinn.

"He's a motorbike mechanic," said Radebe. "It doesn't fit."

Mentz stopped her pacing, nodding. "Rahjev, find out who the owner of the bike shop is."

"Company registrations are not up-to-date. I can poke around but . . ."

Radebe: "I'll send a car over there. Sometimes there are emergency numbers on the door."

"Do it."

She tried to analyze the known facts, angles, and different points of perspective, stumbling on the crime bits of the jigsaw puzzle.

"No record of Mpayipheli with the ANC, MK, PAC, or APLA?" she asked.

"Nothing. But, of course, the ANC systems have had a few knocks. They are not complete. And the PAC and APLA never really had anything. All the PAC info came from the Boers. And there's nothing on Mpayipheli."

"There must be a connection between Mpayipheli and the Kleintjeses."

"Hell," said Quinn, "he could have been their gardener."

Radebe, always careful with what he said, frowned deeply as if he had strong doubts. "She phoned the

Arendse number to find Mpayipheli. Maybe Arendse is the connection."

"Could be." She was walking up and down again, digesting the input, weighing possibilities. Her thirst for information all-encompassing, they had to make a breakthrough, shine a bright light into the haze of ignorance. But how do you get a drug baron to talk?

Another cycle in her traverse of the wall.

"Okay," she said. "This is what we are going to do."

In the dirty toilets of Bellville Station, behind a closed door, he took the pistols out of the rolled-up magazines. Then he went out and placed the different pieces in separate trash cans. He began to walk toward Durban Road. He still had no idea where he was going. He was aware of minutes ticking by and was only ten kilometers closer to Lusaka than when he had been at the airport. The temptation to drop the whole mess and go home lay like yearning on him. But the question kept returning to him: Is that what Johnny Kleintjes did when Thobela needed him? And the answer was always no, no matter how many times he thought about it, no matter how little he wanted to be there, no matter how little he wanted the urgency and tension growing in his belly. He owed Johnny Kleintjes and he would have to move his butt. Turning the corner of Voortrekker and Durban Road, he saw the vehicles at the traffic lights and a light came on in his head, hurrying the tempo of his footsteps as he moved toward the office of the Revenue Services.

There was a taxi rank there. He must get back to the city. Quickly.

For the second time that day Captain Tiger Mazibuko cut his cell-phone connection with Janina Mentz and began barking out orders to Team Alpha: "Let's get these boxes open, there's work to be done. Hecklers, handguns, smoke grenades, bulletproof vests, and night sights. And paint your faces."

They sprang into action with a will, snapped open the equipment cases, flicking glances at him, curious at the type of order, but he gave nothing away while he reflected on his conversation with Mentz. Why had he assaulted an officer this afternoon? Because the fucker had set his German shepherd on Little Joe Moroka. What had Little Joe done? Didn't salute the little lieutenant. Why not? Because Little Joe is Little Joe. So busy inside his head sometimes that he doesn't know what's going on around him. In-a-fog negligence was all that it was. And when the lieutenant confronted him with a stream of obscenities, the outcome was inevitable. Little Joe takes shit from only one person and that's me. That's why we fetched Little Joe out of the MP cells in the first place. Little Joe told him to go do an unmentionable deed with himself or his dog, and the lieutenant encouraged the dog to bite him. Which in any case, militarily speaking, is a contravention of the worst degree. Did the dog bite Little Joe? Yes, the dog bit him in the trousers. Was Little Joe hurt? No. The lieutenant and the dog embarrassed Little Joe. And that is as bad as a bite that draws blood. Worse, in his case. An injustice was perpetrated, however you look at it. Tiger Mazibuko chose not to work through channels to restore the balance because then others would start taking chances with the RU. A point had to be made. And now the Bats were crying.

"Yes, indeed they are crying. They want disciplinary action."

"Then discipline me." Challenging, because he knew the RU was untouchable before he beat up the Bat.

"Not before you've earned your keep." And she gave him the background, the task.

His team handed him his jacket and weapons, the night-sight headset and camouflage paint last. He prepared with deft, practiced movements till the RU stood in line before him and he walked down the row, plucking at a belt, straightening a piece of equipment.

"I have a new name for the Ama-killa-killa," he said. "After tonight you will be known as the Gangsta Busters."

7.

He asked the taxi driver to drop him off in front of the Media 24 building in the Heerengracht. He chose to go east through the Nico Malan, turning left onto Hertzog. Traffic at this time of evening was thin. He deliberately walked without urgency, like a man going nowhere in particular, and turned left again onto Oswald Pirow. As he passed between the petrol pumps, greeting the petrol jockeys through the window of their night room, he saw the car in front of Mother City Motorrad. The lights were on, engine idling, and he saw the intelligence officers in the front seat and his heart sank.

Spooks. They were watching the place.

He opened the door of the petrol attendants' room and went inside, knowing he would be spotted if he stayed outside.

The idling engine was a good sign. If they were keeping the place under surveillance, they would have parked in the cross street with lights and engine off. The attendants were glad to see him; any distraction at this time of night was welcome. What was he doing here, what was in the bag? He made up an answer, a client's motorbike had not been returned after servicing and now he, Mpayipheli, had to sort out the whitey's problems. He had an eye on the car outside, saw it pull away, and tried to keep track of it without raising the suspicions of the petrol jockeys.

Did he have to deliver the bike at this time of night?

Yes, the guy was angry, he needed the motorbike tomorrow morning and the whitey boss was too lazy to go out, so the Xhosa was called out, you know the story. What are you guys watching on TV, a competition? Yes, see, every guy has to pick one of three girls, but he can't see them, he can only ask them questions . . .

The car had gone. He listened politely for a minute or two, then excused himself and left, looking up and down the street, but there was nothing. He crossed, went behind the building into the service alley. He took his wallet from the blue bag, sorting through the leather folds. The silver key to the wooden door lay flat and shiny where he always put it. He was the first one there every morning to sweep up half an hour before the mechanics arrived. He had to put on the kettle and the lights and make sure the display windows were clean. He unlocked the door and typed in the code on the alarm panel. He had to decide whether or not to switch on the lights. The guys at the garage would wonder if he didn't, but he decided against it—he mustn't attract attention.

Next decision: which bike? Lord, the things were big. Would he be able to manage with his Honda 200 experience? He had never been allowed to ride them, he had to push them outside, wash and polish, rub till they shone, push them back in again. Tonight he must get onto one and ride to Johannesburg; but which one?

He felt the weight of the bag dragging at his hand.

The 1200 RS was the fastest, but what about the bag? The LT has luggage space but it was gigantic. The GS demonstration model in the display room had fixed baggage cases on either side of the rear wheel. The machine stood there, chunky and crouched, orangey yellow. The key, he knew, hung in the spares room.

Lord, they were so big.

Despite the concrete walls topped with razor wire and the high gate, despite the early-warning system of human eyes all down the street, and despite the eight men with their collection of weapons inside, it took only seven minutes for Tiger Mazibuko and his Reaction Unit to take the house.

They came through the darkness in three teams of four, four, and five. The two unmarked cars dropped them one block south of the house, and they moved unerringly through gardens and over walls until they could scale the wall of the yard on three sides, quietly and easily cutting the rusty razor wire, their hand signals visible in the light from the street.

The windows were burglarproofed but the large panes were unprotected, and that is how they entered. With smooth, practiced movements of break, dive, and roll, in three separate places, within seconds of one another. When the people inside scrambled to react, panic-stricken, it was too late. Fearful figures with thick welts of camouflage paint, in combat fatigues, forced them adroitly to the floor, pressing chunky Heckler & Koch machine pistols to their temples. Moments of chaos and confusion suddenly turned to quiet, till only one man's voice was heard, clear and in control.

Mazibuko had the captives brought into the front room and forced down on their bellies on the floor with their hands behind their heads.

"Weyers, Zongu, watch the street." Then Mazibuko focused on the bundle of bodies on the floor. "Who's in charge here?" he asked.

Facedown, one or two of the bodies trembled slightly. Seconds passed with no answer.

"Shoot one, Da Costa," said Mazibuko.

"Which one, Captain?"

"Start there. Shoot him in the knee. Fuck up his leg."

"Right, Captain."

Da Costa loudly pulled back the slide of the HK and pressed the barrel against a leg.

"You can't shoot," said a voice in the bundle.

"Why not?"

"There are rules for the SAPS."

Mazibuko laughed. "Shoot, Da Costa."

The shot was a thunderbolt in the room; the man made a deep, curious noise. The smell of cordite filled the room.

"Here's some bad news, assholes. We are not police," said Mazibuko. "Let me ask you again: Who is the chief gangsta here?"

"I am," said the man in the middle, anxiety creasing his face.

"Stand up."

"Are you going to shoot me?"

"That depends, Gangsta. That depends."

Janina Mentz developed her policy on transcripts systematically.

The challenge was to secure information, which in this country leaked like water from an earth dam, through the cracks of old loyalties and new aspirations, filtering away through a sandy bottom of corruption and petty avarice. If something gave off the smell of money, scavengers would emerge from the oddest holes.

From the beginning her method was to trust

nobody too much, to lead no one into temptation, to dampen the smell of the money.

Rahjev Rajkumar had coached her in the vulnerabilities of electronic information. Easy to copy, easy to distribute: floppy disks, zip disks, CD-ROM, FTP, hard drives smaller than half a cigarette pack, e-mail, hacking—because if it was linked it was crackable. If they could get into others' databases, sooner or later with some new ingenious programming, others would get into theirs.

There was only one way to secure information. One copy, on paper: fileable, controllable, limited.

That is why Rajkumar had an extra section to manage. The typists. Four women who played their old-fashioned electric IBM typewriters like virtuosas. Who fingered the keys at the speed of white light in a single video-monitored room on the sixth floor. Who would sign out each digital and magnetic tape, transcribe it, and sign it back in with the single copy on white paper. Paper that would not yellow or decay. So that Radebe and his team could analyze it and then file it away in the access- and temperature-controlled document library, together with the magnetic tapes. The digital tapes were deleted.

By the time the transcript of the interview with Orlando Arendse reached her, forty-seven minutes after it had taken place in Milnerton Ridge, Janina was already familiar with the crucial content.

* * *

Transcript of interview by A. J. M. Williams with Mr. Orlando Arendse, 23 October, 21:25, 55 Milnerton Avenue, Milnerton Ridge

w: I represent the state, Mr. Arendse. I have a few questions about Mr. Thobela Mpayipheli and a Miss Monica Kleintjes . . .

A: I don't work from home. Come and see me at my office in the morning.

w: I am afraid it can't wait that long, Mr. Arendse.

A: Where are your credentials?

w: Here, Mr. Arendse.

A: Drop the "mister"; I can see you don't mean it. This card says nothing. Come see me in the morning, thank you.

w: Maybe you should—

A: Maybe nothing. It's outside my office hours, and you don't have a warrant.

w: I do.

A: Then where is it?

w: Here.

A: That's a cell phone.

w: Just take the call.

A: Good-bye, my brother.

w: It's from a house in Mitchell's Plain that belongs to you.

A: What?

W: Take the call.

A: Hello. Yes . . . Yes . . . The bastards . . . Yes . . . Williams, who the hell are you?

W: Is there somewhere we can talk in private, Mr. Arendse?

A: What do you want?

W: Just some information.

A: Said the spider to the fly. Come in, we will sit in the back.

W: Thank you.

A: You shot my man, Williams.

W: We wanted to get your attention.

A: You can't just shoot. There are rules of engagement.

W: I am sure most of the government departments would agree with you.

A: So who are you?

W: We need some information about a Mr. Thobela Mpayipheli and a Miss Monica Kleintjes.

A: I don't know the lady.

W: And Mr. Mpayipheli?

A: He no longer works for me. Not for two years . . .

W: What sort of work did he do?

A: Now I must ask you to excuse me while I phone my lawyer.

W: I am afraid that will not be possible.

A: Do you imagine, my brown bro, that I will sit here and feed you incriminating evidence because you hold a barrel to my troops' head? My men know the score; they know they can get hurt in our line of work.

w: Mr. Arendse, we know you are involved in organized crime, and the fact of the matter is that we don't care. That is the problem of the SAPS. Do you really think that our actions in Mitchell's Plain, which are hardly in line with the laws of criminal procedure, are part of a plan to bring you to justice?

a: Why do you talk like a whitey? Where are your roots, my bro?

w: Mpayipheli. What did he do for you?

a: Go fuck yourself.

w: Mr. Arendse, my people at the Mitchell's Plain house say there is two hundred kilograms of cocaine in various stages of processing. I am sure it's worth something to you, even if your personnel are not.

[Inaudible]

w: Mr. Arendse?

a: What is your problem with Tiny?

w: Who?

a: Mpayipheli.

w: We just need some background.

a: Why?

w: Routine investigations, Mr. Arendse.

a: At ten o'clock at night? Pull the other one.

w: I am not in a position to discuss our interest in Mr. Mpayipheli with you.

A: Did he go into business for himself?

w: How do you mean?

A: He must have done something to attract your attention.

w: What did he do for you?

A: He was my enforcer.

w: Enforcer?

A: Yes.

w: Could you describe that more fully?

A: Jirre, you talk fancy. The government has taught you well.

w: Mr. Arendse . . .

A: Okay, okay, but don't expect a saga, it's more of a short story. Tiny was firepower and physical intimidation, that's all. He rode shotgun. Sharpshooter like you wouldn't believe. And he was big and strong and he was a mean bastard. You could see it in his eyes—there was a hawk there, he would watch you and look for weakness.

w: How long did he work for you?

A: Six years? I think it was six years.

w: And before that?

A: You should know. He was a soldier in the Struggle.

w: Umkhonto we Sizwe?

A: Exactly.

w: With respect, Mr. Arendse, there are few MK soldiers in Mitchell's Plain.

A: Too true, my bro, they stick to their own. But I got lucky. There was a vacancy and you know how it is—word gets out and the next thing I know this huge Xhosa is standing at the door and he says the vacancy is now filled. Best appointment I ever made.

w: And he told you he was ex-MK.

a: Exactly. I was a bit skeptical, so we drove down to Strandfontein for a proper job interview and we gave him an old AK-47 and a lot of Castle beer bottles at two hundred yards. It may not sound far to you, my brother, but those dumpies were small and he blew them apart with monotonous regularity till the other troops gave him a standing ovation, you understand me?

w: Did he ever use his talents in your service?

a: Speak plain, my bro. Do you want to know if he ever shot someone?

w: Yes.

a: It was never necessary. His hawk look was enough. His mother loved him, but everyone else was scared shitless of him.

w: Where did he serve with MK?

a: How would I know? He never talked about it.

w: Never?

a: Hardly a word. Six years and I never knew him. Kept to himself, always a bit apart like Colin Wilson's Outsider, but who cares, he was a jewel in my crown.

w: Colin who?

a: Literary reference, my bro. You wouldn't understand.

w: And then he left your service?

A: Two years ago, he came in and said he was finished. I thought he was playing me for an increase, but he wasn't interested. Next thing we know, he was working in a motorbike shop, gofer and general cleaner, can you believe it? Works for peanuts; he earned a small fortune with me. But now it seems he was busy with something on the side.

w: So you have had no contact with him the last two years?

A: Sweet fuck all.

w: I won't take up your time any longer, Mr. Arendse.

A: Now there's a relief.

w: You can send medical backup to Mitchell's Plain. We will withdraw from the property.

A: Mr. Williams, you know nothing about Tiny Mpayipheli, am I right?

w: Why do you say that, Mr. Arendse?

A: Just call it a sneaking suspicion. So let me give you some advice: Start ordering the body bags now.

8.

She went quickly to phone from her office. The maid said Lizette was asleep already. She thanked Suthu for the extra bother of sleeping over and asked to talk to Lien.

"I know my work now, Ma, even though you weren't here to help me."

"I knew you could handle it."

"Can I watch *Big Brother* on DSTV, Ma? Till ten?"

Kids. Tried to manipulate every situation to maximum advantage. She wanted to be angry and laugh at the same time.

"You know the rules, Lien. The age restriction is sixteen." And even as she said it she knew exactly what the response would be.

"All my friends watch it, Ma. I'm nearly sixteen. I'm not a child anymore." All three basic arguments in one breath.

"I know you're not a child anymore. You are a wonderful, lovable fifteen-year-old who needs to wait only a couple more months. Then you can watch with your undisciplined friends. Get enough sleep, you need it for the exam."

"Maa-aa . . ."

"And tell Lizette I was just too late to say good night. Tell her I love both of you very much—and I'm very proud of you, too."

"Don't work too hard, Ma."

"I won't."

"We love you, too."

"I know, kid. Sleep well."

"Night, Ma."

She hurried back to the Ops Room, impatience gnawing at her.

"Look again, Rahjev. If he was MK, there must be something," she said as she entered.

"Yes, ma'am." But the Indian's body language said he knew what the result would be.

"You don't believe we will find anything?"

"Ma'am, the methodology we use to search the known data is very refined. There was nothing. I can run it again, but the result will be the same."

"He could have lied to Arendse about his back-ground," said Quinn. "Work was very scarce in the early nineties; people were prepared to say anything."

"Things don't change much," said Radebe drily.

"And now we have a fugitive sharpshooter with two pistols," said Janina.

Rajkumar's brain was working overtime: "The ANC had a paper filing system, too: for Umkhonto we Sizwe. Isn't it on Robben Island?"

"Pretoria," said Radebe. "The MK files are at Voortrekkerhoogte."

"What can you tell us about it?"

"It was never much of a system. With the big influx of recruits after 'seventy-six, there was too much paper and too few administrators. But it could be worth looking."

"What about the old National Intelligence Service's microfiche library? The Boers computerized the index, but it's a secure unconnected system. It's still active, in Pretoria. We can put in a request," said Rajkumar.

It was Radebe who made a disparaging noise, and Janina knew why. Her colleagues at the new National Intelligence Service did not command much respect from her and her people. But she liked the idea.

"If the request comes from high enough up, they will jump to it," she said. "I'm going to talk to the director."

"Ma'am," said Quinn, holding up his hand to stop her.

"What is it?"

"Listen to this." He selected keys, and the electronic hissing of the speakerphone filled the room.

"Tell us again, Nathan."

"We managed to track down the owner of Mother City Motorrad. His name is Bodenstein and he lives in Welgelegen. He says Mpayipheli isn't a mechanic, just a gofer. Quiet man, hard worker, punctual and trustworthy. He knows nothing about a military background."

"Tell us about the alarm again, Nathan."

"While we were busy with the interview, the phone rang. Bodenstein's security company reported that the bike shop's alarm was turned off more than an hour ago and hasn't been reactivated. He said he must go immediately, and we are following him there."

"And what did he say about the key, Nathan?"

"Oh, yes. He says Mpayipheli has a key to the place and he knows the alarm code, because Mpayipheli is the one who opens up in the morning."

Mpayipheli almost fell before he was properly on his way. The power of the huge bike caught him totally unaware as he turned onto Oswald Pirow and opened the throttle. The reaction of this bike was so different from his little Honda Benly that he nearly lost it. And the size—the GS felt massive, heavy and high and unmanageable. He was shocked, adrenaline making his hands tremble, his breath misting the visor of his helmet. He wrestled the bike back in line and this time twisted the throttle with great care and progressed to the traffic lights at the N1. He pulled the front brakes and nearly tipped again, the ABS brakes kicking in hard and urgent. He stopped, breathing heavily, knees trembling, not willing to die on this German machine. The lights turned green, slowly he pulled away, turning slowly to the right with an over-wide arc and exaggerated care, keeping the revs low, through the gears—bloody hell, the thing had power, he was at 100 kilometers per hour before he was properly in third gear, that would be just about the Benly's top speed.

The traffic on the freeway was light, but he was painfully aware of the cars around him. He was riding slower than the flow of traffic, cringing in the left lane, trying to get a feel for the GS; once you were going, the balance was easier, but the handlebars felt too wide, the tank in front of him impossibly big.

He checked again where the blinkers were, how the dims and brights worked, his eyes flicking between the switches and the road ahead, his following distance was long, his speed just under a hundred. He had made a mistake, he had thought this was the way to get a long way from Cape Town very fast; if he could still make Bloemfontein tonight, he would be away because he could catch a plane there, they wouldn't be watching the Bloemfontein airport. But this thing was practically unrideable; he had made a mistake, it would have been quicker to take a mini-bus taxi, and it was dark, too, the lights of Century City reflected off the helmet. Maybe he should ride to Worcester, or only as far as Paarl, and ditch the bloody bike, what could he have been thinking?

At the N7 off-ramp he had to change lanes to let a lorry go past and he accelerated slowly, using the blinkers, changed lanes, swung back into the left one, relaxed a little. Through the long uphill turn at Parow, up the Tygerberg, he knew his body was leaning to the wrong side in the turn, but the bike was so unwieldy, the bend uncomfortable. If only there was less traffic; where were all these people going at this time of night? Down the hill to Bellville's off-ramps and then the streetlights on the freeway became fewer, the traffic dropped off, he saw the signs at the one-stop petrol station beckoning and glanced at the fuel gauge. The tank was full. Thank God. How far could he go on one tank?

His eye caught the speedometer, 110, and he throttled back, felt out of control again—this machine had a life of its own, a wild mustang. All his senses intensely engaged, he knew he must plan ahead. What to do? The tollgate was up ahead, thirty kilometers. What should he do? Avoid the tollgate, go to Paarl, abandon the bike, catch a taxi?

There must be taxis running to Worcester, but it was already very late. And if he stuck with the GS? Take on the Du Toits Kloof Pass with this monster?

The tollgate was a spoor that he would leave; people would remember a big black man on a motorbike, wouldn't they? Lord, he feared the pass in the dark on this thing. But beyond were more passes, more dark roads with sharp turns and oncoming freight trucks. What had possessed him?

What was he going to do?

A taxi was not going to work, not at this time of night.

Look at this positively. He was on the move, on his way. Suppress the desire to get rid of the bike. Use the dark. Use the lead he had. Use the element of surprise. They had no idea, despite the two spooks in the car at the motorbike shop. It would be tomorrow morning before someone realized the GS was gone, he had—

He hadn't reset the alarm. That knowledge came out of the back of his head like a hammer blow. In his hurry and wrestling with the GS, he had forgotten to switch on the alarm.

Jissis, he had gotten sloppy.

By the time he passed the Stellenbosch turnoff, his anger at Johnny Kleintjes and the spooks and at his own stupidity had grown greater than his fear of the motorbike, and he cursed inside the helmet, in all the languages he knew.

"I don't believe it," said Bodenstein. "I bloody don't believe it." They were standing in the showroom of Mother City Motorrad, the two agents and the owner. Bodenstein held out the piece of paper. "Read what he's written. Can you believe this?"

Nathan took the note.

Mr. Bodenstein:

I am borrowing the GS demonstration model for two or three days. I also took a suit and helmet and gloves; that is what the money is for that I left in your desk drawer. Unfortunately, I have to urgently help a friend and I had no other choice. Wear and tear and any damage to the motorbike will be paid in full.

Thobela Mpayipheli

"You think you know someone. You think you know who to trust," said Bodenstein.

"Which one is the GS?" asked Johnny, one of the agents.

"It's that fuckin' huge thing, only yellow," said Bodenstein, pointing to a silver motorbike on the showroom floor. "He's going to fall. Fuckin' hard. It's not a toy. Can you believe it?"

"See reality the way things are, not as you want them to be" is one of the principles of Janina Mentz.

That's why she accepted the developments calmly.

She thought through the happenings while the Ops Room buzzed around her. She stood still, at the end of the long table with her hand on her chin, her elbow propped on her arm, head bowed, a study in calm pensiveness. Aware that the director would hear every word, aware that the way she responded and what decisions she made, her tone of voice and attitude of body, would all create an impression on her team.

Vision: In her mind's eye she saw the road that the evasive persona of Thobela Mpayipheli must travel. He was headed north, and the N1 lay like a fat, twisted artery stretching out ahead to the heart of Africa. The reason for his single-mindedness, the source of his motivation, was unplumbed and now irrelevant. She focused on the route: the implications, the counter-measures, the preventative and limiting steps.

In a soft and even voice she had the big map of the country put up on the wall.

With red ink she drew in the likely route. She defined the role of the Reaction Unit: they would be her net, the welcoming party seventy-seven ki-lometers north of Beaufort West, where the route forked and the possibilities doubled—Kimberley to Johannesburg left, or Bloemfontein to Johan-nesburg right.

She asked Quinn's and Radebe's teams to alert the police stations and traffic authorities along the route, to warn them merely to gather intelligence and not to act, because their armed fugitive was still largely an unknown factor, but they knew he could shoot.

Their ignorance of this factor lay heavily on her, and the next round of instructions must set that right: investigative teams to Miriam Nzululwazi, to Monica Kleintjes. The gloves were off now. Track down the fugitive's family. His parents. His friends. Get information. Who? What? Where? Why? How? She needed to know him, this ghost with the elusive face.

She had the power. She would use it.

Extract from transcript of interview by J. Wilkinson with Mr. André Bodenstein, owner of Mother City Motorrad, 23 October, 21:55, Oswald Pirow Boulevard, Cape Town:

w: What do you know of Mr. Mpayipheli's previous employment?

b: He was a gofer.

w: Gofer?

b: Yes. For a car dealer in Somerset West.

w: How do you know this?

b: He told me.

w: What kind of gofer?

b: A gofer is a gofer. It means you do all the shit jobs that nobody else will.

w: That's all you know?

b: Listen, I don't need a man with a bloody degree to wash the motorbikes.

w: And you trusted him with a key?

b: Not the first day, I'm not a moron.

w: But later on.

B: Hell, he was here on the doorstep every morning when I arrived. Every bloody morning, never sick, never late, never cheeky. He worked—hell, that man can work. Last winter I told him he must open up, he can't stand in the rain like that, he could sweep out and put the kettle on. By the time we arrive, the coffee is made—every fucking morning, the place shines like a new penny. You think you can trust someone. You think you know people. . . .

Twice he was gofer at Killarney when the BMW Rider Academy was coaching well-off, middle-aged white men in the art of motorcycle riding, and now he regretted that he hadn't paid attention, that he hadn't absorbed all that knowledge.

He was riding through Du Toits Kloof Pass in the dark and he was aware that he was a caricature of how it should not be done. Riding jerkily, brakes and throttle and brakes and throttle and switching the light between bright and dim in a battle between good vision and the oncoming traffic, massive, snorting trucks avoiding the toll by using the long route and taking the sharp turns wide or chugging along at a snail's pace ahead of him. He sweated inside the expensive, efficient biker suit, his body heat steaming up the shield with water vapor so that time and again he had to clip it open, always aware of the drop on the left side, the lights very far down below.

Brake, turn, brake, turn, ride, struggling and swearing to the highest point, and then the road swung abruptly east and the lights were gone. For the first time the darkness was complete and the road suddenly quiet, and he became aware of the tremendous tension in his torso, muscles like strung wires, and he pulled over to the side, stopped, yanked the helmet from his head, put the clutch in neutral, took his hands from the handlebars, and stretched, taking in a deep breath.

He must relax, he had to, he was tired already and there were hundreds of kilometers ahead. He had made progress. He had come this far, navigated half the pass in the dark. Despite his ham-fistedness, the monster bike was not impossible. It was being patient with him as though it were waiting for him to try a lighter touch.

Deep breaths, in and out, a certain satisfaction, he had reached this milestone, he was at the top. He had a story to tell Pakamile and Miriam. He wondered if she was asleep. The digital clock on the instrument panel said Miriam had laid out the boy's school things, clothes, and lunch box. If he had been home, his lunch tin would have been packed, the house tidy, the sheets of their bed folded back, and she would have come and lay down with the wonderful smells of the oils and soaps of the bathroom, the alarm set for five o'clock, the light off and her breathing immediately deep and peaceful, the sleep of the innocent, the sleep of the worker.

Behind him he heard a lorry approaching the turn, and he stretched one last time, savoring the night air, clipped the shield down, and pulled away with the knowledge that he had at least mastered the throttle. He deliberately turned it open, felt the power beneath him, and then he was in the next turn and he concentrated on keeping his body relaxed, leaning into the turn as he did with the Benly, carefully, unskilled, but a lot better, more comfortable, more natural, and he accelerated slowly out of the turn, aimed for the next, through the old tunnel, another curve and another, down, down to the valley of the Meulenaars River, down, fighting the urge to stiffen up, keeping himself loose and light, feeling the personality of the bike through his limbs, turn and straighten, over and over, joining up with the toll road, suddenly impossibly luxurious and three lanes wide, the curves wide—the relief was tremendous.

As he looked down at the speedo, it read 130. He smiled inside his helmet at the sensation and the amazing thing that he had accomplished.

9.

"This is not what we were trained to do," said Tiger Mazibuko over the cell phone. He was standing outside next to the runway. He could see his men through the window, they were still pumped after the action they had seen, they talked of nothing else, living it over in the finest detail on the way to the air force base, teasing one another, even him, begging their commander to let them all have a chance to shoot—why only Da Costa? Zwelitini said he was going to send a strongly worded letter to the Zulu king to complain that even in the country's most elite unit there was racial discrimination—only the colonials were allowed to fire, the poor ol' blacks could only watch—and the twelve roared with mirth, but Tiger Mazibuko did not.

"I know, Tiger, but it was very valuable."

"We are not the SAPS. Give us something proper to do. Give us a challenge."

"Does a man that can pick off beer bottles with an AK at two hundred meters sound like a challenge?"

"Only one man?"

"Unfortunately, just one, Tiger."

"No, that doesn't sound like a challenge."

"Well, that's the best I can do. Stand by for an Oryx from Twenty-third Squadron. We are going to pursue the fugitive; you will go on ahead and wait for him."

His quietness displayed his disgruntlement.

When she realized what he was up to, her voice was angry. "If the challenge is not big enough for you, you can always go back to Tempe. I am sure I can find another alternative."

"What do we know about this great shooter of beer bottles?"

"Too little. He might or might not have been MK, he was a sort of bodyguard for organized crime, and nowadays he is a gofer at a motorbike dealer."

"Was he MK, or wasn't he?"

"We are working on it, Tiger. We are working on it."

Transcript of interview by A. J. M. Williams with Mrs. Miriam Nzululwazi, 23 October, 22:51, 21 Govan Mbeki Avenue, Guguletu

w: I represent the state, Mrs. Nzululwazi. I have a few questions about Mr. Thobela Mpayipheli and a Miss Monica Kleintjes.

n: I don't know her.

w: But you do know Mr. Mpayipheli.

n: Yes. He is a good man.

w: How long have you known him?

n: Two years.

w: How did you meet?

n: At my work.

w: What work do you do, Mrs. Nzululwazi?

n: I am a tea lady at Absa.

w: Which branch of Absa?

n: The Heerengracht.

w: And how did you come to meet him?

n: He was a client.

w: Yes?

n: He came to see one of the consultants and I brought him tea. When he was finished he came to look for me.

w: And asked for a date?

n: Yes.

w: And you said yes.

n: No. Only later.

w: So he came back again, after the first time.

n: Yes.

w: Why did you refuse him at first?

n: I don't understand why you wake me up to ask me questions like this.

w: Mr. Mpayipheli is in trouble, Mrs. Nzululwazi, and you can help him by answering the questions.

n: What kind of trouble?

w: He unlawfully took an object that belongs to the state and—

n: He took nothing. That woman gave it to him.

w: Miss Kleintjes?

n: Yes.

w: Why did she give it to him?

n: So that he could take it to her father.

w: But why did she choose him to do this?

n: He owes her father a favor.

w: What kind of favor?

n: I don't know.

w: He didn't tell you?

n: I didn't ask.

w: Do you and Mr. Mpayipheli live together?

n: Yes.

w: As man and wife?

n: Yes.

w: And you didn't ask him why he was receiving stolen property and agreeing to take it to Lusaka?

n: How do you know he is going to Lusaka?

w: We know everything.

n: If you know everything, why are you sitting here asking me questions in the middle of the night?

w: Do you know what Mr. Mpayipheli was involved with before his present work?

n: I thought you knew everything?

w: Mrs. Nzululwazi, there are gaps in our knowledge. I have already apologized for disturbing you so late. As I have explained, it is an emergency and Mr. Mpayipheli is in big trouble. You can help us by filling in the gaps.

n: I don't know what he did.

w: Did you know he worked for organized crime?

n: I don't want to know. He said he had another life, he said he did things that he wants to forget. In this country it wasn't very hard. He would have told me if I had asked him. But I didn't. He is a good man. There is love in this house. He is good to me and to my son. That is all I need to know.

w: Do you know if he was a member of Umkhonto we Sizwe?

n: Yes.

w: Was he?

n: Yes.

w: Did he tell you that?

n: In a way.

w: Did you know where he served?

n: He was in Tanzania and Angola and in Europe and Russia.

w: Do you know when?

n: That is all that I know.

w: But he told you that as a member of MK he—

n: No. He never told stories. I worked it out myself.

w: What do you mean?

n: Like when he talked to Pakamile about other countries.

w: Pakamile is your son?

n: Yes.

w: And this is all you had to go on?

n: Yes.

w: He never actually said he was with MK?

N: No.

[Silence—eight seconds]

W: Mrs. Nzululwazi, the favor he owed Johnny Kleintjes . . .

N: I have already told you I don't know.

W: You didn't find it strange that Miss Kleintjes came in here and Mr. Mpayipheli immediately agrees to undertake a long and dangerous journey on her behalf?

N: Why would it be dangerous to go to Lusaka?

W: You are not aware of the data on the hard drive?

N: What data?

W: The stolen data that he has with him.

N: Why should it be dangerous?

W: There are people that want to stop him. And there are—

N: People like you?

W: No, Mrs. Nzululwazi.

N: You want to stop him.

W: We want to help. We tried at the airport, but he ran away.

N: You wanted to help.

W: We did.

N: You must leave. Now.

W: Madam . . .

N: Get out of my house.

There is a plaque at the entrance to the air force base at Bloemspruit, just outside Bloemfontein. In military terms it is a new plaque, being scarcely three years old. On the plaque are the words 16 SQUADRON and below that, HLASELANI. Black inhabitants of Bloemfontein know what *hlaselani* means, but just to be sure that everyone understands, at the bottom of the plaque in brackets is the word ATTACK.

It is the pilots of the Sixteenth Squadron in particular who look at those words with satisfaction. It defines their purpose, separating them from the winged bus drivers and freight carriers of other squadrons, especially the other helicopter jockeys. They are an attack unit. For the first time in nearly sixty-five years of existence. Forget the quasi bombers like the Marylands, Beauforts, and Beaufighters of the Second World War. Forget the Alouette III helicopters of the bad 1980s.

Their satisfaction was due in large part to the content of the giant hangars: twelve almost brand new AH-2A Rooivalk attack helicopters, impressive air platforms with nose-mounted 20 mm cannon that could fire 740 rounds per minute and the capacity to carry up to sixteen air-to-ground missiles such as the ZT-35 laser-guided antitank missile. And on the wingtips were fittings for the Darter air-to-air missiles to lie snug. Add the Rooivalk's electronic warfare capability, the fully integrated HEWSPS (Helicopter Electronic Warfare Self-Protection Suite) with radar warning, laser warning, and countermeasures system and the pilots felt they were the only ones in the South African Air Force with twenty-first-century technology between their legs, which was their regular joke in the officers' club over their Red Heart rum and Coke.

The call came at 21:59 from General Ben van Rooyen at air force headquarters for two Rooivalk helicopters with extra fuel tanks for an extended operating range of 1,260 kilometers, to take off for Beaufort West as part of a real-life operation (and not the simulated warfare of the past thirty-six months). The biggest dilemma of the Sixteenth Squadron's commander was how to explain to the pilots and gunners who were not chosen how he had made his choice.

"How is it possible that MK has no record of him, Rahjev? If she is right and he was in Russia and Angola, how is that possible?"

"Ma'am, we don't know. We can only look at what is in the databases and analyze it, that's all."

"What is the probability that an MK member is not on record?"

Rajkumar pulled at his ponytail hanging over his shoulder with a plump hand. "Hell, ma'am . . . fifteen percent?"

"Fifteen percent."

"Round about."

"If there were ten thousand MK soldiers, as many as fifteen hundred are not on record?"

"Not on electronic record."

"If there were fifty thousand, are seventy-five hundred just missing?"

"Yes, ma'am."

"But they might be in the files in Voortrekkerhoogte?"

Radebe answered: "I think the odds are greater that they will find him in the Voortrekkerhoogte files."

"How long before we hear?"

"An hour or two. They have three people searching the archives."

"And the Boers' microfiche library?"

Radebe pulled up his shoulders. "It depends how strongly the orders from above came through."

She did a circuit of the room. To be dependent on others was a great frustration. She shook it off.

"What is a motorcycle gofer doing with a consultant at Absa?" Janina asked the Ops Room in general.

"Tell me I can scratch around in the Absa system, ma'am. Please?" Rajkumar stretched his interlaced plump fingers in front of him, cracking his joints in anticipation.

"How much time do you need?"

"Give me an hour."

"Go for it."

"Yeah, yeah, yeah!"

"What is the situation on the road?" she asked Radebe.

"The tollgate says no big bikes have gone north tonight—a few came through south, but no black man. We are working through Police Head Office. They say the local law enforcement and petrol stations as far as Touws River have been alerted. They are phoning Laingsburg, Leeu-Gamka, and Beaufort West now. But if he doesn't take the N1 . . ."

"He will."

He nodded.

She looked at them. They were keen to please.

"Are we making progress with the people that helped Kleintjes with the computer integration?"

"There is a transcript coming, ma'am."

"Thank you."

This is the one, she thought. The one she was waiting for. She looked over the room. They didn't know everything. Only she held all the pieces to this particular jigsaw.

So much careful planning. So much exception management. Long, careful months of fitting the gears one by one into this clock. And now it must all change, thanks to one middle-aged motorbike gofer.

10.

Miriam Nzululwazi lay on the double bed in the dark room, hands folded on her chest, eyes turned to the ceiling. She did not hear the familiar sounds of Guguletu at night, the eternal barking of dogs, the shouts of groups going home from the shebeen, their last fling before the week began again, the revving of a car engine in a backyard repair shop, the insects, music somewhere only audible in bass, the sigh and creak of their house settling for the night.

Her thoughts sought out Thobela and came back every time to the same conclusion: he was a good man.

Why were they chasing him? He was doing nothing wrong.

This country. Would it never stop banging on your door in the middle of the night? Would the ledger of the past never be closed?

Was he doing a wrong thing?

Was Thobela someone else than the man she knew?

"I was different," he had said one afternoon, when their relationship was young, when he had to fight to win her trust.

"I had another life. I am not ashamed. I did what I believed in. It is over. Here I am now. Just as you see me."

That first day in the consultant's office she had not even noticed him, just another client. She had transferred the tea from the trolley onto the tray and slid the tray onto the desk and nodded when the consultant and his client thanked her, and she had pulled the door closed behind her, little knowing that that mundane service would change her life. He had come right into the kitchen looking for her, apparently telling the consultant's secretary he wanted to tell her how good the tea was, and had put out his hand to her and said, "My name is Thobela Mpayipheli." She thought it was a nice name, an honest name—"Thobela" meant "with respect"—but she wondered what he wanted. "I saw you in Van der Linde's office. I want to talk with you."

"What about?"

"Anything."

"Are you asking me out?"

"Yes, I am."

"No."

"Am I too ugly?" he asked, with his smile and broad shoulders.

"I have a child."

"A boy or a girl?"

"I haven't time to talk. I have work to do."

"Just tell me your name, please."

"Miriam."

"Thank you." He had not used any of the popular slang, none of the quasi-American *cool* of the township rakes; he had left and she had gone on with her work. Two days later there was a phone call for her; no one phoned her at work, so she feared someone had died. He had to remind her who he was, he asked her when she took lunch break, she answered evasively and asked him not to phone her at work—there was no outside line to the kitchen, and reception didn't like it if the staff kept the lines busy.

The next day he was waiting outside, not leaning against a wall somewhere but standing right in front of the entrance, his legs planted wide and his arms folded on his chest, and when she sought the sunshine in Thibault Square he was there. "May I walk with you?"

"What do you want?"

"I want to talk to you."

"Why?"

"Because you are a lovely woman and I want to know you."

"I know enough people, thank you."

"You never told me if you have a son or a daughter."

"That's right." He walked next to her, she sat down on a step and opened the waxed-paper wrapping of her sandwich.

"Can I sit here?"

"It's a public place. You can sit where you like."

"I am not a *tsotsi*."

"I can see that."

"I just want to talk."

She let him talk. She was in a dilemma—fear on one hand, loneliness on the other. The experiences behind her argued with the possibilities that lay ahead. She had to shield her child and her heart from the big, handsome, gentle, proper man sitting in the spring sunshine alongside her. Her solution was to wait and see, to be passive. Let him talk, and he did, every other day he was outside, sometimes he brought something to eat, never luxuries: bunny rolls, hot chips with the irresistible flavor of salt and vinegar, sometimes a little bowl of curry and rice or his favorite, a chili bite from the Muslim takeout on Adderley Street, fresh and fragrant and sharp, and he let her taste it. He shared his lunch with her, and slowly she began to melt. Relaxing, she told him about Pakamile and her house for which she had worked so long, how hard it had been to pay it off, and one day he brought a gift for the boy, a jigsaw puzzle, and she said no, that's it, she wouldn't see him anymore, she would not expose Pakamile, men always left. Men never stay, he was a good man, but she thought men couldn't help it. That is how life is: men are temporary. Undependable. Unnecessary. Unnecessary for Pakamile.

Not all men, he had said, and it was on the tip of her tongue to say, "That is what you all say," but there was something in his eyes, in his look, in the set of his mouth and the clenching of his teeth that stopped her, that touched her, and she let it go and then he said, "I had a wild life. I did things. . . ."

"What things?"

"Things in the name of the Struggle. I was different. I had another life. I am not ashamed. I did what I believed in. It is over. Here I am now. Just as you see me."

"We all did things in the name of the Struggle." She was relieved.

"Yes," he said. "I was searching for myself. Now I have found myself. I know who I am and I know what I want. I am not a deserter."

She had believed him. He looked into her eyes and she believed him.

"Rooivalk One, we have a weather situation," said the tower at Bloemspruit. "Trough developing in the west, all the way from Verneukpan to Somerset East and a weak frontal system on the way. It could get wet."

The pilot looked at his flight plan. "Can we get through?"

"Affirmative, Rooivalk One, but you had better shake ass," said the tower, knowing the Rooivalk's operational ceiling was just under twenty thousand feet.

"Rooivalk One ready for takeoff."

"Rooivalk Two ready for takeoff."

"Rooivalk One and Two cleared for takeoff. Make some thunder."

The noise of the double Topaz turboshaft engines was deafening.

He mastered the R 1150 GS just before the Hex River valley. He knew it when he came out of a bend and opened the throttle and there was pleasure in the power. The exhaust pipe snorted softly behind him and he kicked back one gear, chose the line for the curve, tilted the bike, his shoulder dipping into the turn, and there was no discomfort, no fear of the angle between machine and road, just the tingling of pride for a small victory, skills acquired, satisfaction in control of power. He accelerated out of the turn, eyes focused on the next one, taking in the red lights a kilometer ahead, a lorry, aware, in control, bits and pieces, the instructor's voice at the advanced riding school slowly making sense now. He could like this, a little adrenaline, a little more skill, lorry ahead, manipulate clutch and gears and accelerator, a whisper of the front brakes, shoot past, and then he looked up and the moon broke away from the mountain peaks, full and bright, and in that moment he knew it was going to work, the trouble lay behind him, just the twisty, open road ahead, and he opened the taps, and the valley opened ahead of him, a fairyland in the silvery light of the moon.

Monica Kleintjes sat hunched in the sitting-room chair in her father's house, the lines of suppressed tears down her cheeks. Opposite her, Williams sat on the edge of his chair, as if he would reach out to her in empathy. "Miss Kleintjes, I would have done precisely the same if it were my father. It was a noble action," he said softly. "We are here to support you."

She nodded, biting her lower lip, hands clenched in her lap, her eyes large and teary behind the glasses.

"There are just two things we need to shed light on: your father's relationship with Mr. Mpayipheli and the character of the data that he has with him."

"I don't know what is on the hard drive."

"No idea?"

"Names. Records. Numbers. Information. When I asked my father what it was all about, he said it was better if I didn't know. I think . . . names . . ." Her eyes wandered over the wall next to the mantelpiece. There were photos hanging, black-and-white, color. People.

"What names?" Williams followed her gaze, stood up.

"Well-known ones."

"Which?" He looked over the photos. A colored family in Trafalgar Square, Johnny Kleintjes, Monica, perhaps five years old, her little legs stout and very present.

"ANC. The regime . . ."

"Can you remember any specific names?" There were photos of Kleintjes and people now in positions in the government. In Red Square, East Berlin, Checkpoint Charlie and the Wall in the background. Prague. The tourist spots of the Cold War.

"He didn't say."

"Nothing at all?" Williams stared at Johnny Kleintjes's wedding picture. Monica's mother in white, not a beautiful woman but proud.

"Nothing."

He looked away from the pictures, to her. "Miss Kleintjes, it is essential that we know what is in that data. This is in the interests of the country."

Her hands sprang loose from her lap, the tears spilled over the dam wall. "I didn't want to know and my father didn't want to say. Please . . ."

"I understand, Miss Kleintjes."

"Thanks."

He allowed her a moment to calm down. She reached for her tissues and blew delicately.

"And Mr. Mpayipheli?"

"My father knew him in the Struggle."

"Could you be more specific?"

Another tissue. She removed her glasses and wiped carefully under her eyes. "Three weeks . . . two or three weeks ago my father came to me at work. He had never done that before. He had a piece of paper with him. He said it was the name and contact number of someone he trusted completely. If anything should happen to him, I must phone Tiny Mpayipheli."

"Tiny?"

"That is what was on the paper."

"Were you surprised?"

"I was disturbed. I asked him why something should happen to him. He said nothing was going to happen, it was just insurance, like we work with at Sanlam. Then I asked him who Tiny Mpayipheli was, and he said, 'A phenomenon.'"

"A phenomenon?"

She nodded. "Then he said, 'A comrade.' Tiny was a comrade, they served together. He saw Tiny grow up in the Struggle."

"Your father was in Europe during the Struggle?"

"Yes."

"And that is where he got to know Mpayipheli?"

"I assume so."

"And?"

"And should anything go wrong, I should contact Tiny. Then I asked him again what would go wrong—I was worried—but he would say nothing, he wanted to talk about how nice my office was."

"And then when you got the calls from Lusaka, you phoned Mpayipheli?"

"First I opened the safe to get the hard drive. On top of it was a note. Tiny Mpayipheli's name and phone number. So I phoned him."

"And then you took the hard drive to him in Guguletu?"

"Yes."

"And you asked him to take it to Lusaka for you?"

"Yes."

"And he agreed?"

" 'I owe your father,' he said."

"I owe your father."

"Yes."

"Is his photo here?"

She looked at the row of portraits as if seeing them for the first time. She pulled her crutches closer, stood up with difficulty. He wanted to stop her, sorry he had asked. "I don't think so." She looked over the photos. The liquid welled up in her eyes again.

"Have you had any contact with Mr. Mpayipheli since then?"

"You listen to my phone. You know."

"Miss Kleintjes, have you any idea where Mr. Mpayipheli is now?"

"No."

Radebe called her to the Ops Room.

"Yes?"

"The team searching the files in Pretoria, ma'am . . ."

"Yes?"

"There's nothing. They can't find Thobela Mpayipheli."

11.

The agent was from the Eastern Cape Bureau in Bisho. She knew, operationally speaking, that it was the backwoods of South Africa, a professional quicksand where nothing ever happened to give you a chance to rise above, to propel yourself to head-quarters. The longer you remained there, the more you suffocated in the sands of mediocrity.

When Radebe phoned from HQ to order you to interview a subject in Alice, you didn't moan about the lack of information, you put zeal in your voice and hid the gratitude and climbed into the grimy, juddering Volkswagen Golf Chico with 174,000 km on the odometer and you seized the day, because this could be your passport to higher honors.

Then you focused on the questions you were going to ask, the tone of voice to maintain; you prepared until your thoughts began to wander, when you began to daydream about the possibilities this could bring—you saw in your mind's eye Mrs. Mentz reading the report (not knowing what her office looked like, you filled it with chrome and glass) and calling Radebe in to say, "This agent is brilliant, Radebe. What is she doing in Bisho? She belongs here with us."

Before the fantasy could properly take shape, before she could furnish the dream apartment in Sea Point and picture the view, she had arrived. She parked in front of the house in Alice, just a kilometer or so from the lovely new buildings on the Fort Hare campus. There was a light still burning and she knocked politely, her tape recorder and notebook in her handbag, her weapon in the leather holster in the small of her back.

The man who opened the door was silver gray, the wrinkles on his face deep and multiple, the tall body bowed with age, but his "good evening" conveyed only patience.

"Reverend Lawrence Mpayipheli?"

"That is correct."

"My name is Dalindyebo. I need some help."

"You have come to the right place, sister." A strong voice. The minister stepped back and held the door open. Two veined bare feet showed under the burgundy dressing gown.

The agent stepped inside, swept her eyes over the room, the bookshelves along two walls, hundreds of books, the other walls hung with black-and-white and color photos. The room had simplicity, no luxuries, an aura of restfulness and warmth.

"Please sit down. I just want to tell my wife she can go to sleep."

"I apologize for the late hour, Reverend."

"Don't be sorry." The minister disappeared down the passage, bare feet silent on the carpet. The agent attempted to see the photos from her chair. The minister and his wife in the middle, with bridal couples, at synod, with amorphous groups of people. At one side, a family photo, the minister young, tall, and straight. In front of him stood a boy of six or seven, a serious frown on his face, an overbite of new front teeth. The agent wondered if that was Thobela Mpayipheli.

The old man appeared from the passage again. "I have put the kettle on. What do you bring to my house, Miss Dalindyebo?"

For a moment she hesitated, suddenly doubting the prepared phrase on the tip of her tongue. There is something shining out of the old man, a love, compassion.

"Reverend, I work for the state. . . ."

He was about to sit down opposite her when he saw her hesitation. "Carry on, my child, don't be afraid."

"Reverend, we need information about your son. Thobela Mpayipheli."

Deep emotion moved over the old man's face, across his mouth and eyes. He stood still for a long moment as if turned to stone, long enough for her to feel anxiety. Then slowly he sat, as if his legs were in pain, and the sigh was deep and heavy.

"My son?" One hand touched the gray temple, just the fingertips; the other gripped the arm of the chair, eyes unseeing. A reaction she had not expected. She must adjust her timescale and review her questions. But for now she must remain quiet.

"My son," he said, this time not a question, the hand coming loose from the chair and floating to his mouth as if weightless, his gaze somewhere, but not in this room.

"Thobela," he said, as if remembering the name.

It took nearly fifteen minutes for the old man to begin his story. He first asked after the welfare of his son, which she answered with vague lies to spare him anguish. He excused himself to make coffee, treading like a sleepwalker. He brought the tray, which he had arranged with a plate of rusks and biscuits; he dithered about where to begin the chronicle of Thobela Mpayipheli, and then it came out, at first haltingly, a struggle for the right words, the right expression, till it began to flow, to make a stream of words and emotions, as if he were confessing and seeking her absolution.

To understand, you need to go back to the previous generation. To his generation. To him and his brother. Lawrence and Senzeni. The dove and the falcon. Jacob and Esau, if you would forgive the comparison. Children of the Kat River, of poverty, yes, simplicity but pride, sons of a tribal chief who had to do herd duty with the cattle, who learned the

Xhosa culture around the fire at night, who learned the history of the people at the feet of the gray-haired ones, who went through the Xhosa initiation before it became an exploitation of the poor. The difference between them was there from the early days. Lawrence the elder, the dreamer, the tall lean boy, the clever one who was always one step ahead of the others at the mission school with its single classroom, the peacemaker. Senzeni, shorter, muscular, a fighter, a born soldier, impatient, short-tempered, fiery, his attention fully engaged only when the battles were retold, his eyes glittering with fighting spirit.

There was a defining moment, so many years ago when he, Lawrence, had to defend his honor in a senseless adolescent fistfight with another boy, a troublemaker who was jealous of his status as chief's offspring. He was baited with cutting ridicule and within the circle of screaming children had to defend his dignity with his fists. It was as if he were raised above the two boys facing each other in ever diminishing circles, as if he floated, as if he were not really there. And when the blows began to rain down, he could not lift his hand against the boy. He could not ball his hands into fists, could not find the hate or anger to break skin or draw blood. It was a divine moment, the knowledge that he could feel his opponent's pain before it existed, the urge to assuage it, to heal.

Senzeni came to his aid, his little brother. He was staggering and bleeding in the ring of boys, head singing from the blows, blood in his eyes and his nose, and then Senzeni was there, a black tornado of rage ruthlessly thrashing the other boy with frightful purpose.

When it was over he turned to Lawrence with disdain, even a degree of hate, reluctant to accept this new responsibility and questioning without words how they could be brothers.

Lawrence found the Lord at the mission school. He found in Christ all the things he had felt within him that day. Senzeni said it was the white man's religion.

Lawrence received a scholarship through the church, and their mother encouraged him. He studied and married and began the long eternal journey as disciple here among his own people in the Kat River valley. And his brother was always there, a counterweight, by default the next tribal chief, the warrior who fastened onto the rumors of a new movement from the north, who read every word on the Rivonia trials over and over, who became another kind of disciple—a disciple of freedom.

And then there was Thobela.

The Lord made the boy with a purpose. He looked at the ancestors and took a bit here and a little there and sent the child into the world with the presence of his grandfather Mpayipheli, the ability to lead, to make decisions, to see past the angles and sides of a matter and make a judgment. The Lord gave him the body of his father, tall, the same limbs that could run the Ciskei hills with characteristic rhythmic stride, the same facial features so that many, including Thobela's own father, would mistakenly assume the same peacemaker inside.

But God created a predator in him, a Xhosa warrior, the Lord went far back in the bloodline, to Phalo, Rharhabe, Nquika en Maqoma, as he did with Senzeni, and gave Thobela Mpayipheli the heart of the hunter.

In early years his likeness fooled everyone. "His father's son," they said. But the son grew and the truth emerged. His father was the first to know, because he was brother to Senzeni. He knew the signs and he prayed for mercy, because he feared the consequences. He enveloped the boy with love, to create a cocoon to wrap him safely in, but that was not the Lord's will. Too late he came to realize this was his test, this child, too late, because he failed, his wisdom and compassion failed him, his deep love for his son made him blind.

The strife began insignificantly, domestic differences between father and son, and from there, as the years advanced, expanded like the ripples from a pebble dropped in a still pool.

And Senzeni came home to verify the rumors and their fierce hearts recognized each other, Thobela and his uncle, their mouths spoke the same language, their bodies thirsted for the same battlefields, their heads rejected the way of peace and love. And Lawrence Mpayipheli lost his only son.

"In 1976 with the Soweto riots, Thobela was fourteen years old. Senzeni came for him in the night. My brother was forbidden to enter the house because of his influence but he crept in like a thief and took the child and phoned later to say he would bring Thobela home when he had become a man. He had him initiated somewhere, and then took him to every place where Xhosa blood was shed. He filled his head with hate. They were away a long time, three months, and when they returned I did not know my son and he did not know me. Two years we lived like this in the rectory, strangers. He walked his own paths, quiet and secretive, as if tolerating me, waiting.

"In 1979 he was gone. The evening before, he said good night—a rare occurrence—and in the morning his room was empty. The bed unslept in, some clothes missing from the wardrobe. Senzeni came and said my son had gone to the war. There was a terrible row that day. Hard words were spoken. I forgot myself. I was wounded because I could not be a father, because my brother had stolen my son. My words were to Senzeni, but I raged with God. The Lord had let my son leave me. He had drawn the dividing lines of this land and this family in strange places. He made me a man of peace and love, called me to be a shepherd, and then He placed a wolf in the fold so that I was ridiculed, so that the apostate could scorn Him, and that I could not understand.

"Only later did I see it was my test. It was the Lord's way to humble me, to strip me of the illusion that I was more holy than others, to show me my feet of clay. But by then it was too late to save my son, too late to bring him home. Sometimes we had news, sometimes Senzeni would send a message about Thobela, how well he was, that he had been noticed, that the leaders of the Struggle recognized his character, that he had gone to foreign parts to learn to fight for his country.

"Then one evening the message came. The Security Police had taken Senzeni—to Grahamstown. For eight days they beat the life out of him and left his body as rubbish beside the road. And we never heard of our son again."

Beyond Touws River the road shrugged off its bends, and for the first time Thobela's thoughts drifted from the motorbike. He took stock of his position—the implications and what alternatives were available to him. The LCD stripes of the petrol gauge indicated he must refuel. At Laingsburg. After that it was 200 kilometers to Beaufort West, a deadly stretch of highway through the Great Karoo, wide and straight, oppressively hot in daytime, soul-destroying at night. Expected time of arrival: approximately midnight.

From Beaufort West it was another 500 or 550 to Bloemfontein—too far to reach before sunrise? Maybe not, if he pushed on, if he could manage the refueling stops quickly.

He would have to sleep in Bloemfontein, ride into the black township and rest somewhere while the sun shone.

The big question remained: Did they know yet he had taken the bike? Had his error of not turning off the alarm already resulted in consequences? If the answer was no, he had until eight, nine o'clock tomorrow morning before the message went out. And they would have to guess his route.

But if they already knew . . .

He knew the game. He knew how fast the variables multiplied for the hunters and the prey. He knew how they would reason if they already knew. Put their money on the main route, the fastest, shortest road, use resources there because that is where the highest-percentage probability lay, even if it was no more than 50 percent. There were too many longer, lesser routes; the possibilities would drive you out of your mind.

If they knew, the N1 would be their candidate. That's why he needed to use the darkness and the lead he had on them.

He switched the beam of the lights on high, the black ribbon strung out before him, opened the throttle, the needle crept past 140, up the long gradients, 150, his eyes measuring the lit course in front of him. How fast could he safely go at night?

Just over the crest of the next rise a valley opened up before him and the GS moved past the 160 mark. He saw the blue and red revolving lights of the law far ahead in the distance.

He grabbed the front brakes, kicked the back brake, and the ABS shuddered, intense pressure crushing his arms, but he kept the clutch in, for a moment he thought he would lose control, and then he had stopped, in the middle of the road, and there was something he still had to do—what was it? the lights, turn off the lights—searching for the switch in panic, got it, switched it off with his right thumb and suddenly he was night blind, all dark, just himself and the knowledge that they knew, that they were waiting for him, that everything had changed.

Again.

12.

The crime reporter of the *Cape Times* didn't know that the call would be a turning point in her life.

She would never know whether the loss of life would have been less and the outcome very different if she had taken her bag and left for home one minute earlier.

She was by nature a plump woman, cheerful, with wide soft curves and a broad quick smile and a hearty laugh, jolly dimples in her cheeks. If she had been more introspective, she might have wondered if she got on with people so easily because she presented no threat.

Her name was Allison Healy, and when the phone rang on her desk late on a Sunday night, she answered with her usual cheery voice.

"Times," she said.

"Allison, this is Erasmus from Laingsburg." Slightly muffled, as if he didn't want his colleagues to hear. "I don't know if you remember me."

She remembered. The policeman had worked at the Sea Point office. They called him "Rassie." Burned out at twenty-eight in the fight against a declining suburb, he had transferred to more restful pastures. She greeted him happily, asking how he was. As well, he replied, as you could be in a place where the sweet blow all grew a meter high. She laughed her throaty laugh. Then the voice on the line became serious.

"Do you know about the Xhosa on the BMW?"

"No," she said.

"Then I've got a story for you."

CLASSIFIED GRADE ONE

MEMORANDUM

17 NOVEMBER 1984 19:32

STATUS: Urgent

FROM: Derek Lategan, legal attaché, Embassy, Washington

TO: Quartus Naudé

Urgent request from CIA, Langley, Virginia: Any possible information and/or photographic material:

Thobela Mpayipheli, alias Tiny, alias Umzingeli. Suspected previously Umkhonto we Sizwe, probably current operator, Stasi/KGB. Probably operational in UK/Europe. Black male, 2.1 m, 100–120 kg. No further intelligence available.

End

Janina Mentz looked at the fax, the poor reproduction, the handwritten note in the upper right corner barely legible: "Our help with this matter could open doors. Regards, Derek."

She checked the cover page. "Attachments: 1."

"Is this all?" she asked.

"Yes, ma'am, that's all," said Radebe.

"Where's the follow-up? Where's the answer?"

"They say that's the only reference on the microfiche, ma'am. Just that."

"They're lying. Send a request for the follow-up correspondence. And contact details for the sender and addressee of the memorandum: Lategan and Naudé."

Why did they have to struggle for cooperation? Why the endless rivalry and politicking? She was angry and frustrated. She knew the real source was the new information, the caliber of their fugitive and their underestimation of him. This meant escalation. It meant trouble. For her and the project. And if the NIA wanted to play games, she had to get a bigger stick.

She reached for the phone and dialed an internal number. The director answered.

"Sir," she said, "we need help with the NIA. They are not playing ball. Can you use NICoC influence?"

The director, together with the director-general of the National Intelligence Agency, the head of Military Intelligence, the head of the Police National Investigation Service, and the director-general of the Secret Service, was a member of the National

Intelligence Coordinating Committee, under the chairmanship of the minister.

"Let me phone the DG direct," said the director.

"Thank you, sir."

"I am happy to help, Janina."

She took up the fax again. In 1984 the CIA suspected that Mpayipheli was working for the KGB? In Europe?

The CIA?

Urgent request . . . Our help with this matter could open doors.

This man? This middle-aged gofer? The coward from the airport?

She pulled the transcript of the Orlando Arendse interview from the pile in front of her. *So let me give you some advice: Start ordering the body bags now.*

She took a deep breath. No reason to worry. It meant Johnny Kleintjes knew what he was doing. He would not put his safety in amateur hands. They had underestimated Mpayipheli. She would not make that mistake again.

She used the new intelligence, ran through her strategy. More sure than ever that he would use the N1. A cool cat, this one, self-assured: his display at the airport calculated to mislead, the smooth disarming of the agents explained, the choice of motorbike, in retrospect, very clever.

But still they had the upper hand. Mpayipheli did not know that they knew.

And if things went wrong, there was always the leverage of Miriam Nzululwazi. And the child.

He knew he had to get off the road. He couldn't stay where he was in the dark. Or he must turn back, find another route; but he was unwilling, his entire being rejected retreat; he must move on, to the north.

Gradually his eyes adjusted to the darkness. He switched the motorbike on, slowly rode to the side of the highway, looked at the moonlit veld, the wire fence straight as an arrow parallel with the N1. He was looking for a farm gate or a wash under the wire, kept glancing back, unwilling to be caught in the glare of oncoming headlights. He wanted to get off and have a stretch and think.

How far ahead was that roadblock? Four or five kilometers. Closer. Three?

Thank God the GS's exhaust noise was soft. He kept the revs low, scanning the fences, saw promise on the opposite side of the road, a gate and a two-track road into the veld. He rode over, tires crunching on the gravel, stopped, put the bike on the stand, pulled off his gloves, checked the fastening of the gate. No padlock. He pulled the gate open, rode the bike in, and closed the gate behind him.

He must get far off the road, but close enough to still see the lights.

He realized his good fortune: the GS was dual-purpose, made for blacktop and dirt road, the so-called adventure touring bike, spoke wheels, high and well sprung. He turned in the veld so the nose faced the highway, stopped, got off. He pulled the helmet off his head, stuffed the gloves inside, placed it on the saddle, stretched his arms and legs, felt the night breeze on his face, heard the noises of the Karoo in the night.

Blue and red and orange lights.

He heard an oncoming vehicle, from the Cape side, saw the lights, counted the seconds from when it flashed past, watching the red taillights, trying to estimate the distance to the roadblock, but it got lost in the distance, melting into the hazard lights.

He would have to turn back. Take another route.

He needed a road map. Where did his other choices lie? Somewhere there was a turnoff to Sutherland, but where? He did not know that region well. It was on the road to nowhere. A long detour? Tried to recall what lay behind him. A road sign on the left had called out "Ceres" before Touws River even, but it would take him almost back to Cape Town.

He breathed in deeply. If he must, he would go back, whether he wanted to or not. Rather a step backward than wasting his time here.

Stretched, bent his back, touched toes, stretched his long arms skyward, cracked his shoulder joints backward, and took up the helmet. Time to go.

Then he saw the orange flashing lights coming closer from the blockade. Stared rigidly at them.

Yellow? That was not the Law. A possibility whispered; he watched, filling up with hope as the vehicle approached, the noise reaching him, and then it took shape, rumbled past sixty meters from where he stood, and he saw the trailer clearly, the wreck being towed, a car that had rolled, and he knew it was not a roadblock—they were not looking for him.

An accident. A temporary hurdle.

Relief.

He would just have to wait.

"The problem," said Rahjev Rajkumar, "is that Absa keeps only the last two months' statements immediately accessible for any account. The rest are backed up on an offline mainframe, and there is no way to get in there. The good news is that that is the only bad news. Our Thobela had a savings account and a bond on a property. This is where it gets interesting. The balance in the savings account is R52,341.89, which is quite a sum for a laborer. The only income the last two months was from Mother City Motorrad, a weekly payment of R572.72, or R2,290.88 per month—and the interest on the account, just over R440 per month. The debit order from the savings account for the bond repayment is R1,181.59. There is another debit order, for R129 per month, but I can't work out what that is for. That leaves him with R1,385.29 per month to live off. He draws R300 a week from an auto bank, usually the one at Thibault

Square, and it seems like the remaining R189.29 is saved. A disciplined man, this Thobela."

"The property?" Janina prodded.

"That's the funny thing," said Rajkumar. "It's not a house. It's a farm." He raised his head, looking for a reaction from the audience.

"You have our attention, Rahjev."

"Eighteen months ago Mpayipheli bought eight hundred hectares near Keiskammahoek. The farm's name is Cala, after the river that runs there. The bond—listen to this—is just over R100,000, but the original purchase price was nearly half a million."

"Keiskammahoek?" said Quinn. "Where the hell is that?"

"Far away in the old Ciskei, not too far from King William's Town. Seems he wants to go back to his *roots*."

"And the thing is, where did he get the other R400,000?" said Janina Mentz.

"Precisely, ma'am. Precisely."

"Good work, Rahjev."

"No, no," said the fat Indian. "Brilliant work."

Thobela Mpayipheli sat with his back against a rock, watching the lights on the N1.

The night had turned cool; the moon was high, a small round ball on its way, unmarked, to score the goal of the night in the west. His eyes wandered over the desolate ridges, followed the contours of the strange landscape. They said there were rain forests here long ago. Somewhere around here, he had read, they dug up bones of giant dinosaurs that lived between the ferns and short stubby trees, a green pleasure garden of silver waterfalls and thunderstorms that watered the reptilian world with fat drops. Weird sounds must have risen with the vapor from the protojungle: bellows, bugling, clamor. And the eternal battle of life and death, a frightful food chain, terrifying predators with rows of teeth and small, evil eyes hunting down the herbivores. Blood had flowed here, in the lakes and on the plains.

He shifted against the chilly stone. Blood had always flowed on this continent. Here where man at last had shrugged off the ape, where he left his first tracks on two feet in mud that later turned to stone. Not even the glaciers, those great ice rivers that transformed the landscape, that left heaps of unsuspecting rocks in grotesque formations, could staunch the flow of blood. The ground was drenched in it. Africa. Not the Dark Continent. The Red Continent. The Mother. That gave life in abundance. And death as counterweight, creating predators to keep the balance, predators in all their forms, through the millennia.

And then she created the perfect hunter, the predator that upset the balance, that could not be controlled by ice ages and droughts and disease, that kept on sowing destruction, rejecting her power and might. The two-legged predators carried out the great coup, the cosmic coup d'état, conquered all and then turned on one another, white against white, black against black, white against black.

He wondered if there was hope. For Africa. For this land.

Johnny Kleintjes. If steadfast Johnny Kleintjes could bow to temptation, led astray by the rotten stink of money, merely one of the lures of this continent, could there be hope?

He sighed deeply. More lights broke away from the cluster in the darkness; an ambulance siren wailed through the night, coming closer, gone along the road.

Not long now.

It became systematically still again. He heard a jackal howl, far over the ridges, a mockery of the ambulance.

Predators and scavengers and prey.

He was the former. *Was.*

Maybe. Perhaps there was hope. If he had looked into the mirror of his life and found it abhorrent, he who lived his carnivore vocation so mercilessly, then there could be others like him. And perhaps that was all that was needed, one person, first only one. Then two, four, and a handful of people to shift the scales, just a fraction of a millimeter, to reclaim Mother Africa piece by piece, foot by foot, to rebuild, to give a glimmer of hope.

Maybe, if he and Miriam could take Pakamile Nzululwazi away to the Cala River, make a new beginning far from the city, in the landscape of his forefathers, away from the cycle of poverty and soulless travail, the crime, the corruption of empty foreign cultures.

Maybe.

Because nothing in this world could make him as he once was.

The Rooivalk helicopters chose their flight path through the tops of the cumulus nimbus, the white towers majestic in the moonlight, lightning striking silver tentacles kilometers far through the system, turbulence jerking and shaking them, the green, orange, and red flickering of the weather radar screens confirming the system.

"Another ten minutes, then we're through," said the pilot of Rooivalk One. "ETA, twenty-two minutes."

"Roger, One," answered the other.

Just over 160 kilometers east of the two attack helicopters the flight engineer of the Oryx clicked on the intercom.

"Better buckle up, Mazibuko."

"What's up?"

"Weather system. And it looks bad."

"How long still?" asked Tiger Mazibuko.

"Just over an hour. I hope you brought raincoats in those crates."

"We're not scared of a little rain."

Just wait, thought the flight engineer. *Wait till the winds begin tossing us around.*

13.

Allison Healy wrote the story immediately, because the official deadline was already past.

> CAPE TOWN—A manhunt for an armed and danger-ous fugitive is under way after an unknown gov-ernment intelligence agency alerted local police and traffic authorities along the N1 to be on the lookout for a Xhosa man traveling on a big BMW motorcycle.

No, she thought. *Too formal, too official, too crime-reporter. There's a lighter element in this story, something unique.*

> CAPE TOWN—A big, bad Xhosa biker on a huge BMW motorcycle is the subject of a province-wide manhunt, after an undisclosed and top-secret gov-ernment intelligence agency alerted police and traffic officials along the N1 to be on the lookout for what they called "an armed and dangerous fugitive."

Reliable sources told the *Cape Times* the alert was posted around 22:00 last night, but the directive did not provide details about the reason Mr. Thobela Mpayipheli was sought so desperately by what is rumored to be the Presidential Intelligence Unit (PIU).

The fugitive is allegedly in possession of two firearms and one BMW R 1150 GS, all illegally obtained, "but apparently that's not the reason they want to apprehend him," the source said.

Now she had to spin another paragraph or two out of the meager details. That was all the front page would have room for.

The news editor stood impatiently in the doorway. "Almost done," she said. "Almost done." But she knew he would wait, because this was news, good front-page material. "With legs," he had said in his cubicle when she had told him about it. "Nice little scoop, Alli, very nice."

When she had scurried out to begin writing, he had called after her: "We've got a head start. When you're done, go get us more. *Who* is this guy? Why do they want him? And what the hell is he doing on a BMW bike, for God's sake?"

"The Rooivalks are in Beaufort West, ma'am," said Quinn. "They are waiting for your instructions."

"Tell them to get some sleep. If we haven't heard anything by dawn, they can start patrolling the N1 southward. But they must talk with us before they take off. I don't want contact with the fugitive before we are ready."

"Very well, ma'am."

She gave him time to relay the message. She counted hours. He couldn't be close yet, too early. If he made good time on the BMW, he would be somewhere on the other side of Laingsburg. Another two hours to Beaufort West. Not a great deal of time.

"Is the roadblock ready at Three Sisters?"

"The police and traffic people are there already, ma'am. They are moaning. It's raining in the Karoo."

"They'll grumble about anything, Quinn. They know they have to check all vehicles?"

"They know, ma'am."

"How long before Mazibuko gets there?"

"Anytime now, ma'am. Ten minutes, no longer."

Captain Tiger Mazibuko sat with folded hands, eyes closed in the yellow-lit vibrating interior of the Oryx, but he did not sleep.

It was the dawning realization that the Reaction Unit would never come into its own that kept him awake. His teammates were asleep. They were accustomed to the cramped, uncomfortable conditions, able to snatch a few minutes or occasional hour of sleep between events. Mazibuko, too. But rest eluded him; the germ of unease over their deployment had grown since his last exchange with Mentz. He had never thought about it this way before: they were somewhere between a counterterrorist instrument and a hostage rescue unit, cast in the mold of the FBI Hostage Rescue Team and the similar group of the British Special Air Services, the SAS. They had been operational for thirteen months and had done nothing more than simulated training exercises. Until now. Till they had to invade a drug den like fucking blue-trouser cops, and now they were to man a roadblock in this godforsaken desert to wait for a middle-aged fugitive who might once have been an MK soldier.

Maybe he should go see his father and ask him whether, before he sold out to the Boers, before he sang his cowardly song of treason, he had known someone called Thobela Mpayipheli.

His father. The great hero of many kitchen battles with his mother. His father, who beat his wife and who beat his children to the breaking point because he could not live with his humiliation. Because in a Security Police cell he had broken, and the names and places, the methods and the targets had bubbled out over the floor with the spit and the blood and the vomit. And then, deliberately released, the shame shackled to his ankles defined the shuffling course of his life.

His father.

Isn't it time to move out from your father's shadow? Janina Mentz's words could not be blocked out.

Did you know Mpayipheli, Father? Was he one of those you betrayed?

Since the beginning he had had visions, dreams at night and fantasies in his solitary moments. Fired up by the training and Mentz's propaganda, prospects of microbattles, of lightning raids in dark passages, shots cracking, grenades exploding, smoke and cordite and life and death, bullets ripping through him, bursting his head, spattering his rage against the walls. He lived for that, lusted after it. It was the fuel of his zeal, his salvation, the ripping loose from the sins of his father, the destruction of the cells of his brain with the memories, and now he wondered if it would ever happen. Mentz telling him so seriously that the world had become an evil place, presidents and countries not knowing who was friend or foe, wars that would no longer be fought with armies but at the front of secret rooms, the mini-activities of abduction and occupation, suicide attacks and pipe bombs. September 11 was water to her mill, every statement of every radical group she held up as watertight evidence. And where did they find themselves now?

He heard a change in the note of the engines.

Nearly there.

Now they sat in a land the world had passed by. Even the terrorists were no longer interested in Africa.

The Reaction Unit, sent to man a roadblock. The world's best-trained traffic officers.

A good thing the fucker had two pistols. A pity he was alone.

Just after two A.M. he swept easily around the last bend and saw Laingsburg brightly lit before him. Conscious that the dark blanket of night had lifted, he felt his heart beat beneath his ribs. The reserve tank light shone bright orange, leaving him no choice. He slowed down to the legal sixty, saw the big petrol station logo on the left—time to get it over with—turned in, and stopped at a pump, the only vehicle at that time of night.

The petrol jockey came slowly out of the night room, rubbing his eyes.

Thobela put the motorbike on the main stand, climbed off, and removed his gloves. He must get money out.

The jockey was at his side. He saw his eyes widen.

"Can you fill up? With unleaded?"

The man nodded too eagerly. Something was not right.

He unlocked the tank, lifted the valve.

"They are looking for you," said the jockey, his head conspiratorially close, his voice a hoarse whisper as he placed the spout in the tank.

"Who?"

"Police."

"How do you know?"

"They were here. Said we must look for a Xhosa on a motorbike. A bee-em-double-you."

"So what are you supposed to do?"

"I have to phone them."

"And will you?"

"They say you're armed and dangerous."

He looked at the man, into his eyes. "What are you going to do?"

The attendant shrugged his shoulders, staring into the tank.

Just the noise of the fuel running in, the sweet aroma of petrol.

Eventually: "It's full."

The digital figures on the pump read R77.32. Mpayipheli took out two hundred-rand notes. The attendant pulled one only from his fingers.

"I don't take bribes." He took a last look at the man in the helmet, turned on his heel, and walked away.

"Masethla. NIA. I understand you need our assistance," said the voice on the phone without friendliness or subservience.

You need our assistance. "I appreciate your calling," said Janina without appreciation. "We inquired about any references to a Thobela Mpayipheli in the microfiche library and you sent a fax with a 1984 memorandum from Washington."

"That is correct."

"I can't believe that this is the only reference. There must have been a response."

"Possibly. What is it about?"

"Mr. Masethla, I don't see the necessity to explain that. It was an urgent official request in the national interest. We are all working for the same interest. Why can't we get the other documentation?"

"There isn't any."

"What?"

"There isn't any other documentation."

"You say this memorandum is all?"

"Yes."

"I can't believe that."

"You will have to."

She pondered this for a moment. "Mr. Masethla, is your library complete?"

He was silent at the other end.

"Mr. Masethla?"

"It is not my library. It was the Boers'. In the old South Africa."

"But is it complete?"

"We have reason to believe that some films were removed."

"Which films?"

"Here and there."

"By whom?"

"Whom do you think, Mrs. Mentz? Your people."

"The PIU?"

He laughed at her. "No. The whites."

Rage swept over her. She gripped the receiver with whitened knuckles, fighting it back, swallowing it, waiting till her voice would not betray her.

"The sender and receiver of the memorandum. I want their contact details."

"They have left the agency."

"I want their details."

"I will see what I can do."

Then she unleashed her rage. "No, Mr. Masethla. You will not see what you can do. You will have their details to me in sixty minutes. You will get rid of your attitude and you and your people will get to work if you don't want to become another unemployed statistic tomorrow. Do you understand?"

He took just long enough to answer that she thought she had won this round. "Fuck you, you white bitch," he said. Then he put the phone down.

Captain Tiger Mazibuko was first out of the Oryx with a hand on his hat so the rotor blast would not blow it away.

In the pitch dark he saw one white van from the SAPS and one blue and white Toyota Corolla from the provincial traffic authority, blue lights revolving. They were parked beside the road, and a single traffic officer with a flashlight in hand stood on the N1 road surface. A few orange traffic cones indicated a parking area for vehicles. The officer was indicating an 18-wheeler truck to stop.

Mazibuko swore and strode over to the police van, saw one of the occupants opening the door. He stood directly in the opening, one hand on the roof, and leaned in.

"What is going on here?" He had to shout, as the engines of the Oryx were still winding down.

There were two inside, a sergeant and a constable; each had a coffee mug. A thermos stood on the dashboard. Faces looked back at him guiltily.

"We are drinking coffee, what does it look like?" the sergeant shouted back.

"Is this your idea of a roadblock?"

The two policemen looked at each other. "We haven't got a flashlight," said the sergeant.

Mazibuko shook his head in disbelief. "You haven't got a flashlight?"

"That's right."

The helicopter's motors wound down gradually. He waited until he no longer needed to shout. "And what are you going to do when an armed fugitive on a motorbike races through here? Throw the thermos at him?"

"There have been no motorbikes so far," said the constable.

"Lord help us." Mazibuko shook his head from side to side. Then he slammed the door and walked back to the helicopter. The men had disembarked and were standing, waiting, their faces glowing in the reflected blue lights. He barked orders about weapons and equipment and their deployment. Four men must take over for the traffic officer, four must walk a hundred meters up the road as backup, four must put up two tents next to the road as shelter from the rain.

The truck crawled past him. The officer had not even looked in the back. He walked to the dark figure with the flashlight. He saw that the two policemen were out of the van, standing around aimlessly.

"What is your name?" he asked the traffic officer.

"Wilson, sir."

"Wilson, would a motorbike fit in the back of that truck?"

The traffic officer was tall and impossibly thin, a floppy fringe hung over his eyes. "Uh . . . er . . . possibly, but . . ."

"Wilson, I want you to pull your Corolla onto the road here. Block off this lane. Understand?"

"Yes, sir." His eyes glanced from Mazibuko to the helicopter and back, deeply impressed by the importance of the arrivals.

"Then tell your friends to pull their van there, in the other lane, about ten meters farther on."

"Right, sir."

"And then you sit in your vehicles and start the engines every fifteen minutes to keep them warm, do you understand me?"

"Yes, sir."

"Have you got a road map of this area?"

"Yes, sir."

"Can I look at it?"

"Yes, sir."

Pulsating white light suddenly lit up the night around them. Thunder grumbled above, a deep rolling from east to west. A few drops plopped on the blacktop.

"It's getting closer, sir. It's going to be a mother of a storm."

Mazibuko sighed. "Wilson."

"Yes, sir?"

"You don't have to 'sir' me. Call me 'captain' instead."

"Right, Captain." And he saluted him with the wrong hand.

Thobela Mpayipheli saw the far-off flashes of light on the northern horizon, but he didn't know it was the dance of lightning. Above him the starry heavens were clear, but he didn't see them, he rode at 150 km per hour, the headlights illuminating the road straight ahead of him, a bright cocoon in the night, but his gaze was on the rearview mirrors.

What had the petrol attendant done?

There was nothing behind him. They would have to drive to catch him. At 160 or 180, and even then the gap would not close quickly. Or they would radio ahead, to Leeu-Gamka or Beaufort West.

Probably both, a pincer with him in the middle.

They knew. The spooks from the Cape knew about him and the GS. They had guessed his route correctly.

Not bad.

And if the jockey had reported him, they would know he knew they knew. If the man had reported him. He couldn't read his expression; that nothing-to-do-with-me attitude could have been a smoke screen.

They say you're armed and dangerous.

The pistols. That he didn't even have. Well, let them miscalculate. But *dangerous*? What did they know? Possibilities danced through his head and he felt the tension run through his body and then Otto Müller came to visit. In the night on a Karoo road he heard the voice of the Odessa instructor, the East German with the fine, almost feminine features below a grotesque bald head, nearly twenty years past. He heard the heavy Germanic accent, the stilted English. *It is game theory; it is referred to as the Nash equilibrium. When two players have no reason to change from their chosen strategies, they continue with those strategies. The equilibrium. How do you break the equilibrium? That is the question. Not by second-guessing, because that is part of the strategy and therefore part of the equilibrium. In a game of chess, you will lose if you think only of your opponent, think of every option, think of every possibility. You will go crazy. Think what you will do. Think about your strategy. Think how you can change it. How you can dominate. How you can break the equilibrium. Be the actor, not the reaction. That is the key.*

Otto Müller. There was a bond between them; he was one of only ten operators, the rest from the Eastern bloc, Poland, Czechoslovakia, Romania. He was one of the chosen and he fascinated Müller. *I have never taught a schwarze before.*

So he said, *I haff never taken orders from ze whitezer before.* Lord, he was full of fire in those days. Müller laughed at his put-on German accent. *You have the right . . . what is the words . . . attitude?*

He didn't tell the Stasi man he had been born with that *attitude;* he didn't have the self-knowledge then, his *attitude* engulfed him, his *attitude* was him, his complete being.

A month or so ago he had read in a textbook about enzymes, very large molecules in the human cell that elicit a chemical reaction by presenting a surface that encourages that particular reaction. He pondered this, found in himself the metaphor of this biology. His whole life he had floated through the bloodstream of the world with a surface that encouraged violence as a reaction, until that moment when it had made him sick, that moment for the first time in thirty-seven years when he could step back from himself and see and find it repugnant.

The difference was that enzymes cannot change their nature.

People can. Sometimes people must.

In a game of chess, your opponent is looking for patterns of play. Give him the pattern. Give him the Nash equilibrium. Then change it.

But to do that he needed information.

They expected him to follow the N1. He could change this pattern only if he knew what his options were. He needed a good road map. But where on earth could he get one?

Her first impulse after replacing the phone was to be with her children.

She fought it, understanding the need, understanding that Masethla's cutting words made her look for comfort, but her head said she must get used to it, she should have known that Masethla would not like being leaned on from above, would be incapable, too, from a relative position of power of taking orders from a strong woman.

They were all like that.

Lord, why did there have to be men, why did she have to fight against their weak, brittle, fragile egos? That and the sex thing, the one-way traffic of their thoughts—if you were a woman, you were prey. If you didn't give in and jump into bed, you were a lesbian; if you were a woman in authority, you had slept your way to the top; if he was a man with more authority, then you were screwable.

She had learned these lessons hard. A decade ago, after a long, frustrating, and even painful realization that she would have to live with a constant of overt and covert innuendo and sexual advances, she had taken stock of herself and pinpointed her two physical assets. Her large mouth, wide and full-lipped, white and regular teeth, and her bust, impressive without being excessive. She had developed a deliberate style: no lipstick; small, severe steel-rimmed glasses, and hair always drawn back and fastened; outfits never too formfitting, neutral colors, mostly gray, white, and black. And her actions, interactions, communications, were refined until eventually the volume of erotic interest was turned down to acceptable, manageable levels.

But about the other thing, the ego, she could do nothing.

That is why she forced her thoughts away from her children, stood up and straightened, brushing the wrinkles from her skirt, smoothing her hair.

Rajkumar brought a result. "The other debit order, ma'am, the R129 per month?"

"What?" she said, not in the present right then.

"The other debit order on Mpayipheli's bank account. The clearance code . . . I ran it down. We know where the money is going."

"Yes?"

"To the CCE. The Cape College of Education."

"For the child?"

"No. It's a correspondence college. For adults."

"Oh."

"High school education. Grade ten to twelve. Someone is doing a course with them."

There was little new in the information. "Thanks, Rahjev."

Her cell phone rang. She checked the screen, which read MAZIBUKO.

"Tiger?"

"I am letting Bravo come down from Bloemfontein. In our vehicles."

"What for?"

"There's nothing happening here. Two policemen and a speed cop with two vehicles. There's a big thunderstorm on the way that looks bad, and there are two or three roads off the N1 between here and Beaufort West and who knows how many farm roads."

"He's on a motorcycle, Tiger."

"I know. But if he spots the blockade and turns back, how do we pursue him?"

"With the Rooivalks."

"In the rain?"

"How sure are you that it will rain?"

"Ma'am, it's raining already."

"It's a five-hour drive from Bloemfontein, Tiger."

"That's why I want them to leave at once."

She decided. "Okay, let them come."

"Mazibuko out."

"Tiger?"

"I'm here."

"Mpayipheli. He might have been more than MK."

"More?"

"Don't underestimate him."

"What do you mean? What have you found?"

"He . . . We don't know enough yet. Just don't underestimate him."

"He's still only one man."

"That's true."

"Mazibuko out."

She pressed the END button on the cell phone. Her eye caught the fax machine printing out a document. Stepping up to it she read the heading as she waited for it to finish. NIA.

"Well, well," she said softly, keeping her fingertips on the paper till it finished and then picking it up.

Last known address—Derek Lategan: Orange River Wine Exports, P.O. Box 1798, Upington, Northern Cape
Last known address—Quartus Naudé: 28 Four-teenth Avenue, Kleinmond, Western Cape

Masethla had supplied the information. She could imagine his internal struggle, his reluctance, irritation, and fear that his outburst would be reported. A small victory for her. She found no pleasure in it.

Frowning, Radebe came over the floor to her with another document in his hand. "Here's an odd one,

ma'am. This report came in from Pretoria, but we
hadn't given instructions."

She took it from him.

Transcript of interview by V. Pillay with Mr. Gerhardus Johannes Groenewald, 23 October, 21:18, 807
Dallas Flats, De Kock Street, Sunnyside, Pretoria

P: You were on the integration team with Johnny
     Kleintjes?
G: I was second in command.

"It was on my orders, Vincent."

"Ma'am?"

"I phoned Pillay direct. Groenewald was in our
records."

Radebe looked at her, frowning still.

"I'm sorry, Vincent. I ought to have told you."

"Ma'am, that's not it. . . ."

"What is it?"

"I thought I knew all our agents."

She kept eye contact with him, smiling reassur-
ingly. "Pillay doesn't work full-time for us, Vincent.
I don't want to interfere with your people."

The frown lifted.

"Ma'am, there's something else. . . ." His voice was
soft, as if he didn't want the others to hear.

"Talk to me."

"Mpayipheli, ma'am. We are treating him like a criminal."

"He *is* one, Vincent."

It seemed that he wanted to contradict her but thought better of it.

"He disarmed two of our agents, refusing a legal request to hand over state property. He stole a motorcycle."

Radebe's gaze was far-off. He nodded, but she did not feel that he agreed. He turned around. She watched him thoughtfully until he sat down.

Transcript of interview by V. Pillay with Mr. Gerhardus Johannes Groenewald, 23 October, 21:18, 807 Dallas Flats, De Kock Street, Sunnyside, Pretoria

P: You were on the integration team with Johnny Kleintjes?

G: I was second in command.

P: Did you have access to the same material?

G: Yes.

P: Did you know Mr. Kleintjes had made backups of certain sensitive records?

G: Yes.

P: Tell me about it, please.

G: It's ten years ago.

P: I know, Mr. Groenewald.

G: Most of that data is useless now. The people . . . Things have changed.

P: We need to know.

G: Those were strange times. It was . . . To suddenly see what the enemy had on you, to show them what we had, it was surreal. Your enemy was no longer your enemy. After all those years. To work with them, it was difficult. For everyone. Both sides.

P: You worked for the National Party government, before 1992?

G: Yes.

P: Proceed, Mr. Groenewald.

G: Some people on the team couldn't handle it. It was conditioning, hammered into you for so many years, the secretiveness, the idea of us against them. Stuff disappeared.

P: What sort of stuff?

G: Operational records. The kind of stuff individuals didn't want counting against them. When Johnny Kleintjes realized that people were deleting stuff, he began to make backups. We worked together, as fast as we could. And when one of the backup tapes disappeared, he started taking work home.

P: Did you know what material he took home?

G: He never hid anything from me.

P: What was it?

G: There were the X-lists of the politicians, judges, and intelligence people. You know . . . who is sleeping with whom, who has financial troubles, who's in league with the opposition. And the E-lists. "E" for elimination. Who was killed. Who was to be taken out next. And the Zulu dossier.

P: The Zulu dossier?

G: You know, the Zulu nationalists.

P: I don't know, Mr. Groenewald.

G: You must know that in the Zulu ranks there is a conservative nucleus that still dreams of Zulu independence?

P: Proceed, Mr. Groenewald.

G: They supported the former regime's policy of separate development. They saw it as the way to their own sovereign Zulu state. Elements in the old regime were only too eager to help, promises were made, they worked intimately together. And then F. W. de Klerk went and cheated them by unbanning the ANC and allowing free elections.

P: Yes?

G: The Zulu dossier contains names of the secret Organization for Zulu Independence, the OZI. There are politicians, businessmen, and a lot of academics. The University of Zululand was a breeding ground. If I remember rightly, the head of the History Department was head of OZI for years.

P: Is that all? Just a list of OZI members?

G: No, there was more. Weapons caches, strategy, plans. And the name of Inkululeko.

P: You'll have to explain.

G: Inkululeko. A code name. It's the Zulu word for *freedom*. A member of the OZI who infiltrated the ANC years back. A mole. But high up. There was talk that he also worked for the CIA during the Cold War. Lately I heard a rumor that considering the present government's attitude to Libya and Cuba, for example, he was still helping the Americans.

P: Do you know who it is?

G: No.

P: But Johnny Kleintjes knows?

G: Johnny knew. He saw the list.

P: Why did he never expose it?

G: I don't know. I wondered about that. Remember the violence in Kwa-Zulu, Pillay? Remember the political murders, the intimidation?

P: I remember.

G: I wondered if he didn't use the list as a trump card in negotiations. You know, a sort of "stop your nonsense or I will leak the list" type of thing. The unrest decreased, later.

P: But that is rather unlikely, isn't it?

G: Yes. It is.

P: What do you think the real reason is?

G: I think Johnny Kleintjes knew Inkululeko personally. I think he was a friend.

14.

Through the lens of a hidden camera or the eyes of a voyeur the scene would have been sensual. Allison Healy sat before the hi-fi in her restored duplex in Gardens. She was naked. Her plump body glowed from the hot bath, the creams and oils she was massaging into her skin. The CD playing was *Women of Blue Chicago:* Bonnie Lee, Karen Carroll, Shirley Johnson, and her favorite, Lynne Jordan. Music about women's trouble with men. There was a cigarette in the ashtray on the small table next to the navy blue easy chair, smoke trailing upward in a tall, thin column. The room was softly lit by one table lamp alongside the small television.

Despite the potential an eye could find in this stage, her thoughts were far from sexual. She was considering a motorcyclist speeding through the night, a mysterious man hunted by law enforcement and intelligence officers. She wondered why.

Before she left the office she had phoned Rassie Erasmus of the Laingsburg police again. Asked questions. There was mischief in their talk, as if they were co-conspirators against the secret forces of the state, but the chat had yielded little new information.

Yes, the request to be on the lookout had come from the regional police head office. And the order to report there if they spotted something. No, it was never explicitly stated that it was the Presidential Intelligence Unit looking for Mpayipheli, but the police had their own language, their own references, their jealousies and envy. He was fairly certain it was the PIU. And from what he could gather, the fugitive had something the PIU was after.

"Any news on Mpayipheli, Rassie?"

"No. Not a word."

She reached for the journalist's study bible—the telephone directory. There were three Mpayipelis and four Mpayiphelis listed. All in Khayalitsha or Macassar, but none had the initial T. She phoned every number, aware of the late hour, knowing she would be disturbing hardworking people in their sleep, but she had a job to do, too.

"I am so sorry to bother you so late, but can I speak to Thobela, please?"

Every time the same response: a sleepy voice saying, "Who?"

Just to be sure, she had searched with Ananzi and Google on the Internet, typed in "Thobela Mpayipheli" and to be thorough, "Thobela Mpayipeli" and clicked on SEARCH.

Your search—Thobela Mpayipheli—does not appear in any documents.

So she had turned off the computer, took her handbag, said good-bye to the few colleagues still at work, and come home to a long hot bath, half a glass of red wine, her skin-care routine, music, and a last cigarette.

She rose to pack away the bottles and jars in the bathroom and returned to lie back in the chair, drawing deeply on the tobacco, closing her eyes to let Johnson's "As the Years Go Passing By" flow over her. It evoked nostalgia in her, for Nic, for the intensity of those moments. No. Longing for a journey. To the smoky blues bars of Chicago. To a world of pulsing, moaning rhythms, sensual voices, and strange new experiences, a new uncontaminated life.

Focused on the music. Sleep was near. The prospect of a long, well-deserved rest. She wasn't due back at work until noon.

Where was he now, the big, bad Xhosa biker?

He was two kilometers from Leeu-Gamka, the headlights turned off, the GS standing in the veld a few hundred meters from the road. He stripped off the suit, locked it in one luggage case, put the helmet in the other, and began walking toward the lights.

The night air was sharp and cool, carrying the pungent scent of Karoo shrubs crushed under his

boots. The weariness of the last fifty or sixty kilometers had invaded his body, his eyes were red and
scratchy, he was thirsty and sleepy.

No longer twenty, his body complained. He knew
he had been running on adrenaline, but the levels
were running low. He knew the next few hours till
dawn would be the most difficult. He walked briskly
to get his circulation going, his boots crunched gravel
on the road verge rhythmically. Lights from the petrol station on the right and the police station on the
left of the highway came steadily closer. There was
no movement, no sign of life, no roadblock or other
indications of a search. Had the petrol jockey in
Laingsburg said nothing? He owed him, he thought.
It was so difficult to read people, how oddly they
behaved. Why did the man not tell him he would
keep quiet? Why keep him worrying? Was he still
making up his mind?

He walked into the petrol station. There was
a twenty-four-hour kiosk, a tiny café. Behind the
counter was a black woman, fast asleep with her
chin dropped onto her chest, mouth half open. He
took two cans of Coca-Cola from the fridge, a few
chocolate bars from the shelf. Behind her on the wall
he saw the rack of road map books.

He cleared his throat. Her eyes opened.

"Sorry, sister," he said softly, smiling sympathetically at her.

"Was I asleep?" she asked, baffled.

"Just resting a bit," he said.

"What time is it?"

"Just after three," he said.

She took the cool drinks and chocolate and rang them up. He asked for a map book.

"Are you lost?"

"No, sister, we are looking for a shortcut."

"From here? There are no shortcuts here." But she took the book down from the shelf and put it in the plastic bag with the other things.

He paid and left.

"Drive safely," she called after him, and settled back in her chair.

He looked back once he was a little way off. He could see through the window that her head had dropped again. He wondered if she would remember he was there, in case anyone asked.

Halfway back to the bike he popped open a can of Coke, drinking deeply, burped the gas, drank again. The sugar would do him good. He emptied the can, opened a Milo bar, pushing the chunks into his mouth. A white Mercedes flashed past on the highway, spoiling his night vision for a while. He put the empty can and candy wrappers back into the plastic bag.

He would have to inspect the map book. He had no flashlight. The moon gave less light now, almost setting in the west. He should have bought a flashlight.

Perhaps the moonlight was sufficient. He left the road, cutting across the veld, for the first time thinking of puff adders. The night was cold, they shouldn't be active. He reached the GS and took the book out of the bag.

The routes and roads were a spiderweb of alternatives, spooky-looking in the dim light. He strained to see, the moon cast a shadow of his head over the page, forcing him to shift around, his eyes irritatingly close to the page. He found the right page.

There was a road from there, from Leeu-Gamka to Fraserburg.

Fraserburg?

The direction was wrong, too far west, too few possibilities. He must go north.

He saw there were two additional routes from Beaufort West, snaking threads to Aberdeen in the east and Loxton approximately north-northwest. That might do. He turned to the next page to follow it. Loxton, Carnarvon, Prieska. Too far west.

Paging back, he followed the N1 to Three Sisters. The road forked there. To Bloemfontein or Kimberley. Paging on, he found the Kimberley route, traced it with his finger. Promising. Many more options.

In a game of chess, your opponent is looking for patterns of play. Give him the pattern. Then change it.

"We will change it at Three Sisters, herr obergruppenführer," he said softly.

He would have to fill up in Beaufort West. He would ask how far it was to Bloemfontein, what the road was like. With any luck, the spooks would hear about it. And at Three Sisters he would take the road to Kimberley.

He took out the second can of Coke.

It was raining in the Great Karoo. The weather had rolled in over the plains, rumbling and spitting like some giant primordial predator, visible in the night sky only when lightning came searching in fantastic forms, and now here it was above them, the rains of Africa, extravagant and pitiless.

Captain Tiger Mazibuko cursed, splashing through ankle-deep puddles, wiping water from his face. The rain fell in dark sheets; thunder growled continuously.

He had been checking the maps in the traffic officer's car. There were at least two side roads they would have to block. Halfway between the roadblock and Beaufort West one turned east to Nelspoort, the other was closer, forking west to Wagenaarskraal. Unfamiliar routes, but alternatives available to a fugitive. And they had too few men and too few vehicles. He would have to deploy four RU members; the police van would have to drop them off, minimizing the effect of his roadblock here. They would have to guard the roads in pairs. They would be on foot, while he had a motorbike. Visibility was terrible in this weather. It was a fucking fiasco. But that was typical. Backward. Everything was backward. You could say what you liked about the Americans, but if the FBI Hostage Rescue Team had been here, it would have been four-wheel drives and armored vehicles and helicopters. He knew because he had been there, in Quantico, Virginia, for four months; he had seen it with his own eyes. But no, in Africa things worked differently; here, we fucked up. Here, we putter around with a bloody bakkie and a Corolla and a frightened traffic cop and two Boers who worry about their caps getting rained on and just one fucking middle-aged Xhosa on a motorbike—jissis, couldn't the fucker get a more respectable form of transport? Even the bad guys were backward in Africa.

He shook his fist at the heavens, which for a moment were still. He screamed his frustration, an uncanny sound, but the rain drowned it out.

He pushed his head into the tent. Four soldiers looked dumbstruck at him.

"I have to send you out," he said, calm and under control.

The early hours began to take their toll in the Ops Room; urgency had leaked away.

She struggled to decide whether to send people to Derek Lategan and Quartus Naudé tonight.

They weren't compelled to cooperate. They were retired agents, had taken the package, probably not benign to the present government. A visit at this time of night would just complicate matters. She weighed that against the need for information. What could they contribute? Could they confirm that Mpayipheli had worked for the KGB? What difference would that make to the investigation?

Let it wait, she thought. She looked up at the big chart of southern Africa on the wall.

Where are you, Mpayipheli?

Are you on the N1? How strong is your motivation? Are you sleeping somewhere in a hotel room while we make the wrong assumptions about you?

No. He was out there, somewhere; he couldn't be far from Mazibuko now. Contact. That is what they needed to shake off the lethargy, to regain momentum, to be in control again.

Contact. Action. Control.

Where was Thobela Mpayipheli?

She stood up. There was another job to do.

"May I have your attention, everyone," she said.

Unhurried, they turned to her.

"This time of night is always the worst," she said. "I know you've had a long day and a long night, but if our calculations are right, we can finish this before eight o'clock."

There was little response. Blank faces gazed back at her.

"I think we must see how many people we can relieve for an hour or two. But before we decide who is going to take a nap, there are some who wonder why we regard this fugitive as a criminal. I can understand why."

Bloodshot eyes looked back at her. She knew she was making no impression.

"But we must also wonder where all that money came from. We must remember he worked for organized crime. Remember that he hired out his talents for the purpose of violence and intimidation. That he stole two firearms, after rejecting the chance to work with the state. See the nature of the man."

Here and there a head nodded.

"We must be professional. There are too many gaps in our knowledge, too many questions unanswered. We have a very good idea now of what is on that hard drive. And that news is not good. We are talking about information on a mole at the highest level, code name Inkululeko. We are talking about very, very sensitive information that can cause untold damage in the wrong hands. Our job is to protect the state. Sympathy has no place in this. If we put everything into the balance, there is only one choice: be professional. Keep focused. Look at the facts, not the people behind them."

She looked over the room.

"Have you any questions?"

No reaction.

But no matter. She had planted the seed. She had to force herself not to look up at the ceiling where she knew the microphones were hidden.

15.

His thoughts roamed freely, for this road did not require much concentration. He thought of this and that, knowing he must get some sleep but not wanting to waste the darkness. Somewhere beyond Three Sisters once the sun was up he would find a screened and shaded place in the veld for a few hours' rest. He was familiar with the landscape of sleep deprivation, knew the greatest danger was poor judgment, bad decisions. His thoughts jumped around: Who were the spooks that were after him? How desperate were they? What was the whole purpose, the stuff on the drive that cast a hex over him?

In one month's time Pakamile would be finished with grade one. They could leave the township. How long had they been talking of this?

She didn't want to. She always wanted to stick to the known, afraid of change. As she had been with him, when he had started courting her. When he had first seen her, that time in the investment consultant's office, her hands—such deft, slim hands—her grace and pride, had been like a beacon to him. She wasn't even aware of him, but he could barely hear what the man was saying, she had consumed him so. He had been in love before, now and then, sometimes lust, sometimes more than that, but never absolutely right, never the way it was with Miriam, and she wanted nothing to do with him at first. The father of her child had put her off men, but he couldn't think of anything but her—Lord, to be in love like a teenager at his age, sweaty palms and heart beating haywire when he sat with her in Thibault Square in the bright sun and watched the cloud on the mountain grow and shrink and grow and he tried to hide the longing, afraid to scare her, his desire to touch her, to hold her hand, to press her against him and say, "I love you, you belong to me, let me keep you safe, I will chase away your fears like an evil spirit, I will cherish you, hold you and honor you."

He had to wait a year before he could make love to her, a year, twelve months of sighs and dreams, not at all what he had expected, soft and slow, quenching, and later his fingers on her body, no longer a young woman's body, found the traces of motherhood and he was overwhelmed with compassion, his hands traced the marks in awe at this thing that she had accomplished, the life she had created and carried and borne; in her and on her she carried the fullness of her vocation, and he could only trace it with his fingertips, so conscious of his incompleteness, so filled with the urge to find his own.

How would he tell her of the land he had bought? He already knew how she would react, how she clung to the things she had control over, because there was so much she could not control. The battle she had fought to get where she was, in her house with her son, had been so long, so hard in a world of poverty and violence. Her work, her house, her daily routine—it was her sanctum, her shield, her very survival.

One Saturday he had looked up from the mathematics textbook he was studying and decided that today was the day. She had her needlework in her hands, he had turned down the radio and told her that in that time when he had stared into his own eyes, his urge had been to get away, to go back to where he came from, to continue his life's journey back to the source, to begin again, a new life. To build something with his own hands—hands that had broken—perhaps a house, with his sweat and muscle and concentration, a place to live. To dig his fingers into the ground, to turn the earth and to plant and grow. He began to search, and weeks later he found it in the Cala valley, a beautiful place where the mist rose up against the mountain slopes in winter, where as far as the eye could see, the veld was an undulating green of fertility, Xhosa country, the landscape of his youth and his people.

He was on his way, busy with the final arrangements, when Miriam had crossed his path, and now, months later, the urge remained. But he could no longer do it alone, for he was no longer alone. He asked her to come with him. Her and Pakamile. They would take the child out of this harsh world and show him his heritage, let him learn other values, give him a carefree youth. There were schools there, in town, where he would get his education. She wouldn't have to work. It would be just the three of them; he could provide, he would provide, he would build this new life for them.

She was quiet for a long time, the needle and thread moving rhythmically in her hands. Then she said she needed to think about it—it was a big decision—and he nodded, grateful that she would at least consider it, that her first answer had not been no.

The lightning brought him back. It seemed there was rain up ahead. He looked at the odometer, another sixty to Beaufort West. The fuel was below half. The eastern horizon was changing color, he had to make town before daybreak to refuel. He opened the throttle, 160, feeling the tiredness in his body, 170, he checked the figures on his digital watch, 04:43, the night was nearly over, he had not come very far and there was a long way to go today. Kimberley—if he could get there, he could get a plane, 180, perhaps to Durban, to break the pattern, from Durban to Maputo, Maputo to Lusaka or something, but keeping flexible, 190, be adaptable, get this thing over and then go back, so Miriam would see he would never desert her, 200, the white lines on the road flew past, too fast, he had never gone so fast. Yes, the new day was a red ribbon in the east.

Two more vehicles arrived, an Opel Corsa and an Izuzu bakkie, policemen climbing out stiff-legged, pulling their raincoats tight around their bodies, irritated by the early call out and the rain. They walked over to Mazibuko.

"The sergeant called over the radio to say he has dropped off your men."

"I know. We have radio contact. Where's the sergeant now?"

"They have gone home. Their shift is over."

"Oh."

"The road will get very busy once it's light. Are you stopping everything?"

"Just the necessary. Are you here to help?"

"Yes."

"Then you must move your vehicles."

"How?"

He directed them. He wanted a formation that would make running the roadblock impossible. They followed his instructions, pulling their vehicles into the road while he waded through puddles to the helicopter and pulled open the door. The flight engineer lay asleep in the back with mouth agape. The pilot was up front, awake.

"Do you have a weather report?" asked Mazibuko.

"Yes," said the pilot. "Rain. Any minute now." He smiled broadly at his own joke.

"The rest of the day?"

"The system will move east. It will clear in the afternoon."

"Fuck."

"You can say that again."

Mazibuko pulled his cell phone from under his jacket and punched in a number.

"How far are you?" he asked.

"Just beyond Richmond," said Lieutenant Penrose, second in command of the Reaction Unit.

"You must move."

"We are driving as fast as we can, Captain."

"Is it raining there?"

"Not yet, but we can see it coming."

"Fuck," said Tiger Mazibuko.

"You can say that again," mumbled the pilot in the Oryx.

The consignment of Cape newspapers landed in a pile on the desk of the news editor of the SABC's morning television program in Auckland Park, Johannesburg, yesterday's *Argus* and this morning's *Burger* and *Cape Times*. It was one of his moments of truth every morning: how well the news team in the south had fared against the competition, but also a window to another strange world, ships sinking in storms, Muslim extremists, gangs in the Cape Flats, the ongoing political circus.

MORE NNP LEADERS CROSS OVER read the *Burger*'s headline in Afrikaans. No surprises there. Nor in the rugby analysis: SKINSTAD: WE HAVE NO EXCUSE. He overlooked the usual manipulative Christmas Fund article and skipped to the last front-page story of a thirteen-year-old cricket protégé. Mmmm. Country story, from Barrydale. He circled it with a thick red marker for follow-up.

Pulled the *Times* from the stack. NEW ALLIANCE FOR PROVINCE? the headline cried. And THERE GOES THE RAND AGAIN. Then his eye fell on the third front-page story. SPOOKS SEEK BIG, BAD BMW BIKER by Allison Healy. He read it.

"Molly," he called, but there was no response.

"Molly!"

A face appeared at the door.

"Get that asshole in the Cape on the line. Right now."

"Rooivalk One, this is Ops Control, come in, over." There was urgency in Quinn's voice. He waited a moment, got no reaction He made sure the frequency on the digital panel was correct, called again. "Rooivalk One, this is Ops Control, come in, over."

"This is Rooivalk One, Ops Control. What have you got for us? Over." The voice was a little sleepy.

"We have contact, Rooivalk One. Repeat, we have contact. Subject is four minutes out of Beaufort West on the N1 on the way to Three Sisters. We want you in the air. Do you read me? Over."

"We read you, Ops Control, we read you. Rooivalk One and Two operational. Over."

"What is your expected time of interception, Rooivalk One? Over."

"Expected time of contact, ten minutes, Ops Control, repeat, ten minutes. Over."

Quinn clearly heard the big engines being started up in the background. He spoke louder automatically. "We just want to chase him on to Three Sisters, Rooivalk One. We want presence, but no contact. Do you understand? Over."

"No contact, Rooivalk One confirming, no contact."

The pitch of the engines hit high. "Are you aware of the weather status, Ops Control? Over."

"We know it's raining at Three Sisters, Rooivalk One. What is your situation? Over."

"The rain is threatening, Ops Control. There's a helluva system up north. Over."

"Rooivalk One on the way, Ops Control. Over."

"Rooivalk Two ditto, over."

"We will keep contact, Rooivalk One, the channels stay open. Report when you intercept. Ops Control over and out."

"Roger, Ops Control. Rooivalk One over and out."

Quinn leaned back and looked around. Janina Mentz was busy on the cell phone with Tiger Mazibuko. The few people who had rested since four A.M. were back at their posts. There was a tingling in the air. The Ops Room was awake.

Allison Healy was dreaming of her mother when the phone rang. The dream was an argument, a never-ending, disconnected fight over nothing, and she was relieved by the sound. In her dream she lifted the instrument to answer, but it continued ringing.

She made a noise, a groan of reluctance to rise out of the deep sleep, sitting half upright in bed, the sheet falling away to bare her rounded nakedness to the room.

"Hullo."

"Allison?" It was the voice of a colleague, she couldn't place which one.

"What?"

"Are you awake?"

"Sort of."

"You had better come down here."

"What's going on?"

"There's a shoeshine man downstairs. He wants to talk to you."

"A shoeshine man?" She wondered if she was awake.

"He's a friend of your big, bad Xhosa biker."

"Oh shit," she said. "I'm coming."

16.

He had drunk coffee and swallowed an uninteresting sandwich at the petrol station while the attendant filled up, and he had asked how far it was to Bloemfontein and if there were police on the road. He had tried to look like an "armed and dangerous" fugitive and had no idea if anyone would take the bait. The jockey was jumpy as a cat in a dog run, but that meant nothing and now the dark bank of clouds hung before him, twenty, thirty kilometers away, and the road stretched out before him, the light washing the Karoo in pastels. He rode fast, 185, because he wanted to pass Three Sisters on his way to Kimberley before they could react, and the caffeine had awakened anxiety that he should have felt since Laingsburg. If they knew he had taken the motorbike and knew he was on the N1, why had there been no attempt to stop him, why were they not waiting for him?

Never mind, he thought, *never mind.* He was here and he had done all he could to establish Bloemfontein as his destination. All he could do now was ride as hard as he could, try 200 kilometers per hour; in daylight perhaps it would be less terrifying. He kicked down to fifth and twisted the ear of the great machine, feeling the vibration of the two flat cylinders, the boxer engine—strange name. He was consumed with urgency, anxiety. Where were they? What were they up to? What were they thinking? And when he heard the thunder, his first instinct was that it had come from the heavy clouds up ahead, but the noise was continuous and his heart turned cold. It was an unnatural thunder and then a dark thing swept over him, a huge shadow whose noise drowned out the boxer beneath him and he knew they were here; he knew what they were up to.

Miriam Nzululwazi was rinsing Pakamile's porridge bowl in the kitchen. She missed Thobela, he was the one who brought good humor to the morning. Before, it had been a silent, almost morbid rush to be ready before the school bus came and she had to catch the Golden Arrow to the city. Then had come the man who swung his feet off the bed at the crack of dawn with a lust for life, who made the coffee and carried the fragrant steaming mugs to the bedrooms, singing all the way—not always in tune, but his deep voice buoyed up the house in the morning.

She had said the boy was too young for coffee, but he said he would make it especially weak. She knew that hadn't lasted long. She had said she didn't want to hear that Afrikaans radio announcer in her house, but he said he and Pakamile couldn't learn to be farmers by listening to the music of Radio Metro every morning. They listened to the weather forecast and the market prices and the talk about farming topics, and the child was learning another language, too. He kept Pakamile on the go with RSG when the boy dawdled, saying, "Pakamile, it's raining on the farm," or "The sun is shining on the farm today, Pakamile, you know what that means?" And the boy would say, "Yes, Thobela, the plants are growing with chlorophyll," and he would laugh and say, "That's right, the grass is getting green and sweet and fat, and the cattle are going to swish their tails."

This morning she had switched on the radio to compensate for his absence, to restore normality. She listened to the weather forecast from habit, wanting to shake her head—here was Miriam Nzululwazi listening to Afrikaans; Thobela had changed so many things. She must go and see how far along Pakamile was. "Pakamile, have you brushed your teeth?"

"No, Ma."

"It's going to be hot on the farm today."

"Oh." Uninterested. He was missing Thobela, too. The time signal sounded on the radio, time for the news, she must hurry. The newsreader's somber voice sounded through the house, America in Afghanistan, Mbeki in England. The rand had dropped again.

"Don't dawdle, Pakamile."

"Yes, Ma."

Petrol was going up. Thobela would always talk back to the announcers and newsreaders, would always say when petrol prices were announced each month, "Get to the diesel price—Pakamile and I have a tractor to run," and then he and the boy would grin at each other and Pakamile would mimic the Afrikaans word *trekker,* rolling the *r*s that drew out each end of the word.

"According to a Cape newspaper, intelligence authorities are hot on the trail of a fugitive, Mr. Thobela Mpayipheli, who allegedly stole a motorcycle in Cape Town and is thought to be heading . . ." She ran to the kitchen and snapped off the radio before Pakamile could hear. Stole a motorcycle. *Stole a motorcycle, Thobela?* Her hands trembled; her heart beat in her throat.

What had he done?

In the Ops Room the voice of the pilot came clearly over the speakers. "Rooivalk One to Ops Control. We have intercepted. Thirty kilometers outside Beaufort West, fugitive on a yellow motorcycle, estimated speed 200 kilometers per hour. This guy is sending it. Over."

They applauded, the entire room, punching the air, shouting. Janina Mentz smiled broadly. She had been right, but mostly she felt relief, more than anything else, enormous relief.

"Ops Control to Rooivalk One, we hear you, interception verified. Just stay behind him, Rooivalk One. Do not attempt contact."

"Confirm no contact, Ops Control. We are just chasing him on."

"Ma'am," said Radebe, but over the applause she couldn't hear him.

"Ma'am?"

"Vincent?"

"The vehicle team says we must get hold of a *Cape Times*."

"Why?"

"They say there are posters all over town, ma'am."

It took an effort to change gears, to make the shift and understand what he was saying. "What do they say, Vincent?" The anxiety in her voice quickly silenced the entire room, only the radio static hissed.

SPOOKS

SEEK

BIG, BAD

BIKER

It was like a blow to her chest.

"Will you get us a paper, Vincent?"

"Yes, ma'am."

"Quinn, tell Mazibuko the subject is on his way, he must confirm contact with him. Rahjev . . ."

"Yes, ma'am?"

She looked up at the bank of television screens on the wall. "Put on TV2 for us. And eTV. And please ask someone to monitor the radio news."

"Okay, ma'am."

The police. She knew the leak came from the police.

Luckily, this thing was almost over.

The helicopter flew low over him, its dark belly scarcely a hundred meters above his head, and then it swooped back behind him and when he looked around he saw there were two of them, side by side, predatory birds biding their time behind him. He could feel the vibrations of their great engines in his body; the adrenaline ran thickly in his veins; the accelerator was fully open, but he knew it was in vain—these things were much faster. A truck came from ahead. The driver with disbelieving eyes nearly swerved in front of him. Why were they hanging back?

The needle was just beyond 200, the cloudbank loomed. Oncoming traffic had windshield wipers and lights on; he began to hope: How deep was this weather? How hard was it raining? Would the helicopters follow him in? He wanted to pass a car, the driver confused by the tremendous noise from above, brake lights—oh God, here's trouble—he swerved just in time, spray hit the helmet visor—shit—he was going too fast, he saw the rain ahead, a dense curtain, spatter became drops, hard to see, dying to lift a hand and wipe, but at this speed . . . A truck in front of him, he couldn't maintain this speed, couldn't see, he braked, closed the throttle, then the rain hit, sheets, gusts, the drops hard and stinging on his body, the truck's tires spurting up plumes of mist, he couldn't see oncoming cars, slower, slower, at last wiping his visor, just rearranging the water patterns. The rain was harder now, African rain, the lorry moved over, he went down a gear, accelerated, past but not fast, visibility was terrible—what to do?—and then he realized the helicopters' noise was fading, they were no longer with him.

"My name is Immanuel," he said to Allison Healy. "I'm the shoeshine man."

She put out her hand to him. "Hullo, Immanuel."

"I get the *Cape Times* every morning. I fetch my lot at the back here, I sell them. And when I have set out all my stuff, then I read it because there are not many clients so early."

"I understand," she said patiently.

"So this morning I read about Thobela."

"Mpayipheli?"

"He is my friend. And the things you wrote about him are not right."

"What do you mean?"

"He is not a 'big, bad biker.' "

"Uh . . . It's just a way of writing, Immanuel."

"But it's not true. He's a good man. He's a war veteran."

"A veteran?"

"That's right. He was a soldier in the Struggle. He fought in lands far away. Russia and Germany."

"MK?"

"He fought for all of us."

"You say he was an MK fighter?" This was news. Big news.

Immanuel just nodded.

"Why did he steal the motorcycle?"

"That's not true. Thobela doesn't steal."

"How do you know, Immanuel?"

"I know him. He's my friend. We talk, three, four times a week. He is an honest man. A family man."

"He has a family?"

"It's the most important thing in his life. Why would he steal?"

"Where can I find his family?"

"It's impossible. Ops Control, visibility is too poor. Heavy turbulence. We have to turn back. Over." Static crackled on the radio connection, the voice breaking up.

Quinn looked to Janina Mentz. She shook her head; he translated: "Negative, Rooivalk One, stay with him. Over."

"Ops Control, visibility is zero. We don't know where 'with him' is. We don't even have visual contact with each other. These are nonoperational conditions. Over."

He looked at Janina. She stood with folded arms, her lips thin. "How many million rand did it cost to develop these machines? And they can't fly through rain."

Quinn waited.

"Tell them to turn around. Tell them to make sure he doesn't go back."

Her cell phone rang in her pocket. She looked over the bank of televisions, where the country's channels were flickering: early-morning cartoons, local news, sports, CNN, the voices and music whispering. On TV2 the newsreader was talking. Behind him was a graphic of a man on a motorbike.

The cell phone rang.

Rahjev Rajkumar touched a panel, and the sound filled the room: "*. . . somewhere in the Western Cape on a stolen motorcycle. Considered to be armed and dangerous, it is not clear why authorities are seeking Mr. Mpayipheli at this time.*"

She felt like swearing. She picked up her phone.

"Mentz," she said grimly.

"Ma, Lien says I'm fat," said her daughter in a whiny tone.

He crept forward at fifty kilometers per hour, the leather gloves were sodden, his hands cold although he had turned on the electric heaters in the handgrips.

His biggest problem was seeing the road ahead, the inside of his helmet was steamed up and rain poured down the outside, the road was slippery. How to see the traffic ahead in time. The urge for speed and distance gnawing at him. At least the helicopters were quiet, but he knew they were out there somewhere. He had to get away.

They must want him very badly to use that sort of technology.

Johnny Kleintjes, what is on that hard drive?

They had waited for daylight, patient and easy, like a cat for a mouse, waited for the early morning, knowing he would be tired, knowing that the helicopters were excessive, that they would intimidate and conquer.

They were not fools.

The helicopters had stayed behind him.

Like dogs herding a sheep.

Into the pen.

They were waiting for him. Somewhere up ahead they were waiting.

Allison Healy's finger ran down the pages of the phone book, found "Nzululwazi," found "M. Nzululwazi, 21 Govan Mbeki Avenue." She scribbled the number down in her notebook, pulled the phone closer, and dialed.

It rang.

A war veteran. A family man. A good man.

Still ringing.

What was going on here? Why were they after him?

Ring, ring, ring. There was nobody home.

Time to ring Laingsburg again. Perhaps there was news.

17.

Seventeen kilometers south of the Three Sisters roadblock the gravel road turns west off the N1, an insignificant branch going nowhere, merely a connection that ends in a T junction at the normally dusty route between the forgotten villages of Sneeukraal and Wagenaarskraal.

Two soldiers were standing nearly three hundred meters from the paved road where the police van had dropped them off in the bend of the first turn. Little Joe Moroka and Koos Weyers were dry under their plastic raincoats, but the cold had seeped through their camouflage uniforms. Their faces were wet; water ran down the barrels of the R6 assault rifles and from there streamed down to the ground.

In the hour before dawn they had talked about sunrise and the light that would bring relief, but the rain still poured down. The only improvement was the visibility extending another forty or fifty meters to expose the low thorn trees and Karoo veld, the stony ridges and pools of mud.

It had been twenty-four hours since they slept, if you could even count that restless dozing on the Oryx. Their exhaustion was showing in the feebleness of their legs and the red scratchiness of their eyes, in the dull throbbing in their temples. They were hungry. Conversation ran to a fantasy of hot, sweet coffee, sausage, eggs and bacon, and toast with melting butter. They could not agree on the necessity for fried mushrooms. Moroka said fungus was snail food; Weyers responded that when taste was at issue, 60 million Frenchies couldn't be wrong.

They did not hear the motorbike.

The rain was a soundproof blanket. The exhaust of the GS fluttered softly at the low revs needed for the muddy road. The soldier's senses were dulled by weariness and tedium, and their voices drowned out the last chance of warning.

Later, when Little Joe Moroka gave his full report in the face of the spitting fury of Captain Tiger Mazibuko, he would attempt to break down and reconstruct each moment: They should not have stood so close to each other. They should not have been talking, should have been more alert.

But there are some things you cannot plan for, such as the fact that the fugitive had lost control. The straight just before the bend had a good surface where the bike would have accelerated; the turn would have been sudden and unexpectedly sharp. And just in front of them it was muddy, thick snotty porridge where a boot would sink twenty centimeters deep. The rider had followed the contour of the road formed by the regular traffic, but in the mud the front wheel had lost its grip at the critical moment.

They saw him—saw the light over the predatory beak of the monster machine and heard the engine when it was right in front of them, an apparition. Moments, fractions of moments, within which the senses register, signals are sent, the brain interprets and searches via a network of tired synapses for the right reaction in the memory banks of endless training.

In reflection Little Joe Moroka would will himself to react faster, but in the real moment he registered the uniform snicking of safety catches as he and Weyers reacted in unison, conditioned by training, the motorbike sliding, iron and steel colliding with Weyers. The rider falling away from the machine, Moroka staggering, slipping, falling on his back, finger in the guard of the R6 pulling the trigger unwilled, shots in the air, rolling, jumping up. The shoulder of the fugitive driving into his midriff, falling again, winded. *Captain, that man, I don't know how he did it. I saw him fall, I saw him falling over the front of the bike to the right of Weyers, but when I stood up he hit me, he was so fast. . . .*

He's fucking forty years old, Mazibuko would scream at him, the commander's face centimeters from his.

Rain in his eyes, gasping for air, boots kicking for a grip to get up, the rider on top of him, bashing him in the face with the helmet, pain coursing through him. The man grabbed his firearm, pulled, jerked and twisted it from his grip. Blood, his blood, against the front of the helmet, then the barrel of the R6 in his eye and he could only lie there in the mud until the man pushed up the helmet visor and said, "Look what you're making me do." He heard Weyers groaning, "Joe." Weyers calling him but he could not turn his head to his mate. "Joe?" A weird expression on the face of the man above him, not anger—sorrow almost. "Joe, I think my leg is broken."

"Look what you made me do."

The digital radio at Tiger Mazibuko's hip came to life and he heard an unexpected word: "Hello." Immediately temper flamed up in the tinder of his frustration and discomfort and exhaustion.

"Alpha One receiving and why the fuck aren't you using radio protocol? Over."

"What is your name, Alpha One?" He didn't know this voice. It was deep, strange.

"This is a military frequency. Please get off the air immediately, over."

"My name is Thobela Mpayipheli. I am the man you are looking for. Who are you?"

It was a bizarre moment, because there was joy in it, tempered with a sudden deep apprehension. He knew something had happened to one of his teams, but that would take some level of skill. It would take a worthy opponent.

"My name is Captain Tiger Mazibuko," he said. "And I am talking to a dead man. Over."

"No one needs to die, Captain Tiger Mazibuko. Tell your masters I will do what I have to do, and if they leave me alone, there will be no blood. That is my promise."

"Who did you steal that radio from, you bastard?"

"They need medical help here, west of the N1, the Sneeukraal turnoff. Your men will tell you the serious injury was an accident. I am sorry for it. The only way to avoid that is to avoid confrontation. I am asking you nicely. I don't want trouble."

A wonderful thing happened in Tiger Mazibuko's head as the meaning of the man's words was assimilated and processed, like tumblers falling into place. The end result was the synaptic equivalent of an explosion of white fire. "You're dead. You hear me, you're dead." He ran toward the nearest vehicle. "You hear me, you cunt, you fuckin' shit." No, the helicopter. He spun around. "If it's the last thing I do, you're gone, you cunt, you fuckin' dog." The help-lessness of the distance between them was driving him insane. "Get this thing going, now," he told the pilot. "Da Costa, Zongu, get everybody," he shouted. "Now." Back to the pilot: "Get this fucking chopper in the air." He touched the weapon at his belt, the

Z88 pistol, jumped out of the helicopter again, ran to the tent, pulled open a chest, grabbed the R6 and two spare magazines, ran back. The Oryx engines turning, Team Alpha came running. He held the radio to his lips. "I'm going to kill you, I swear, as God is my witness, I'm going to kill you, you fucking piece of shit."

Like a condemned man, Rahjev Rajkumar read the words on www.bmwmotorrad.co.za to the whole room, knowing the tidings he brought would not be welcome. "At home all around the world. Adventures are limitless with the BMW R 1150 GS, whether on hard surfaces, pistes or gravel tracks. Uphill and downhill, through valleys and plateaus, forests and deserts—the R 1150 GS is the perfect motorcycle for every adventure."

"He can ride dirt roads," said Janina.

The people in the Ops Room were quiet, the murmur of voices from the television bank suddenly audible.

"It's my fault," she said. "I take responsibility for this one."

She ought to have made sure. She should have had questions asked. Should never have accepted the conventional thinking.

She walked over to the big map of the country hanging on the wall and checked the distance between the turnoff and the roadblock. It was so near.

She had been right. About everything. He had taken the N1. He was an hour later than she had predicted, but he was there. But for the rain . . .

She looked at the great stretches of the North West Province.

What now? Mpayipheli's choices multiplied with every thin red stripe that represented a road, no matter what the surface. Even with Team Bravo in action, there were simply too many holes, too many crossroads and junctions and turnoffs and options to cover.

What to do now?

She needed a hot bath, needed to wash the night out of her hair and scrub it from her body. She needed new clothes and fresh makeup. A good breakfast.

Her eyes wandered to the final destination. Lusaka.

She knew one thing. He had turned west. Written off the direct route through Bloemfontein. She traced a new line. Through Gaborone, Mmabatho, Vryburg, and Kimberley.

That was the strongest possibility.

The storm had saved him, but now it was his enemy. They knew the system was two hundred kilometers wide, but he could only guess. He had fallen on the gravel road, not too skilled. He would have to ride slowly in the mud, carefully. He would consider his choices. He would wonder where they were. He would look over his shoulder for the helicopters, check the road ahead for soldiers. He was tired and cold and wet. Sore from the fall.

Five, six hundred kilometers to Kimberley. How fast could he go?

She checked her watch. Of the seventy-two hours, twelve had passed. Sixty remaining. Six, seven, eight hours to reach Kimberley. A lot could happen in that time.

She looked around at the waiting faces throughout the room. Anxious. Tired. Chagrined. They needed rest, to regain their courage. A hot shower and a hot breakfast. Perspective.

She smiled at the Ops Room. "We know where he is, people. And he has only one place to go. We'll get him."

At the T junction he nearly fell again. As he braked sharply the motorbike slid and he had to wrench his body to stay upright. Pain focused in his shoulder. The signpost opposite him said Loxton to the left, Victoria West to the right. He hesitated for long seconds, wavering. Instinct made him turn left because it was the only unpredictable option he could make. He kept moving, the events that lay behind him resting heavily on him; he would have to check the map again.

He would have to sleep.

But it was raining, he couldn't just park in the veld and lay his head down, he needed a tent.

The dirt road was bad, the surface erratic, where it dipped it was easy to expect the soft mud; he kept to the middle. His hands were freezing; his head dull now that the adrenaline had worked itself out of his system. He wanted to defer thinking about the two soldiers and his own deep disappointment when he picked up the motorbike and got going again, fleetingly surprised at the lack of damage, at the engine that sprang to life at the first turn, taking off with back wheel waggling in the sodden ground. He was disappointed in himself, over the incredible hatred that had come over the radio, but he didn't want to think of that now.

He made a list of his problems. They knew where he was. They would count his options on a map. They were using the army, unlimited manpower, helicopters. Vehicles? He was weary, a deep fatigue, his shoulder muscles were damaged or badly bruised, his knee less so. He had been driven from the highway, the fast route was denied. It was raining.

Lord, Johnny Kleintjes, what have you got me into? I want to go home. Add that to the list: he had no stomach for it; he wanted to go home to Miriam and Pakamile.

He saw the homestead out of the corner of his eye. To the left of the road, a ruin between stony ridges and thorn trees that suddenly made sense. It altered the predictable, offered a solution and rest. He pulled the brakes carefully, turned about slowly, and rode back to the two-track turnoff. The gate lay open, ramshackle and neglected. He went slowly up the rocky track, the handlebars jerking in his hands. He saw the cement reservoir and the windmill, the old house, windows filled with cardboard, walls faded by the Karoo sun, tin roof without gutters, the water running off in streams. He rode around to the back and stopped.

Did anyone live here? No sign of life, but he remained on the bike, hand on the accelerator. No washing on a line, no tracks, no vehicle.

He turned the key, switched off the engine, clipped open the helmet.

"Hullooooo . . ."

Just the sound of rain on the roof.

He climbed stiffly off, put the bike on the stand, careful to prevent it from tipping over in the soft ground. Pulled off the sodden gloves and the helmet.

There was a back door, paint long since peeled away. He knocked, the sound was hollow—"Hullo"—he turned an antique doorknob—was it locked?—put his good shoulder to the door, pushed, no luck.

He walked around, checking the road. No sound or sign of traffic.

No door on that side. He walked back, tried to peer through a window, through a crack between cardboard and frame, but it was too dark inside. He went back to the door, turning the knob, bumped hard with his shoulder, a bang, and it swung wide open. A field mouse scurried across the floor, disappearing into a corner; the smell was of abandonment, musty.

The small coal stove against the wall was once black, now dull gray, the handle of the coal scuttle was broken off. A dilapidated cupboard, iron bedstead with a coir mattress. An ancient wooden table, two plastic milk crates, an enamel basin, dust and spiderwebs.

For a moment he stood there, considering. The motorbike could not be seen from the road. Nobody had been there in weeks.

He made up his mind. He fetched his bag from the bike, closed the door properly, and sat down on the mattress.

Just for an hour or two. Just to ease the fatigue.

He pulled off the leathers and boots, found warm clothes in his bag, shook the worst dust from the mattress, and lay down with the bag as his pillow.

Just an hour or two.

Then he would study the map and define his options.

The news that the fugitive had outmaneuvered the helicopters and the roadblock, that one Special Forces soldier was being flown to Bloemfontein by helicopter, spread through the law enforcement community like a brushfire. By the time Allison Healy contacted her source in Laingsburg, it had garnered the baroque embellishments of a legend in the making.

"And he is ex-MK. He's a forty-year-old has-been fucking up the spies left, right, and center," Erasmus told her with relish so that she could have no doubt that the police were enjoying every minute of the drama.

"I know he's a war veteran," she said, "but why are they after him?"

"How did you know that?" Erasmus was hungry for more gossip.

"I had a visitor. An old friend. Why are they chasing him?"

"They won't say. That's the one thing the fuckers won't say."

"Thanks, Rassie. I have to go."

"I'll phone you if I hear something more."

She put the phone back in her bag and walked in to the Absa offices in the Heerengracht. At the information desk she had to wait in line. The newest information milled in her head. The phone rang again.

"Allison."

"Hi, Allison, my name is John Modise. I do a talk show for SAFM."

"Hi, John."

"You broke the story about the black guy on a motorcycle."

"Yes."

"How would you like to be on the show this morning? Telephone interview."

She hesitated. "I can't."

"Why not?"

"It would compromise my position, John. You are competition media."

"I understand, but your next edition is only tomorrow morning. A lot can happen . . ."

"I can't."

"Did you know this guy was Umkhonto we Sizwe?"

"I did," she said with a sinking heart. Her lead was disappearing. "How did you find out?"

"My producer got it from the Beaufort West police. He slipped through their fingers just an hour ago."

Now they were all singing like canaries.

"I know."

"You see, it's public knowledge. So there's no harm in being on the show."

"Thanks, but no thanks."

"Okay, but if you change your mind before eleven, you call me."

"I will."

It was her turn at the desk. "Hi," she said. "I'm looking for a Ms. Miriam Nzululwazi. She works here."

18.

I am finished with all these things. I am finished with fighting, with the violence, with shooting and beating and hate. Especially the hate. Finished," he said.

That was in the hospital in Milnerton, beside the bed of his white friend Zatopek van Heerden, the two of them full of medication and bandages and pain and the shared trauma of a strange and violent experience that he and the ex-policeman had gone through together by sheer chance. That was while he worked for Orlando Arendse. He had felt an inner glow, a Damascus experience of a new life vision, pumped up by the *lucidum intervallum*. Van Heerden had stared expressionlessly at him, just his eyes betraying a hint of empathy.

"You don't believe I can change?"

"Tiny, it's hard."

Tiny. That was his name. He had rejected it in the metamorphosis, part of the process of killing off the past, like a snake shedding its skin and leaving it behind as a ghostly reminder. He had become Thobela. It was his christened name.

"If you can dream it, you can do it."

"Where do you get that populist crap?"

"Read it somewhere. It's true."

"That's Norman Vincent Peale or Steven Covey, one of those false prophets. Great white witch doctors."

"I don't know them."

"We are programmed, Tiny. Wired. What we are, we are, in sinew and bone."

"We are growing older and wiser. The world is changing around us."

Van Heerden was always excruciatingly honest. "I don't believe a man can change his inherent nature. The best we can do is to acknowledge the balance of good and evil in ourselves. And accept it. Because it's there. Or at least the potential for it. We live in a world where the good is glorified and the bad misunderstood. What you can do is to alter the perspective. Not the nature."

"No," he had said.

They left it there, agreeing to differ.

When he was discharged and left the white man behind in the hospital, he said good-bye with so much enthusiasm for reinventing himself, on fire for the new Thobela Mpayipheli, that Zatopek had taken his hands and said, "If anyone can do it, you can." There was urgency in his voice, as if he had a personal stake in the outcome.

And now he lay on a dusty, musty coir mattress in the middle of the Karoo and sleep eluded him because the scene with the two soldiers played over and over in his head. He sought the singularity, the moment when he had regressed, when that which he wanted to be had fallen away. The high blood of battle rising so quickly in his head, his hands so terribly ready to kill, his brain clattering out the knowledge of the vital points on the soldier's body like machine-gun fire, despairing—don't, don't, don't—fighting with himself, such deep disappointment. If Pakamile could see him . . . and Miriam, how shocked she would be.

"Look what you made me do." The words had come out before they were formed. Now he knew it was displacement of blame; he needed a sinner, but the sinner lay within. Wired.

What could you do?

If Van Heerden was right, what could you do?

They went to visit Van Heerden once, he and Miriam and Pakamile, on a smallholding beyond Table View, at a small white house—his mother lived in the big white house. A Saturday afternoon, the family from the townships picked up at the taxi rank in Killarney, Van Heerden and Thobela chatting straight off, the bond between them as strong as it always is for people who have faced death together. Miriam was quiet, uncomfortable; Pakamile's eyes wide and interested. When they arrived Van Heerden's mother was there to sweep the child away: "I've got a pony just for you." Hours later when he came back, the boy's eyes were shining with excitement. "Can we have horses on the farm, Thobela, please, Thobela?"

The attorney, Beneke, was also there, she and Miriam had spoken English, but it wouldn't work, lawyer and tea lady, the gulf of color and culture and three hundred years of African history gaped in the uneasy silences between them.

Van Heerden and he had made the fire for the barbecue outside. He stood around the fire, he told stories of his new job, of motorbike clients, middle-aged men looking for remedies for male menopause, and they had laughed by the burning *rooikrans* logs, because Thobela had a talent for mimicry. Later, when the coals were glowing and Van Heerden was turning the sausage and chops with a practiced hand, he had said to his friend, "I am a new man, Van Heerden."

"I'm glad."

He laughed at the man. "You don't believe me."

"It's not me who must believe, it's you."

They hadn't visited like that again. Rather, he and Van Heerden went somewhere to eat and talk once a month. About life. People. About race and color, politics and aspirations, about the psychology that Van Heerden had begun studying intensely to try and tame his own devils.

He sighed, turned onto his back, the shoulder aching more now. He had to sleep; he had to get his head clear.

What could you do?

You could walk away from circumstances that brought out the worst in you. You could isolate yourself from them.

The hatred in Captain Tiger Mazibuko's voice over the radio. Pure, clear, sheer hate. He had recognized it. For nearly forty years it had been his closest companion.

It's not me who must believe, it's you.

It took Allison nearly fifteen minutes to convince the Xhosa woman that she was on Thobela's side. Miriam's mouth remained stern, her words few; she evaded questions with a shake of the head but finally gave in: "He's helping a friend, that's what. And now look what they're doing."

"Helping a friend?"

"Johnny Kleintjes."

"Is that the friend's name?" Allison did not write it down, afraid to intimidate the woman. Instead, she memorized it feverishly, repeating the name in her head.

Miriam nodded. "They were together in the Struggle."

"How is he helping him?"

"Kleintjes's daughter came around yesterday evening to ask Thobela to take something to him. In Lusaka."

"What did she want him to take?"

"I don't know."

"Was it a document?"

"No."

"What did it look like?"

"I didn't see it."

"Why didn't she take it herself?"

"Kleintjes is in trouble."

"What sort of trouble?"

"I don't know."

Allison drew a deep breath. "Mrs. Nzululwazi, I want to be sure I've got this straight, because if I make a mistake and write something that is not true, then I and the newspaper are in trouble and that won't help Thobela. Kleintjes's daughter came to your house yesterday evening, you say, and asked him to take something to her father in Lusaka?"

"Yes."

"Because her father is in trouble?"

"Yes."

"And Thobela agreed because they are old comrades?"

"Yes."

"And so he took the motorcycle . . ."

The tension and confusion were too much for Miriam. Her voice broke. "No, he was going to take the plane, but they stopped him."

For the first time the reporter saw the stubbornness in the light of deep worry and put her hand on the thin shoulder. For a moment Miriam stood stiff and humiliated before leaning against Allison, letting her arms fold around her, and the tears ran freely.

For two hours Janina slept on the sofa in her office, a deep dreamless sleep until the cell phone's alarm went off. Her feet swung to the ground immediately and she stood up with purpose, the rest a thin buffer against fatigue and tension, but it would have to suffice. She showered in the big bathroom on the tenth floor, enjoying the tingling water, the scent of soap and shampoo, her thoughts going on to the next steps, laying out the day like a map.

She pulled on black trousers and a white blouse, black shoes, wiped the steam from the mirror, brushed her hair, made up her face with deft movements of fingers and hands, and walked first to her office for the dossiers and then to the director's door.

She knocked.

"Come in, Janina." As if he had been waiting for her.

She opened the door and entered. He was standing at the window, looking out over Wale Street toward the provincial government buildings and Table Mountain behind. It was a clear and sunny morning with the flags across the street waltzing lazily in the breeze.

"I have something to confess, sir."

He did not turn. "No need, Janina. It was the rain."

"Not about that, sir."

When he stood etched against the sky like that, his hunchback was obvious. It was like a burden he carried. He stood so still, as if too tired to move.

"The minister has phoned twice already. She wants to know if this thing will become an embarrassment to us."

"I am sorry, sir."

"Don't be, Janina. I am not. We are doing our job. The minister must do hers. She is paid to handle embarrassments."

She placed the dossiers on the desk. "Sir, I involved Johnny Kleintjes in this."

He did not move. The silence stretched out between them.

"On March seventeenth this year a Muslim extremist was arrested by the police on charges of possession of unlicensed firearms. One Ismail Mohammed, a leading player, probably a member of Pagad, Quibla, and/or MAIL. He repeatedly requested a meeting with a representative of the intelligence services. We were fortunate that the police approached us first. I sent Williams."

The director turned slowly. She wondered if he had slept last night. She wondered if it was the same shirt he had been wearing yesterday. His face betrayed no weariness.

He walked over to the chair behind his desk, not meeting her eyes.

"Here is the full transcript of the interview. Only Williams, the typist, and myself know about this."

"I am sure you had a reason for not showing me this, Janina." Now for the first time she could see that he was tired, the combination of inflection and body language and the dullness in his eyes.

"Sir, I made a choice. I think you will eventually agree it was a reasonable one."

"Tell me."

"Mohammed had information about Inkululeko."

It was a moment she had waited a long time for. He showed no reaction, said nothing.

"You know there have been speculations and suspicions for years."

The director seemed to sigh as if releasing internal tension. He leaned back in his chair. "Do sit down, Janina."

"Thank you, sir."

She pulled the chair closer, drawing a breath to proceed, but he held up a small hand, the palm rose-colored, the nails perfectly manicured.

"You kept this from me because I am under suspicion." Not a question, a mild statement.

"Yes, sir."

"Was that the right thing to do, Janina?"

"Yes, sir."

"I think so, too."

"Thank you, sir."

"No need to thank me, Janina. It is what I expect from you. That is how I have taught you. Trust no one."

She smiled. It was true.

"Do you think it necessary now for me to know everything?"

"I think you need to know about Johnny Kleintjes."

"Then you may tell me."

She considered awhile, collecting her thoughts. The director would know of Inkululeko's history back through the eighties, when the rumors in the leaders' circle of the ANC were put down to counterintelligence maliciously planted by the regime to damage the unity between Xhosa and Zulus in the organization. But even after 1992 the rumors persisted, the violence in Kwa-Zulu, the Third Force. And since the 1994 elections the feeling that the CIA were too well informed.

She tapped the dossier in front of her. "Ismail Mohammed says in the interview that Inkululeko is a senior member of the intelligence arm. He says he has proof. He says Inkululeko is working for the CIA. Has been for years."

"What proof?"

"Not one big thing. Many small ones. You know the Cape Muslim extremists have connections with Qaddafi and Arafat and bin Laden. He says they deliberately fed misinformation into the system here and watched things unfold in the Middle East. He says there is no doubt."

"And we must assume they have decided to remove Inkululeko by giving us information."

"We must consider that possibility at least, sir."

He smoothed his tie slowly as if removing imagined wrinkles. "I think I understand now, Janina. You fetched Johnny Kleintjes out of retirement."

"Yes, sir. I needed someone credible. Someone who would have had access to the data."

"You sent him to the American consulate."

"Yes, sir."

"He was to tell them he had data he wanted to sell. And if it had been me, I would have told Johnny to use the September eleventh attacks as motivation. Something like 'I can no longer sit back and watch these things happen while I have information that can help you.'"

"Something like that."

"And the name of Inkululeko as an afterthought, an incidental extra?"

She merely nodded.

"So that they can know we know. Clever, Janina."

"Apparently not clever enough, sir. It may have backfired on us."

"I would guess you had a few names you wanted to experiment with, a few possible Inkululekos? To test reactions?"

"Three names. And a lot of harmless information. If the Americans said the data is nonsense, we would know he is not one of those three. If they pay, we know we are on target."

"And my name was one of them."

"Yes, sir. After Johnny's visit to the consulate, the CIA reacted as we expected. They told Johnny not to make direct contact again, that the building is being watched. Don't call us, we'll call you. I arranged for his phone to be monitored. A week ago they called, a smoke screen for a meeting in the gardens at the art museum. There they asked Johnny to take the info to Lusaka."

"What went wrong, Janina?"

"We think Johnny used his own initiative, sir. We think the hard drive he took was empty. Or filled with pointless data."

"Johnny Kleintjes," said the director with nostalgia. "I think he did not completely trust you, Janina."

"It's possible. It took a lot of persuading to get him to go along. The three names . . ."

"He knows all three."

"Yes, sir."

"And he does not believe any one of the three is Inkululeko."

"That's right."

"Typical of Johnny. He would want to check things through first. But with an escape route if the Yanks got serious."

"I suspect Thobela Mpayipheli has the real hard drive."

"The one you prepared."

"Yes, sir."

"And you do not want that data to reach Lusaka."

"I thought we would stop Mpayipheli at the airport. I wanted to send the drive with one of my own people. That is still the plan."

"More control."

She nodded. "More control."

The director pulled open a drawer in the big desk. "I too have a confession, Janina," he said, lifting out a photograph, a dog-eared color snapshot. He held it out to her. She took it carefully, holding it up to her eyes with her fingertips on the edges of the faded card. The director, young—easily twenty years ago. He had his arm around a tall broad-shouldered black youth, supple and muscular, regular features, a strong line to mouth and chin, determined. In the background was a military vehicle.

"Dar es Salaam," said the director. "Nineteen eighty-four."

"I don't understand, sir."

"The other man in the photo is Thobela Mpayipheli. He was my friend." There was a faint smile lingering on the small Zulu's mouth.

A chill swept over her. "That is why you let the Reaction Unit come."

He looked up at the ceiling, his thoughts in another time. She waited patiently.

"He is a ruthless man, Janina. A freak of nature. He is . . . he was only seventeen when he enlisted. But they picked him out from the start. While the others had general infantry training in Tanzania and Angola, he was sent with the elite to the Soviet Union. And East Germany. The KGB fell in love first and kept us up-to-date with his training. The Germans pinched him. They knew . . ."

"That's why there is no record."

The director was still somewhere in the past. "He was everything they needed. Dedicated, intelligent, strong—mentally, too. Fast . . . He could shoot, ah, Tiny could shoot . . ."

"Tiny?"

A dismissive gesture. "That is a story in itself. But above all he was unknown in their world, a wild card that the Americans and Brits and even Mossad knew nothing of. A black unknown, a brand-new player, an unrecorded assassin with the hunger . . ." The director pulled himself back to the present, his eyes slowly focusing on hers.

"They bought him from us, Janina. With weapons and explosives and training. There was one small problem. He was unwilling. He wanted to come back to South Africa, to shoot Boers and blow up the SADF. His hate was focused. They sat with him for nearly two weeks, trying to explain that he would make a contribution, that the CIA and MI5 were hand in glove with the Boers, that war against one was war against the others. Two weeks . . . until they turned his head."

She pushed the photo back across the desk. She met the director's eyes and they sat, staring, testing, and waiting.

"He makes me think of Mazibuko," she said.

"Yes."

"Was he the so-called Umzingeli?"

"I don't know the whole story, Janina."

She stood up. "I can't afford to let him reach Lusaka."

The director nodded. "He is the sort of man who will retrieve Johnny and the data."

"And that would not do."

"No, that would not do."

Silence descended between them as each considered the implications, till the director said: "I want you to know I am going home for some rest. I will be back later. Will you be sending the usual team to watch me?"

"It will be the usual team, sir."

He nodded wearily.

"That is good."

19.

The editor of the *Cape Times* looked at the rounded figure of Allison Healy and thought once more, *If she could lose ten or fifteen kilograms* . . . She had a sensuality about her. He wondered if it was the curves, or the personality. But there was a beautiful slender woman somewhere inside there.

". . . and nobody else knows about this Johnny Kleintjes, which gives us a great angle for tomorrow's story. I've got his address, and I will get an interview with the daughter. And this afternoon, we'll get a pic of Mrs. Nzululwazi and the boy. Exclusive."

"Right," said the editor, wondering if she was a virgin.

"But there's more, Chief. I know it. And I want to use this radio show to put some bait in the water. Stir the pot."

"You're not going to leak our scoop, are you?"

"I'm going to be all coy and clever, Chief."

"You're always coy and clever, Allison."

"Fair enough," she said, and he laughed.

"Just make sure you plug the newspaper. And if you can let it slip that we will be revealing a lot more tomorrow morning . . ."

Self-assured, at ease, Janina sat at the big table.

"Can you hear us, Tiger?" she asked.

The entire room listened to the captain's voice as it came over the speakerphone. "I can hear you."

"Good. What is your status?"

"Team Bravo has arrived with our vehicles. We expect the Oryx back any moment and another is on the way from Bloemfontein." She could hear the impatience in Mazibuko's voice, the suppressed anger.

"What's the weather doing, Captain?"

"It's not raining so hard anymore. The air force says the system is moving east."

"Thank you, Tiger." She went to stand alongside Vincent Radebe. "We have established beyond reasonable doubt that Thobela Mpayipheli was an MK member who received specialized training in the Eastern bloc. There are still some details outstanding, but he is a worthy opponent, Tiger. Don't be too hard on your team."

Just hissing on the line, no response.

"The point is, he is not an innocent citizen." She looked pointedly at Radebe, who boldly met her eyes.

"He knows how serious we are about that data and he did not scruple to use violence. He chose confrontation. He is dangerous and he is determined. I hope we all understand this."

Some heads nodded.

"We also know now that the data he is carrying is of an extremely sensitive nature for this government and especially for us as an intelligence service. So sensitive that you have the right to use any necessary force to stop him, Tiger. I repeat. Any necessary force."

"I hear you," said Captain Tiger Mazibuko.

"In the next half hour I will be requesting the mobilization of the available manpower from the army bases at De Aar, Kimberley, and Jan Kempdorp. We need more feet on the ground. There are too many possible routes to watch. Tiger, I want you centered in Kimberley so that you can respond quickly. Given the background of the fugitive, we will need a concentration of highly mobile, well-trained men when he makes contact again. Let the police and the army watch the roads. I will ask that the entire Rooivalk Squadron be moved to Kimberley on standby."

"How certain are you of Kimberley," Mazibuko's voice came back over the ether.

She thought a little before answering, "It's an informed guess. He's tired, he's wet, hungry, and the rain is slowing him down. He hears the clock ticking and his time running away. Kimberley is the closest to a straight line between him and Botswana, and he will see Botswana as freedom and success."

She saw one of Rahjev Rajkumar's people whispering in his ear.

"Is there something, Raj?"

"Radio program, ma'am. SAFM."

"Any questions?" She waited for a reaction from Radebe and Mazibuko.

"Mazibuko out," said the captain over the speakerphone. Radebe sat and stared at the digital instruments before him.

"Switch on, Raj," she said.

. . . joined by Allison Healy, crime reporter from a Cape Town newspaper, who broke the saga of the big, bad Xhosa biker in her newspaper this morning. Welcome to the show, Allison.

Thanks, John, it is a privilege to participate.

You have interesting new information about our fugitive motorcyclist?

I have, John. We have information that casts a new light on Mr. Mpayipheli's motivation, and it seems this is something of a mercy mission. His motive, it seems, might just be noble.

Please go on.

I'm afraid that's about all I can say, John.

And how did you get that information, Allison?

From a source very close to him. Let's call it a love interest.

"Quinn," said Janina with suppressed rage.

"Yes, ma'am?"

"Bring her in."

He looked bewildered.

"Miriam Nzululwazi. Bring her in."

"Very well, ma'am."

. . . on the side of the fugitive?

It is not for me to choose sides here, John, but there are two things that I find puzzling. According to information provided to the police by what is allegedly the Presidential Intelligence Unit, Mr. Mpayipheli stole the BMW motorcycle. But that seems to be untrue. No charges have been filed with the police, there is no theft investigation, and I spoke to the owner of the dealership just five minutes ago, and the truth is that Mr. Mpayipheli left a note behind, saying he had no choice but to borrow the machine and will pay for the privilege. That does not sound like theft to me.

And the second thing, Allison?

The Cape Times *broke the story more than five hours ago, John. If the fugitive is guilty of anything, why has the government not stepped forward to set the record straight?*

I see where you are going. What do you think is happening here?

I think the government is once again trying to cover up, John. I wouldn't be surprised if some form of corruption or something similar is involved. I'm not saying that's it. I'm just saying I will not be surprised. I'm working on several new leads, and the Cape Times *will have a full story tomorrow morning.*

Thank you very much, Allison Healy, crime reporter of a Cape-based newspaper. This is John Modise and you are tuned to SAFM. The lines are open now; if you have an opinion on the matter, please call us. And remember, the subject this morning is the fugitive motorcyclist, so let's stick to that . . .

"Monica Kleintjes," said Janina. "We will have to bring her in, too. Before the media flock to her door."

"Right, ma'am," said Quinn. "But what about her telephone, if they call again from Lusaka?"

"Can you redirect the line here?"

"I can."

Janina's thoughts were jumping around. How had the Healy woman got that information? How had she made the connection between Mpayipheli and Nzululwazi? What could be done to slow her down?

. . . Pretoria chapter of the Hell's Angels. Good morning, Burt.

Good morning, John. What we want to know is where the man is. Do you have information?

We know he was in the vicinity of Three Sisters at six o'clock this morning, Burt. Where he is now is anybody's guess. Why are you asking?

Because he's our brother, man. And he's in trouble.

Your brother?

All bikers are part of a greater brotherhood, John. Now, you may have heard a lot of untruths about the Angels, but I can tell you, when one of our brothers is in trouble, we help.

And how do you think you will be able to help?

Any way we can.

Rajkumar made a deprecating sound and turned the volume down. "All the worms are creeping out of the woodwork," he said.

"No," said Janina. "Leave it on."

He dozed shallowly, fitfully crossing the border of sleep, dreams and reality mixing. He was riding the GS down infinite roads, feeling the faint vibration of the bike in his legs, talking to Pakamile, hearing the rain on the roof of the cottage and then the sucking sound of tires in the mud, an engine at low revs, but he only really woke up to the bang of a car door. He rolled off the mattress, continued rolling up to the wall beneath the window.

Anonymous from Mitchell's Plain, go ahead, you are on the air.

Hello, John, can you hear me?

You are on the air, go ahead.

I'm on the air?

Yes, Anonymous, the whole country can hear you.

Oh. Well. I just wanted to say this Mpayipheli is not the hero you make him out to be.

We are not making him into a hero. We are letting the facts speak. What have you got for us?

I don't know if it is the same guy, but there was a Thobela Mpayipheli working for a drug dealer in Mitchell's Plain. Big black man. Mean as a junkyard dog. And they were saying he was ex-MK. They used to call him "Tiny."

Working for a drug gang?

Yes, John. He was what we call an "enforcer."

"We," Anonymous? Who are "we"?

I used to be a drug dealer in the Cape Flats.

You were a drug dealer?

Yes.

In Mitchell's Plain?

No. I worked from the southern suburbs.

Sounds like a franchise business. And what does an "enforcer" do, Anonymous?

He makes sure the dealers pay the supplier. By beating them up or shooting them. Or their families.

And Mpayipheli worked as an enforcer for a supplier?

He worked for the biggest supplier in the Peninsula at the time. That was before the Nigerian Mafia came to town. These days, they run the show.

The Nigerian Mafia? We must have you back for a radio show all of your own, Anonymous. So what made you quit dealing?

I did time. I'm rehabilitated now.

There you have it. Strange but true.
This is a strange country, John, believe me.
Amen, brother.

He lay on the floor, breathing the dust. Footsteps sounded as if they were circling the motorbike. Then a voice called.

"Helloooo . . ."

Instinctively he looked around for a weapon, cursing himself for not keeping the soldier's assault rifle. He could break a leg off the table. He stopped one stride away. No more violence, no more fighting. Implications ran through his mind. Did this mean the journey was over, could he go home? It meant Johnny Kleintjes was fucked; he stood in limbo between instinct and desire.

"Hello, the house . . ." A man's voice. Afrikaans. Was it the farmer?

His hands hung by his sides but were clenching open and shut.

"Thobela?" he heard the voice say his name. "Thobela Mpayipheli?"

Soldiers, he thought, adrenaline flowing through his veins. One step to the table, he grabbed one wooden leg in his hands and pressed his foot against the tabletop. *No,* said his mind, *no, let it be over.*

Go ahead, Elise, what is your take on this unfolding drama?

Two things, John. First, I don't believe this drug business at all. Why is it that people always want to drag someone down the moment they hit the limelight? Second, I am the secretary of the Pretoria BMW Motorcycle Club, and I just want to say we don't need the Hell's Angels to act on our behalf. Mr. Mpayipheli is riding a BMW, and if anybody helps him, it will be the BMW motorcycle fraternity. I don't know how the Hell's Angels with their Harleys are going to travel on the gravel roads of the Northern Cape.

So the fugitive is a member of a BMW club?

No, John, but he rides a BMW.

And that gives you ownership.

We don't own him, John. But neither do the Hell's Angels.

What's this about gravel roads?

Mr. Mpayipheli slipped through the roadblocks by traveling on gravel roads. He's on a GS, you know.

And what is a GS?

It's an on road/off road motorcycle.

Like a scrambler?

No. Yes, I suppose you could call it a scrambler with a thyroid condition.

Ha. Now there's the quote of the day. How do you know he slipped through a roadblock?

It is all on our website, John.

Your website?

Yes. www.bmwmotorrad.co.za. We have inside information.

And just how is your website getting inside information?

Oh, policemen ride BMWs, too, you know.

"I'm coming inside, Thobela, don't shoot. I'm your friend."

Don't shoot. They still thought he was armed.

"I'm on my own, Thobela, be nice."

The door opened.

"I'm on your side, my brother."

He waited the space of a single heartbeat and dropped his shoulder in readiness.

"I can't get it," said Rahjev Rajkumar. The web browser showed an error message: *The page cannot be displayed. The page you are looking for is currently unavailable. The website might be experiencing technical difficulties, or you may need to adjust your browser settings.*

"Motorrad has two *r*s," said Vincent Radebe softly.

"How do you know?" said Rajkumar nastily.

"It's German for 'motorcycle.' "

He typed in the new address. This time the website loaded. At the top, under the page title were the words FOLLOW THE GS FUGITIVE—AN INSIDE STORY.

He stood with his feet apart, shoulder lowered, the internal battle raging, knowing it was his moment of truth, knowing this was where he would win or lose—on so many levels.

The door swung slowly wider. The voice was soft and soothing. "I am a man of peace."

A colored man, dressed in tattered suit, anonymous gray shirt, and a bow tie that could have been red in a previous era. His eyes were wide and he held his hands up in front protectively.

"Who are you?"

"I am Koos Kok," he said very carefully. "You won't kill me now, hey?"

"How do you know my name?"

"Just one look at that big motorbike. You are all over the radio. The 'big, bad Xhosa biker.'"

"What?"

"Everyone is very excitable about you."

"What are you doing here?" Mpayipheli straightened up.

"I was lonely for my winter house," he said, motioning at the cottage. "I came to keep myself warm."

"'They had a roadblock at Three Sisters, manned by an army unit, some SAPS and traffic authorities, and a big helicopter. They also had some Rooivalk attack helicopters at Beaufort West who tried to follow the GS, but the rain forced them back,'" Rajkumar read aloud from the website, and he wondered why fate had singled him out to be the bearer of bad news.

"Shit," said Quinn.

"Go on," said Janina.

"'Apparently, the GS took a side road, presumably the Sneeukraal turnoff, and went through a two-soldier roadblock, hurting one badly. Then he disappeared. That is all I have at the moment.

"'The only way we can help this guy is if all BMW owners in the country unite. We must all gather at Three Sisters and try to find him. That way, we can help him get through to wherever he is going.'"

"They want to help him," said Quinn.

"Who wrote that?" asked Janina.

"'An Insider.' That is all they say."

"Fucking policeman," said Quinn, and saw Janina's disapproving eye. "I beg your pardon, ma'am."

"Is there any more?" she asked Rajkumar.

"There are a few messages from guys who say they are going to help."

"How many?"

He counted. "Eleven. Twelve."

"Not many," said Quinn.

"Too many," said Janina. "They'll get in the way."

"Ma'am," said Vincent Radebe.

"Yes?"

He held out the phone to her. "The director."

She took the receiver. "Sir?"

"The minister wants to see us, Janina."

"In her office?"

"Yes."

"Shall I meet you there, sir?"

*   *   *

*We have time for one more call. Burt from the Hell's
Angels, you back again?*

*Yes, John. Two things. We don't ride Harleys. Well,
a few members do, but only a few. And this thing that
the black guy belongs to the BMW people is bullshit.*

Let's watch the language, Burt. This is a family show.

*I'm sorry, but they're nothing but a bunch of fair-
weather, breakfast-run weekend wannabe bikers.*

*What happened to the great brotherhood of motor-
cycle riders, Burt?*

*Real bikers, John. Not these Beemer sissies. That
Mpheli . . . Mpayi . . . that guy out there is a real biker.
A war veteran, a warrior of the road. Like us.*

And you can't even pronounce his name.

20.

They got two ministers for the price of one.

The minister of intelligence was a woman, lean, as fitted her office, a forty-three-year-old Tswana from the North West Province. The minister of water affairs and forestry sat in the corner, a gray-haired white man, an icon of the Struggle. He said not a word. Janina Mentz did not know why he was there.

The director and she sat down in front of the desk. Janina glanced briefly at the director before she began to speak. He indicated with a minimal nod that she must hold nothing back. She filled in the background first: the Ismail Mohammed interview, the counterintelligence operation, and the things that had gone wrong.

"Have you seen the TV news?" asked the intelligence minister coldly.

"Yes, Minister." Resignedly. Not for the first time did Janina wonder why politicians were more sensitive about TV than about newspapers.

"Every half hour there is something new over the radio. And the more they talk, the more he becomes a hero. And we look like the Gestapo." A dainty fist emphasized her words on the wood of the desktop, her voice rose half an octave. "This cannot continue. I want solutions. We have a public relations crisis. What do I tell the president when he calls? And he will call. What do I say?"

"Minister . . . ," said Janina.

"Two agents at the airport. Two Rooivalk helicopters and a whole brigade at Three Sisters and you don't even know where he is."

Janina had no answer.

"And everyone wonders why the rand falls and the world laughs. At Africa. At bungling, backward Africa. I am tired of that attitude. Sick to death of it. This cabinet"—the minister stood up, too angry to sit, her hands bracketing her words—"labors night and day, battling the odds, and what support do we get from the civil service? Bungling. Lame excuses. Is that good enough?"

Janina stared at the carpet. The minister drew a deep breath, collected herself, and sat down again.

"Minister," said the director in his soft, diplomatic tones, "while we are speaking frankly, may I place a few points on the record. This is the first well-planned counterintelligence operation we have attempted, and may I say it is high time. It is not only necessary but also ingenious. Creative. Nothing that has happened has jeopardized the purpose of the mission. On the contrary, the longer this develops, the more genuine it will look to the CIA. Granted, things haven't unfolded as planned, but that is the way life goes."

"Is that what I must say to the president, Mr. Director? That is the way life goes?" Her tone was sarcastic and cold.

The director's tone echoed hers: "Minister, you know shifting blame is not my style, but if the members of the police service were loyal to the collective state, the media would not be having a field day. Perhaps we should place the blame where it belongs: at the door of the minister of safety and security. It is high time he sorted this out."

"This operation is my responsibility. My portfolio." She had calmed down, but the mood was fragile.

"But the behavior of another department is jeopardizing the operation. Undermining it. We don't shirk taking our punishment, but it must be deserved. The circumstances at the airport were such that we wanted to avoid an incident. Our people acted with circumspection. As for the weather: our influence does not stretch that far." Janina had never heard the director speak with such passion.

The minister was silenced. The director continued: "Consider for a moment the possibility that we can make a fool of the mighty CIA. Think what it would be worth on every conceivable level. Let them laugh at Africa. We will laugh last."

"Will we?"

"We will conclude the operation successfully. And speedily. But someone must deal severely with the police."

"How quickly can you conclude this operation?"

Janina knew it was her call: "Two days, Minister. No more."

"Are you sure?"

"Minister, if the Department of Defence and the police work together, I will stake my professional reputation on it." Janina heard herself say it and wondered if she believed it.

"They will cooperate," said the minister fiercely. "What do I tell the media?"

Janina had the answer. "There are two possibilities. One is to say nothing."

"Nothing? Have you any idea how many phone calls this office has had this morning?"

"Minister, no country in the world allows the media to interfere with covert operations. Why should we allow it here? Whatever you say, the media will write and broadcast what they wish; they will twist your words or use them against us. Ignore them; show them we will not be intimidated. Tomorrow, the day after, there will be some other event to attract their attention."

The minister thought a long time. "And the second possibility?"

"We use the media to our advantage."

"Explain."

"The line between hero and villain is very narrow, Minister. It often depends on how the facts are interpreted."

"Go on."

"The fugitive was previously a member of a drug network that contributed to the collapse of the social structure and ruined the children on the Cape Flats. He misused his MK training for intimidation and violence. We suspect he is still involved—there are large unexplained sums of money in his bank account. He is a man who does not hesitate to parasitize an innocent woman and her child; he does not even have his own house. A reckless man who has seriously injured a young white soldier with deliberate intent, a man who twice chose to obstruct the purposes of the state when he had the chance to surrender himself. Innocent people, good citizens, or heroes do not become fugitives. There are many ex-MK who followed another path. Who chose to build this nation, not break it down. Who even now fight the good fight in the midst of unemployment and poverty. And all we need to do is turn the facts over to the media."

The minister of intelligence nudged the gold-rimmed glasses farther up the bridge of her nose, thoughtful.

"It can work," she said.

"You prefer the second option?"

"It is more . . . practical."

From the corner sounded the melodious voice of the minister of water affairs and forestry. "We must remember one thing," he said.

All the heads turned.

"We are talking about Umzingeli."

Talking nonstop, Koos Kok had unloaded two chairs from the back of his dilapidated twenty-five-year-old Chevrolet El Camino van, and now they were seated at the table, eating bread and tinned pilchards in rich chili tomato sauce and drinking cheap brandy out of enamel mugs.

"I am the great Griqua troubadour," he introduced himself in his Griqua dialect, "the guitar player that David Kramer overlooked, *skeefbroer* by birth, hardly *voorlopig* a child, always *vooraan* since I was little, *norring* crazy for music, *langtanne* to go to school . . ."

"I can't understand what you're saying," Thobela said, halting him.

"I don't speak Xhosa, my brother, *sôrrie,* it's a *skanne,* and Great-Granpa Adam Kok went to live with you and all."

"You're not speaking Afrikaans, either."

"Dutchman Afrikaans? Well, I can." And his story emerged on a flood of shamelessly self-centered words, the wrinkled, weathered face animated with the telling in conventional language until he reverted to the tongue of his people and Thobela had to frown and put up his hand to get a translation. Here was the

Troubadour of the Northern Cape, the entertainer of the "townies" who frequented the dance halls, where he sang of the landscape and the people with his guitar and his verses. "But I don't see a chance for the *drukmekaar* squeeze, I travel in summer, in winter this is my home, I make a fire and write more songs, and now and again when the feeling is too strong I will go *jongman-jongman* with the girls in Beaufort West."

That morning he had had the radio on in his rusty old Chevy bakkie when he heard the news and later listened to John Modise, so he knew about the big, bad Xhosa biker running around loose in the area, and when he saw the motorbike behind his winter quarters, he knew straightaway. It was the work of the Lord, it was divine guidance, and he was not going to look on with *paphanne,* no, he was going to help.

"You are going to help me?" asked Thobela, his belly properly full and the brandy in his blood.

"*Ja,* my brother. Koos Kok has a plan."

Tiger Mazibuko called Team Alpha together at the open door of the Oryx helicopter. The rain had diminished; blue cracks shone through the clouds, the drops were fine, and the wind restless.

"This morning I crapped out Little Joe in front of you all and I want to apologize. I was wrong. I was angry. I should have stayed calm. Joe, it wasn't your fault."

Little Joe Moroka nodded silently.

"I just can't handle it when something happens to one of my men," Mazibuko said uncomfortably. He could see the fatigue drawn on their faces.

"We are going to Kimberley. Anti-Aircraft School. There will be hot food and warm beds. Team Bravo will do first standby. The army and police will do the roadblocks."

A few faint smiles. He wanted to say more, to restore the bond and minimize the damage. The words would not come.

"Climb up," he said. "Let's get some sleep."

Allison Healy drove to the southern suburbs, to Johnny Kleintjes's house, as it was in the telephone book. She used the hands-free cell-phone attachment to call the office for a photographer and then dialed Absa's number. She wanted to ask Miriam about Thobela's alleged drug involvement. She did not believe it. The radio contribution was thin on facts, heavy on insinuation.

"Mrs. Nzululwazi is not here," said the receptionist.

"Can you tell me where she is?"

"They came to fetch her."

"Who did?"

"The police."

"Police?"

"Can I take a message?"

"No." She felt like pulling over but she was on De Waal Drive with the Cape stretched spectacularly before her. There was no road shoulder: she had to keep going, but her hands began to tremble. She searched for the number of the SAPS liaison officer and pressed the button.

"Nic, this is Allison. I need to know if you have taken Mrs. Miriam Nzululwazi in for questioning."

"I wondered when you would phone."

"So you have got her?"

"I don't know what you're talking about, Allison."

"She is the common-law wife of Thobela Mpayipheli, the man on the motorcycle. Her employers said the police fetched her at work."

"I know about him, but I don't know about her."

"Can you find out?"

"I don't know . . ."

"Nic, I'm asking nicely . . ."

"I'll look into it. And get back to you."

"Another thing. There are rumors that Mpayipheli was involved with drugs on the Cape Flats . . ."

"Yes?"

"Who would know?"

"Richter. At Narcotics."

"Would you?"

"Okay."

"Thanks, Nic."

"Till the day I die I will feel responsible for that man," said the minister of water affairs and forestry. He sat silhouetted against the window, the late-morning light forming a halo around him. Janina wondered if it was sorrow that made his voice so heavy.

"I was chief of staff: operations. I had to make the decision. We owed the Germans so much."

He rubbed his hands over his broad face, as if he could wipe something away. "That's not relevant now," he said, leaning forward with his elbows on his knees. He folded his hands as if to pray.

"Once every six months I had a visitor from Berlin. A goodwill visit, you might say. A verbal progress report, nothing on paper, a diplomatic gesture to let me know how Tiny was getting on. How pleased they were with him. 'He is a credit to your country.' It was always a tall, lean German. They were all lean. 'Yond Cassius has a lean and hungry look; He thinks too much: such men are dangerous.' Every time they would update the score. Like a sport. 'He has done six.' Or nine. Or twelve."

The minister of water affairs and forestry unfolded his hands and crossed his arms on his chest.

"They used him seventeen times. Seventeen." His eyes leaped from the minister to the director to Janina. "The one they couldn't talk enough about was Marion Dorffling. CIA. A legend. Thirty or forty eliminations—it boggles the mind. Those were strange times, a strange war. And Umzingeli got him. Sniffed him out, tracked him for weeks."

He smiled with fond nostalgia. "That was my suggestion, Umzingeli. The hunter. That was his code name."

He shook his head slowly from side to side; the memories were incredible. He had forgotten them; for a minute or longer he was absent from the room. When he began to speak again his voice was lighter.

"He came to see me. Two months before the 'ninety-four elections. My secretary, well, there were so many people wanting to talk to me, she didn't tell me. She thought she was doing right to keep them away. Late one afternoon she came in and said, 'There's this big guy who won't go away,' and when I went to see, there he was, looking apologetic and saying he was sorry to bother me."

The head shook again. "Sorry to bother me."

Janina Mentz wondered where this was leading, whether there was a point to all this meandering. Impatience welled up in her.

"I was ashamed that day. He told me what had happened since the fall of the Wall. His German masters had disappeared overnight. His pay had dried up. He didn't know where to turn. And it was open season on him, because the West had ahold of the Stasi dossiers and he knew they would come after him. It was a new world and everyone wanted to forget, except the ones who were hunting him. No one at our London office knew him; they were new personnel, knew nothing about him and didn't want to know. He lay low for a while, and when he eventually came home and came to me for work, I said I would help, but the elections came and the new government and I forgot about him. I simply forgot."

The minister of water affairs and forestry stood suddenly, giving Janina a fright. "I am wasting your time," he said. "It is my fault, I must take the blame. It is my fault he found another livelihood. But I want to say this. Something happened to that man, because if he were still Umzingeli, there would be at least four dead bodies for you to explain. If you can work out why he spared them, you have a chance of bringing him in."

21.

"Thank you, sir," she said to the small Zulu on the stairs outside.

He stopped with a serious frown on his face. "Not at all, Janina. I was just being honest. I really do think it is an ingenious operation."

"Thank you, sir."

"Why didn't you say anything?"

"About your name being on the list?"

He nodded.

"I didn't think it relevant to the purpose of the meeting."

He nodded again and walked slowly down the steps. She stayed where she was.

"Are you Inkululeko, sir?"

He walked to the bottom and turned and looked up at her with a faint smile before setting off on the long walk back to the office.

He lay in the back of the El Camino on an old mattress alongside the R 1150 GS lying incongruously on its side. The baggage cases were removed and it lay next to the carton of stolen mutton ("A little something toward redistribution of wealth, I'm a *skorriemorrie*," Koos Kok had said), between bits of rickety furniture—two chairs, a coffee table with three legs, and the headboard of a bed. Four shabby suitcases were filled with clothes and documents. All this under a paint-flecked dirty canvas tarpaulin. The bakkie's shocks were gone and the dirt road was very bumpy, but the mattress made it bearable. He lay curled in a fetal position in the cramped space. The rain was almost over, just the occasional shower against the tarp and the water dripping through holes.

He was thinking of the moment when the door had opened, thinking of his self-control, his victory of reason over instinct, suppressing the almost irresistible impulse, and he was filled with satisfaction. He felt like telling Miriam. Sometime he would phone her and tell her he was okay. She would be worried. But what tales he would have to tell Pakamile in the evenings. Koos Kok the Griqua. "Don't you know about Adam Kok, Xhosa? He went to live with you guys." And he heard the short version of that history.

The brandy had made him drowsy, and as they turned toward Loxton on the tar road between Rosedene and Slangfontein, the soft rocking of the Chevy lulled him to sleep. His last thoughts were of a river god. Otto Müller had told of the theory of two British scientists that animals deliberately behave unpredictably in order to survive, the way the hare flees from the dog. *Does it run in a straight line? Of course not. If it runs in a straight line, it will be caught. So it zigzags. But not predictably. Now zigging, then zagging, the dog always guessing, never knowing. The British scientists called it protean behavior.* After the Greek god Proteus, who could change his form at will from a stone to a tree, from a tree to an animal, in order to confound his enemies.

The big, bad Xhosa biker had become the big, bad Xhosa passenger. Müller would have approved of the change of form to avoid the opponent.

His last conscious thought as he slipped into a deep, restful, satisfying sleep was of his friend Zatopek van Heerden, who would not believe that he had become the Proteus of his inherent nature.

Allison Healy had knocked, walked around the house, knocked again, but there was no life there. She leaned against her car in the driveway and waited. Perhaps Monica Kleintjes had gone out for a while. The photographer had come and left again, saying he could not wait, he had to get to the airport—Bobby Skinstad was arriving after the losing rugby tour to Europe. He took some pictures of the house, just in case. It was not an unusually large house, pretty garden, big trees, tranquilly unaware of the drama that surrounded the occupants.

She lit a cigarette. She was comfortable with her habit, ten a day, sometimes less. Nowadays there were few places where one could smoke. It was her appetite suppressant, her consolation prize, an escape to small oases through the day.

She had learned it from Nic.

Nic had seduced her while he was still married.

Nic said he had the hots for her from day one when she had walked into the SAPS office to introduce herself. He said he couldn't help it.

The affair had lasted sixteen months. An uncomplicated, chain-smoking man, a good man, basically, if you left his unfaithfulness to his wife out of the equation. Emotionally needy, not very attractive, an unexceptional lover. But then she was no great judge of that. Five men, since that first time at university.

She and Nic in her flat once or twice a week. Why had she let it happen?

Because she was lonely.

A thousand acquaintances and not one bosom friend. This was the lot of the fat girl in a world of skinny standards. Or was that just her excuse?

The truth was that she could not find her place. She was a round peg in a world of square holes. She could not find a group where she felt at home among friends.

Not even with Nic.

It felt better after he left, lying naked alone on the bed, sexually sated, with music and a cigarette, than it did in the moment of passion, the peak of orgasm.

She did not love him. Just liked him a lot. She did still, but after the divorce and the guilt he carried around like a ball and chain, she had ended the relationship.

He still asked every now and then. "Could we start again? Just one more time?" She considered it. Sometimes seriously because of the desire to be held, to be caressed . . . He had liked her body. "You are sexy, Allison. Your breasts . . ." Maybe that was the thing, he had accepted her body. Because she could not change it, the curves were genetic, passed on from grandmother to mother to daughter in an unbroken succession, stout people, plump women, regardless of the best efforts of diets and exercise programs.

She crushed the cigarette into the grass with the tip of her shoe. The butt lay there like a reproach. She picked it up and threw it behind a shrub in a bed of daisies.

Where was Monica Kleintjes?

Her cell phone rang.

"It's the boss, Allison. Where are you?"

"Newlands."

"You had better get back. The minister is doing a press conference in fifteen minutes."

"Which one?"

"Intelligence."

"I'm on my way."

During the design and equipping of the interview/ interrogation room of the Presidential Intelligence

Unit, Janina Mentz has asked why a table was necessary. Nobody could give her an answer. That is why there wasn't one. She had asked why the chairs should be hard and uncomfortable. Why the walls must be bare except for the one with the one-way mirror. She asked whether a stripped, unpleasant, chilly room yielded better results than a comfortable one. Nobody could answer that. "We are not running a police station" was her argument. So there were three easy chairs of the sort that Lewis Stores or Star Furnishers sold in the hundreds for people's sitting rooms. They were upholstered in practical brown and treated with stain-resistant chemicals. The only difference was that these chairs could not be moved, so no one could prevent or delay entry to the room by pushing the chairs under the door handle. The chairs were bolted down in an intimate triangle. The floor was covered in wall-to-wall carpet, uniform *beige,* not khaki, not pumpkin, but exactly to Janina's specification: *beige.* The microphone was concealed behind the fluorescent light in the ceiling, and the closed-circuit television was in the adjoining observation room, pointing its cyclopean eye through the one-way glass.

Janina stood by the camera and looked at the woman in one of the chairs. Interesting that everyone brought in chose the chair half turned away from the window. As if they could sense it.

Was this the result of too many television serials?

She was Miriam Nzululwazi, common-law wife of Thobela Mpayipheli.

What had Umzingeli seen in her?

She did not seem a cheerful type. She looked like someone who was chronically unhappy, the permanent lines of unhappiness around her mouth. No laugh lines.

She predicted that the woman would not cooperate. She expected her to be tense and hostile. Janina sighed. It had to be done.

Allison's phone rang as she climbed the stairs.

"It's Nic."

"Any news?"

"We don't have your Mrs. Nzululwazi."

"Well, who has?"

"I don't know."

"Can the intelligence services detain people? Without trial?"

"There are laws that are supposed to regulate them, but the intelligence people do as they please, because it is in the interest of the state and the people they work with are not the sort who run to the courts over irregular treatment."

"And the drug angle?"

"I talked to Richter. He says Mpayipheli is well known. He worked for Orlando Arendse when he was Prince of the Cape Flats. No arrests, no record, but they were aware of him."

"And Orlando Arendse was a dealer?"

"An importer and distributor. A wholesaler. Mpayipheli was a deterrent for dealers who would not pay. Or who did not reach their targets. It's another kind of business, that."

"Where do I get hold of Arendse?"

"Allison, these are dangerous people."

"Nic . . ."

"I'll find out."

"Thanks, Nic."

"There's something else."

"Not now, Nic."

"It's not about us."

"What is it?"

"Memo from the minister. Strong steps if they catch anyone leaking information on the Mpayipheli affair to the media. Full cooperation with our intelligence colleagues, big mobilization in the Northern Cape."

"You were not supposed to tell me that."

"No."

"I appreciate it."

"I want to see you, Allison."

"Good-bye, Nic."

"Please." In a little-boy voice.

"Nic . . ."

"Please, just once."

And she weakened in the face of . . . everything.

"Maybe."

"Tonight?"

"No."

"When then?"

"The weekend, Nic. Coffee somewhere."

"Thanks." And he sounded so sincere that she felt guilty.

It had been fifteen years since Miriam Nzululwazi's terrible night in the Caledon Square cells, but the fear she felt then made the jump to the present, here to the interrogation room. Her hands gripped the arms of the chair, but her eyes were blind to the wall they faced. She remembered one woman in the cell kept screaming, screaming, a sound that penetrated marrow and bone, a never-ending lament. The red-faced policeman, who opened the cell door and cleared a way through the perspiring bodies to the screaming one with his truncheon, raised the blunt object high above his head.

She was seventeen, on her way home to the thrown-together wooden hut on an overpopulated dune at Khayalitsha, her week's wages clasped in her handbag, on the way to the buses at the Parade when the mass of demonstrators blocked the road. A seething mass like a noisy pregnant python curling past the town hall, banners waving, whistling, chanting, toyi-toyiing, shouting, a swinging carnival of protest over pay in the clothing industry or something. She had joined in, as they were flowing in her direction, laughing at the young men cavorting like monkeys, and suddenly the police were there, the tear gas, the charge, the water cannon—the python had borne chaos.

They pushed her into the back of a big yellow lorry, pulled her out at the cells with the rest of the horde, shoved them into a cell, too full, nobody could sit and the screaming woman, wailing something about a child, she must go to her sick child, the red-faced white man threatening with the truncheon above his head, shouting, voice lost in the din, the arm dropping, again and again, and terror had overwhelmed Miriam—she needed to escape, she pushed against the others, through the screaming women till she reached the bars, put her hands through them, and there were more policemen shouting, too, faces wild, till someone pulled her back, the lamenting voice suddenly quiet.

She felt the same fear now, in this closed space, the locked door, the locking up without reason, without guilt. She jumped as the door opened. A white woman entered, went to sit opposite her.

"How can I convince you that we want to help Thobela?" Janina Mentz used his first name deliberately.

"You can't keep me here." Miriam heard the fear in her own voice.

"Ma'am, these people are misusing him. They are putting him in unnecessary danger. They have lied and misled him. They are not good people."

"I don't believe you. He was Thobela's friend."

"He was. Years ago. But he has gone bad. He wants to sell us out. Our country. He wants to hurt us and he is using Thobela."

She could see uncertainty in Miriam's face; she would capitalize on it. "We know Thobela is a good man. We know he was a hero of the Struggle. We know he wouldn't have got involved if he knew the whole story. We can sort this out and bring him home safely, but we need your help."

"My help?"

"You talked to the media . . ."

"She also wanted to help. She was also on Thobela's side."

"They are manipulating you, ma'am."

"And you?"

"How will the media be able to bring Thobela home? We can. With your help."

"There is nothing I can do."

"Do you expect Thobela to phone?"

"Why do you want to know?"

"If we could just give him a message."

Miriam glanced sharply at Janina, at her eyes, her mouth, her hands.

"I don't trust you."

Janina sighed. "Because I am white?"

"Yes. Because you are white."

Captain Tiger Mazibuko could not get to sleep. He rolled about on the army bed. It was muggy in

Kimberley, not too hot, still overcast, but the humidity was high and the room poorly ventilated.

What was this hate that he felt for Mpayipheli?

The man was in the Struggle. This man had not sold out his comrades.

Where did this hate come from? It consumed him, it influenced his behavior; he had not treated Little Joe well. He had always had the anger, but it had never before affected his leadership.

Why?

This was just a poor middle-aged man who had a moment of glory a long time ago.

Why?

Outside there was a rumbling that grew louder and louder.

How was he supposed to sleep?

It was the Rooivalks. The windows shook in their frames, the deep bass note of the motors reverberated in his chest. Earlier it had been the trucks, departing one after another with single-minded purpose. Soldiers were being deployed to set up the roadblocks on the dirt and blacktop roads. The net was cast wider to catch a single fish.

He turned over again.

Did it matter where the hate came from? As long as he could control it. Channel it.

Any necessary force, Janina Mentz had said. In other words, shoot the fucker if you like.

Lord, he looked forward to it.

2 2.

The six-man team searched the house in Guguletu with professional skill.

They took video footage and digital stills before they began so that everything could be replaced exactly where it had been. Then the methodical, laborious search began. They knew the hidey-holes of amateurs and professional frauds, no nook or cranny was left unsearched. Stethoscopes were used on walls and floors, powerful flashlights in the spaces between roof and ceiling. The master keys they had brought for cupboards and doors were not required. One of the six men was master of the inventory. He murmured into a palm-size tape recorder like a businessman dictating a letter.

It was a small house with not much inside. The search took 130 minutes. Then they were gone in the microbus they had arrived in. The master of inventory phoned his boss, Vincent Radebe.

"Nothing," he said.

"Nothing at all?" asked Radebe.

"No weapons, no drugs, no cash. A few bank statements. The usual documentation. Mpayipheli is taking his high school equivalency, there is correspondence and books. Magazines, cards—sentimental love notes to the woman in her clothes drawer. 'From Thobela. To Miriam. I love you this, I love you that.' Nothing else. Ordinary people."

In the Ops Room Vincent shook his head. He had thought so.

"Oh, one other thing. A veggie garden out back. Very neat. Best tomatoes I have seen in years."

The trick at a news conference is to phrase your questions in such a way as not to disclose to the other media the information you have.

That was why, after the minister had read the prepared statement on the stormy life and violent criminal times of Thobela Mpayipheli and had responded to a horde of questions from radio, newspaper, and television journalists almost without exception with "I am not in a position to answer that question, due to the sensitive nature of the operation," Allison Healy asked: "Is anybody else connected with this operation being detained at the moment?"

And because the minister did not know, she hesitated. Then she gave an answer that would cover her if the opposite were true. "Not to my knowledge," she said.

It was an answer she would later wish with all her heart never to have uttered.

*   *   *

They brought Miriam coffee and sandwiches in the interrogation room. She asked when they would let her go. The food bearer did not know. He said he would ask.

She did not eat or drink. She tried to overcome her fear. The walls suffocated her, the windowless room pressed down on her. Tonight it was she who needed to go to her child, tonight it was she who wanted to cry out with a high frightened voice, "Let me out." She must go fetch Pakamile. Her child, her child. Her work. What were the bank people thinking? Did they think she was a criminal? Were they going to fire her? Would someone here go and explain to the bank people why they had come to fetch her?

She needed to get out.

She must get out.

And what about Thobela? Where was he now? Was it true what the white woman said, that he was in danger?

She had not asked for this.

Janina Mentz waited until everyone who had been resting was back before she gathered them around the table.

Then she told them almost the whole story. She did not mention that the director's name was on the list, but she confessed that she had set up the operation from the start. She did not apologize for keeping them in the dark. She said they should understand why she had done it that way.

She described the meeting with the minister, the confirmation that Thobela Mpayipheli, code name Umzingeli, was a former MK operative, that he had received advanced training, that he was a dangerous opponent, and that it was of cardinal importance that he be stopped.

"We will waste no more time finding out who he was. We are going to focus on finding out who he is now. With his background, his behavior the past eighteen hours makes no sense. He has deliberately refrained from violence. At the airport he said, I quote, 'I don't want to hurt anybody.' In the confrontation with two Reaction Unit members he said, 'Look what you made me do.' But at neither of these occasions did he give himself up. It doesn't make sense to me. Does anyone have an opinion here?"

She knew Rajkumar would have an opinion. He always had an opinion. "Escalation," he said. "He's not a moron. He knows if he shoots someone, things will escalate out of his control."

Radebe said nothing, but she had her suspicions. So she drew him out. "Vincent?"

Radebe sat with his palms over his cheeks, fingertips on his temples, and his eyes on the big table. "I think not."

"What do you mean?" asked Rajkumar irritably.

"Put everything together," said Radebe. "He left the drug work. Of his own free will. Orlando Arendse said he just left without explanation. He deliberately chose an occupation without violence, probably at a much-reduced salary. He begins a relationship with a single mother, lives with her and her child, enrolls in a high school correspondence course, buys a farm. What does that tell us?"

"Smoke screen," said Rajkumar. "What about all the money?"

"He worked for six years in the lucrative drug industry. What could he spend his money on?"

"A thousand things. Wine, women, song, gambling."

"No," said Radebe.

"What do you think, Vincent?" asked Mentz softly.

"I think he began a new life."

She watched the faces around the table. She wanted to test the support for Radebe. She saw none.

"Why not give himself up then, Vincent?" Rajkumar asked with a flamboyant gesture.

"I don't know," said Radebe. "I just don't know."

Rajkumar leaned back as if he had won the argument.

"A leopard doesn't change its spots," said Janina. "He was out of the big game for ten years. But now he's back. I think he is enjoying it."

* * *

He awoke with a start, immediately aware that the El Camino was no longer moving and the engine was off. He heard voices.

"Koos Kok, get out."

"Why?"

"We want to see if you are smuggling a man with a motorbike."

Under the tarpaulin, he was blind to the action.

"Ja, okay, you got me. Have mercy, it's just a dwarf on a fifty cc."

Roadblock. His heart thundered in his ears, his breathing sounded very loud, he wondered if he had made any noise waking up.

"You always were a smooth-mouthed bastard, Koos. All your life."

"And you are a *ghwar,* Sarge, even for a Dutchman."

"*Ghwar?* What's a *ghwar?*"

"Just playing, Sarge, what's with you today?"

"How many sheep have you got in the back, Koos?"

"I'm not in that business anymore, Sarge."

"You lie, Koos Kok. You will be a sheep stealer till the day you die. Lift up that sail."

How many men were there? Would he be able to . . . ?

"Leave the man, Gerber, we've got more important things to do."

"He's a thief. I bet you there's meat here."

Thobela Mpayipheli heard the man's voice right by him, heard the rustle of a hand over the canvas.

Lord, he was helpless, weaponless, he was lying down without a chance.

"You can look, it's just my furniture," said Koos Kok.

"Where are you moving to?"

"Bloemfontein. I'm looking for a proper job."

"Ha! You lie like a dentist!"

"Let him go, Gerber, he's blocking the road."

"I tell you there are sheep here. . . ."

"Let him go."

"Okay, Koos, get your *skedonk* out of the road."

"But what about the dwarf with the motorbike? He can't ride in the back there all the way."

"Fuck off, Koos, before you get in trouble."

"Okay, okay, Sarge. I'm going." And the springs of the bakkie shifted as Koos Kok got in and then the engine fired and the big six-cylinder rumbled.

"Jissis, Koos, you must work on that exhaust."

"Just as soon as I've dropped off the motorbike," said Koos Kok, and he pulled away with spinning tires.

Quinn set the first issue of the *Argus* carefully before her.

FUGITIVE BIKER WAS MK HERO

The fugitive motorcyclist now hunted nationally by intelligence agencies, the military, and the South

African Police Service was a top Umkhonto we Sizwe soldier who served the Struggle with great distinction, says a former SANDF colonel and comrade of Mr. Thobela Mpayipheli.

"Although I lost track of Thobela's military career during the latter part of the struggle against apartheid, there is no doubt that he was an honorable soldier," says Col. "Lucky" Luke Mahlape, who retired as second in command at First Infantry Battalion in Bloemfontein last year.

Col. Mahlape, now living in Hout Bay, called the *Argus* to set the record straight after news of Mr. Mpayipheli's high-speed cross-country dash on a big BMW motorcycle caught local headlines earlier today.

They will have to change their tune now, she thought. *If the minister does her part thoroughly.*

He did not sleep again but shook on the mattress, the adrenaline dammed up, wondering if there would be more roadblocks, because his nerves could not take it. He wanted to get out from under the tarpaulin, wanted to get on the bike and have control—he could not be this helpless, wondering where they were, how long he had been sleeping.

It was practically dark where he lay, the hands of his watch invisible. He turned so he could lift the canvas, realized it had stopped raining, managed an opening. Twenty past twelve. Lowered the sail again.

Two hours on the road at an average of ninety, a hundred kilometers per hour. Richmond, that is where he guessed the roadblock had been. It was one of the danger spots they had discussed in the house when they had hunched over the map. He wanted to go to De Aar; Koos Kok said no, the army was there, let's go through Merriman to Richmond and then take the back roads to Philipstown, and there you were through the worst, Petrusville, Luckhoff, Koffiefontein, perhaps some danger at Petrusburg because it was on the main route between Kimberley and Bloemfontein, but after that it was a straight run, Dealesville, Bloemhof, Mafikeng, and Botswana and nobody would be the wiser.

He was not so sure. Kimberley was the straight line. And that is where they would wait for him. On a motorbike, not in the back of an El Camino.

And eventually decided the risk was too high.

The bakkie lost speed.

What now?

Stopped.

Lord.

"Xhosa," said Koos Kok.

"What?"

"Don't worry. I have to fill up."

"Where?"

"Richmond. It's just here."

Lord.

"Okay, fine."

Koos Kok pulled away again.

He should have added: "No jokes about the man on the motorbike."

But it probably wouldn't have made any difference.

23.

She was naive when she joined the *Cape Times,* an alumna of Rhodes University's journalism program with stars in her eyes and a burning desire to live out her romance with words at *Cosmo* or *Fair Lady* but prepared to serve her apprenticeship at a daily. She trusted everyone, believed them, looked with wide-eyed wonder at the famous whom she came into contact with in her daily rounds.

But disillusionment followed, not suddenly or dramatically—the small realities slowly took over uninvited. The realization that people are an unreliable, dishonest, self-centered, self-absorbed, backstabbing, violent, sly species that lie, cheat, murder, rape, and steal, regardless of their status, nationality, or color. It was a gradual but often traumatic process for someone who wished only to see good and beauty.

Miriam Nzululwazi and Immanuel the shoeshine man had argued with such conviction that Mpayipheli was a good man. The minister had sketched another picture, the tragedy of the once trustworthy soldier gone bad. Very bad.

Where was the truth?

Will the real Thobela Mpayipheli please stand up.

The only way to find the truth, she knew, was to keep on digging. Keep asking questions and sift the wheat from the chaff.

Eventually Nic phoned in Orlando Arendse's contact numbers. "You can try, but it won't be easy," he said.

She began phoning, one number after another.

"Orlando who?" was the reaction without exception. She would tell her story, in a breathless hurry before they broke the connection: it was about Thobela Mpayipheli, she just wanted background, she would protect her source.

"You have the wrong number, lady."

"So what is the right number?"

Then the line would go dead and she would ring the next one. "My name is Allison Healy, I'm with the *Cape Times,* I would really like to talk to Mr. Orlando Arendse in absolute, guaranteed confidence . . ."

"Where did you get this number?"

She was taken unaware; "from the police" was on the tip of her tongue, but she bit it back. "I'm a reporter, it's my job to find people, but, please, it's about Thobela Mpayipheli . . ."

"Sorry, wrong number."

She rang all five numbers without success and slammed the flat of her hand down on the desk in frustration and then went to have a smoke on the sidewalk outside, short, angry drags on the cigarette. Maybe she should threaten. "If Arendse does not speak to me, I will put his name and occupation in every article I write about this. Take your choice."

No. Better to try again.

When she pulled the notebook of numbers toward her, the phone rang.

"You want to speak to Mr. O?"

For a second she was lost. "Who?" she said, and then hurriedly, "Oh, yes. Yes, I do."

"There's a blue-whale skeleton in the museum. Be there at one o'clock."

Before she could respond, the phone went dead.

The big whale hall was in twilight, dim blue light represented the deep, the taped sounds of the massive animals lent a surreal atmosphere as the colored couple, a young man and girl, wandered hand in hand from one display to the next. She did not consider them until they were right next to her, when the man said her name.

"Yes?" she answered.

"I have to search your handbag," he said apologetically, and she stood rooted until insight caught up with her.

"Oh." She handed over the bag.

"And I have to frisk you," said the girl with a suggestion of a smile. She was nineteen or twenty, with long pitch-black hair, full lips, and tasteful but heavy makeup. "Please raise your arms."

She reacted automatically, feeling the hands skillfully sliding over her body; then the girl stepped back.

"I'm going to keep this until after," said the man, holding up her tape recorder. "Now please come with us."

Outside, the sunlight was blinding. Ahead lay the Kompanje gardens, pigeons and fountains and squirrels. They walked wordlessly on either side of her, leading her to the tea garden, where two colored men sat, somewhat older with stern faces.

Heads were nodded, the two men stood, the girl indicated to Allison to sit. "Nice meeting you," she said, and they were gone. Allison sat with her handbag pinched under her arm, feeling that she would not be surprised if Pierce Brosnan loomed up beside her and said, "Bond. James Bond."

She waited. Nothing happened. Families and businesspeople sat at the other tables. Which of them were Orlando Arendse's? She took out her cigarettes and put one to her lips.

"Allow me," said a voice beside her, and a lighter appeared. She looked up. He looked like a schoolmaster in a tailored suit, blue shirt, red spotted bow tie, hair graying at the temples, but the deep brown face was etched with the lines of a hard life.

While she held her cigarette in the flame he said: "Please forgive the cloak-and-dagger. But we needed to be sure." He sat down opposite her and said, "Rubens."

"I beg your pardon?"

"A game, Miss Healy, Rubens would have painted you. I like Rubens."

"He's the one who liked fat women." She was insulted.

"No," said Arendse. "He is the one who painted perfect women."

She was off-balance. "Mr. Arendse . . ."

He pulled out the chair opposite her. "You may call me Orlando. Or Uncle Orlando. I have a daughter your age."

"Is she also in the . . ."

"Drug business? No, Miss Healy. My Julie is a copywriter at Ogilvie. Last year she won a Pendoring Award for her work with the Volkswagen Golf campaign."

Allison blushed deeply. "Please excuse me. I had the wrong impression."

"I know," he said. "What will you drink?"

"Tea, please."

He gestured to a waiter with the air of a man accustomed to giving orders. He ordered tea for her, coffee for himself. "One condition, Miss Healy. You will not mention my name."

Her eyebrows asked the question.

"To throw my weight around in the newspaper is one way to draw the attention of the SAPS," he said. "I can't afford that."

"Are you really a drug baron?" He did not look like one. He did not speak like one.

"I always found that name amusing. Baron."

"Are you?"

"There was a time in my life, when I was young, I would have answered that with a long rationalization, Miss Healy. How I merely fulfilled the need of people to escape. That I was merely a businessman supplying a product greatly in demand. But with age comes realism. I am among other things a supplier. An illegal importer and distributor of banned substances. I am a parasite living off the weakness of man." He spoke softly, without regret, merely stating the facts. Allison was amazed.

"But why?"

He smiled at her in a grandfatherly way at an obvious question. "Let us blame apartheid," he said, and then laughed softly and privately and switched to a Cape Flats accent and nuances like speaking another language. "Crime of opportunity, *mêrrim, djy vat wat djy kan kry, verstaa' djy.*"

She shook her head in wonder. "The stories you could tell," she said.

"One day, in my memoirs. But let us talk about the man of the moment, Miss Healy. What do you want to know about Tiny Mpayipheli?"

She opened her notebook. She explained about the minister's declaration, the allegations that Mpay-ipheli was a fallen hero, misusing his skill. She was interrupted by the arrival of the tea and coffee. He asked her if she took milk, poured for her. He put milk and three spoons of sugar with his, sipped it.

"The spooks came to me last night. Asking questions with that attitude: 'we have the power and the right.' It is interesting to me, the way everything changes but nothing changes. Instead of chasing the Nigerians that are taking over here. How is one supposed to make a living? Nevertheless, it made me think, last night and this morning, when Tiny was in the news. I thought a lot about him. In my line you see all kinds. You learn to recognize people for what they are, not for what they are trying to show you. And Tiny . . . I knew he was different from the moment he walked in my door. I knew he was just passing through. It was as if he was there, but not his spirit. For years I thought it was because he was a Xhosa in a colored people's world, a fish out of water. But now I know that was not so. He was never an enforcer at heart. He is a warrior. A fighter. Three hundred years ago he would have been the one in front, charging the enemy with spear and shield, the one who reached the lines while his comrades fell around him, the one who kept stabbing until there was only blood and sweat and death."

He came back to reality. "I am a romantic at heart, my dear, you must excuse me."

"Was he violent?"

"*Now there's a question.* What is 'violent'? We are all violent, as a species. It simmers just below the surface like a volcano. The lucky ones go through their entire lives without an eruption."

"Was Thobela Mpayipheli more inclined to violence than the average person?"

"What are we trying to prove here?" he said with some anger.

"Have you seen today's *Argus*?"

"Yes. They say he is a war hero."

"Mr. Arendse . . ."

"Orlando."

"Orlando, the intelligence services are pursuing this man over the length and breadth of the country. If he is a violent and criminal man, it places a whole different perspective on what they are doing. And how they are doing it. The public needs to know."

Orlando Arendse grimaced until the lines of his face creased deeply.

"That is my problem with the media, Miss Healy. You want to press people into packages, that is all there is time and space for. Labels. But you can't label people. We are not all good or bad. There is a bit of both in all of us. No. There is a lot of both in all of us."

"But we don't all become murderers or rapists."

"Granted." He took a packet of sugar in his fingers, twirling it around and around. "He never sought violence. You must understand, he was big. Six foot five. If you are a dealer on the Flats and this big black bugger walks in the door and looks you in the eye, you see your future and it doesn't look good. Violence is the last thing you want to provoke. He carried the threat of violence in him."

"Did he resort to violence sometimes?"

"Lord, you won't give up until you have the answer, the sensation you are looking for."

She shook her head, but he continued before she could protest.

"Yes, sometimes he did use violence. What do you expect, in my line of business? But remember, he was provoked. In the days before the Nigerians started messing us around, it was the Russians who tried to get control of the trade. And they were racist. Tiny worked a couple of them over right into intensive care. I wasn't there, but the men told me, whispering with big eyes as if they had seen something otherworldly. The intensity was awesome. Raw. What frightened them most—they said he enjoyed it. It was as if a light shone out from him."

She scribbled in her notebook, hurrying to keep up.

"But if you want to define him like that, you will be making a mistake. He has a lot of good in him. One bad winter we were in the city late at night, other side of Strand Street in the red-light district, collecting protection money, and he was watching the street kids. And then he went over and gathered them up—there must have been twenty or thirty—and took them to the Spur Steakhouse and told the management it was their birthday, all of them and each one must get a plate of food and a sparkler and the waiters must sing 'Happy Birthday.' That was a party for you."

She glanced up from her writing. "He made a choice in those days. He came to work for you. I can't understand why an MK veteran would go to work for a drug baron."

"That is because you were never an MK veteran out of work in the new South Africa."

"Touché."

"If you committed your life to the Struggle and won, you'd expect some kind of reward. It's human, an inherent expectation. Freedom is an ephemeral reward. You can't grasp it in your hand. One morning you wake up and you are free. But your township is just as much a ghetto as yesterday, you are just as poor, your people are as burdened as before. You can't eat freedom. You can't buy a house or a car with it."

He took a big swallow of coffee. "Madiba was Moses and he led us to the Promised Land, but there was no milk or honey."

He put his cup down.

"Or something like that." And he smiled gently. "I don't know what to say to you. You are looking for the real Tiny, and I don't think anyone knows who that is. What I can say is that in the years he worked for me, he was never late, he was never sick; he did not drink or sample the produce of the trade. Women? Tiny is a man. He had his needs. And the girls were mad about him, the young ones—seventeen, eighteen— they ran after him, pursued him with open desire. But there was never any trouble. I can tell you his body was in the work, but his mind was elsewhere."

Orlando Arendse shook his head in recall. "Let me tell the thing with the French. One day we were walking in the city, down St. George's, and there were these tourists, French, standing with a map and wondering, and they called me over in their bad English and they were looking for a place. The next thing big, black Tiny starts babbling in French like you won't believe. There in front of my eyes he became another person, different body, different eyes, another language, another land. Suddenly he was alive, his body and mind were in one place together. He was alive."

The material in his memory bank made him laugh. "You should have seen their faces, those tourists nearly hugged him, they chattered like starlings. And when we walked away I asked him, 'What was that?' And he said, 'My previous life'—that's all, 'My previous life'—but he said it with longing that I can still feel today, and that is when I realized I didn't know him. I would never know him. Some more tea?"

"Thank you," she said, and he did the honors. "And then he left your service?"

Orlando Arendse drank the last of his coffee. "Tiny and I . . . There was respect. We looked each other in the eye, and let me tell you it doesn't happen often in my business. Part of that respect was that we both knew the day would come."

"Why did he leave?"

"Why? Because the time had come, that is probably the simplest answer, but not the whole truth. The thing is: I loaned him out, just before he resigned. Long story. Just call it business, a transaction. There was a shooting and a fight. Tiny landed in the hospital. When he came out, he said he was finished."

"Loaned out?"

"I'm honor-bound, my dear. You will have to ask Van Heerden."

"Van Heerden?"

"Zatopek van Heerden. Former policeman, former private eye, now he's like a professor of psychology at the university."

"The University of Cape Town?"

"The Lord works in mysterious ways, *verstaa' djy,*" said Orlando Arendse with a twinkle in his eye, and beckoned the waiter to bring the check.

Vincent Radebe closed the door of the interview room behind him. Miriam Nzululwazi stood by the one-way window, a deep frown on her face.

"When can I go home?" she asked in Xhosa.

"Won't you sit down, sister." Soft, sympathetic, serious.

"Don't 'sister' me."

"I understand."

"You understand nothing. What have I done? Why are you keeping me here?"

"To protect you and Thobela."

"You lie. You are a black man and you lie to your own people."

Radebe sat down. "Please, ma'am, let us talk. Please."

She turned her back on him.

"Ma'am, of all the people here, I am about the only one who thinks that Thobela is a good man. I think I understand what happened. I am on your side. There must be some way I can make you believe that."

"There is. Let me go. I am going to lose my job. I have to look after my child. I am not a criminal. I never did anything to anyone. Let me go."

"You won't lose your job. I promise you."

"How will you manage that?"

"I will talk to the bank. Explain to them."

She turned around. "How can I believe you?"

"I am telling you. I am on your side."

"That is exactly what the white woman said."

Mentz is right, he thought. It was not easy. He had offered to come talk to her. He was uneasy that she was there, that she was being detained. His thoughts were with her, his empathy, but the damage had already been done. He let the silence grow.

She gave him an opening: "What can I say to you? What can I do so you will let me go?"

"There are two things. This morning you spoke to the newspapers . . ."

"What did you expect me to do? They come to my work. They also say they are on my side."

"It was not wrong. Just dangerous. They write crazy things. We—"

"You are afraid they will write the truth."

He suppressed his frustration, kept his head cool. "Ma'am, Thobela Mpayipheli is out there somewhere with a lot of information that a few people want very badly. Some of them will do anything to stop him. The more the papers write, the more dangerous the things that they will do. Is that what you want?"

"I won't talk to them again. Is that what you want?"

"Yes, that is what I want."

"What else?"

"We need to know why he has not given himself up yet."

"That you must ask him yourself." Because if everything was as they said, then she did not understand, either.

"We would dearly love to. We hoped you would help us to get him to understand."

"How can I? I don't know what he thinks. I don't know what happened."

"But you know him."

"He went to help a friend, that is all I know."

"What did he say before he left?"

"I have already told the colored man who came to my house. Why must I say it again? There is nothing more. Nothing. I will keep quiet, I will talk to nobody, I swear it to you, but you must let me go now."

He saw she was close to breaking, he knew she was telling the truth. He wanted to reach out and comfort her. He also knew she would not tolerate it. Radebe stood. "You are right, ma'am," he said. "I will see to it."

24.

He had to stretch his legs, the cramps were creeping up on him, and his shoulder throbbed. The nest under the tarpaulin was too small now, too hot, too dusty. The shuddering over the dirt roads—how far still to go?—he needed air, to get out, it was going too slowly, the hours disappearing in the monotonous drone of the Chevy. Every time Koos Kok reduced speed he thought they had arrived, but it was just another turn, another connection. His impatience and discomfort were nearly irrepressible, and then the Griqua stopped and lifted the sail with a theatrical gesture and said, "The road is clear, Xhosa, *laat jou voete raas.*"

He was blinded by the sudden midday sun. He straightened stiffly, allowing his eyes to adjust. The landscape was different, less Karoo. He saw grass veld, hills, a town in the distance.

"That's Philipstown." Koos Kok followed his gaze.

The road stretched out before them, directly north.

They wrestled the GS off the El Camino, using two planks as a ramp that bent deeply under the weight, but it was easier than the loading. They worked hurriedly, worried about the possibility of passing traffic.

"You must wait until sunset," said Koos Kok.

"There's no time."

The GS stood ready on its stand; Thobela pulled on the rider's suit, opened the sports bag, and counted out some notes, offering them to Koos Kok.

"I don't want your money. You paid for the petrol already."

"I owe you."

"You owe me nothing. You gave me the music."

"What music?"

"I am going to write a song about you."

"Is that why you helped me?"

"Sort of."

"Sort of?"

"You have two choices in life, Xhosa. You can be a victim. Or not." His smile was barely discernible.

"Oh."

"You will understand one day."

He hesitated a moment and then pushed the cash into Kok's top pocket. "Take this for wear and tear," he said, handing over a couple of hundred rand.

"Ride like the wind, Xhosa."

"Go well, Griqua."

They stood facing each other uncomfortably. Then he put out his hand to Koos Kok. "Thank you."

The Griqua shook his hand, smiled with a big gap-toothed smile.

He put the bag in the side case, pushed his hands into the gloves, and mounted. Pushed the starter. The GS hesitated a second before it caught and then he raised his hand and rode, accelerating gradually through the gears, giving the engine time to warm up. It felt good, it felt right, because he was in control again; on the road, fourth, fifth, sixth, 140 kilometers per hour, he shifted into position, found the right angle with most of his torso behind the windshield, bent slightly forward, and then let the needle creep up and looked in the rearview mirror to see that Koos Kok and the El Camino had become very small behind him in the road.

The digital clock read 15:06 and he made some calculations, visualizing the road map in his mind, two hundred kilometers of blacktop to Petrusburg—that was the dangerous part, in daylight on the R48—but it was a quiet road. Petrusburg by half past four, five o'clock. Refuel and if he was reported, then there was the network of dirt roads to the north, too many for them to patrol, and he would have choices, to go through Dealesville or Boshof, and his choices would multiply and by then it would be dark and if all went well, he could cross the border at Mafikeng before midnight. Then he would be away, safe, and he would phone Miriam from Lobatse, tell her he was safe, regardless of what they said over the radio.

But first he had to pass Petrusville and cross the Orange River.

If he were setting up a roadblock, it would be at the Big River, as Koos Kok called it. Close the bridge. There were no other options according to the map, unless you were willing to chance your luck in Orania.

The thought made him smile.

Odd country, this.

What would the Boers of Orania think if he pulled up in a cloud of dust and said, "I am Thobela Mpayipheli, chaps, and the ANC government would love to get their hands on me"? Would it be a case of "if you are against the government, you are with us"? Probably not.

He had to pass a sheep lorry, slowing down and using his blinkers like a law-abiding citizen, sped up again, leaning the bike into the turns where the road twisted between the hills, aware of the landscape. Beautiful country, this. Colorful. That is the difference, the major difference between this landscape and the Karoo. More color, as if God's palette was increasingly used up on the way south. Here the green was greener, the ridges browner, the grass more yellow, the sky more blue.

Color had messed up this land. The difference in color.

The road grew straight again, a black ribbon stretching out ahead, grass veld and thorn bush. Cumulus clouds in line, a war host marching across the heavens. This was the face of Africa. Unmistakable.

Zatopek van Heerden said it was not color, it was genes. Van Heerden was big on genes. Genes that caused the Boers of Orania to pull into the defensive *laager*. Van Heerden said racism is inherent, the human urge to protect his genes, to seek out his own so the genes could propagate.

Thobela had argued because Van Heerden's philosophy was too empty. Too damning. Too easy.

"So, I can do as I please and shrug my shoulders and say, 'It's genes'?"

"You must differentiate between genetic programming and morality, Thobela."

"I don't know what you mean."

Van Heerden had bowed his shoulders as if the weight of knowledge were too heavy to bear.

"There is no easy way to explain it."

"That is usually the case with absolute drivel."

Laughing: "That's fucking true. But not in this case. The problem is that most people won't accept the big truths. You should see them fighting in the letters page of the *Burger* over evolution. And not just here. In America they don't want to allow evolution into the classroom even. In the twenty-first century. The evidence is overwhelming, but they fight to the bitter end."

Van Heerden said accepting evolution was the first step. People are formed through natural selection, their bodies and thoughts and behavior. Programmed. For one thing alone: the survival of the species. The preservation of the gene pool. The white man had laid down evidence before him in one motivated layer after another, but eventually, though Thobela had conceded that there was some truth in what Van Heerden said, it could not be the whole truth. He knew that, he felt it in his bones. What of God, what of love, what of all the strange, wonderful things that people were capable of, things we do and experience and think?

Van Heerden waved his hand and said, "Let's forget about it."

And he had said: "You know, whitey, it sounds like the new excuse to me. All the great troubles of the world have been done in the name of one or other excuse. Christianization, colonialism, herrenvolk, communism, apartheid, democracy, and now evolution. Or is it genetics? Excuses, just another reason to do as we wish. I am tired of it all. Finished with that. I am tired of my own excuses and the excuses of other people. I am taking responsibility for what I do now. Without excuse. I have choices; you have choices. About how we will live. That's all. That's all we can choose. Fuck excuses. Live right, or get lost."

He spoke with fervor and conviction. He had been loud, and heads turned in the coffee shop where they sat, but he didn't care. And now, in this desolate piece of Africa at 160 kilometers per hour, he knew he was right and it filled him with elation for what he must do. Not just the thing in the bag, but afterward. To live a life of responsibility, a life that said if you want change, start here, inside yourself.

"Ma'am, let us let her go." Vincent Radebe sat next to Janina Mentz, speaking softly to keep the potential for conflict between them low-key. He knew she was keeping an eye on him, knew she had doubts about his attitude and his support for her. But he had to do what he must do.

She sat at her laptop at the big table. She finished typing but did not turn to him.

"Ai, Vincent," she said.

"She knows nothing. She can't add value," he said.

"But she can do damage."

"Ma'am, she understands she must not talk to the media."

Janina put her hand on Vincent Radebe's arm compassionately. "It is good that you are part of the team, Vincent. You bring balance. I respect and value your contribution. And your honesty."

He had not expected that. "Can I go and tell her?"

"Let me give you a scenario to think over. We drop Mrs. Nzululwazi at her house. She fetches her child, and a photographer from the *Cape Times* photographs them standing hand in hand in front of their little house. Tomorrow the picture is on the front page. With the caption 'Mother and child wait anxiously for fugitive's return'—or something like that. Do we need that? While the minister works to explain Mpayipheli's true colors to the media? She has already done damage. You heard the reporter on the radio. 'His common-law wife says he is a good man.'"

He could see what she meant.

"In any case, Vincent, what guarantee do you have that she will not talk to the media again? What happens when they start pulling out checkbooks?"

"I have summed her up differently," he said.

She nodded in thought. "Perhaps you are in a better position to make this decision, Vincent."

"Ma'am?"

"The decision is yours."

"You mean I can decide if she can go or not?"

"Yes, Vincent, just you. But you must bear the responsibility. And the consequences."

He looked at her, searching for clues in her eyes, suddenly wary.

"I will have to think about it," he said.

"That is the right thing to do."

He slowed down when he saw Petrusville. He had hoped the road would bypass the town, but it ran directly through. Koos Kok was right, it would have been better at night, but there was no helping it now, he must gut it out. He checked the fuel meter—still over half. Keeping the needle on sixty, he rode into town, one- and two-story buildings, bleached signboards, Old World architecture. From the corner of his eye he could see black faces from the lower town turning, staring. He was colorless, without identity under the helmet, thankfully. He stopped at the four-way stop. A car pulled up alongside him, a woman, fat and forty. She stared at the bike, at him. He kept his eyes forward, pulled away, excruciatingly aware of the attention. There was a sprinkling of activity in the hot, sleepy afternoon. Pedestrians. Cars, bakkies, bicycles. He rode with his ears pricked for alarm signals, his back tense as if waiting for a bullet. Kept to sixty, revs low, trying not to make a racket, to be invisible, something impossible on this vehicle. He passed houses and children by the road, a few fingers pointed—did they recognize him, or was it the motorbike? Town boundary, a sign saying he could ride 120 again. He accelerated slowly, uncertain, keeping watch in the rearview mirror.

Nothing.

Was it possible?

A car beside the road. White people under a thorn tree, a thermos of coffee on the concrete table. They waved. He lifted his left hand.

Signboard saying Vanderkloof Dam to the right.

He continued straight on.

Somewhere up ahead was the turnoff to Luck-hoff—and the bridge over the Orange.

Trouble must be waiting there.

*   *   *

Fourteen kilometers south of Koffiefontein the official of the Free State Traffic Authority sat at his speed trap.

"Department of Psychology," said the woman's voice over the phone.

"Hi. May I speak to Mr. Van Heerden?"

"You mean Dr. Van Heerden?"

"Oh. Zatopek van Heerden?"

"I'm afraid Dr. Van Heerden isn't in. May I take a message?"

"This is Allison Healy of the *Cape Times*. Do you know how I can get hold of him?"

"I'm afraid I'm not at liberty to provide his home number."

"Does he have a cell number?"

The woman laughed. "Dr. Van Heerden is not keen on cell phones, I'm afraid."

"May I leave my number? Will he call me back?"

"He will be in again tomorrow."

Thobela Mpayipheli knew the bridge must be within a kilometer or two, according to the map.

A Volkswagen Kombi approached from the front. He watched the driver, looking for signs of blockades, the law, or soldiers.

Nothing.

He saw the green seam of the river, knew the crossing was just ahead, but there was no sign of activity.

Was he far enough east? Was that why they were not here?

The road straightened and the bridge came into view, two white railings, double lane, open, clear.

He accelerated, leaving the Northern Cape, looked down at the brown waters flowing strongly, the midday sun reflecting brightly off the ripples. The sluices of the dam must be open, he surmised. Probably because of the rain. Over the bridge, over the Orange.

Free State.

Relief flooded through him. They had slipped up.

What about . . . His head jerked up to the sky, searching for the specks of helicopter, ears straining for their rumble above the noise of the motorbike.

Nothing.

Had the ride in the back of the El Camino slipped him through the net?

It didn't matter. The initiative was with him now; he had the lead and the advantage.

He must use it.

He used the torque with purpose, felt the power flow to the rear wheel, how the steering rod got lighter.

He wanted to laugh.

Fucking beautiful German machine.

Fourteen kilometers south of Koffiefontein the official of the Free State Traffic Authority sat reading.

The white patrol car was behind the thorn trees that grew by the dry wash, his canvas chair positioned so that he could see the reading on the Gatsometer and the road stretching out to the south. The book was balanced on his lap.

So far it was an average day. Two minibus taxis for speeding, three lorries from Gauteng for lesser offenses. They thought if they came through here, avoiding the main routes, they could overload or get away with poor tires, but they were wrong. He was not overenthusiastic. He enjoyed his work, especially the part that allowed him to sit in the shade of an acacia on a perfect summer's day, listen to the birds chattering, and read Ed McBain. But when it came to enforcing traffic ordinances, he was probably a tad stricter with vehicles from other provinces.

He had pulled over a few farmers in their bakkies. One didn't have his driver's license with him, but you couldn't just write a ticket for these gentlemen, they had influence. You gave them a warning.

Two tourists, Danes, had stopped to ask directions. An average day.

He checked his watch again. At quarter to five he would start rolling up the wires of the Gatsometer. Not a minute later.

He looked up the road. No traffic. His eyes dropped back to the book. Some of his colleagues from other towns listened to the radio. When there were two officers stationed together, they talked rubbish from morning to night, but he preferred this.

Alone, just him and McBain's characters, Carella and Hawes and the big black cop, Brown and Oliver Weeks and their things.

An average day.

25.

Everything happened at once.

The director walked into the Ops Room and everyone was astounded, Janina Mentz's cell phone rang, and Quinn, headphones on his ears, suddenly started making wild gestures to get her attention.

She took the call because she could see from the little screen who it was.

"It's Tiger," said Mazibuko. "I am awake."

"Captain, I will phone you right back," she said, and cut the connection. "What have you got, Rudewaan?" she asked Quinn.

"Johnny Kleintjes's house number. We relayed it here."

"Yes?"

"It's ringing. Continuously. Every few minutes they phone again."

"Where is Monica Kleintjes? Bring her down."

"In my office. Is she going to answer?"

A nervous question because of the director's presence, the figure at the margins, the big boss they almost never saw. They couldn't afford a mess-up now.

Mentz's voice was reassuring. "Perhaps it's nothing. Maybe it's the media. Even if it is the people in
Lusaka—by now they must know something is going
on, with all the media coverage."

Quinn nodded to one of his people to go fetch
Monica Kleintjes.

She turned to the director and stood up. "Good
afternoon, sir."

"Afternoon, everyone," the small Zulu said, smiling like a politician on election day. "Don't stand up,
Janina. I know you are busy." He went and stood by
her. "I have a message from the minister. So I thought
I would come down. To show my solidarity."

"Thank you, sir. We appreciate it."

"The minister has asked the Department of Defence to track down people who worked with Mpayipheli in the old days and, shall we say, do not have
fond memories of him."

"She is a woman of initiative, sir."

"That she is, Janina."

"And did she find someone?"

"She did. A brigadier in Pretoria. Lucas Morape.
They trained together in Russia, and he describes
our fugitive as, I quote, 'an aggressive troublemaker,
perhaps a psychopath, who was a continuous embarrassment to his comrades and the Movement.'"

"That is good news, indeed, sir. From a public
relations angle, of course."

"It is. In the course of the afternoon the brigadier will release a short report to the media." He prepared to leave. "That is all I have at the moment, Janina. I won't disturb you further."

"I truly appreciate it, sir. But may I ask one more favor? Could you pass on this news to Radebe personally?"

"Is he somewhat skeptical, Janina?"

"One could say that, sir."

The director turned and walked over to where Radebe was sitting at the communication banks. Mentz concentrated on her cell phone, getting Mazibuko on the air.

"You must know we are working with a bunch of morons here," said Tiger Mazibuko.

"How so?"

"Jissis," he said. "So many egos. So much politicking. Free State Command wants to run the show and so does Northern Cape. They don't even have enough radios for all the roadblocks, and Groblershoop is not covered, because the trucks have broken down."

"Slow down, Tiger. Where are you?"

"Anti-Aircraft School. Kimberley."

"Is that where the Rooivalks are?"

"Yes. They are waiting in a row here. My people, too."

"Tiger, according to my information, Free State Command is covering the N8 from Bloemfontein to

Perdeberg, and Northern Cape is responsible for the rest, up to Groblershoop. With the police as backup."

"In theory."

"What do you mean, 'in theory'?"

"In the Free State things look okay: they have fourteen roadblocks and things look right on the map. But between us and Groblershoop there are about twenty roads that cross the N8. The little colonel here says they have only sixteen roadblocks, and four of them have not reported back yet because they haven't received radios yet, or they don't work."

"Do you include the police in that?"

"The police are using their own network. The co-ordination stinks."

"You would expect that, Tiger. This thing came down on them out of the blue."

"They are going to let the fucker slip through, ma'am."

"Captain . . ."

"Sorry."

She saw Monica Kleintjes coming in with an urgent limp, Quinn's assistant behind her.

"Let me see what I can do, Tiger. I'll phone you back."

She stood up and went to Quinn. "Are they still calling?"

"Not at the moment."

"How are you feeling, Monica?"

"Scared."

"There is nothing to be afraid of. Our people are already in Lusaka, and we will handle this thing."

The colored woman looked at her with hope.

"If it is the media, say you don't know what they are talking about. If it is the people from Lusaka, tell them the truth. With one exception: tell them you are at home. Don't tell them we brought you here. Understand?"

"I must say I gave the hard drive to Tiny?"

"The whole truth. Tell them why you gave it to him, when you gave it to him, everything. If they ask you if it is the man who is so much in the news, say yes. Keep to the truth. If they ask you if we have contacted you, say yes, there was a man who came to question you. Admit you told him everything. If they ask how we knew, tell them you suspect your phone was tapped. Keep to the truth. Just don't tell them you are here."

"But my father . . ."

"They are after the data, Monica. Never forget that. Your father is safe as long as that is the case. And moreover, we have teams in Lusaka. Everything is under control."

Monica's eyes stayed wide, but she nodded.

You are not your father's child, thought Janina. There was nothing of Johnny Kleintjes's quiet strength. Perhaps that will work in our favor.

"Ma'am," said Rahjev Rajkumar, "something is brewing."

She looked at the Indian tapping a fat finger on the computer screen of one of his assistants.

"I'm coming," she said. "Quinn, let Monica answer if they phone again."

"Very good, ma'am."

As she moved toward Rajkumar, she could see the director and Radebe deep in conversation in the corner at the radio panel. She could see Radebe talking fervently, waving his hands, the director small and defenseless against the onslaught, but she could not hear a single word. Let him see what she had to deal with. Let him see how she was undermined. Then there would be no trouble when she transferred Vincent Radebe to lighter duties.

The Indian shifted his considerable bulk to make room for her. On the screen was the BMW motorcycle website.

"Look at this," he said. "We have been monitoring them all afternoon."

She read. Messages, one after another.

This is going to be better than the annual gathering. We are four guys, leaving at 13:00. See you in Kimberley.

—John S., Johannesburg

I'm leaving now, will take the N3 to Bethlehem, then Bloemfontein and on to Kimberley. I'm on a red K 1200 RS. If there's anybody who wants to come along for the ride, just fall in behind me. If you can keep up, of course.

—Peter Strauss, Durban

See you at Pietermaritzburg, Peter. We are on two R 1150s, a F 650 and a new RT.

— Dasher, PM

We are three guys on 1150 GSs, just like the Big Bad Biker. We will meet you at the Big Hole, will keep the beers cold, it's just over the hill for us.

—Johan Wasserman, Klerksdorp

"How many are there?" asked Janina.

"Twenty-two messages," said Rajkumar's assistant. "More than seventy bikers who say they are on the way."

"That doesn't bother me."

Rajkumar and his assistant looked at her questioningly.

"It's just a lot of men looking for an excuse to drink," she said. "Seventy? What are they going to do? Carry out a coup d'état at Northern Cape Command with their scooters?"

"Department of Psychology."

"This is Allison Healy of the *Cape Times* again. I wonder if —"

"I told you, Dr. Van Heerden will be in tomorrow."

"You did. But I was wondering if you could call him at home and tell him it is in connection with Thobela Mpayipheli."

"Who?"

"Thobela Mpayipheli. Dr. Van Heerden knows him well. The man is in trouble, and if you could call him and tell him, I can leave you my number."

"Dr. Van Heerden does not like to be disturbed at home."

"Please."

There was silence on the end, followed by a dramatic sigh. "What is your number?"

She gave it.

"And your name again?"

The Reaction Unit's members sat around in groups defined by the shade of the acacias next to the hard-baked red and white parade ground of the Anti-Aircraft School, between the vehicles and boxes. The row of trees provided ever shifting shelter from the merciless sun and dominating heat of thirty-four degrees Celsius. Two tents had been erected—just the roof sections, like enormous umbrellas. Shirts were off, torsos glistening with sweat, weapons were being cleaned, a few of Team Alpha lay sleeping, others chatted, here and there a muffled laugh. A radio was playing.

As Captain Tiger Mazibuko approached, he heard

them fall silent as a news bulletin was announced. He checked his watch. Where had the day gone?

Four o'clock on Diamond City Radio and here is the news, read by René Grobbelaar. Kimberly is the focal point of a countrywide search for MK veteran Thobela Mpayipheli, who evaded law enforcers yesterday evening in Cape Town on a stolen motorcycle. According to Inspector Tappe Terblanche, local liaison officer for the police, a joint operation between the army and SAPS has been launched to intercept the fugitive. He is probably somewhere in the Northern Cape. A similar operation is under way in the Free State.

During a news conference earlier today the minister of intelligence revealed that Mpayipheli, who is armed and considered dangerous, is in possession of extremely sensitive classified information that he has illegally obtained. In reply to a question on the nature of the information, the minister replied that it was not in the interest of national security to reveal details.

Members of the public who have had contact with Mpayipheli, or who have information that could lead to his arrest, are advised to call the following toll-free number. . . .

With my luck, thought Tiger Mazibuko, *some idiot will force Mpayipheli off the road with his souped-up Opel and demand the reward, too.*

He sat down beside Lieutenant Penrose. "Is Bravo ready?"

"When the signal comes, we can be rolling in five minutes, Captain."

"If the signal comes." He motioned toward the building behind him where the operation was coordinated. "This lot of monkeys couldn't find a turd in a toilet."

The lieutenant laughed. "We will get him, Captain. You'll see."

Fourteen kilometers south of Koffiefontein the Gatsometer gave its fine electronic scream and the officer closed the book in one flowing motion, checked the speed reading, stood up, and walked into the road. It was a white Mercedes-Benz, six or seven years old. He held up his hand and the car immediately began to brake, stopping just next to him. He walked around to the driver's side.

"Afternoon, Mr. Franzen," he greeted the driver.

"You got me again," said the farmer.

"A hundred and thirty-two, Mr. Franzen."

"I was in a bit of a hurry. The kids forgot half their stuff on the farm and tomorrow is rugby practice. You know how it is."

"Speed kills, Mr. Franzen."

"I know, I know. It's a terrible thing."

"We'll look the other way this time, but you must please respect the speed limit, Mr. Franzen."

"I promise you it won't happen again."

"You can go."

"Thank you. Cheers, *boet.*"

He doesn't even know my name, the officer thought. *Until I write him a ticket.*

Quinn motioned for everyone to keep quiet before he allowed Monica Kleintjes to answer. She had a headset on, earphones and microphone, and then he pressed the button and nodded to her.

"Monica Kleintjes," she said in a shaky voice.

"You have a lot of explaining to do, young lady." Lusaka. The same unaccented voice of the first call.

"Please," she said.

"You gave the drive to the guy on the motorbike?"

"Yes, I—"

"That was a very stupid thing to do, Monica."

"I had no choice. I . . . I couldn't do it on my own."

"Oh, no, Monica. You were just plain stupid. And now we have a real problem."

"I'm sorry. Please . . ."

"How did the spooks find out, Monica?"

"They . . . the phone. It was tapped."

"That's what we thought. And they're listening right now."

"No."

"Of course they are. They are probably standing right next to you."

"What are you going to do?"

The voice was still calm. "Unlike you, my dear, we are sticking to the original deal. With maybe a few codicils. You have forty-eight of the seventy-two hours left. If the drive isn't here by then, we will kill your father. If we see anything that looks like an agent in Lusaka, we will kill your father. If the drive gets here and it is more bullshit, we will kill your father."

Monica Kleintjes's body jerked slightly. "Please," she said despairingly.

"You should know, Monica, that your daddy is not a nice man. He talked to us—with a little encouragement, of course. We know he is working with the intelligence people. We know he tried to palm off bullshit data. That's why we ordered the real thing. So here's the deal for you and your friends from Presidential Intelligence: if the motorbike man does not make it, we kill Kleintjes. And we'll give the bullshit drives and the whole story of how they abused a pensioner to the press. Can you imagine the headlines, Monica? Can you?"

She was crying now, her shoulders shaking, her mouth forming words that could not escape her lips.

And then everyone realized the connection was broken, and the director was looking at Janina Mentz with a strange expression on his face.

26.

He was doing nearly 180 when he saw the double tubes of the Gatsometer on the road in front of him and grabbed a handful of brakes and pulled hard, a purely instinctive reaction. The ABS brakes kicked in, moaned; one eye on the instrument panel, one eye on the tubes, still too fast, somewhere around 140, he saw the man run over the road, hand raised, and he had to brake again to avoid contact, realizing it was traffic police, one man, just one man, a speed trap. He must decide whether to run or stop, the choice too suddenly on him, the causality too wide; he chose to run, turned the throttle, passed the traffic officer and one car on the right, under the tree, only one car; he made up his mind, heart in his throat, and pulled the brakes again, bringing the motorbike to a standstill on the gravel verge. It didn't make sense, a lone traffic cop, one car, and he turned to see the man jogging toward him, half apologetic, and then he was standing there, saying, "Mister, for a minute there I thought you were going to run away."

* * *

For the first time she felt fear as she climbed the stairs with the director to his office.

In that moment when he had looked at her in the Ops Room, something had altered between them, some balance. He had made a small movement with his head and she knew what he meant and followed, her staff unknowing but silently watching them.

It was not the change in the balance of power between her and the Zulu that clamped around her heart, it was the knowledge that she was no longer in control, that perception and reality had drifted apart like two moving targets.

He waited until she was inside, closed the door, and stood still. He looked unblinkingly at her. "That is not the CIA, Janina," he said.

"I know."

"Who is it?"

She sat down, although he had not invited her. "I don't know."

"And the drive that Mpayipheli has?"

She shook her head.

He walked slowly through the room, around the desk. She saw his calm. He did not sit, but stood behind his chair, looking down at her.

"Have you told me everything, Janina?"

One man, the situation was surreal. He was moving in a dream world as he climbed off the motorbike, pulled off his gloves and helmet. "That's a beautiful bike," said the traffic officer.

For a moment he considered the irony: the traffic cop saw the removal of his accessories as submission; he knew he did it for ease of movement, should he need to react. Retreating from the threat of violence, he forced himself into pacifist mode. He could see the weapon in the shiny leather holster on the officer's hip.

"We don't see many of those around here."

The blood was pulsing through him, he was aware of his readiness. As long as he recognized it, he could control it. He still felt unreal; the conversation was impossibly banal. "It is the biggest-selling bike bigger than seven-fifty cc in the country," he said, keeping his voice even with difficulty.

"You don't say?"

He didn't know how to answer. The motorbike was between them—he wanted to reduce the gap but also maintain it.

"You were going quite fast."

"I was." Was he going to get a ticket? Would it be as ridiculous as that?

"Let me see your driver's license."

Suspicion: he must know something, he could not be alone. "Of course." He took the key from the ignition, unlocked the luggage case, tried to scan the line of thorn trees and bushes surreptitiously. Where were the others?

"Lots of packing space, hey?" There was an ingenuous quality in the man, and the question loosened something in his belly, a strange feeling.

He zipped open the blue sports bag, looking for his wallet, took out the card, and handed it over. He kept a vigilant watch on the officer's face, looking for covertness or deceit.

"Mpay—"

"Mpayipheli." He helped the man pronounce it.

"Is this your motorbike, Mr. Mpayipheli?"

Then he knew what was happening, and the urge to giggle was overwhelming, pushing up in him without warning as his brain grasped the possibility that this provincial representative had absolutely no idea. It almost overcame him. He allowed it to bubble up modestly, careful not to lose it but suddenly relaxing, laughing heartily, "I could never afford one of these."

The officer laughed along with him, bonding— two middle-class men admiring the toys of the rich. "What do these things cost?"

"Just over ninety thousand."

The man whistled through his teeth. "Whose is it?"

"My boss's. He has an agency in the Cape. For BMW." And again the laugh bubbled up in him, any minute now he was going to wake up under the tarpaulin of the El Camino, these moments of drama could not be real.

The traffic officer handed back his driver's license. "I rode a Kawasaki when I did traffic in Bloemfontein. A seven-fifty. Big. I don't see a chance for that anymore." Trying to strengthen the bond.

"I've got a Honda Benly at home."

"Those things last forever."

They both knew the moment of truth was coming, a defining factor in the budding relationship. It hung in a moment of silence between them. The officer shrugged his shoulders apologetically. "I really should ticket you."

Fuck, he could not hold it in. It was filling his body with the urgency of a call of nature. "I know" was all he could manage.

"You'd better go, before I change my mind."

He smiled perhaps too widely, put out his hand. "Thank you." He turned away quickly, putting away the license in the wallet, wallet in the bag, bag in the motorbike.

"And take it easy," came the voice over his shoulder. "Speed kills."

He nodded, put on the helmet, and pulled on his gloves.

"You know all that I know," said Janina Mentz, but she lied. "I planned the operation on Ismail Mohammed's testimony. I recruited Johnny Kleintjes. Me alone. No one else knew anything. We compiled the data together. It is false but credible, I am sure of that. He contacted the Americans. They showed interest. They invited him to Lusaka. He went, and then the call came to his house."

"And she got Mpayipheli."

"Unforeseen."

"Unforeseen, Janina? According to the transcript of Monica's interview, Johnny came to her work two weeks before he left for Lusaka and said if something happened to him, Mpayipheli is the man. And more-over, on top of the hard drive in his safe was a note with Mpayipheli's phone number."

Then she saw what the director saw, and the hand around her heart squeezed a little tighter. "He knew."

The director nodded.

She saw from a wider perspective. "Johnny Kleintjes sold us out."

"Us and the Americans, Janina."

"But why, sir?"

"What do you know of Johnny Kleintjes?"

She threw up her hands. "I studied his file. Activist, exile, ANC member, computers . . ."

"Johnny is a communist, Janina."

She sprang up, frustration and fear the goads. "Mr. Director, with respect, what does that mean? We were all communists when it suited us to have the help of the Eastern bloc. Where are the communists now? Marginalized dreamers who no longer have a significant influence in the government."

She stood with her hands on the desk and became conscious of the distaste in the Zulu's demeanor. When he eventually answered, his voice was soft. "Johnny Kleintjes may be a dreamer, but you were the one who marginalized him."

"I don't understand," she said, removing her hands and stepping back.

"What don't you understand, Janina?"

"Sir," she said, sinking slowly into the chair, "to whom could he go? To whom did he sell us out?"

"That is what we must find out."

"But it makes no sense. Communism . . . There's nothing left. There's no one anymore."

"You are too literal, Janina. I suspect it's more a question of 'the enemy of my enemy.'"

"You must explain."

"Johnny always had a special hatred for the Americans."

Insight came slowly to her, reluctantly. "You mean . . ."

"Who does the CIA currently view as threat number one?"

"Oh, my God," said Janina.

A bespectacled black soldier with the epaulettes of the Anti-Aircraft School on his shoulders came to fetch Captain Tiger Mazibuko under the tree. "The colonel asks the captain to come quickly."

He jumped up. "Have they got him?" He jogged ahead, aware of the expectations of the RU behind him.

"I don't think so, Captain."

"You don't think so?"

"The colonel will tell you, Captain." He jogged into the building. The colonel stood at the radio, microphone in hand.

"We have a situation."

"What?"

"There are thirty-nine Hell's Angels on motorbikes at the Windsorton Road roadblock. They want to come through."

"Where the hell is Windsorton Road?"

"Forty-five kilometers north, on the N12."

"The Johannesburg road?"

The colonel nodded.

"Fuck them. Send them home."

"It's not that simple."

"Why?"

"They say there are another fifty on the way. And when they arrive they are going through and if we want to stop them, we will have to shoot them."

Tiger reconsidered. "Let them through."

"Are you sure?"

Mazibuko smiled. "Very."

The colonel hesitated a moment and then depressed the SEND button on the microphone. "Sergeant, let them through whenever they want."

"Roger and out," came the response.

"What is your plan, Captain?" the colonel asked just before Mazibuko walked out with a certain zip in his step.

He did not look up, but kept walking. "Diversion, Colonel. Nothing like a bit of diversion for a bunch of frustrated soldiers," he said.

The traffic officer was carefully rolling up the tubes of the Gatsometer. It was a tedious job on his own, but he did it mechanically, without bitterness, just another part of his easy routine. His thoughts were occupied with the black motorcyclist.

Strange, that. A first. Black man on a big motorbike. You don't see many of those.

But that wasn't all.

The thing was, when he rode off, the BMW's flat, two-cylinder engine made a nice muffled sound. He could swear he heard the man laugh, a deep, thundering, infectious, paralyzing laugh.

Must be his imagination.

"Who?" asked Janina Mentz. "Al Qaeda? How, sir? How?"

"My personal feeling is Tehran. I suspect Johnny had made a contact or two some way or another. Perhaps through the local extremists. But in my opinion, that is not the burning question, Janina."

She drew a deep breath to damp the growing unease. She was watchful for what would follow.

"The question we must ask ourselves now is, What is on the hard drive?"

She knew why the balance had shifted. He was not the Zulu source, he was not Inkululeko. He was free. Of suspicion, misunderstanding, circumstantial evidence. He was pure.

The director leaned toward her and said, with great tenderness: "I had hoped you would have some ideas."

The lieutenant of First Infantry Battalion had put a lot of thought into the roadblock at Petrusburg. His problem was that the place had a proliferation of roads leading like arteries out of the heart of the town in every direction—three dirt roads north, the east-west route of the N8 to Kimberley and Bloemfontein, the R48 to Koffiefontein, another dirt road south, and then the paved road to the black township, Bolokaneng.

Where to put up the blockade?

His eventual decision was based on the available intelligence: the fugitive was heading for Kimberley. That is why the roadblock was just four hundred meters outside the town boundary on the Kimberley side, on the N8. For extra insurance, the SAPS, who provided two vans and four policemen, according to the agreement, were sitting on the gravel road that ran parallel east-west and joined the N8 farther along toward the City of Diamonds.

Now the lieutenant had a more difficult decision to make. One thing was for sure: if you are a member of the military faced with a complicated choice, your first option is to pass the decision up the chain of command. That is how you cover your back.

So he did not hesitate to resort to the radio.

"Oscar Hotel," he said to the ops commander at the Anti-Aircraft School. "I have stopped nineteen riders on BMW motorbikes here. One says he is a lawyer and will get an injunction against us if we don't let them through. Over."

He could swear he heard the colonel say, "Fuck," but perhaps the radio reception was not clear.

"Stand by, Papa Bravo." *Papa Bravo.* Military abbreviation for Petrusburg. There was once a time when he had felt like a clown using these terms, but it had passed. He waited, looking out of the tent that stood beside the road. The BMWs stood in ranks of two, all with headlights on and engines idling. Where the fuck were they going? His men stood with their assault rifles over their shoulders, looking on curiously. There is something about a group of bikers. Like a Mongol horde of Genghis Khan on the way to cause desolation . . .

"Papa Bravo, this is Oscar Hotel Quebec, come in, over."

"Papa Bravo in, over."

"Are you sure there are no black guys on any of the BMWs, over."

"We are sure, Oscar Hotel, over."

"Let them through, Papa Bravo. Let them through. Over."

"Roger, Papa Bravo over and out."

27.

In the editorial office of the *Cape Times* Allison Healy read the story that had come in from the *Star*'s offices in Johannesburg.

"A violent man, an aggressive troublemaker, perhaps a psychopath" is how a former comrade-in-arms of the fugitive Thobela Mpayipheli describes the man now being sought across three provinces by intelligence authorities, the SA National Defence Force, and the SAPS.

According to Brig. Lucas Morape, a senior member of the Supply and Transport Unit at SANDF headquarters in Pretoria, he served with Mpayipheli in Tanzania and at a Kazakhstan military base in the former USSR, where Umkhonto we Sizwe soldiers were trained as part of Eastern bloc support for the Struggle in the eighties.

"In one instance, he almost beat a Russian soldier to death in a messroom fistfight. It took the leadership weeks to repair the diplomatic damage done by this senseless act of brutality."

Mpayipheli allegedly received sensitive intelligence data from his Cape Town employer and is heading north. He slipped through a military cordon at Three Sisters early this morning during a heavy thunderstorm. His current whereabouts are unknown.

In an issued statement, Brig. Morape goes on to describe Mpayipheli as a compulsive brawler who became such a problem to the ANC that he was removed from the training program. "I am not surprised by allegations that he worked for a drug syndicate in the Cape. It fits his psychopathic profile perfectly."

"Psychopathic profile," she said softly to herself, and shook her head. Suddenly everyone was a psychiatrist.

How well the brigadier's opinion fitted in with the efforts of the minister.

The wheels were rolling, the great engine of the state was building up steam. Mpayipheli did not stand a chance.

And then her cell phone rang.

"Allison Healy."

"This is Zatopek van Heerden. You were looking for me." The tone was belligerent.

"Thank you for returning my call, Doctor." She kept the tone cheery. "It is in connection with Mr. Thobela Mpayipheli. I would like to ask a few—"

"No." The voice was brusque and irritable.

"Doctor, please . . ."

"Don't 'doctor' me."

"Please help, I—"

"Where did you hear that I know him?"

"Orlando Arendse told me."

He was silent for so long that she thought he had hung up on her. She wanted to say, "Doctor," or something again and was wondering how to address him when he asked: "Did you say Orlando Arendse?"

"That's right, the . . . um . . ."

"The drug baron."

"Yes."

"Orlando talked to you?"

"Yes."

"You have guts, Allison Healy."

"Um . . ."

"Where do you want to meet?"

Thirty minutes south of Petrusburg, just across the Riet River, the road curves lazily between the Free State kopjes, a few wide sweeping curves before it returns to straight as a die. Enough to draw his concentration back to the motorbike again; the engine was running optimally in the heat, a reassuring constant, tangible heartbeat beneath him. This extension of his body lent him security. It was the moment he realized he could keep on riding, past Lusaka, continuing north, day after day, he and the machine and the road to the horizon. It was the moment when he understood the addiction the white clients had spoken of.

It was that time of day.

The sun shone a benign orange, as if it knew the day's task was nearly done.

He had discovered the magic of late afternoon in Paris, during his two years of desolation after the Wall had fallen. He had fallen, too, his lot inextricably entangled with the Berlin barrier, from celebrated assassin, the darling of the Stasi and KGB, to uneducated unemployed. From wealthy man of the world to the disillusionment of knowing that the thirty dollars in his account was the last and there would be no more income. From arrogance to depression, angrily and reluctantly accepting the new reality in between. Until he picked himself up from self-pity and went door-to-door looking for work like any lowly laborer. Monsieur Merceron had asked to see his hands— "These hands have never worked, but they are built to work"—and he got the job, just west of the Gare du Nord in Montmartre, gofer at the bakery, sweeper of floury floors, bearer of sacks and boxes, scrubber of the big mechanical blenders, early-morning deliverer of baguettes, with arms full of loaves. In the winter the steam rising from the warm bread into his nostrils had become the fragrance of Paris, fresh, exotic, and wonderful. And in the late afternoon when the sun angled down and the whole city was in transition between work and home, he would go back to his first-story apartment near the Salvador Dalí museum. Every day he walked the long route, first up the steps on the hill to the Sacré-Coeur, the Basilica of the Sacred Heart, and went to sit right at the top, his body delightfully weary, and watched the evening claim the city like a jealous lover. The sounds rose up, the shadings slowly shifting to grays, the crouching mass of Notre-Dame, the twisting Seine, the sun sparking gold off the dome of Les Invalides, the dignified loneliness of the Eiffel Tower and in the east the Arc de Triomphe. He sat till every landmark disappeared in the dark and the lights flickered like stars in the city firmament, the scene changing to a wonder world without dimension.

Then he would rise and go into the church, allowing the peace of the interior to fill him before lighting a candle for each of his victims.

The memory filled him with a deep nostalgia for the simplicity of those two years, and he thought that with the money in the sports bag, if he kept the nose pointing north, he could be there in a month.

He smiled sardonically in the helmet—how ironic, now he wished to be there. When the one thing, the single lack, the great desire, when he had been there was this very landscape that stretched out before him; how many times had he wished he could see the umbrella of a thorn tree against the gray veld, how he had longed for the earthshaking rumble of a thunderhead, the dark gray anvil shape, the lightning of a storm over the wide-open, endless plains of Africa.

Vincent Radebe was waiting for her at the door of the Ops Room and said, "Ma'am, I will bring in a camp bed for Mrs. Nzululwazi; I realize now we can't let her go," and Janina put her hand on the black man's shoulder and said, "Vincent, I know it wasn't an easy decision. That's the trouble with our work: the decisions are never easy."

She walked to the center of the room. She said every team must decide who would handle the night watch and who would go home to sleep, so that there would be a fresh shift to start the day in the morning. She said she was going out for an hour or two to see her children. If there was anything, they had her cell phone number.

Radebe waited until she was out before slowly and unwillingly walking to the interview room. He knew what he must say to the woman; he needed to find the right words.

When he unlocked the door and entered, she sprang up urgently.

"I have to go," she said.

"Ma'am . . ."

"My child," she said. "I have to fetch my child."

"Ma'am, it is safer to stay here. Just one night . . ."

He saw the fear in her face, the panic in her eyes.

"No," she said. "My child . . ."

"Slow down, ma'am. Where is he?"

"At the day care. He is waiting for me. I am already late. Please, I beg you, you can't do this to my child."

"They will take care of him, ma'am."

She wept and sank to her knees, clutching his leg. Her voice was dangerously shrill. "Please, my brother, please . . ."

"Just one night, ma'am. They will look after him, I will make sure. It is safer this way."

"Please. Please."

Thobela saw the sign beside the road that said only ten kilometers to Petrusburg. He drew a deep breath, steeling himself for what lay ahead, the next obstacle in his path. There was a main route that he had to cross, another barrier before he could spill over into the next section of countryside with its dirt roads and extended farms. It was the last hurdle before the world between him and the Botswana border lay open.

And he needed petrol.

The traffic officer of the Free State Traffic Authority stopped at the office in Koffiefontein. He opened the trunk of the patrol car, removed the Gatsometer in its case and carried it inside with difficulty, put it down, and closed the door.

His two colleagues from Admin were ready to leave. "You're late," said one, a white woman in her fifties.

"You didn't catch the biker, did you?" asked the other, a young Sotho with glasses and a fashionable haircut.

"What biker?" asked the traffic officer.

Allison Healy found the plot at Morning Star with difficulty. She did not know this area of the Cape; no one knew this area of the Cape.

"When you drive through the gate, the road forks. Keep left, it's the small white house," Dr. Zatopek van Heerden had said.

She found it, with Table Mountain as a distant backdrop. And far out to sea a wall of clouds stretching as far as the eye could see hung like a long gray banner in front of the setting sun.

Lizette ran out of the house before she had stopped the car, and when Janina opened the car door, her daughter threw her arms around her theatrically. "Mamma." A dramatic cry with the embrace and she felt like laughing at this child of hers in that uncomfortable stage of self-consciousness. With arms around her neck she felt the warmth of her daughter's body, smelled the fragrance of her hair.

"Hullo, my girl."

"I missed you." An exaggerated exclamation.

"I missed you, too." Knowing the hug would go on too long, that it was as it should be, she would have to say, "Wait, let me get out," and Lizette would ask, "Aren't you going to put the car away?" and she would say no, I have to go back soon. She looked up and Lien stood on the steps of the veranda, still and dignified just to make the point that she could control her emotions, that she was the elder, stronger one, and Janina felt that her heart was full.

"Mamma," Lien called from the veranda, "you forgot to turn off your blinker light again."

Vincent Radebe carefully closed the door of the interview room behind him. He could no longer hear the sobs.

He knew he had made the wrong decision. He had realized it inside there, with her face against his knees. She was just a mother, not a player; she had one desire, and that was to be with her child.

He stood still a second to analyze his feelings, because they were new and unfamiliar to him, and then he understood what had happened. The completion of the circle—he had finally become what he did not want to be and just now realized he must get out of here, away from this job, this was not what he wanted to do. Perhaps it was something he could not do. His ideal was to serve his country, this new fragile infant democracy, to raise up and build, not to break down—and look at him now. He made up his mind to write his letter of resignation now and put it into Janina Mentz's hand, pack his things, and leave. He expected to feel relief, but it was absent. He went over to the stairs, the darkness still in his mind.

Later he would wonder if his subconscious had made him leave the door unlocked.

Later he would run through his exit of the room in his head, and every time he would turn the key.

But it would be too late.

Captain Tiger Mazibuko put away the gun cloths and oil in the olive green canvas bag and stood up. He walked purposefully over to where Little Joe was sitting with Zongu and Da Costa. He still felt guilty about shouting at Moroka.

"Do you feel like a bit of fun?" he asked.

They looked up at him, nodding and expectant.

"How many of us can take on forty Hell's Angels?" he asked.

Da Costa got it immediately and laughed, "Hu-hu."

"Just one or two," said Little Joe, looking for his approval.

"Take the whole of Alpha, Captain," said Zongu. "We deserve it."

"Right," said Mazibuko. "Don't make a big issue of it. Get the men together quietly."

That was when they heard running steps and turned around. It was the bespectacled soldier, the colonel's messenger.

"Captain, the colonel . . . ," he said, out of breath.

"What now? Guys on Hondas?"

"No, no, Captain, it's Mpayipheli," and Mazibuko felt that internal shock.

"What?" Too nervous to hope.

"The colonel will tell you —"

He grabbed the soldier by the shirt. "Tell me now."

The eyes were frightened behind the glasses, the voice shook. "They know where he is."

28.

He recognized the symptoms, the heart rate increasing steadily, the soft glow of heat, the fine perspiration on palms and forehead, and the vague light-headedness of a brain that could not keep up with the oversupply of oxygen. He reacted out of habit, drew a deep breath, and kept it all under control. He pulled in at the first petrol station in the main street of Petrusburg and watched two F 650 GS riders pull away. He stopped at the pumps, the engine still running when the petrol jockey said, "Can you believe it, black like me."

He did not react.

"Do you know what bee-em-double-you stands for?" asked the jockey, a young black guy of eighteen or nineteen.

"What?"

"*Bankrot maar windgat,* that's what the Boers say. Bankrupt but boastful."

He tried to laugh, switched off the bike.

"Fill up?"

"Please." He unlocked the fuel cap.

"What are you going to do when you find the Xhosa biker?" the jockey asked in Tswana as he pushed his electronic key against the petrol pump. The figures turned back to zeroes.

"Excuse me?"

"You guys are just going to be in the way. That man needs a clear road."

"The Xhosa biker," he repeated, and understanding came to him slowly. He watched the tumbling numbers on the pump.

Eventually the attendant asked: "So where are you from?"

The pump showed nineteen liters and the petrol was still running.

"From the Cape."

"The Cape?"

"I am the Xhosa biker," he said on inspiration.

"In your dreams, brother." Twenty-one liters and the tank was full. "The real one is at Kimberley and they are never going to catch him. And you know what? I say good luck to him, because it's high time somebody stopped the gravy train."

"Oh?"

"It doesn't take a rocket scientist to work out what he's got. It's the numbers of the government's Swiss bank accounts. Maybe he will draw the money and give it to the people. That would be real redistribution of wealth. You owe me R74.65."

Thobela Mpayipheli handed over the money. "Where's the roadblock?"

"There are two, but the BMWs can go through. They shouldn't, because you guys are just going to get in the way."

He put away the wallet and locked the case. "Where?" His voice was serious.

The jockey's eyes narrowed. "The Kimberley side. Turn left at the four-way stop." He indicated up the street.

"And the other one?"

"On the Paardeberg gravel road. It's farther on, other side the co-op, then left."

"And if I want to go to Boshof?"

"What is your name?" asked the man in Xhosa.

"Nelson Mandela."

The jockey looked at him, and then the smile spread broadly across his face. "I know what you are planning."

"What?"

"You want to wait for him on the other side of Kimberley."

"You are too clever for me."

"Boshof is straight ahead via Poplar Grove for about twenty kilos, then turn left other side the Modder and right again at the next bridge."

"The Modder?"

"The mighty Modder, Capie, the Modder River."

"Thank you." He had the helmet on, just pushed his fingers into the gloves.

"If you see him, tell him, 'Sharp, sharp.'"

"Sharpzinto, muhle, stereke." He pulled away.

"You speak the language, my bro, you speak the language," he heard the jockey calling after him.

Miriam Nzululwazi knelt by the chair in the interview room and wept. Her tears began with the fear that had grown too big, the weight of the walls too heavy so that she slid from the chair, her eyes shut so that she could not see them closing in on her, the memories of the Caledon Square cells that echoed in her head. The fear had grown too great and with it the knowledge that Pakamile would wait and wait and wait for his mother to fetch him, for the first time he would wait in vain because she was never late, in six years she had always been there to pick him up. But today he would not know what was wrong, the other children would be fetched, one after the other except him—please God—she could see him, she could feel her child's fear, and it crushed her heart. Gradually her weeping included the wider loss of her life with Thobela, the lost perfection of it, the love, the security in every day, the predictability of a man who came home evening after evening and held her tight and whispered his love to her. The scene of him and her son in the vegetable garden behind the house, the block of man on his haunches by the small figure of the boy, close together, and her Pakamile's undisguised hero worship. The loss of those evenings when they sat in the kitchen, he with his books that he had studied and read with a thirst and a dedication that was scary. She had sat and watched him, her big, lovely man who now and again would look up with that light of new knowledge in his eyes and say, "Did you know . . . ," and express his wonderment of the new world he was discovering. She would want to stand up and throw herself down before him and say, "You can't be real." When they lay in bed and he shifted his body close to hers and with his arm over her pulled her possessively tight against himself, his voice would travel wide paths. He would share with her what was in his heart, so many things, the future, the three of them and a new beginning on a farm that lay waiting, green and misty and beautiful. About their country and politics and people, his often weird observations at work, his worry over the violence and poverty of the townships, the filtering away of Xhosa culture in the desert sands of wannabe American. And sometimes, in the moments before they drifted into sleep, he would speak of his mother and father. How he wished to make peace, how he wished to do penance, and now she wept because it was all gone, lost—nothing would ever be the same. The sobs shook her, and the tears dampened the seat of the chair. Eventually she calmed, emptied of crying, but one thing remained—the impulse to get out.

She did not know why she stood up and tried the door. Maybe her subconscious had registered no sound of a key turning with that last exit, maybe she was merely desperate. But when she turned the handle and the door gave to her fingers, she was shocked and pushed it shut again. She went back and sat in the chair, on the edge, and stared at the door, her heart beating wildly at the possibilities awaiting her.

Allison sat on the veranda of the little white house with its green roof. She sat in a green plastic garden chair opposite Dr. Zatopek van Heerden, captivated by his lean body and his intense eyes and energy locked up in him like a compressed spring, plus something indefinable, unrecognizable but familiar.

It was hot and the light was soft in the transition from afternoon to evening. He had a beer and she drank water with tinkling ice cubes. He had cross-examined her for all she knew, hovering like a falcon over her words, ready to swoop on nonsense, and now he had heard her chronological story and he asked, "What now? What do you want?"

She was discomfited by the intensity of his gaze—he looked right inside her, those eyes never still, over her and on her, searching and measuring, evaluating. With his psychological expertise, could he multiply the fractions of her voice and body language to a sum of her very thoughts? Strangely there was a sexuality in him that reached out and lured an involuntary response from deep in her body.

"The truth," she said.

"The truth." Cynical. "Do you believe there is such a thing?" He did not look away, as other people did when they talked. His eyes never left her face. What was it, this thing she felt?

"Truth is a moving target," she admitted.

"My dilemma," he said, "is loyalty. Thobela Mpay-ipheli is my friend."

Four Rooivalk attack helicopters flew low over the flat earth, crossing the boundary between Northern Cape and the Free State Province. Behind flew two Oryx, slow and cumbersome by comparison, each carrying four members of the RU's Team Alpha in its constricted interior. The men were in full kit for the job: bulletproof vests, steel helmets mounted with infrared night sights, weapons held comfortably clasped with both hands between knees. In the leading Oryx, Tiger Mazibuko tried to conduct a cell-phone conversation over the roar of the engines.

Janina Mentz was in the dining room of her house, between the school homework books of her daughters. She could barely make out Mazibuko's words.

"Where, Tiger? Where?"

"Somewhere near Pe—"

"I can't hear you." She was practically shouting.

"Petrusburg."

Petrusburg? She had no idea where that was.

"I'm going back to the Ops Room, Tiger. We will try the radio."

". . . get him . . ."

"What?"

The signal was gone.

"What's that about Petrusburg, Ma?" asked Lien.

"It's work, sweetie, I've got to go."

The tension he felt going into the petrol station had resurrected a memory, brought it back from the past, the same trembling in his hands and perspiration on his face during that first time, that first assassination. He was in Munich with the SVD in his hands, the long sharpshooter's weapon, the latest model with the synthetic nonfolding stock, a weapon whose deadly reach was 3,800 meters. The crosshairs looked for Klemperer, the double agent who should come out a door a kilometer away.

He felt as if Evgeniy Fedorovich Dragunov were lying beside him, the legendary modest Russian weapons developer. He had met him briefly in East Germany when he and the other students of the Stasi sharpshooters school were helping test an experimental SVDS. Comrade Evgeniy Fedorovich was fascinated by the black student with the impossible groupings. At two thousand meters with a crosswind of seventeen kilometers per hour and the poor light of an overcast winter's day, Thobela Mpayipheli had shot a R100 factor of less than 400 mm. The stocky aging Russian had said something in his mother tongue and pushed up his black-framed eyeglasses onto his forehead before reaching out and gripping the Xhosa's shoulder, to feel if he was real, perhaps.

He wanted to dedicate this one to Dragunov but, dear God, his heart bounced so in his ribs on this, his first blooding, his fingers and palms were wet with sweat. On the practice range it was the testosterone of competition, but this was real, a man of flesh and blood, a bald middle-aged West German who was feeding on both sides of the fence. The KGB had earmarked him for elimination, and it was time for the ANC's exchange student to earn his keep. There was steam on the telescopic lens; he dared not take his eye from the door. It opened.

Miriam sat on the chair, staring at the door, trying to recall the route they had followed bringing her here. Was there another way out? It was so quiet in the building, just the soft sound of the air conditioner and now and then the creak of metal expanding or contracting. She could not wait much longer.

"I don't want to be on the record," said Dr. Zatopek van Heerden. "That is the condition."

"I will show my story to you first." She hoped for a compromise, but he shook his head.

"I am not anti-media," he said. "I believe every country gets the media it deserves. But Thobela is my friend."

Allison had to make a decision, and eventually she said, "It's a deal." Then Van Heerden began to speak, his eyes never leaving her face.

Tiger held the light of the little flashlight to the map before him. The fucking problem was that the R48 forked beyond Koffiefontein, the R705 went to Jacobsdal, the R48 going on to Petrusburg. He had ordered four Rooivalks south to Jacobsdal, the other four with the two Oryx to the more likely east, but the problem was that the damn traffic officer had alerted them too late. By Mazibuko's reckoning, the fugitive could be past Petrusburg but where? Where the fuck? Because the roadblocks, two bloody roadblocks, said a horde of BMWs had gone through, but not one had a black guy, and the possibilities were legion. Where are you going, you dog? Dealesville or Boshof? His finger traced the routes farther, and he gambled on Mafikeng and the Botswana border. That made it Boshof. But had he crossed the Modder River yet? The Rooivalks would each have to follow a dirt road; there were too many alternatives.

"He is not a complex man, but that is precisely where you can make a mistake," said Van Heerden. "Too many people equate uncomplicated with simple or a lack of intelligence. Thobela's noncomplexity lies in his decision-making abilities, he is a man of action, he examines the facts, he accepts or rejects, he does not worry or agonize over it. If Miriam told you he was helping a friend by taking something to Lusaka, then he made the decision that his loyalty lay with his friend, regardless of the consequences. Finished and *klaar*. They are going to battle to get him to stop. They are going to have their hands full."

Only part of his attention was on the long lit path that the double lamps of the GS shone through the growing dark. The dirt road was a good one, reddish brown and hard-surfaced. He kept his speed down to sixty or seventy. That fall in the Karoo storm still bothered him. The rest of his mind was in Munich, on his first assassination. Somewhere in the back of his mind he was aware that during the past twenty-four hours he was reliving the past, as if he was some-how reactivated. He let it flow, let it out, perhaps it was part of a healing process, a changeover, a closure so that he could shake it off, a period at the end of a paragraph in his metamorphosis.

The door had opened and his finger had curled around the trigger, the SVD became an extension of his being. In his mind's eye he could see the bullet waiting for metal to hit the percussion cap, the 9.8 gram steel of the 7.62 mm bullet waiting to be spun through the grooved tunnel of the 24 cm barrel, through the silencer, and then in a curved trajectory, irrevocably on its way. Pressure on the trigger increased, a woman and child appeared in the lens, freezing him, the cross rested on her forehead, right below the band of the blue wool cap, he saw the smoothness of her face, the bright healthy skin, laugh lines at her eyes, and he blew out his breath and the tempo of his heart accelerated some more.

Tiger Mazibuko screamed orders into the microphone. There were three routes to Boshof: from Paardeberg, Poplar Grove, and Wolwespruit. Two Rooivalks on the first, his primary choice, one each on the other two, flying north—he wanted them to start searching from Seretse.

"I am putting the TDATS on infrared," said the pilot over the radio, and Mazibuko had no idea what he was talking about. "That means we will see him even if his lights are off."

29.

Miriam Nzululwazi stood up suddenly and opened the door and went out, closing it quietly behind her.

The passage was empty. Gray cold tiled floor stretched left and right. She had come from the left; there were offices and people that way. She turned right, the flat heels of her shoes audible, tip-tap, tip-tap. She walked with purpose until she saw another door at the end of the passage.

She could just make out the letters, in faded peeling red paint: FIRE ESCAPE.

"How well was he trained as a soldier?" asked Allison.

"Soldier? He was never a soldier."

"But he was in Umkhonto."

He looked at her in surprise. "You don't know?"

"Don't know what?"

"He was an assassin. For the KGB."

She knew her face betrayed her shock and dismay.

"And now you are going to judge him. You think that changes everything?"

"It's just . . ."

"Less honorable?"

She searched for the right words. "No, no, I . . . ," but he did not give her time.

"You formed a picture in your head of a foot soldier of the Struggle, a relatively simple man, maybe something of a rebel who broke out now and again, but nothing more than that. Just an ordinary soldier."

"Well, yes. No. I didn't think him ordinary. . . ."

"I don't know the whole story. The Russians discovered him. Shooting competition in Kazakhstan, some base in the mountains where the ANC men were trained. Probably he shot the hell out of the commies and they saw possibilities. He had two years of training in East Germany, at some special spy school."

"How many people did he . . ."

"I don't remember precisely. Ten, fifteen . . ."

"My God." She blew out a breath. "Are we still off the record here?"

"Yes, Allison Healy, we are."

"My God." She would not be able to write this.

He had given the lens a quick wipe with the soft cloth and lined up his eye behind it again. Not too close, just the right focus length, checked his adjustments again, and waited for the door. Beads of sweat ran down his forehead—he would have to get a sweatband, it was going to sting his eyes. The door, dark wood, was shut again, his palms were wet and the temperature inside the warm clothes still rising. He became aware of a distaste for what he was doing. This was not the way to wage war, it was not right; this was not the way of his people.

There was a bar on the door, white letters on a green background that read PUSH/DRUK, and Miriam obeyed. There was a snap as the lock disconnected and the door creaked and groaned as the unused hinges protested, and she saw she was outside, she saw the night and she heard the city sounds and stepped forward and closed the door behind her. She looked down, and far below there was an alley but right here in front of her was a metal rail and the rusty wounds of a sawed-off metal stairway. She realized she was in a dead end. The door had clicked shut behind her and there was no handle on the outside.

The light flashed on the access control panel and the official picked up the internal phone and called the Ops Room.

It was Quinn who answered.

"Fire door on the seventh floor. The alarm has been activated," said the official.

Quinn raised his voice. "Who is on the seventh floor? The fire door has been activated."

Six meters from him Vincent Radebe sat listening to the crackle of the Rooivalk radios more than a thousand kilometers north, and he only half registered what Quinn had said, but the hair rose on his neck.

"What?" he said.

"Someone has opened the fire door on seven." Quinn and Radebe looked at each other and understood, and Radebe felt an icy hand knot his innards.

"You are a journalist. You should know that concepts of good and bad are relative," said Zatopek van Heerden. He was up and moving to the edge of the veranda, looking out at the night sky. "No, not relative. Clumsy. Insufficient. You want to take sides. You want to be for him or against him. You need someone to be right, on the side of justice."

"You sound like Orlando Arendse," she said.

"Orlando is not a fool."

"How many people did he murder?"

"Listen to yourself. *Murder.* He murdered no one. He fought a war. And I don't know how many of the enemy died at his hand, but it must have been many, because he was good. He never actually said, but I saw him in action and his ability was impressive."

"And then he became a gofer at a motorbike dealership?"

Van Heerden moved again, this time closer to her, and for Allison it was equally stimulating and threatening. He passed close by her and leaned back on the white plastic garden table and sat on it. She smelled him; she swore she could smell him.

"I wondered when you would get to the crux of the matter."

"What do you mean?"

"The question that you and the spooks must ask is why Thobela left Orlando. What changed? What happened?"

"And the answer is?"

"That is his Achilles' heel. You see, his loyalty was always complete. First, it was the Business. The ANC. The Fight. And when it was all over and they left him high and dry, he took his talents and found someone who could use them. He served Orlando with an irreproachable work ethic. And then something happened, something inside him. I don't know what it was—I have my suspicions, but I don't know precisely. We were in the hospital, he and I, beaten and shot up, and one day just before six he came to my bed and said he's finished with violence and fighting. I still wanted to chat, to pull his leg, the way we did, but he was serious, emotional, I could see it was something to him. Something big."

"And that is his Achilles' heel?"

Van Heerden leaned forward and she wanted to retreat from him.

"He thinks he can change. He thinks he has changed."

She heard the words, registered the meaning, overwhelmingly aware, too, of the subtext between them, and in that moment she understood the attraction, the invisible bond: he was like her, somewhere inside there was something missing, something out of place, not quite at home in this world, just like her, as if they didn't belong here.

And then the door opened and the bald man appeared, eyes blinking in the bright light of the street outside, and Thobela's finger caressed the trigger and the long black weapon jerked in his hands and coughed in his ears, and a heartbeat later the blood made a pretty pattern on the wood. In the forty-seven seconds it took to dismantle the weapon and pack it away in the bag, he knew he could not wage war like this. There was no honor in it.

The enemy must see him. The enemy must be able to fight back.

Miriam Nzululwazi knew there was only one way out. She had to climb, she had to get over the railing and hang from the lowest bar and then let herself drop the extra meter to the lower-story fire escape and then repeat the process till she was there where the sawed-off stairs resumed and zigzagged down to the ground.

She pulled herself up over the rail. She did not look down but swung her leg over, then her body, seven floors above the dirty, smelly alley.

"Ma, you're never home anymore," said Lien, outside by the car.

"Ai, my child, it's not because I *want* to be at work. You know I sometimes have to work extra hours."

"Is it the motorbike man, Mamma?" asked Lizette.

"You watch too much television." Stern.

"But is it, Mamma?"

She started the car and said softly: "You know I can't talk about it."

"Some people say he's a hero, Mamma."

"Suthu says she battles to get you to go to bed. You must listen to her. You hear?"

"When will we see you again, Ma?"

"Tomorrow, I promise." She put the car in reverse and released the clutch. "Sleep tight."

"Is he, Mamma? Is he a hero?" But she backed out, in a hurry, and did not answer.

Quinn and Radebe ran, the black man ahead up the stairs, their footfalls loud in the quiet passage. How was it possible, how could she have escaped? It could not be her. They ran past the door of the interview room; he saw it was shut, which gave him courage. She must be there, but his priority was the fire-escape door. He bumped it open and at first saw nothing, and relief flooded over him. Quinn's breath was at his neck, and they both stepped out onto the small steel platform.

"Thank God," he heard Quinn say behind him.

"As long as he believes it," said Zatopek van Heerden, "things shouldn't get out of hand. They even have a chance to persuade him to turn back. If they approach him correctly."

"You sound skeptical," said Allison.

"Have you heard of chaos theory?"

She shook her head. The moon lay in the east, a big round light shining down on them. She saw his hand lift from the table and hang in the air; for a moment she thought he was going to touch her and she wanted it, but the hand hung there, an aid in the search for an explanation. "Basically, it says that a minute change in a small local system can expand to upset the balance in another larger system, far removed from it. It is a mathematical model; they replicate it with computers."

"You've lost me."

His hand dropped back and supported his position on the table. "It's difficult. First, you have to understand who he is. What his nature is. Some people, most people, are passive bending reeds in the winds of life. Resignedly accepting changes in their environment. Oh, yes, they will moan and complain and threaten, but eventually they will adjust and be sucked along by the stream. Thobela belongs to the other group, the minority, the doers, the activators, and the catalysts. When apartheid threatened his genetic fitness index, he resolved to change that environment. The apparent impossibility of the challenge was irrelevant. You follow?"

"I think so."

"Now, at this moment he is suppressing that natural behavior. He thinks he can be a bending reed. And as long as the equilibrium of his own system is undisturbed, he can do it. So far it has been easy. Just his job and Miriam and Pakamile. A safe, closed system. He wants to keep it like that. The problem is life is never like that. The real world is not in balance. Chaos theory says in the balance of probability, something should happen somewhere to ultimately change that environment."

Vincent Radebe looked down just before he was about to go back through the fire door, and that's when he saw her. She was suspended between heaven and earth below him. Their eyes met and hers were full of fear. Her legs were a pendulum swinging out over the drop and back over the lower platform.

"Miriam," he cried with utter despair, and bent to grab her arms, to save her.

"And then what?" asked Allison. "If this theoretical thing happens and he comes back to what he is?"

"Then all hell will break loose," said Dr. Zatopek van Heerden pensively.

Her reaction was to let go, to open her cramping fingers.

The pendulum of her body took her past the platform of the sixth floor. She fell. She made no sound.

Vincent Radebe saw it all, saw the twist of her body as it slowly revolved to the bottom. He thought he heard the soft noise when she hit the dirty stone pavement of the alley far below.

He cried once, in his mother tongue, desperately to heaven.

Thobela Mpayipheli absorbed the world around him, the moon big and beautiful in the black heaven, the Free State plains, grass veld stretching in the lovely light as far as the eye could see, here and there dark patches of thorn trees, the path that the headlights threw out before him. He felt the machine and he felt his own body and he felt his place on this continent and he saw himself and he felt life coursing through him, a full, flooding river; it swept him along and he knew that he must cherish this moment, store it somewhere secure because it was fleeting and rare, this intense and perfect unity with the universe.

30.

Janina Mentz's cell phone rang twice as she drove back to Wale Street Chambers. The first caller was the director.

"I know you are enjoying a well-earned rest, Janina, but I have some interesting news for you. But not over the phone."

"I'm on my way back now, sir." They were both aware of the insecurity of the cellular network. "There are other things happening, too."

"Oh?"

"I will fill you in."

"That is good, Janina," said the director.

"I will be there in ten minutes."

Barely three minutes later it was Quinn. "Ma'am, we need you."

She did not pick up the depression in his voice at first. "I know, Rudewaan, I am on the way."

"No. It's something else," he said, and she now registered his tone. Worry and frustration colored her answer. "I am coming. The director wants me, too."

"Thank you, ma'am," he said.

She ended the call.

The children, the job. Eternal pressure. Everyone wanted something from her, and she had to give. It was always that way. Ever since she could remember. Demands. Her father and mother. Her husband. And then single parenthood and more pressure, more people, all saying, "Give, more"; there were moments when she wanted to stand up and scream, "Fuck you all!" and pack her bags and leave because what was the use? Everyone just wanted more. Her parents and her ex-husband and the director and her colleagues. They demanded, they took, and she must keep giving; the emotions built up in her, anger and self-pity, and she looked for comfort where she always found it, in the secret places, the clandestine refuge where no one went but her.

He saw the helicopter silhouetted against the moon, just for a moment, a pure fluke, so quick that he thought he had imagined it, and then his finger reached feverishly for the headlight switch, found it and switched off.

He pulled up in the middle of the dirt road and killed the engine, struggled with the helmet buckle, took the gloves off first, and then pulled off the helmet. Listened.

Nothing.

They had searchlights on those things. Perhaps some form of night vision. They would follow the roads.

He heard the deep rumble, somewhere ahead. They had found him and he felt naked and vulnerable and he must find a place to hide. He wondered what had happened, what had tipped them off to look for him here. The petrol jockey? The traffic officer? Or something else?

Where do you hide from a helicopter at night? Out in the open plains of the Free State?

His eyes searched for the lights of a farmhouse in the dark, hoping for sheds and outbuildings, but there was nothing. Urgency grew in him—he couldn't stay here, he had to do something, and then he thought of the river and the bridge, the mighty Modder, it must be somewhere up ahead, and its bridge.

Under the bridge would be a place to shelter, to hide away.

He must get there before they did.

Quinn and Radebe waited for her at the elevator and Quinn said, "Can we talk in your office, ma'am," and she knew there was a screw loose somewhere because they were grim, especially Radebe—he looked crushed. She walked ahead, opened the office door, went in, and waited for them to close the door behind them.

They stood, conventions of sitting irrelevant now. The two began to speak simultaneously, stopped, looked at each other. Radebe held up his hand. "It is my responsibility," he said to Quinn, and looked at

Janina with difficulty, his voice monotone, his eyes dead, as if there was no one inside anymore. "Ma'am, due to my neglect, Miriam Nzululwazi escaped from the interview room." She went cold.

"She reached the exterior fire escape and tried to climb down. She fell. Six floors down. It is my fault, I take full responsibility."

She drew breath to ask questions, but Radebe forged ahead. "I offer my resignation. I will not be an embarrassment to this department anymore." He was finished, and the last vestige of dignity left his body with those words.

Eventually Janina said, "She is dead."

Quinn nodded. "We carried her up to the interview room."

"How did she get out?"

Radebe stared at the carpet, unseeing. Quinn said, "Vincent thinks he did not lock the door behind him."

Rage welled up in her, and suspicion. "You think? You think you didn't?"

There was no reaction from him, which fueled her rage. She wanted to snarl at him, to punish him; it was too easy to stand lifelessly and say he thought he hadn't locked the door—she had to deal with the consequences. She bit back a flood of bitter words.

"You may go, Vincent. I accept your resignation."

He turned around slowly, but she was not finished. "There will be an inquiry. A disciplinary hearing."

He nodded.

"See that we know where to find you."

He looked back at her, and she saw that he had nothing left, nowhere to go.

Dr. Zatopek van Heerden walked her to her car.

She was reluctant to leave; the nearing deadlines called, but she did not want to be finished here.

"I don't entirely agree," she said as they reached the car.

"About what?"

"Good and evil. They are very often absolute concepts."

She watched him in the moonlight. There was too much thought in him; perhaps he knew too much, as if the ideas and knowledge built up pressure behind his mouth and the outlet was too small for the volume behind. It caused strange expressions to cross his face but found some release in the movements of his body. As if he wrestled to keep it all under control.

Why did he turn her on?

Ten to one he was a bastard, so sure of himself. Or was he?

She had always been sensual, deep inside. She saw herself that way. But a woman learned with the years that that was only a part of the truth. The other part lay outside, in the way men saw you. And women, who measured and compared and helped put you in your place in the long food chain of love play. You learned to live with that, adjusted your expectations and dreams and fantasies to protect a sensitive heart whose wounds of disappointment healed slowly. Until you were content with the now and then, the sometimes reasonable intensity of stolen moments with a bleached policeman, someone else's husband. And here tonight, she wished she were tall and slim and blond and beautiful, with big breasts and full lips and a cute bottom, so that this man would propose something improper.

And what did she do?

She challenged him intellectually. She. Who was so average—in everything.

"Name me someone evil," he said.

"Hitler."

"Hitler is the stereotypical example," he said. "But let me ask you: Was he worse than Queen Victoria?"

"I beg your pardon?"

"Who fed Boer women and children porridge with glass in it? What about the scorched-earth policy? Maybe it was her generals. Maybe she had no idea. Just like P. W. Botha. Denying all knowledge, and therefore good? What of Joseph Stalin? Idi Amin? How do we measure? Are numbers the ultimate measure? Is a sliding scale of the numbers of victims the way we determine good or evil?"

"The question is not who is the worst. The question is, Are there people who are absolutely evil?"

"Let me tell you about Jeffrey Dahmer. The serial murderer. Do you know who he is?"

"The Butcher of Milwaukee."

"Was he evil?"

"Yes." But there was less assurance in her voice.

"The literature says that for seven or nine years, I can't remember, let's say seven years, Dahmer suppressed the urge to kill. This broken, fucked-up, pathetic wreck of a man kept the nearly inhuman drive bottled up for seven years. Does that make him bad? Or heroic? How many of us know that sort of drive, that intensity? We who can't even control basic, simple urges like jealousy or envy."

"No," she said. "I can't agree. He murdered. Repeatedly. He did terrible things. It does not matter how long he held out."

Zatopek smiled at her. "I give in. It is an endless argument. It rests ultimately on so many personal things. I suspect it rests ultimately on the undebatable. Like religion. Norms, values. The way you see yourself, the way you see others and what we are. And what you have experienced."

She had no answer to that and just stood there. Her face was expressionless, but her body felt too small to contain all she felt.

"Thank you," she said to break the silence.

"Thobela Mpayipheli is a good man. As good as the world allows him to be. Remember that."

* * *

He was busy putting the R 1150 GS down when he heard the drone of the helicopter coming closer.

He had battled to negotiate the steep bank of the river down toward the water, then he had ridden it up with spinning rear wheel through the grass and bushes directly under the concrete of the bridge. It would be difficult to spot there. Neither the side stand nor the main stand would work there, and he had to lay the bike on its side. It was difficult, the secret was to turn the handles up and hold the end, let your knees do the work, not your back. The big engines of the helicopter were ever nearer. Somehow or other they must have spotted him.

He placed the helmet on the petrol tank, removed the jacket and trousers—they were too lightly colored for the night. He tried to see where the aircraft was, and when he looked around the edge of the bridge, he saw it was only thirty or forty meters away, not far off the ground. He could feel the wind of the great rotors against his face, saw the red and white revolving lights, and saw through the open door of the Oryx four faces, every one beneath an infrared night sight.

Da Costa, Little Joe Moroka, Cupido, and Zwelitini waited till the Oryx landed and the great engines had quieted before jumping down.

The helicopter had landed in a piece of open veld, bordered by the river and road and thorn trees. The first thing they did was to walk to the river, drawn by the ancient magnetism of water. Behind them the main rotor turned ever more slowly and stopped. The night sounds took over, frogs that had been still, insects, somewhere far away a dog barked.

Da Costa walked to the water, opened his fly, and urinated a fat shiny stream in the moonlight.

"Hey, the farmers have to drink that fucking water," said Cupido.

"The Boers drink brandy and Coke," said Da Costa, and spat his chewing gum in an impressive arc.

"Not bad," said Zwelitini. "For a whitey."

"So, can you do better?"

"Naturally. Didn't you know we Zulus have lips like these so we can spit on whiteys and Xhosas?"

"Put your money where your lips are, Your Highness."

"Ten rand says I can do better than that."

"Best of three."

"Fair enough."

"Hey, what about us?" asked Cupido.

"This is the RU, my bru'. Come and spit with us."

"Wait," said Da Costa. "I must radio the captain first. Tell him we are in position."

"Take your time. The night is young."

And so they bantered and teased and spat, ignorant of their prey only twelve meters away, unaware that one of them would not see the sun rise.

31.

She told the director in his office of Miriam Nzu-lulwazi's death and she could see how the news upset him, how the stress of the whole affair slowly crept up on him. The little smile was gone, the compassion and consideration for her was less, the cheerfulness had been swept away.

He is feeling the strain, she thought. The snow-white shirt had lost its gleam; the wrinkles were like cracks in his armor, barely visible.

"And Vincent?" he asked in a weary voice.

"He offered his resignation."

"You accepted it."

"Yes, sir." There was finality in her voice.

The Zulu closed his eyes. He sat motionless, hands on his lap, and for a moment she wondered if he was praying, but she knew it was just his manner. Other people would have gestures or blow out their breath or sag in the shoulders. His way was to shut out the world momentarily.

"There are always casualties in our work," he said softly.

She did not think he expected her to respond. She waited for the eyes to open, but it did not happen.

"This is the part I don't like. It is the part I hate. But it is inevitable."

The eyes opened. "Vincent." A hand gesture at last, a vague wave. "He is too idealistic. Too soft and emotional. I will get him a transfer. Somewhere we can channel that dedication."

She still had no idea what to say, for her opinion differed. Vincent had failed. For her he no longer existed.

"What are we going to do with . . . Mrs. Nzululwazi?"

With the body? Why didn't he say it? She was learning a lot tonight. She saw weakness.

"I will arrange to have her sent to the morgue, sir. No questions asked."

"And the child?"

She had forgotten about the child.

"Sir, the best would be for family to look after him. We are not . . . we don't have the facilities."

"That is true," he said.

"You said over the phone you had some interesting news."

"Oh. Yes. I have. I had a call from Luke Powell."

It took a while to sink in. "Luke Powell?" she repeated, mainly to gain time, to make the mental adjustments.

"He wants to meet us. He wants to talk."

She smiled at the director. "This is unexpected, sir. But not an unpleasant prospect."

He answered her smile with one of his own. "It is, Janina. He is waiting for us. At the Spur on the waterfront."

"Oh, he wants to play a home game," she said, and waited for the director to acknowledge the joke, but he did not.

Allison Healy made two calls before she began to type the lead story for the next day's *Cape Times*. The first was to Rassie Erasmus of the Laingsburg police.

"I tried twice this afternoon, but your cell was off," he said reproachfully.

"I had an interview with a difficult man," she said. "Sorry."

"Three things," he said. "The thing this morning at Beaufort West. They say the biker held a gun to one soldier's head, he could have shot them both to hell, but he let them go and said something like 'I don't want to hurt anybody.'"

"I don't want to hurt anybody," she repeated as she made frantic notes.

"Number two: it's a rumor but the source is good, an old pal of mine in Pretoria. That brigadier who said over the news that the biker was such a fuckup in the Struggle, you know who I mean, the one in the army?"

"Yes?" She sifted through the documents on her desk for the fax.

"Apparently, there's a case pending against him. Sexual harassment or something. They say he's talking now because the sexual harassment thing against him may just go away if he's helpful enough."

"Wait, wait, wait, Rassie." She found the paper and ran her finger down it. "You say the brigadier, here it is, Lucas Morape, you say he's lying about this to save his own skin?"

"I'm not saying he's lying. I'm saying he's helping them. And that's not a fact, it's a rumor."

"So what's the third thing?"

"They've cornered the biker in the Free State."

"Where in the Free State?"

"Petrusburg."

"Petrusburg?"

"I know, I know, between bugger all and nowhere, but that's what the guy says."

"You said they've cornered him."

"Wait, let me explain. This afternoon he went through a speed trap this side of Petrusburg, and the speed cop wrote him a fucking ticket without a clue who he was and then let him go. When the poor fool got back to the office, the bomb burst. They thought he must have slipped through Petrusburg because of all the other BMW motorbikes, but now they've blocked all the holes. Apparently, there's a whole squadron of Rooivalks waiting for him with guided missiles."

"Rassie, don't be ridiculous."

"Sweetness, have I ever lied to you?"

"No . . ."

"I tell you like I hear it, Allison. You know that. And I've never let you down."

"That's true."

"You owe me."

"Yes, I owe you, Rassie." She hung up and shouted at the news editor: "I'm going to need some help on this one, Chief."

"What do you need?"

"People to make some calls."

"You've got it," he said, and crossed over to her desk.

She had already dialed the next number. It was to the house of Miriam Nzululwazi in Guguletu. "I need someone to call Defence Force Media Relations and ask them to confirm or deny the fact that Brigadier Lucas Morape has a sexual harassment case pending."

The phone rang in Guguletu.

"What brigadier?"

"The guy who put out the press release about how bad the biker really is."

"Check," said the news editor.

"And I need someone to call that Kimberley number and ask them to confirm or deny that Thobela Mpayipheli has been trapped near Petrusburg."

"Good girl," said the news editor.

The phone still rang.

"And I need someone to try and find a list of child day-care centers in Guguletu and start calling. We need to know if a Pakamile Nzululwazi has been picked up by his mom today."

"It's eight-thirty."

"It's Guguletu, Chief. Not some cozy white suburb where everybody goes home at five o'clock. We might get lucky. Please."

The phone rang and rang.

Tiger Mazibuko sat in the copilot's seat of the Oryx. It had landed beside the R64, halfway between Dealesville and Boshof.

He had the radio headset on, listening to the Rooivalk pilots calling in from each sector they had searched as clear. He marked them off on a chart.

Could the dog be through already, beyond Boshof?

He shook his head.

Impossible. He couldn't ride that fast.

They would get him. Even if he got lucky, there was a last resort. Beyond Mafikeng there were only two roads over the Botswana border. Just two. And he would close them off.

But it would probably not be necessary.

At first there was relief. The Oryx had not landed here because they had spotted him. Now there was the frustration of being trapped.

He lay beside the GS under the bridge and dared not move, he dared not make a sound, they were too close, the four romping young soldiers. The copilot had come down, too, and now they were skipping flat stones over the water. The one with the most skips before the stone sank would be the champion.

He had recognized one of the soldiers, the young black fellow. This morning he had held a rifle to his head.

He saw himself in them. Twenty years ago. Young, so very young, boys in men's bodies, competitive, idealistic, and so ready to play soldier.

It was always so, through the ages, the children went to war. Van Heerden said it was the age to show off what you had, to make your mark so you could take your place in the hierarchy.

He was even younger when he had left home, seventeen. He could remember it well, in his uncle Senzeni's car, the nighttime journey, Queenstown, East London, Umtata; they had talked endlessly, without stopping, about the long road that lay ahead. Senzeni had repeated over and over that it was his right and his privilege, that the ancestors would smile on him, the revolution was coming, injustice would be swept away. He remembered, but as he lay here now, he could not recall the fire that burned in his soul. He searched for that zeal, that Sturm und Drang that he had felt, he knew it had been there, but as he tried to taste it, it was only cold ash. He had caught the bus in Umtata; Senzeni had hugged him long and hard and there were tears in his uncle's eyes and his farewell was "Mayibuye." It was the last time he had seen him—had Senzeni known? Had he known his own battle would be the more dangerous, working inside the lion's den, with so much greater risk? Was the desperation of Senzeni's embrace because of a foreboding that he would die in the war on the home front?

The bus ride to Durban, to Empangeni, was a journey into the unknown; in the earliest hours before dawn, the enormity of that journey ahead became a worm in his heart that brought with it the corruption of insecurity.

Seventeen.

Old enough to go to war, young enough to lie awake in the night and fear, to long for the bed in his room and the reassurance of his father in the rectory, young enough to wonder if he would ever feel his mother's arms again.

But the sun rose and burned away the fears, it brought bravado, and when he got off at Pongola he was fine. The next night they smuggled him over the border to Swaziland, and the following night he was in Mozambique and his life was irrevocably changed.

And here he was now, using a skill the East Germans had taught him. To lie still, that was the art of the assassin and sniper, to lie motionless and invisible for hours, but he had been a younger man—this one was forty years old, and his body complained. One leg was asleep, the stones under the other hip were sharp and unbearably uncomfortable, the fire in his belly was quenched, and his zeal was gone. It was fifteen hundred kilometers south in a small house on the Cape Flats beside the peaceful sleeping body of a tall slim woman, and he smiled to himself in the dark, despite his discomfort, he smiled at the way things change, nothing ever stays the same and it was good, life goes on.

And with the smile came the realization, the suspicion, that this journey would change his life, too. He was on the way to more than Lusaka.

Where would it take him?

How could anyone know?

She worked on the lead story, knowing it was going to be a difficult job tonight.

A squadron of Rooivalk attack helicopters cornered the fugitive motorcyclist Thobela Mpayipheli near the Free State town of Petrusburg late last night amid conflicting reports from the military and unofficial sources.

She read her introductory paragraph. Not bad. But not quite right. The *Burger* and television and radio could have the same information. And by tomorrow morning he might have been arrested.

She placed the pointer of the computer screen on the end of the paragraph and deleted it. She thought, she rephrased, testing sentences and construction in her mind.

A new drama surrounding the fugitive motorcyclist Thobela Mpayipheli unfolded late last night with the mysterious disappearance of his common-law wife, Mrs. Miriam Nzululwazi.

This was where her scoop lay. She went on.

Authorities, including the SAPS and the Office of the Intelligence Ministry, strongly denied that Mrs. Nzululwazi was in government custody. Yet colleagues say the Absa employee was apprehended by unidentified law enforcement officials at the Heerengracht branch yesterday.

The military reaction on persistent rumors that a squadron of Rooivalk attack helicopters had cornered Mpayipheli near the Free State town of Petrusburg after sunset yesterday was "no comment."

That's better, she thought. *Two birds with one stone.*
"Allison . . ."
She looked up. A black colleague stood beside her.
"I've got something."
"Shoot."
"The kid. I found him. Sort of."

"You did!"

"A woman at the Guguletu Preschool and Child Care Center says he's a regular there. And the mother never turned up tonight."

"Shit."

"But some sort of government guy did." The man looked at his notes. "Said his name was Radebe; flashed a card at her and said there had been some sort of accident and he was there to take the kid into his care."

"Ohmigod. Did he say whom he worked for? Where was he taking the kid?"

"She says the card he showed her just said he was Department of Defence."

"And she let the kid go?"

"He was the last one left."

"The last one left?"

"He was the last kid to be fetched, and I think the lady just wanted to go home."

Vincent Radebe could not tell the boy his mother was dead. He did not know how.

"Your mother has to work late" was the best he could do, in the car. "She asked me to look after you."

"Do you work with her?"

"You could say that."

"Do you know Thobela?"

"Yes, I do."

"Thobela has gone somewhere and it's our secret."

"I know."

"And I'm not going to tell anybody."

"That's good."

"And he's coming back tomorrow."

"Yes, he's coming back tomorrow," he had said on the way to Green Point, where his flat was. There were moments in the car that his guilt, the heaviness of spirit, became nearly too much for him, but now in McDonald's opposite the Green Point athletic stadium he had control of himself. He watched Pakamile devour the Big Mac and asked: "Have you got other family here in the Cape?"

"No," said the boy. There was tomato sauce on his forehead. Radebe took a napkin and wiped it off.

"Nobody?"

"My granny lived in Port Elizabeth, but she's dead."

"Have you got uncles or aunts?"

"No. Just Thobela and my mother. Thobela says there are dolphins in Port Elizabeth and he is going to show us at the end of the year."

"Oh."

"I know where Lusaka is. Do you?"

"I know."

"Thobela showed me. In the atlas. Did you know Thobela is the cleverest man in the world?"

32.

Luke Powell's official title was economic attaché of the American consulate in Cape Town.

But his unofficial office, as everyone in the intelligence community was well aware, had little to do with the economy. His actual rank was senior special agent in charge of the CIA in southern Africa, which included everything this side of the Sahara.

In the politically correct terminology of his country, Luke Powell was an *African American,* a jovial, somewhat plump figure with a round, kind face who wore (to the great mortification of his teenage daughter) large gold-rimmed eyeglasses that had gone out of fashion ten years ago. He was no longer young, there was gray at his temples, and his accent was heavy with the nuances of the Mississippi.

"I'll have a cheddamelt and fries," said Powell to the young waiter with the acne problem.

"Excuse me?" said the waiter.

"A cheddamelt steak, well done. And fries."

The frown had not disappeared from the waiter's forehead. Every year they were younger. *And dimmer,* thought Janina Mentz. "Chips," she said in explanation.

"You want only chips?" the waiter asked her.

"No, I want only an orange juice. He wants a cheddamelt steak and chips. Americans refer to chips as fries."

"That's right. French fries," said Luke Powell jovially, smiling broadly at the waiter, who was properly confused now, the pen poised over the order book.

"Oh," said the waiter.

"But they're not French, they're American," said Powell with a measure of pride.

"Oh," said the waiter.

"I'm just going to have a plate of salad," said the director.

"Okay," said the waiter, relieved, and scribbled something down, hovered a moment, but as no one said anything more, he left.

"How are y'all?" asked Luke Powell with his smiling mouth.

"Not bad for a developing Third World nation," said Janina, and opened her handbag, taking out a photograph and handing it to Powell.

"We'll get right to the point, Mr. Powell," she said.

"Please," he said. "Call me Luke."

The American took the black-and-white photo. He saw the front door of the American consulate in it, and the unmistakable face of Johnny Kleintjes leaving the building.

"Ah," he said.

"Ah, indeed," said Janina.

Powell removed his gold-rimmed eyeglasses and tapped them on the photo.

"We might have something in common on this one?"

"We might," said the director softly.

He's good, this American, thought Janina Mentz, considering the lightning adaptation to changes, the poker face.

An innocent six-year-old boy from Guguletu has become a pawn in the nationwide manhunt for Thobela Mpayipheli, the fugitive motorcyclist being sought by intelligence agencies, the military, and police.

"Now you're cooking," said the news editor, tramping around nervously behind Allison as the deadline loomed.

Pakamile Nzululwazi was taken from a day-care center for preschoolers late last night by an official from the "Department of Defence." He is the son of Mpayipheli's common-law wife, Miriam Nzululwazi, who also mysteriously disappeared from the Heerengracht branch of Absa, where she is an employee.

"Cooking with gas," said the news editor, and she wished he would sit down so she could concentrate in peace.

"What happened in Lusaka?" asked Janina Mentz.

Luke Powell looked at her and then he looked at the director and then he replaced the glasses on his face.

What a strange game this is, thought Janina. He knew they knew and they knew he knew they knew.

"We're still trying to find out," said Powell.

"So you got stung?"

Luke Powell's kind face betrayed nothing of the inner battle, of the humiliation of admitting the superpower's little African expedition had gone wrong. As always, he was the professional spy.

"Yes, we got stung," he said evenly.

Now they sat in a circle on the grass, chatting, the four soldiers, the pilot and copilot.

Thobela Mpayipheli was relieved because now they were at a safer distance. He could hear their voices but not their words. He could hear laughter bursting out, so he assumed they were telling jokes. He heard the periodic crackle of the radio that would hush them every time until they were certain the message was not for them.

The adrenaline had left his body slowly, discomfort had grown, but at least he could move now, shift his limbs and work away the stones and grass tufts that bothered him.

But he had a new worry now: How long?

They were obviously waiting for a signal or alarm. And he knew he was the object of that alarm. The problem was, as long as he lay pinned down under this bridge, there would be no call. Which meant they would not leave. Which meant it would be a long night.

But more crucial were the hours lost, hours in which he should be burning up the kilometers to Lusaka. Not yet a crisis, still enough time, but better to have time in the bank, because who knew what lay ahead. There were at least two national borders to cross, and although he had his passport in the bag, he did not have papers for the GS. The African way would be to put a few hundred rand notes in the pages of the passport and hope it would do the trick, but the bribery game took time for haggling and you could run up against the wrong customs man on the wrong day—it was a risk. Better to find a hole in the border fence, or make one and go your way. The Zambezi River, however, was not so easy to cross.

He would need those hours.

And then, of course, the other little problem. As long as it was dark, he was safe. But tomorrow morning when the sun came up, this hiding place in the deep shadow of the bridge would be useless.

He had to get out.

He needed a plan.

"There is one thing I have a problem understanding, Luke," said the director. "Inkululeko, the alleged South African double agent, works for you. So why offer to buy the intelligence off Johnny Kleintjes?"

Powell merely shook his head.

"What do you care if we think we know who he is?" asked the director, and Janina was surprised at the direction the questions had taken. The director had confessed nothing to her of his suspicions.

"I don't think that is a sensible line of questioning, Mr. Director," said Powell.

"I think it is because the smell of rat is fairly strong in this vicinity."

"I have no comment. I am willing to discuss our mutual Lusaka problem, but that's it, I'm afraid."

"It does not make sense, Luke. Why would you take the risk? You knew it was there, from the moment Kleintjes walked into the consulate. You know we have a photographer outside."

Powell was spared for a moment by the waiter bringing the food—a cheddamelt steak for the American, a plate of chips for Janina, and an orange juice for the director.

"I did not . . . ," Janina began, and then decided to let it go, it would not help to correct the waiter. She took the orange juice and placed it in front of her.

"I'm going to get some salad," said the director, and stood up.

"May I have some ketchup?" asked Powell.

"Excuse me?" said the waiter.

"He wants tomato sauce," Janina said, irritated.

"Oh. Yes. Sure."

"Why do you do that?" she asked Powell.

"Do what?"

"Use the Americanisms."

"Oh, just spreading a little culture," he said.

"Culture?"

He just smiled, the waiter brought the tomato sauce, and he poured a liberal amount over his chips, took his fork and stabbed some and put them in his mouth.

"Great fries," Powell said, and she watched him eat until the director returned with a full plate of salad.

"Have you any idea who burned you in Lusaka?" Janina asked.

"No, ma'am," said Powell through a mouthful of steak.

The waiter materialized at the table. "Is everything all right?"

She wanted to snap at the pimple face that all was not right, that she did not order chips, that he'd better not come flirting for a tip but rather leave them in peace, but she did not.

"Steak's fantastic," said Powell, and the waiter grinned, relieved, and went away.

"How's your salad, Mr. Director?" asked Powell.

The director placed his knife and fork precisely and neatly on his plate. "Luke, we have people in place in Zambia. The last thing we need is to run into a team of yours."

"That would be unfortunate."

"So you have a team there, too?"

"I am not at liberty to say."

"You said you were willing to discuss our mutual Lusaka problem."

"I was hoping you had information for me."

"All we know is that Thobela Mpayipheli is on his way there with a hard drive full of who knows what. You are the one who knows what happened there. With Johnny."

"He was, shall we say, intercepted."

"By parties unknown?"

"Exactly."

"And you don't even have a suspicion?"

"I wouldn't say that."

"Enlighten us."

"Well, frankly, I suspected that you were the fly in the ointment."

"It's not us."

"Maybe. And maybe not."

"I give you my personal guarantee that it was not my people," said Janina Mentz.

"Your personal guarantee," said Powell, smiling through a mouthful of food.

"It's going to get crowded in Lusaka, Luke," said the director.

"Yes, it is."

"I am asking you, as a personal favor, to stay away."

"Why, Mr. Director, I did not know South Africa had right-of-way in Lusaka."

There was a chill in the director's voice. "You have botched the job already. Now get out of the way."

"Or what, Mr. Director?"

"Or we will take you out."

"Like you're taking out the big, bad BMW biker?" asked Powell, and put another piece of steak loaded with cheese and mushroom in his mouth.

The big, bad BMW biker had his plan thrust upon him.

Fate played an odd card beside the mighty Modder.

33.

Had it not been for the singing, Little Joe Moroka might never have stood up from the ring of jokers.

Cupido started the whole thing with one of those teasing statements—"You whiteys can't . . ."— and it eventually ended up with a singsong, and that is when the pilot and copilot, white as lilies, burst forth with "A bicycle built for two" in perfect harmony, a cappella, and filled the night with melody.

"Jissis," said Cupido when they had finished and the rowdy applause had faded. "Where the fuck did you learn to sing like that?"

"The air force has culture," said the pilot, acting superior.

"In striking contrast with the other branches of the SANDF," confirmed his colleague.

"All sophisticated people know this."

"No, seriously," said Da Costa. "Where does it come from?"

"If you spend enough time in the mess, you discover strange things."

"It wasn't bad," said Little Joe. "For whitey harmony."

"Ooh, damning with faint praise," said the pilot.

"But can the darkie sing?" asked the copilot.

"Of course," said Little Joe. And that is how it began, because the pilot said, "Prove it," and Little Joe Moroka smiled at them, white teeth in the darkness. He stretched his throat, tilted his head up as if his vocal cords needed free rein, and then it came, warm and strong, "Shosholoza," the four notes in pure bravura baritone.

Thobela Mpayipheli could not hear the conversation from under the bridge, but the first song of the two pilots had reached him, and although he did not consider himself a music fanatic, he found pleasure in it despite his position, despite the circumstances. And now he heard the first phrase of the African song and his ears pricked up, he knew this was something rare.

He heard Little Joe toss the notes into the night like a challenge. He heard two voices join in without knowing whose they were, the song gained meaning and emotion, longing. And then another voice, Cupido's tenor, round and high as a flute, it hung for a moment above the melody and then dove in. The final ingredient was Zwelitini's adding his bass softly and carefully so that the four voices formed a velvet foundation for Moroka's melody, the voices intertwining, dancing up and down the scales. They sang without haste, carried by the restful rhythms of a whole continent, and the night sounds stopped, the Free State veld was silent to receive the song, Africa opened her arms.

The notes filled Thobela, lifted him up from under that bridge and raised him to the patch of stars in his vision; he saw a vision of black and white and brown in a greater perfect harmony, magical possibilities, and the emotion in him was at first small and controllable, but he allowed it to bloom as the music filled his soul.

And another awareness grew—it had been hiding somewhere, waiting for a receptive spirit, and now his head cleared and he felt for the first time in more than a decade the umbilical drawing him back to his origin, deeper and further, back through his life and the lives of those before him, till he could see all, till he could see himself and know himself.

As the last note died away over the plains, too soon, there was a breathless quiet as if time stood still for a heartbeat.

He discovered the wetness in his eyes, the moisture running in a long silver thread down his cheek, and he was amazed.

The night sounds returned, soft and respectful, as if nature knew she could not compete now.

Wordlessly, Little Joe Moroka stood up from the circle at the helicopter.

From habit he slung the Heckler & Koch UMP submachine pistol over his shoulder and he walked.

No one said a word. They knew.

Little Joe walked down the bank. It had been a bittersweet day and he wanted to cherish the sweet a little longer, taste the emotions a little more. He walked down to the river, stood gazing into the dark water, the HK harmlessly behind his back. He did not want to stand still but walked toward the bridge, thinking of everything, thinking of nothing, the sounds reverberating in his head—damn, it was good, like when he was a kid—aimlessly wandered into the dark under the bridge. He saw the dull gleam of the stainless-steel exhaust pipe, but it did not register because it did not belong, he looked away, looked again, a surreal moment with a tiny wedge of reason, a light coming on in his brain, one step closer, another, the shiny object took shape, lines, tank and wheel and handlebars, and he made a noise, surprised, reached for his weapon, swung it around, but it was too late. Out of the moon shadow came a terrifyingly fast movement, a shoulder hit him for the second time that day, but his finger was inside the trigger guard, his thumb already off the safety, and as his breath exploded over his lips and he tumbled backward, the weapon stuttered out on full automatic, loosing seven of its nineteen rounds.

Five hit the concrete and steel, whining away into the night. Two found the right hip of Thobela Mpayipheli.

He felt the 9 mm bullets jerk his body sideways, he felt the immediate shock; he knew he was in trouble but he followed the fall of Moroka, down the steep bank to the river. He heard the shouts of the group

at the helicopter but focused on the weapon—Little
Joe was winded, Thobela landed on top of him, his
hand over the firearm, jerked it, got it loose, his
fingers sought the butt, his other forearm against the
soldier's throat, face-to-face, heard the approaching
steps, comrades shouting questions, pressed the barrel of the HK against Moroka's cheek.

"I don't want to kill you," he said.

"Joe?" called Da Costa from above.

Moroka struggled. The barrel pressed harder, the
weight of the fugitive heavy on him; the man hissed,
"Shhh," in his face, and Little Joe submitted because
where could the fucker go, there were six of them
against one.

"Joe?"

Mpayipheli rolled off Moroka, moved around
behind him, pulled him up by the collar to use him
as a shield.

"Let's all stay calm," said Thobela. The adrenaline
made the world move in slow motion. His hip was
wet, blood running in a stream down his leg.

"Jissis," said Cupido above. They could see now.
Little Joe with the gun to his head, the big fucker
behind him.

"Put down your weapons," said Mpayipheli. The
shock of the two 9 mm rounds combined with the
chemistry of his body to make him shake.

They just stood there.

"Shoot him," said Little Joe.

"No one is getting hurt," said Thobela.

"Kill the dog," said Little Joe.

"Wait," said Da Costa.

"Put it down," said Mpayipheli.

"Please, man, shoot him," Little Joe pleaded. He could not face Tiger Mazibuko's anger again, no more humiliation. He writhed and struggled in the grip of the fugitive and then Thobela Mpayipheli hit him with the butt of the HK where the nerves bunch between back and head, and his knees sagged, but the arm locked around his throat and held him up.

"I will count to ten," said Mpayipheli, "and then all the weapons will be on the ground," and his voice sounded hoarse and strange and distant, a desperate man. His mind was on the helicopter: Where was the pilot? Where were the men who could use the radio to send a warning?

They put their weapons down, Da Costa and Zwelitini and Cupido.

"Where are the other two?"

Da Costa looked around, betraying their position.

"Get them here. Now," said Mpayipheli.

"Just stay calm," said Da Costa.

Little Joe was beginning to come around and started wriggling under his arm. "I am calm, but if those two don't get here now . . ."

"Captain," Da Costa called over his shoulder.

No answer.

He's using the radio, Mpayipheli knew; he was calling in reinforcements.

"One, two, three . . ."

"Captain." There was panic in Da Costa's shout.

"Four, five, six . . ."

"Shit, Captain, he's going to shoot him."

"I will. Seven, eight . . ."

"Okay, okay," said the pilot as he and his colleague walked over the rim of the riverbank with their hands up.

"Stand away from the weapons," said Mpayipheli, and they all moved back a few steps. He shoved Little Joe up the bank so he could see the helicopter better. The soldier was unsteady on his feet but still mumbled, "Shoot him," and Mpayipheli said, "You don't want me to hit you again," and the mumbling stopped.

They stood, the fugitive with his hostage, the other five in a bunch.

In his head a clock ticked.

Had the pilot got a message out? How much blood had he lost? When would he feel the light-headedness, the loss of concentration, and the loss of control?

"Listen carefully," he said. "We have a bad situation. Don't make it worse."

No response.

"Is his name Joe?"

Da Costa was the one to nod.

He felt the armor of the Kevlar vest under Little Joe's shirt. He chose his words carefully. "The first shot goes in Joe's shoulder. The second in his leg. You understand?"

They did not answer.

"You three"—he gestured with the barrel—"get the motorbike."

They just stood there.

"Hurry up," he said, and pressed the barrel against Little Joe's shoulder joint.

The soldiers moved down to the bottom of the bridge.

"You haven't got a chance," said the pilot, and Thobela knew then for sure the man had used the radio.

"You have thirty seconds!" he screamed at the three at the motorbike. "You"—he motioned to the copilot—"fetch the helmet and my suit. They are over there. And if I think you are wasting time . . ."

The man's eyes were wide; he jogged off, past the men struggling to push the motorbike up the incline.

"Help them to get it in the helicopter," he said to the pilot.

"You're fucking insane, man. I'm not flying you anywhere," and that is when Little Joe suddenly jerked out of his grasp with a drop and a twist of the shoulders and dove toward the pile of weapons on the ground. Thobela followed him with the Heckler's barrel as if in slow motion, saw him grab a machine pistol, roll over, fingers working the mechanisms with consummate skill. He saw the barrel turn toward him, saw everyone else frozen, and he said softly to himself, once, "No," and then his finger pressed the trigger as the choice was no longer to shoot or not, but to live, to survive. The shots cracked; he aimed for the bulletproof vest, and Little Joe jerked backward, Mpayipheli moved toward Little Joe, right leg caving in (how much damage?), and jerked the weapon out of the young soldier's hands, threw his own down, looked up. The others still stood transfixed; he looked down, three shots were harmlessly to the chest, and one was in the neck, ugly, blood spurting.

He took a deep breath; he must control himself. And them.

"He needs to get to the hospital. You determine how fast," he said. "Load the bike."

They were shocked now.

"Move. He will die."

Little Joe groaned.

The GS was at the open door of the Oryx.

"Help them," he said to the pilot.

"Don't shoot," said the copilot, coming up the bank with the helmet and clothes.

"Put it in."

The four battled with the heavy machine, but the adrenaline in their arteries helped them lift first the front and then the back.

"Do you have first aid equipment?"

Cupido nodded.

"Put a pressure bandage on his neck. Tight."

He walked to the Oryx, his steps wobbly, the pain in his hip throbbing and sharp, demanding. He knew he was nearly out of time.

"We must go," he said, looking at the two air force pilots.

34.

In the second Oryx, which stood beside the R64, halfway between Dealesville and Boshof, Captain Tiger Mazibuko was the one who heard the emergency signal. "Mayday, Mayday, Mayday. They are shooting here below, I think we've found him. . . ."

And then it was quiet.

First, he shouted outside where the helicopter crew stood around, smoking and chatting to the other members of Team Alpha. "Come!" he screamed, and then over the radio: "Where are you? Come in. Where are you?" But there was silence and his heart began to race and frustration was the bellows of his rage.

"What?" said the pilot, now beside him.

"They've found him; someone called in Mayday," he said. "Come in, Mayday, where are you, who signaled?"

The officer had his headset on in the control cabin.

"Rooivalk One to Oryx, we heard it, too."

"Who was it?" asked Mazibuko.

"Sounded like Kotze, over."

"Who the fuck is Kotze?"

"The pilot of the other Oryx."

"Come!" yelled Tiger Mazibuko, but his pilot had the engines running already. "I want all the Rooivalks, too," he said into the mouthpiece. "Do you know where Kotze and them are?"

"Negative, Oryx, over."

"Fuck," said Mazibuko, struggling with the map in the dark cabin.

"Show me," said the copilot. "Then I'll give the coordinates."

"Here." He jabbed the map with his index finger. "Right here."

They tore over the landscape and the pilot shouted, "Where?" and he shouted back above the racket, "Botswana," and the captain shook his head.

"I can't cross the border."

"You can. If we keep low, the radar won't pick us up."

"What?"

The pain in his hip was enormous, throbbing; his trousers were soaked in blood. He had to have a look. But there were more urgent things.

"I want a headset," he said, and gestured.

The copilot got it, hands trembling and eyes on the HK in Mpayipheli's hands. He got earphones and passed them over, plugging the wire in somewhere. Hissing, voices, the Rooivalks were talking to each other.

"Tell them about the wounded man," said Thobela Mpayipheli in the microphone to the copilot, "and nothing else. Understand?"

The man nodded.

Thobela searched the instrument panel for the compass. He knew Lobatse was north, almost directly north. "Where's your compass?"

"Here," said the pilot.

"You lie."

Their eyes met, the pilot assessing him, glancing down at his wounds and his trembling hands, like a predator eyeing its prey. Mpayipheli listened while the copilot called in the news about the wounded soldier. "Oryx Two to Oryx One, we have a casualty, repeat, we have a casualty, we need help immediately."

"Where are you, Oryx Two?" Mpayipheli recognized the voice. It was the one from this morning, the crazy guy.

"That's enough," he said to the copilot, who nodded enthusiastically.

"Listen carefully," he said to the pilot. "I need only one pilot. You saw what happened to the soldier. Do you want me to shoot your partner, too?"

The man shook his head. No.

"I want to see the compass. And I want to see the ground, all the time, understand?"

"Yes."

"Show me."

The pilot touched the top of the instrument. 270, it read.

"Do you think I am a stupid *kaffir*?"

Voices talked on the radio, Mazibuko's incessantly calling, "Oryx Two, come in. Oryx One to Oryx Two, come in." The pilot said nothing.

"You have ten seconds to turn north."

A moment of hesitation, then the pilot turned the helicopter, 280, 290, 300, 310, 320, the instrument swung under its cover, white letters on a black background, 330, 340, 350, 355.

"Keep it there."

He must take care of his wounds. Stop the bleeding. He must drink something, the thirst made his mouth like chalk, he had to stay awake, he must stay ready.

"How long to Lobatse?"

"Hour, hour and a quarter."

The atmosphere in the Ops Room was morbid.

Janina Mentz sat at the big table, trying to keep the tension off her face. They were listening to the cacophony over the radios. *It is chaos up there,* she thought, chaos everywhere, the meeting with the American was chaos, the ride back with the director was not good, and what she found back here was a demoralized team.

Everyone knew of the death of Miriam Nzululwazi now, everyone knew Radebe had gone, everyone knew one of the RU members was badly wounded, and the fugitive—no one knew where the fugitive was.

Chaos. And she had no idea what to do.

In the car she had tried to talk to the director, but there was distance between them, a breach of confidence, and she couldn't understand it. Why had his circle of suspicion extended to include her? Or was it a case of kill the bearer of bad news?

Or did the director see all this chaos as a threat to his career? Was he thinking ahead, to explaining this mess to the minister?

She heard the first Rooivalk arriving at the wounded soldier.

She heard Da Costa report in over the radio of the Rooivalk.

Thobela Mpayipheli had hijacked the Oryx.

Her heart sank.

She heard Tiger Mazibuko's reaction, the cursing tirade.

He is not the right man for the situation, she thought. Rage would not help now. She would have to step in. She was about to get up when she heard Mazibuko call the other Rooivalks. "The dog is going to Botswana. You must stop him. Get that Oryx."

One by one, the attack helicopters confirmed their new bearings.

What are you thinking, Tiger? Are we going to shoot down the Oryx, with our people and all?

A terrible choice.

"And get Little Joe to a hospital," said Mazibuko over the radio.

"Too late, Captain," said Da Costa.

"What?" said Mazibuko.

"He's dead, Captain."

For the first time, the ether was still.

Vincent Radebe looked at the sleeping child in the sitting room of his Sea Point flat. He had made up a bed on the sofa and put the TV on, skipping through the channels for something suitable.

"I don't want to watch TV," said Pakamile, but he couldn't keep his eyes off the screen.

"Why not?"

"I don't want to go stupid."

"Stupid?"

"Thobela says it makes people stupid. He says if you want to be clever, you must read."

"He's right. But it's too much television that makes you stupid. We are just going to watch a little bit." *Please, Lord*, he prayed silently, *let me keep the child occupied, let him go to sleep so I can think.*

"Just a little?"

"Just until you go to sleep."

"That must be okay."

"I promise you it will be okay."

But what do you let a child watch?

And there, on one of the SABC channels, was a series on a pride of lions in the Kalahari and he said, "This will make you clever, too, because it's about nature," and Pakamile nodded happily and rearranged himself. Vincent had watched as sleep drew an invisible veil over the boy's face, slowly and softly, till the eyes fell shut.

Radebe switched off the TV and the sitting-room light. The one in the open-plan kitchen he left on so the child would not be bewildered if he woke up in the night. He stood on the balcony and thought, because it was a horrible mess.

He would have to tell him his mother was dead.

Sometime or other. It was not right to lie to him.

He had to get the boy clothes. And a toothbrush.

They couldn't stay here; Mentz would find out that he had collected the child, and she would take him away to that little room.

Where could they go?

Family was no good. That was the first place Mentz would look. Friends were also dangerous.

So where?

Allison Healy lit a cigarette in her car before turning the key. She inhaled the smoke and blew a stream at the windshield, watching the smoke dissipate against it.

A long day. A strange day.

Woke up and looked for a story and found a complication.

Moments of truth. Tonight she had wanted to write another intro.

Thobela Mpayipheli, the fugitive motorcyclist, is a former hit man for the KGB.

No.

Thobela Mpayipheli, the man the media had dubbed the "big, bad BMW biker," is a former KGB assassin.

She had broken off-the-record agreements before. It was a nebulous agreement at best. People didn't always mean what they said. The source talked and talked and talked, and somewhere along the way said, "You can't write that," and in the end no one remembered what was on the record and what was off. Of course, the really juicy bits, the real news, lay in those areas. Some people used it as a "cover my ass" mechanism but actually wanted you to write it as long as they could protest, "I told her it was off the record."

Sometimes you wrote regardless.

Sometimes you trespassed knowingly, weighing up the consequences, and *publish and be damned* and if people were angry—they would get over it, because they needed you, you were the media. With others it didn't matter—let them be angry, they got what they deserved.

Tonight the temptation was exceedingly strong.

What had prevented her?

She took out her cell phone. She felt her heart bump in her chest.

She searched for the number under RECEIVED CALLS. Pressed the button and put the phone to her ear.

Three, four, five rings. "Van Heerden."

"There is something you said that I don't understand."

He did not answer immediately. In the silence there was meaning.

"Where are you?"

"On the way home."

"Where do you live?"

She gave him the address.

"I'll be there in half an hour."

She put the phone in her bag and pulled deeply on the cigarette.

Dear God, what am I doing?

35.

It was difficult to watch the compass, to gauge their altitude, keep an eye on the crew, and get the sports bag out of the luggage case while juggling the HK in one hand.

He did it step-by-step, aware of the need to concentrate. Nothing need happen quickly, he just had to stay alert and monitor all the variables. He placed the bag next to him.

He pulled up the shirt to get at the wound. It did not look good.

He heard the first Rooivalk arriving at the scene, listened to the reports. Heard the Rooivalk's orders to come after them.

They knew he was going to Botswana.

It was the voice from this morning.

My name is Captain Tiger Mazibuko. And I am talking to a dead man.

Not yet, Captain Mazibuko. Not yet.

Mazibuko barking out, *And get Little Joe to a hospital.*

Too late, Captain.

What?

He's dead, Captain.

It was the pilot who looked around, disgusted at
the Xhosa's presence here. The injustice registered
with Thobela, but that was irrelevant now.

But his status *was* relevant. And that had changed
dramatically. From illegal courier, in their perspective, to murderer. Although it was in self-defense,
they would not see it like that.

He looked down at the wound.

He must concentrate on survival.

Now more than ever.

He could see now that it was more than one bullet: one had taken a chunk of flesh out just below the
hip bone, the other had gone in and out on a skewed
trajectory—it must have struck the hip bone. Blood
was thick over the wounds. He pulled a shirt from the
bag and began to clean it up, first looking up to see the
copilot watching him, seeing the wounds, the man was
pale. Checked the compass, looked outside, below he
could see the landscape flashing by in the moonlight.

He looked around the interior. Some of the
soldiers' gear had been left inside: backpacks, two
metal trunks, a paperback. He pushed the backpacks
around with his left foot. Got hold of two water
bottles and loosened them from the packs.

"I need bandages," he said. The copilot pointed.
At the back was a metal case with a red cross painted
on it screwed to the body of the helicopter. Sealed.

He stood up and unplugged the headset. He broke the seal of the case and opened it. The contents were old, but there were bandages, painkillers, ointment, antiseptic, syringes of drugs he did not recognize, everything in a removable canvas bag. He took it out and moved back to his seat, replaced the headset, went through the checklist of crew, altitude, and direction. He placed the bandages aside, trying to make out the labels on the tubes of ointment and packets of pills in the poor light. He put what he needed to one side.

He had never been wounded before.

The physical reaction was new to him; he vaguely recalled the expected pathology: there would be shock, tremors, and dizziness, then the pain, fatigue, the dangers of blood loss, thirst, faintness, poor concentration. The important thing was to stop the bleeding and take in enough water; dehydration was the big enemy.

He heard his mother's voice in his head. He was fourteen, they were playing by the river, chasing iguanas, and the sharp edge of a reed had sliced open his leg like a knife. At first all he felt was the stinging. When he looked down, there was a deep wound to the bone, he could see it, above the kneecap, pure white against the dark skin, he could see the blood that instantaneously began seeping from all sides like soldiers charging the front lines. "Look," he said proudly to his friends, hands around the leg, the wound long and very impressive, "I'm going home, so long," limping back to his mother, watching the progression of blood down his leg with detached curiosity as if it wasn't his. His mother was in the kitchen, he needed to say nothing, only grinned. She had a shock—"Thobela," her cry of worry. She let him sit on the edge of the bath and with soft hands and clicking tongue disinfected the wound with snow-white cotton balls, the smell of Dettol, the sting, the bandages and Band-Aid, his mother's voice, soothing, loving, caressing hands—the longing welled up in him, for her, for that carefree time, for his father. He jerked back to the present, the compass was still at 355.

He got to his feet, pressed the HK against the copilot's neck. "Those helicopters. How fast can they fly?"

"Aah . . . uum . . ."

"How fast?" And he jabbed the weapon into the man's cheek.

"About two-eighty," said the pilot.

"And how fast are we going?"

"One-sixty."

"Can't we go faster?"

"No," said the pilot. "We can't go faster." Unconvincingly.

"Are you lying to me?"

"Look at the fucking aircraft. Does it look like a greyhound to you?"

He sagged back to his seat.

The man was lying. But what could he do about it? They wouldn't make it; the border was too far. What would the Rooivalks do when they intercepted?

He unclipped another water bottle from one of the rucksacks and opened the cap, brought it to his lips and drank deeply. The water tasted of copper, strange on his tongue, but he gulped greedily, swallowing plenty. How the bottle shook in his big hand—hell—he trembled, trembled. He breathed in slowly, slowly breathed out. If he could just make it to Botswana. Then he had a chance.

He began to clean the wound slowly and meticulously.

Because if he were still Umzingeli, there would be at least four dead bodies for you to explain.

That is what the minister of water affairs and forestry had said, and now there was one body and Janina Mentz wondered if the gods had conspired against her. For what were the odds that the perfect operation, so well planned and seamlessly executed, would draw in a retired assassin?

And in the moment of self-pity she found the truth. The foundation of reason that she could build upon.

It was not by chance.

Johnny Kleintjes had instructed his daughter to involve Thobela Mpayipheli if something happened to him. Was it a premonition? Did the old man expect things to go wrong? Or was he playing some other game? Someone had known about the whole thing, someone had waited in Lusaka and taken the CIA out of the game, and the question, the first big question was, Who?

The possibilities, this is what drove her out of her head, the multiple possibilities. It could be this own country's National Intelligence Agency, it could be the Secret Service, or Military Intelligence—the rivalry, the spite, and corruption were tragic in their extent.

The contents of the hard drive was the second big question, because that was a clue to the who.

If Johnny Kleintjes had contacted someone else . . . an old colleague now at the NIA or SS or MI, said this is what the people at PIU are planning . . . But I have other data.

Impossible.

Because then this thing of the phone calls to Monica Kleintjes, the threats to kill Johnny Kleintjes, would never have happened. Why complicate it so? Why endanger his own daughter?

Johnny could just have given copies of the data to the NIA.

It had to be someone else.

She had recruited Kleintjes, she had explained the operation to him, she had seen his eagerness, estimated his loyalty and patriotism. They had watched him in those weeks, listened to his calls and followed him, knew what he did, where he was. It made no sense. Kleintjes could not be the leak.

Where then? With the CIA?

Perhaps a year or two ago, but not since September 11. The Americans had retreated into the *laager;* they played a serious, pitiless game, cards close to the vest. Took no chances.

Where was the leak?

Here she was the only one who knew.

Here. Quinn and his teams had trailed Kleintjes and tapped his phone without being briefed with the whole picture. Only she knew the whole story. Everything.

Who? Who, who, who?

Her cell phone rang and she saw that it was Tiger. She did not want to speak to him right now.

"Tiger?"

"Ma'am, he's on the way . . ."

"Not now, Tiger, I'll call you back."

"Ma'am . . ." Desperation, she could understand that. One of his men was dead, murder burned in his heart, someone had to pay. First she had to think; she pressed the button, cutting him off.

When she entered the Ops Room she felt despair. She no longer felt up to the task. She recognized the feelings of self-pity. The director was the source of that. He had withdrawn his support and trust, and now she felt suddenly alone and aware of her lack of experience. She was a planner, a strategist, and a manipulator. Her skill was in organization, not crisis management. Not violence and guns and helicopters.

But the fact remained, this was not about the crisis of the fugitive and a dead soldier.

Don't get caught up in the drama. Maintain perspective. Think. Reason, let her strong points count.

The hard drive.

Johnny Kleintjes had done what any player with a lifetime of sanctioned fraud behind him would do: left an escape route, a bit of insurance. Thobela Mpayipheli was that insurance, but Kleintjes had not even left the man's proper address or telephone number with Monica—it was out-of-date. If he really expected trouble, he would have taken more trouble, probably gone to see Mpayipheli himself. At least made sure of where his old friend was.

No, it was out of habit, not foreknowledge.

The same went for the hard drive. It was a piece of insurance from the days when he was coordinator for the amalgamation of the awful stuff. Old forgotten intelligence on political leaders' sexual preferences and suspected traitors and double agents. Negligible. Irrelevant, just something that Kleintjes had thought of when he was knee-deep in trouble, a way of using his insurance. Don't focus on the hard drive; don't be misled by it. She felt relief growing, because she knew she was right.

But she need not disregard it; she could play more than one game.

She must concentrate on Lusaka. She must find out who was holding Johnny Kleintjes. If she knew that, she would know where the leak was, and in that knowledge lay the real power.

Forget the director. Forget Thobela Mpayipheli. Focus.

"Quinn," she called out. He sat hunched over his panel and jumped when he heard his name.

"Rahjev."

"Ma'am?"

"Don't look so depressed. Come, walk with me." There was strength in her voice and they heard it. They looked to her, all of them.

By the time he knocked on the door, Allison had showered, dressed, put on music, agonized over the brightness of the lights, lit a cigarette, and sat down in her chair in the sitting room, trying to attain a measure of calm.

But the minute she heard the soft knock, she lost it.

Janina Mentz walked in the middle, the two men flanking her—Quinn, the brown man, lean and athletic; Rajkumar impossibly fat—a pair of unmatched bookends. They walked down Wale Street without speaking, around the corner at the church toward the Supreme Court. The only sound was Rajkumar's gasping as he struggled to keep up. The two men knew she had got them out to avoid listening ears. As participants in the plot, they accepted her lead.

They crossed Queen Victoria and went into the Botanical Gardens, now dark and full of shadows of historic trees and shrubs, the pigeons and squirrels quiet. She had brought her children here with her ex-husband on days of bright sunshine, but even in daylight the gardens whispered, the dark corners created small oases of complicity and secretiveness. She walked to one of the wooden benches, looked at the lights of Parliament on the other side, and the homeless figure of a *bergie* on the grass.

Ironic.

"Good," she said as they sat. "Let me tell you how things stand."

Zatopek van Heerden had brought wine that he opened and poured into the glasses she provided.

They were uneasy with each other, their roles now so different from that afternoon, the awareness they shared was avoided, sidestepped, ignored like a social disease.

"What is it that you don't understand?" he asked as they sat.

"You talked of genetic fitness indicators."

"Oh. That."

He studied his glass, the red wine glowing between his hands. Then he looked up and she saw he wanted her to say something else, to open a door for him, and she could not help herself, she asked the question of her fears. "Are you involved?" Realized that was not clear enough. "With someone?"

36.

No," he said, and the corners of his mouth turned up.

"What?" she asked unnecessarily, because she knew.

"The difference between us. Between man and woman. For me it is still . . . enigmatic."

She smiled with him.

He looked at his glass as she spoke, his voice quiet. "How many times in one person's life will you know that the attraction is mutual? In equal measure?"

"I don't know."

"Too few," he said.

"And I need to know if there is someone else."

He shrugged. "I understand."

"Doesn't it matter to you?"

"Not now. Later. Definitely later."

"Odd," she said, drawing on her cigarette, taking a swallow of wine, waiting. He stood up, placed the glass on the coffee table, and went to her. She waited a moment, then bent down to stub out her cigarette.

Tiger Mazibuko sat in the Oryx, alone. Outside at the bridge where Little Joe died, the men stood waiting, but he did not think of them. He had the charts with him, maps of Botswana. He hummed softly as his fingers ran over them, an unrecognizable, monotonous refrain, busy, busy when the phone rang. He knew who it would be.

"What I really want to do," he said straightaway, "is to blow the fucker out of the sky with a missile, preferably this side of the border." His voice was easy, his choice of words deliberate. "But I know that's not an option."

"That's right," said Janina Mentz.

"I take it we are not going to call in the help of our neighbors."

"Still right."

"National pride and the small problem of sensitive data in strange hands."

"Yes."

"I want to ambush him, ma'am."

"Tiger, that's not necessary."

"What do you mean, 'not necessary'?"

"This line is not secure, take my word for it. Priorities have changed."

He nearly lost it just then, the rage pushed up from below like lava. *Priorities have changed:* jissis, he had lost a man, he was humiliated and sent from pillar to post, he had endured the chaos and the fucking lack of professionalism, and now someone in a fucking office had changed the fucking priorities. It wanted to explode out violently, but he held it in, choked it back, because he had to.

"Are you there?"

"I am here. Ma'am, I know what route he will use."

"And?"

"He's going to Kazungula."

"Kazungula?"

"On the Zambian border. He won't go through Zimbabwe, too many border posts, too much trouble. I know this."

"It doesn't help us. That's in Botswana. Even if it comes from the top, official channels will take too long."

"I didn't have anything official in mind."

"No, Tiger."

"Ma'am, he's wounded. The way Da Costa talks—"

"Wounded, you say?"

"Yes. Da Costa says it's serious, his stomach or his leg. Little Joe got some rounds off before he was shot. It will slow him down. He has to rest. And drink. That gives us time."

"Tiger . . ."

"Ma'am, just me. Alone. I can be in Ellisras in two hours. In three hours at Mahalapye. All I need is a vehicle. . . ."

"Tiger . . ."

"It gives you an extra option." He played his trump card.

She vacillated and he saw opportunity in that. "I swear I will keep a low profile. No international incident. I swear."

Still she hesitated and he drew breath to say more but stopped. Fuck her, he would not plead.

"On your own?"

"Yes. In every way."

"Without backup and communications and official approval?"

"Yes." He had her; he knew he had her. "Just a car. That's all I ask."

"Oryx Two, this is Rooivalk Three. We are two hundred meters behind you with missiles locked in. Land, please, there's lots of places down below."

He had swallowed the painkillers with lukewarm water, but they had not kicked in yet. The wound was clean now, the bandage stretched tight around his middle, pulling heavily on his side. It was still bleeding in there, he did not know how to stop it, hoped it would just happen. The pilot asked, "What now?"

"Stay on course."

"Oryx Two, this is Rooivalk Three. Confirm contact, please."

"How far are we from the Botswana border?"

The two officers merely stared ahead. He cursed quietly, stood up, feeling the wounds—Lord, he should keep still. He hit the copilot against the forehead with the barrel of the Heckler, drew blood, and shook the man who raised his hands protectively. "I am tired of this."

"Seventy kilometers," said the pilot hurriedly.

Mpayipheli checked his watch. It could be true. Another half an hour.

"Oryx Two, this is Rooivalk Three. We have you in our sights, you have ninety seconds to respond."

"They are going to shoot us down," said the co-pilot. He had wiped his forehead and was looking at the blood on his hand now, then at Mpayipheli, like a faithful dog that has been kicked.

"They won't," he said.

"How do you know?"

"Sixty seconds, Oryx Two, we have permission to fire."

"I'm going down," said the pilot with fear.

"You will not land," said Thobela Mpayipheli, the HK against the copilot's neck.

"Do you want to die?"

"They won't fire."

"You can't say that."

"If you do anything but fly straight, I will shoot off your friend's head."

"Please, no," said the copilot, his eyes screwed shut.

"Thirty seconds, Oryx Two."

"You're fucking crazy, man," said the pilot.

"Stay calm."

The copilot made a strangled noise.

"Oryx Two, fifteen seconds before missile launch, confirm instruction, I know you can hear me."

Two innocent lives and a helicopter of millions of rand, they would not shoot, they would not shoot, they would have heard an official order over the radio, this kind of decision was not made at the operational level, they could not shoot. The seconds ticked by, they waited for the impact, all three rigid, instinctively bracing for the bang, for a sign, waiting. They heard the Rooivalk pilot. "Fuck," he said.

Relief.

"You've got balls, you black bastard, I'll give you that," said the Rooivalk pilot.

37.

He made the Oryx land near a road sign to make sure they were over the border. The Rooivalks had turned back; the main route between Lobatse and Gaborone was quiet and the night warm. He made the men lie facedown on the blacktop while he struggled mightily to get the big GS up from the floor of the helicopter. There was no help for it, he would have to start it and ride it out, hoping not to fall in the jump from aircraft to the ground half a meter down. He had a slight fever leaving a thin transparent membrane between him and reality. The painkillers had kicked in and he moved studiously, every step ticked off against a checklist in his mind, lest he forget something.

If he fell, they would leap up—the pilot was the danger, the officer's hate for him was like a beacon.

He got the motorbike on the side stand, checked that the sports bag was in the luggage case, locked. What was he forgetting? He mounted and pressed the starter; the engine turned and turned but would not take.

He pressed the choke up and tried again. This time it took with a roar and a shudder. He lifted the side stand with a foot and turned the steering. He couldn't ride out slowly; he would accelerate powerfully and let momentum carry him out. The helicopter was beside the road, engines still on, the blades sweeping up a whirlwind around the resting bird. He must be sure the GS's engine was sufficiently warmed up enough and he revved.

The pilot lay watching with an expressionless face.

He drew a breath, now or never, clutch in, first gear, turned the throttle, and released the clutch. The GS shot forward and out, the front wheel dropped, hit the ground, shocks banging, the force shooting up his arms and making him lose balance, the rear wheel came down and with the throttle still wide open he shot forward, straight across the road, braked to stop going into the veld and came to a halt. His heart pounded—dear Lord—he looked around, the pilot had leaped up and was running to the helicopter, the Heckler lay there inside, that's what his head had been trying to tell him—don't forget the machine pistol—but now it was too late, there was only one option. He rode as fast as the motorbike would accelerate, lying flat without looking back, a smaller target, ears pricked, second, third, fourth gear, something struck the bike, fifth, 160 kilometers per hour, still accelerating—what had the pilot hit?

Then he knew he was out of range and kept the speed there, and he wondered if the pilot's hate was great enough to follow him with the Oryx.

Janina Mentz carried out her plan meticulously.

She fetched the director from his office; she could see he was tired now, his whole body expressed it. "I want to talk, sir, but not here."

He nodded and stood up, taking his jacket from where it hung neatly on a hanger, took his time putting it on, and then held the door for her. They rode down in the elevator and left the building, he a courteous step behind her. She led him up Long Street, knowing the Long Street Café would be open still. This part of the city was still alive, young people, tourists with backpacks, Rikki taxis, scooters. Nightclub music pounded from an upper floor. The director was short and bowed beside her, and she was once again conscious of the spectacle they presented—what would people think seeing the white woman in a business suit walking with the little hunchbacked black man?

There was an open table at the back near the cake display.

He held the chair for her, and for an instant she felt his courtesy irritating, she wanted to be accepted or rejected, not live in this no-man's-land.

He did not look at the menu. "You believe we are being bugged?"

"Sir, I have considered all the evidence, and some-where there is a leak. With us, or with Luke Powell."

"And you don't believe it is with them?"

"It's not impossible, just improbable."

"What has happened to our Johnny the com-munist theory?"

"The more I think about it, the less it makes sense."

"Why, Janina?"

"He would not endanger his own daughter. He would not leave an outdated address and phone number for Mpayipheli with her. If he wanted to threaten the CIA, there are other ways. To tell the truth, nothing about it makes sense."

"I see."

"You still think it's Johnny?"

"I no longer know what to think." The weari-ness was undisguised in his voice, and she saw him with greater depth then. What was he? Somewhere on the shady side of fifty, he carried the burden of the invisible, endless decades of intrigue behind him. While a young waitress with dark secret eyes took their order, she studied him. Did he once have dreams and ambitions for greater things? Had he seen himself as material for the inner circle, to wear the head ring of the stalwart? Was he on the verge of that once in his wanderings during the Struggle? He was a clever man whose potential they would have recognized. What had held him back, kept him out, so that now he sat here, a worn-out old man holding on to his status as senior civil servant with titles and white silk shirts?

He misinterpreted her examination. "Do you really suspect me, Janina?"

She sighed deeply. "Sir . . ."

There was compassion in the set of her mouth. "I had to consider it."

"And what was your conclusion?"

"Another improbable."

"Why?"

"All you could know was that Johnny Kleintjes was one of a large number of people we were keeping tabs on. I was the only one who knew why."

He nodded slowly, without satisfaction; he knew that would be the result. "That goes for all of us, Janina."

"That is what puzzles me."

"Then the leak is not with us."

"I don't know. . . ."

"Unless, of course, it is you."

"That's true. Unless I am the one."

"And that couldn't be, Janina."

"Sir, let me speak frankly. I feel our relationship has altered."

The coffee arrived, and her words hung in the air until the waitress left.

"Earlier today when we met Powell, after that," she said.

He took his time, tore open the sugar packet, and stirred the sugar into his coffee. He looked up at her. "I don't know whom to trust anymore, Janina."

"Why, sir? What has changed?"

He brought the cup to his lips, testing the heat carefully, sipped and replaced the porcelain cup carefully back in the saucer. "I don't have an empirical answer to that. I can't set out the points one by one. It is a feeling, Janina, and I am sorry that you felt it includes you, too, because that is not necessarily the case."

"A feeling?"

"That I am being led down the garden path."

When Thobela dismounted from the R 1150 GS before the Livingstone Hotel in Gaborone, he could barely stand. At first he held on to the saddle with a thousand stars swimming in his vision, bending over it until balance and sight returned.

When he moved around the bike, he saw the damage for the first time.

The 9 mm bullets had struck the right-hand luggage case, two small neat holes in the black polyvinyl. The sports bag was in there.

He unclipped the case and took out the bag. Two holes, perfectly round.

He locked everything and crossed the pavement and entered the door.

The night porter sat sleeping in his chair. Thobela had to ding the bell with his palm before the man stood up groggily and pushed the register over the desk. He filled in his particulars.

"Will you take South African rand?"

"Yes."

"Can I still get something to eat?"

"Ring room service. Nine one. Passport, please."

He passed it over. The man's bloodshot eyes barely looked at it, just checking the number against the one he had written down. Then he pulled a key out of the lockup cupboard behind him and passed it over.

Before the rattling elevator had reached the ground floor and opened for Umzingeli, the man was asleep again.

The room was large, the bed heavenly under its multicolored spread, and the pillows billowy and tempting.

First, a shower. Redress the wound. Eat, drink. And then sleep—dear God, how he would sleep.

He zipped open the sports bag. Time to review the damage. He shook the contents onto the double bed. Nothing to mention, even his toilet bag was whole. Then he picked up the hard drive and held it in his hands and saw that it was destroyed. The Heckler & Koch rounds had hit the middle of the almost square box, where metal and plastic and integrated circuits came together. The data was lost forever.

No wonder the bang had been so loud.

* * *

Heads together, voices low, Janina Mentz and the director looked like lovers in the Long Street Café. She said the hard drive was the wrong focus, containing nothing of importance, old stale intelligence locked up in a safe by an old man who wanted to feel he still had a part in the game, suddenly dug up when he was in trouble. Thobela Mpayipheli was no longer important; he had become a marginal figure, an irritation at worst. Let him go, the action was in Lusaka, the answers lay waiting there.

"We already have four operatives there. We are going to send another twelve, the best we have. We want to know who is holding Johnny Kleintjes hostage and we want to know how they knew of this operation. I considered sending the RU to Lusaka, but we don't want an incident; we need a low profile, to work subtly. We need silent numbers, not fireworks."

"And what about the leak?"

"I am only involving four people here—myself, you, sir, Quinn, and Rajkumar. We keep it small, we keep it intimate, and we get the answers."

"Does Tiger know?"

"Tiger knows only that priorities have changed. Anyway, he is on a mission of his own. Apparently, he is going to stop Mpayipheli. In Botswana."

"And you let him go?"

She thought this over before answering carefully. "Tiger has earned his chance, sir. He is alone."

The director shook his head. "Tiger has the wrong motives, Janina."

"He has always had the wrong motives, Mr. Director. That is why he is such an asset."

They lay beside each other in the dark, she on her back, he on his side next to her, stroking her body, getting to know it from her neck to her toes. His touch was paradise, absolute acceptance. She had asked him when the perspiration and the passion had cooled and his palm was absently stroking over her full breasts and she felt the warmth of his breath on her nipples, she had asked him if he liked her body and he had said, "More than you will ever know," and that was the end of her fears for tonight. She knew there was one more up ahead, but that could wait until tomorrow; she wanted to experience this moment without anxiety. His voice was gentle, his head in her neck, his hand never stopped stroking, and he spoke to her, told her everything, opening a new world to her.

Captain Tiger Mazibuko crossed the border an hour after midnight. He was driving a 1.8-liter GTI Turbo Volkswagen Golf. He had no idea how Janina Mentz had organized it: it was waiting for him at the police station at Ellisras, and the keys were handed to him at the desk of the charge office once he had shown his passport. Now he was in Botswana and he drove as fast as the narrow road and the darkness allowed in this other country, with cattle and goats grazing beside the road. He had made his calculations. Everything depended on the dog's progress, but the injuries would hold him up. The pilot of the Oryx had spoken with him over the cell phone; they had their hate for Mpayipheli in common. The pilot said the wound was bad and the fugitive would not last the night on the motorbike. He was close to falling when he came out of the helicopter, and there were more shots fired, perhaps he had taken another bullet or two.

Let's say the fucker was tougher than they thought; let's say he kept going . . .

Then Mpayipheli would be ahead of him. At least two hours ahead.

Would he be able to catch him?

It depended on how fast the bugger could ride— he had to eat, he had to rest, he had to drink and fill up with petrol.

It was possible.

Maybe he slept somewhere and then Tiger would wait for him. At the bridge over the Zambezi, just beyond the place where the waters of the great river and the Chobe merged.

A good place for a death in Africa.

* * *

Before he turned off the light and sank into the soft-
ness of the double bed, he sat staring at the telephone. His longing for Miriam and Pakamile was
overwhelming—just one call, "Don't worry about the
reports over the radio, I am okay, I am nearly there,
I love you," that was all he wanted to say, but if they
had tapped the line, they would know immediately
where he was and they would come get him.

If only he could contact someone and say the terrible information on your piece of computer equipment is destroyed, your dark secrets are safe and
threaten no one, leave me alone, let me go help an
old friend, and then let me go home.

Tomorrow he would be there, late tomorrow afternoon he would ride into Lusaka. He had read
the signs—no roadblocks outside Gaborone, no hot
pursuit by the Oryx, obviously they did not want to
involve the Botswana government, they wanted to
keep it in the family. Probably they were waiting for
him in Lusaka, but that was good, he could handle
that, he was trained in the art of urban warfare. Tomorrow it would all be over. He felt as if he were
sinking into the bed, deeper and deeper, so weary,
his whole body exhausted, but his brain was flashing
images of the day behind him. He was aware of the
physiology of the bullet wounds, the feverishness,
the effects of the painkillers and four cans of cola and
the brandy he had after his room service meal. *We have
a club sandwich and chips or a cheeseburger and chips,*

take your pick. He could rationalize his emotions, but he could not suppress them, he felt so alone.

Not for the first time. Other cities, other hotel rooms, but that was different, there had been no Miriam before.

There had never been a Miriam before he had found her. There were other women; at Odessa there were the prostitutes, the official Stasi-approved whores to see to their needs, to keep the levels of testosterone under control so they would pay attention to their training. Afterward he was under instructions—don't get involved, don't get attached, don't stay with a woman. But his Eastern bloc masters had not reckoned on the Scandinavians' obsession with black men. Lord, those Swedish women, shamelessly hot for him, on his first visit in '82, three of them had approached him in a coffee shop in Stockholm, one after another until he had fled, sure of a plot, some NATO counterintelligence operation. Eventually, a year later, Neta had explained it to him: it was just a thing they had, she couldn't say why. Agneta Nilsson, long fine blond hair and two wild weeks of passion in Brussels until the KGB had sent a courier to say that was enough, you are trespassing, looking for trouble. He, Thobela Mpayipheli from the Kei, had eaten white bread, the whitest to be had, sated himself to the bursting point but not his heart, his heart remained empty until he had seen Miriam. Not even in '94 had his heart been so empty, waiting

for the call from a man who was now minister, waiting for his reward, waiting to be included in the victory, to share the fruits, waiting. Days of wandering
the streets, a stranger in his own land, among his
own people. He had thought of his father in those
weeks, played with the idea of taking the train to visit
his parents, to stand in the doorway and say, "Here
I am, this is what happened to me," but there was
too much baggage, the gulf was too wide to cross,
and in the evenings he went back to the room and
waited for the call that never came—rejected, that is
how he felt, a feeling that slowly progressed to one
of betrayal. They had made him what he was, and
now they didn't want to know. Eventually he went
to Cape Town so he could hear the tongue of his
ancestors again, until he decided to offer his services
where they would be appreciated, where he would
be included, where he could be part of something.

It had not worked out as he thought it would.
The Flats had been good to him, but he remained
the outsider, still alone, alone among others.

But not so lonely as now, not like now. Fevered
chills, strange dreams, a conversation with his father
that never ended, explanation, justification, on and
on, words flowing out of him, and his father reced-
ing, shaking his head and praying, and then he forced
himself to wake up, sweating, and the pain in his hip
was a dull throbbing and he got up and drank from
the tap in the bathroom of the cold sweet water.

* * *

Somewhere in the predawn Allison Healy awoke from sleep momentarily, just enough to register one thought: the decision to withhold the information that he had given her was the best decision of her life.

Had she known, in those moments when she had to decide? Had she known despite her fears and insecurities?

It no longer mattered. She rolled over, pressing her voluptuousness against his back and thighs, and sighed with joy before she softly sank away in sleep again.

38.

When Lien and Lizette crept into the double bed beside her, Janina Mentz woke up and rubbed her eyes. "What time is it?" she asked.

Lien said, "It's early, Ma, sleep a little longer."

She checked the clock radio. "It's half past six."

"Very early," said Lizette.

"Time to get ready," she said without enthusiasm. She could sleep for another hour or two.

"We're not going to school today," said her younger daughter.

"Oh, really?"

"It's National Keep Your Mother at Home at Any Cost Day."

"Hah!"

"Failure to obey is punishable with a fine of five hundred rands' worth of new clothes for every descendant."

"That will be the day."

"It is the day. National Keep Your Mum —"

"Put on the TV."

"Watching TV so early in the morning is harmful to the middle-aged brain. You know that, Ma."

"Middle-aged, my foot. I want to see the news."

"Maaa . . . leave the work until we go to school."

"It's not work, it's a healthy interest in my environment and my world. An attempt to demonstrate to my darling daughters that there are more things in life than Britney Spears and horny teenage boys."

"Like what?" said Lien.

"Name one thing," said Lizette.

"Put on the TV."

"Okay, okay."

"Middle-aged. That's a new one."

"People should be comfortable with their age."

"I hope I see the same level of wisdom on your report cards."

"There you go—the middle-aged brain's last resort. The school report."

Lien pressed the button on the small color television. A sports program on M-Net appeared slowly on the screen.

"The middle-aged brain wants to know who has been watching TV in my room."

"I had no choice. Lien was busy entertaining horny teenage boys in the sitting room."

"Put it on TV2 and stop talking rubbish."

"Isn't there an educational program—"

"Shhh . . ."

. . . details about the South African weapons scandal. The newspaper quotes a source saying the data

Mpayipheli is carrying contains the Swiss bank account details of government officials involved in the weapons deals, as well as the amounts allegedly paid in bribes and kickbacks. A spokesperson for the Office of the Minister of Defence strongly denied the allegations, saying it was, quote, another malicious attempt by the opposition press to damage the credibility of the government with deliberate lies and fabrications, unquote.

The spokesperson also denied any military involvement in the disappearance of Mrs. Miriam Nzululwazi, the common-law wife of the fugitive Mpayipheli, and her six-year-old son. According to the Cape Times, *a man identifying himself as an employee of the Department of Defence took young Pakamile Nzululwazi into his custody last night, after his mother was arrested at her place of work, a commercial bank, earlier in the day.*

Meanwhile, rival motorcycle groups seemingly supporting Mr. Mpayipheli clashed in Kimberley last night. Police were called in to break up several fights in the city. Nine motorcyclists were treated for injuries at a hospital.

Moving on to other news . . .

The other fear embraced her when she awoke and found Van Heerden gone. No note, nothing, and she knew the fear would be her constant companion until she heard from him again. Until she saw him again, the impulse to dial his number, to seek reassurance and confirmation, would strengthen through the day, but she must resist at all costs.

She stood up, looking for salvation in routine, swung the gown over her shoulders, put on the kettle, opened the front door, and retrieved the two newspapers. Went back to the kitchen, scanned the *Times,* everything was as she had written it, the main story, the boxes, the other two stories. She glanced quickly at pages two and three, did not see the small report hidden away, unimportant.

LUSAKA—Zambian police are investigating the death of two American tourists after their bodies were found by pedestrians on the outskirts of the capital yesterday.

A law enforcement spokesman says that the tourists died of gunshot wounds, and the apparent motive was robbery. The names of the two men are expected to be released today, after the American embassy and relatives have been notified.

No arrests have been made.

She was in a hurry to get to the *Burger.* She opened the newspaper on the breakfast bar.

Weapons Scandal:
MOTORCYCLE MAN HOLDS THE KEY

CAPE TOWN—Full particulars of the South African weapons scandal, including names, relevant sums, and Swiss bank account numbers of government officials are allegedly contained in the computer hard drive in the possession of the fugitive Mr. Thobela Mpayipheli—the motorcyclist who still evades arrest by the authorities.

Sweet lord, she thought, *where did this come from?*

According to advocate Pieter Steenkamp, previously of the Directorate for the Investigation of Serious Economic Crimes (Disec), there was frequent mention of the hard drive during the hearing of evidence relating to alleged irregularities in the weapons transaction of R43.8 billion last year.

"Come on," murmured Allison.

"We conducted more than a hundred interviews and according to my notes, at least seven times there was mention made of complete electronic data in the possession of an intelligence agency," said Advocate Steenkamp, who joined the Democratic Alliance in November last year.

"My allegations will probably be dismissed as petty politicking. We will just see more cover-up. It is in the interest of the country and all its people that Mr. Mpayipheli is not apprehended. His journey has more significance than that of Dick King who rode on horseback from Durban to Grahamstown in 1842 to warn the English of the Boer siege."

The fugitive motorcyclist was still on the loose at the time of going to press after leaving Cape Town on a stolen BMW R 1150 GS (see article below) the day before yesterday. According to a SAPS source, Mpayipheli evaded government authorities at Three Sisters during one of the worst thunderstorms in recent memory (article on p. 5, weather forecast on S8).

An extensive operation at Petrusburg in the Free State also failed to apprehend the Umkhonto veteran last night. Unconfirmed reports claim that he crossed the border into Botswana late last night.

Allison Healy considered the report, staring at the magnets on her fridge.

Not impossible.

And if they were right, she had been scooped. Badly.

She looked down at the page again. There was another article, presented in box form beside the picture of a man standing next to a motorcycle.

By Jannie Kritzinger, Motoring editor
This is the motorcycle that created a sensation last year by beating the legendary sports models like the Kawasaki ZX-6R, Suzuki SV 650 S, Triumph Sprint ST, and even the Yamaha YZF-R1 in a notorious

alpine high-speed road test run by the leading German magazine, *Motorrad*.

But the BMW R 1150 GS is anything but a racing motorcycle. In truth, it is the number one seller in a class or niche that it has created—the so-called multipurpose motorcycle that is equally at home on a two-track ground road or the freeway.

While the GS stands for "Gelände/Strasse" (literally, "veld and street"), the multipurpose idea has expanded to include models from Triumph, Honda, and Suzuki, which all use drive-chain technology.

She scanned the rest, wanting to turn to the promised article on page two (MOTORCYCLIST IS PSYCHOPATH, SAYS BRIGADIER and MPAYIPHELI MUTILATED ME—REHABILITATED CRIMINAL TELLS ALL and THE BATTLE OF KIMBERLEY: BIKER GANGS HAND-TO-HAND), but her cell phone rang in the bedroom and she ran, praying, *Please, let it be him.*

"Allison, I have a guy on the phone who says he rescued the boy last night. Can I give him your number?"

Thobela's plate was filled with sausage and eggs, fried tomato and bacon, beans in tomato sauce, and fried mushrooms. Hot black bitter coffee stood steaming on the starched white tablecloth, and he ate with a ravenous appetite.

He had overslept, waking only at twenty to seven, his wounds excruciating, wobbly on his feet, hands still trembling but controllable like an idling engine. He had bathed without haste, carefully inspected the bloody mass, covered it up again, taking only one pill this time, dressed, and come down to eat.

In the upper corner of the dining room the television was fixed to a metal arm. CNN reported on share prices and George Bush's latest faux pas with the Chinese and on the European Community that had turned down yet another corporate merger, and then the newsreader murmured something about South Africa and he looked up to see the photo of his motorbike on the screen and froze. But he could not hear, so he went forward till he was directly under the screen.

> . . . *the fugitive's common-law wife and her son have since gone missing. Mpayipheli is yet to be apprehended. Other African news: Zimbabwean police arrested another foreign journalist under the country's new media legislation, this time the* Guardian *correspondent Simon Eagleton* . . .

Gone missing?

What the fuck did they mean by "gone missing"?

Captain Tiger Mazibuko ate in the Golf. He had pulled off the road two hundred meters south of the Zambezi bridge and he had the tasteless hamburger on his lap and was drinking out of the Fanta orange can. He wished he could brush his teeth and close his eyes for an hour or two, but at least he was reasonably sure the dog had not passed there yet.

He had stopped at every filling station, Mahalapye, Palapye, Francistown, Mosetse, Nata, and Kasane, and no one had seen a motorbike. Every petrol attendant he had gently nudged awake or otherwise woken had shaken his head. Last week, yes, there had been a few. Two, three English but they were going down to Johannesburg. Tonight? No, nothing.

So he could wait, his furry mouth could wait for toothpaste, his red eyes for healing water, his sour body could wait for a hot, soapy shower.

When he had eaten, he unlocked the trunk, lifted the cover of the spare tire, loosened the butterfly nut, lifted the tire, and extracted the parts of his weapon.

It took two trips to transfer the parts of the R4 to the front seat without obviously holding a firearm in his hands. There were people walking and cars passing continuously between the border post a kilometer or so north and the town of Kasane behind him. He assembled the assault rifle, keeping his movements below the steering wheel, away from curious eyes.

He would use it to stop the cunt. Because he had to come this way, he had to cross this bridge, even if he avoided the border post.

And once he had stopped him . . .

39.

The battle raged in him as he stood in front of the hotel, booted and spurred, ready to ride. The urge to turn around, to go back, was terrifically powerful. If they harmed Miriam and Pakamile . . . *Gone missing.* He had tried to convince himself that she could have taken her child and fled; if the media knew about them, there would be continuous calls and visitors—and he knew Miriam, he knew what her reaction would be. He had phoned from his hotel room, first her house, where it rang without ceasing. Eventually he gave up and thought desperately whom he could call, who would know at eight in the morning. Van Heerden—he could not remember the number, had to call international Information, give the spelling and hold on for ages. When it came he had to write hurriedly on a piece of torn-off hotel stationery. He phoned but Van Heerden was not at home. In frustration, he threw the phone down, took his stuff, paid the account, and went and stood by the motorbike. Conflicting urges battled within him, he was on the point of going back, Lobatse, Mafikeng,

Kimberley, Cape Town. No, maybe Miriam had fled; it would take him two days, better finish one thing, what if . . .

Eventually he left, and now he was on the road to Francistown, barely aware of the long straight road. Worry was one traveling companion, the other was the truth that he had uncovered through an African song under the Modder River bridge.

"I want to bring the boy to you," said Vincent Radebe to her over the phone.

"Where is he?"

"He's waiting in the car."

"Why me?"

"I read your story in the paper."

"But why do you want to bring him to me?"

"Because it is not safe. They will find me."

"Who?"

"I'm in enough trouble already. I cannot tell you."

"Do you know where his mother is?"

"Yes."

"Where?" He answered so quietly that she could not hear. "What did you say?"

"His mother is dead."

"Oh, God."

"I haven't told him yet. I can't."

"Oh, my God."

"He has no family. I would have taken him to family, but he says there is no one. And he is not safe with me; I know they will find me. Please help."

No, she wanted to say, no, she couldn't do this, what would she do, how would she manage?

"Please, Miss Healy."

Say no, say no.

"The newspaper," she said. "Please take him to the office, I will meet you there."

All the directors were there—NIA, Secret Service, Presidential Intelligence—heads of Defence and Police, and the minister, the attractive Tswana minister, stood in the center and her voice was sharp and cutting and her anger filled the room with shrill decibels because the president had called her to account, not phoned but called her in. Stood her on the red carpet and dressed her down. The president's anger was always controlled, they said, but it had not been that morning. The minister said the president's anger was terrible, because everything hung in the balance, Africa stood with a hand out for its African renaissance plan and the USA and the EU and the Commonwealth and the World Bank had to decide. As if all the misunderstandings and undermining with the whole AIDS mess was not enough, now we are abducting women and children and chasing war veterans across the veld on a motorbike, of all things, and everyone who has a nonsensical theory about what is on the hard drive is creeping out of the woodwork and the press are having a field day, even the *Sowetan,* that damned assistant editor's piece, he was with Mpayipheli at school, he talked to the man's mother. How does that make us look?

The minister was the torchbearer of the president's anger and she let it burn high, sparing no one, focusing on no one; she addressed them collectively, and Janina Mentz sat there thinking it was all in vain because there were twenty agents in Lusaka and within the hour they would storm the Republican Hotel and put an end to it. And sometime today, Tiger Mazibuko would shoot the big, bad biker from his celebrated fucking BMW and then it would no longer matter that the woman was dead and the child gone and it would be business as usual again in Africa. Tomorrow, the day after, there would be other news, the Congo or Somalia or Zimbabwe, it was just another death in Africa; did the minister think America cared? Did she think the European Union kept count?

The telephone rang on the minister's desk and she glared at it; Janina was amazed that the phone neither shrank nor melted. The minister went to the door and yelled, "Did I not tell you to hold all calls?" and a nervous male voice answered. The minister said, "What?" and an explanation followed. She slammed the door and the telephone continued to ring and the minister went to her desk and in a tone lost between despair and madness said, "The boy. They have the boy. The newspaper. And they want to know if the mother is dead."

CIA

EYES ONLY

FOR ATTENTION: Assistant Deputy Director (Middle East and Africa) CIA HQ, Langley, Virginia

PREPARED BY: Luke John Powell (Senior Agent in Charge—Southern Africa) Cape Town, South Africa

SUBJECT: Operation Safeguard: the loss of four agents in the protection of South African source Inkululeko

I. BACKGROUND TO OPERATION SAFEGUARD

Inkululeko is the code name for a source the CIA acquired in 1996 in the South African government. The source was secured after tentative signals from subject during an embassy function were explored. Subject's motivation at the time was stated as disillusionment with SA government's continued support of rogue states, including Iraq, Iran, Cuba, and Libya. This author recruited subject personally, as it was the first acquisition inside the ANC/Cosatu Alliance that was not previously Nationalist government–aligned. Subject's motivation was suspicious at the time, but has since proved valuable as a source.

Exact motivation still unknown.

*   *   *

It took the leader of the operation seven minutes and five thousand American dollars to buy over the manager of the Republican Hotel and pinpoint the room where Johnny Kleintjes was being held.

He had a team of twenty agents, but he chose just five to accompany him to 227. The others were ordered to man the entrances, the fire escape, and elevators, to watch windows and balconies from outside, or to sit in one of the vehicles with engines idling, ready for the unpredictable.

The leader had a key in his hand, but he sprayed silicon in the keyhole, using a yellow can with a thin red pipe on the cap. His colleagues stood ready at his back with firearms pointing at the roof. The leader fitted the key carefully and quietly turned it. The lubricated mechanism opened soundlessly. The leader gave the signal and opened the door in one smooth motion, and the first two agents rolled into the room, but all they saw was the body of an old colored man with gruesome wounds all over his body.

On Johnny Kleintjes's lap lay two hard drives and on his chest a word was carved with a sharp instrument.

KAATHIEB.

"Leave him with me," said the black male secretary of the minister, and Allison Healy bent down and said to Pakamile Nzululwazi, who gripped her hand, "We have to go and talk in there, Pakamile. Will you stay with this nice man for a while?" The child's body expressed anxiety, and her heart contracted. He looked at the secretary and shook his head. "I want to stay with you." She hugged him to her, not knowing what to do.

The secretary said something in Xhosa, in a quiet voice, and she said sharply, "Talk so I can understand."

"I only said I will tell him a story."

Pakamile shook his head. "I want to stay with you." She had become his anchor when Radebe handed him over to her; he was confused, afraid, and alone. He had asked for his mother a hundred times, and she didn't know how much more of this she could stand.

"He had better come along," said her editor to the secretary.

They were a delegation of four, not counting the boy. The editor and her and the managing director and the news editor, not one of whom had ever been there before. The door opened and the minister stood there and looked at Pakamile and there was so much compassion in her eyes.

She held the door for them, and Allison and the child walked ahead, the men behind. Inside, a white woman and a black man were already seated. The man stood up and she saw he was small and there was the bulge of a hump at his neck.

*   *   *

He stopped at Mahalapye for petrol and crossed over to the small café in search of a newspaper, but the small local paper had nothing and so he went on. The African heat reflected sharply from the blacktop and the sun was without mercy. He ought to have taken more pills, as the pain of the wound was paralyzing him. How badly was he damaged?

Huts, small farmers, children cavorting carefree beside the road, two Boer goats sauntering to greener pastures across the road—oh, Botswana, why couldn't his own country lie across the landscape as easily, so without fuss? Why couldn't the faces of his people remain as carefree, as easily laughing, as at peace? What made the difference? Not the artificially drawn lines through the savannah that said this country ends here and that one begins there.

Less blood had flowed here, for sure; their history was less fraught. But why?

Perhaps they had fewer reasons to shed blood. Fewer gripping vistas, less succulent pastures, fewer hotheads, less valuable minerals. Perhaps that was the curse of South Africa, the land where God's hand had slipped, where He had spilled from the cup of plenty—green mountains and valleys, long waving grass as far as the eye could see, precious metals, priceless stones, minerals. And He looked over it and thought, *I will leave it so, let it be a test, a temptation; I will put people here with a great thirst, I will let them come out of Africa and the white north and I will see what they do with this paradise.*

Or perhaps Botswana's salvation was merely that the gap between rich and poor was so much smaller. Less envy, less hatred. Less blood.

His thoughts were invaded again. *Gone missing:* the refrain ran in his mind; *gone missing:* it blended with the monotonous drone of the GS's engine, the wind that hissed on his helmet, the rhythms of his heart pushing blood painfully through his hip. He sweated; the heat increased with every kilometer, and it came from inside him. He would have to be careful, keep his wits; he would need to rest, take in fluids, shake the dullness from his head. His body was very sick. He counted the kilometers, concentrated on calculations of average speed, so many kilometers per minute, so many hours left.

He eventually stopped at Francistown.

He dismounted with difficulty at the petrol station, put the bike on its stand. There was a slippery feel to the wound, as if it was opening up.

The petrol jockey's voice was distant. "Your friend was looking for you early today."

"My friend?"

"He went through here early this morning in a Golf." As if that explained everything.

"I don't have a friend with a Golf."

"He asked if we'd seen you. A black man on a big orange BMW motorbike."

"What did he look like?"

"He's a lion. Big and strong."

"Which way did he go?"

"That way." The man pointed his finger to the north.

40.

Allison the onlooker.

She was always good at that, to look on from the outside, to be part of a group but in her head to be apart. She had worried about it, thought it over for hours at a time, analyzed it for years, and the best conclusion she had come to was that that was how the gears and springs and levers of her brain were put together, a strange and accidental product, no one's fault. Yesterday afternoon already she had known that he was like that, too. Two freaks who had sniffed each other out in a sea of normality, two islands that had improbably collided. But once again she found herself with that distance separating her from others, the itch of it was a gnawing voice of conscience that it was a form of fraud, to pretend you were part when you did not fit. You knew you did not belong here. The advantage was that it made her a good reporter because she saw what others were blind to.

There was an undercurrent to the negotiations.

The communication was stilted, in English, grown-ups speaking grown-up language so the child would be protected and the painful truths delayed.

The conversation was not for the record, the minister said. The nature of it was too sensitive, and she wanted agreement on that from all the parties.

One after another they nodded.

Good, she said. We will proceed. There was a child psychologist on the way. Also two women from the day-care center, as the therapist said familiar figures would be a cushion when the news was broken to him. Also a man and a woman from Child Welfare would be arriving soon. Senior people, very experienced.

Everything would be done, everything the state had access to, and the full machinery would be turned on, because what we had here was a tragedy.

Allison read the subtext. The minister watched the other woman, not continuously, but as staccato punctuation in the discourse, as if she were checking that she was on the right path.

This other woman. Not officially introduced. Sat there in her business suit like a finalist for Business-woman of the Year, gray trousers, black shoes, white blouse, gray jacket, hands manicured but without color on the nails, makeup soft and subtle, hair tied back, eyes without expression, a hint of beauty in a face with stern, unapproachable lines, but it was the body language that spoke louder, of control, a figure of authority, driven, self-assured.

Who was she?

A tragedy, the minister was saying, carefully choosing adult words and phrases, euphemisms and figurative speech to spare the child. Innocent people who were involved through chance. She wished she could tell the media everything, but that was impossible, so she had to make an appeal. They would have to trust her that you couldn't make an omelette without breaking eggs, and that made Allison shiver; we live in a dangerous world, a complicated world, and to help this young democracy to survive was much more difficult than the press could ever imagine.

There was the operation, a sensitive, necessary, well-planned operation, fully within the stipulation of the National Strategic Intelligence Act of 1994 (Act 94-38, 2 December 1994, as amended) and in the national interest; she did not use the term lightly, knowing how often it had been abused in the past, but they would have to take her word for it. National interest.

She wanted to make one thing clear: the operation as planned by the intelligence services did not require the involvement of innocent parties. To be frank, great efforts were made to avoid that. But things had gone wrong. Things that nobody could have foreseen. The operation that had run so smoothly had been derailed. Civilians were drawn in by underhanded methods; an innocent bystander was sucked into the vortex by an evil force, a third party, resulting in tragedy. If she could turn back the clock and change it, she would, but they all knew that was beyond the realm of possibility. A tragedy, because a civilian had died, possibly

by her own hand; the motivation, the precise circumstances were not wholly clear, but for the minister
that was one civilian too many and she mourned,
she could tell them she mourned for that life that had
been blotted out. But (a) it had nothing to do with
any weapons scandal, of that she was absolutely sure;
(b) there would be a complete, official, and rigorous
inquiry into the great loss; (c) if there was any responsibility or negligence on the part of any official, they
would proceed relentlessly with a disciplinary hearing
according to Article 15 of the Intelligence Services Act
of 1994 (as amended); and (d) the young dependent
would receive the best care available, after ascertaining
beyond a doubt whether any relatives existed, and if
there were none, the state would fulfill its responsibili-
ties, that was her personal promise, she would stake
her entire reputation, her career even, on that.

The minister looked at everyone, and Allison
knew she was trying to gauge whether they accepted
her explanation.

What would have happened if Pakamile had not
been dropped off at the *Cape Times* offices? She knew
the answer. It would have been hushed up. Wife and
child? What wife and child? We know nothing about
that. But there was a righteousness in the minister,
a desperation to her honor.

"Madam Minister," said the editor, the bespectacled, dignified colored man whom Allison greatly

respected. "Let me just say that we are not the monsters politicians always make us out to be."

"Of course," said the minister.

"We have sympathy for your role and your position."

"Thank you."

"But we do have one small problem. Having now gone on record that these two civilians have gone missing, and in the light of the huge tragedy that is, to some extent at least, public knowledge, if you are going to involve two ladies from the child-care center, we cannot write absolutely nothing."

Inkululeko is the Zulu word for "freedom," and there's an interesting historical footnote to this code name: apparently, there were constant rumors in the seventies and eighties that a mole of Zulu origin existed in the echelons of the ANC/SA Communist Party Alliance—a mole who allegedly leaked information to both the CIA and the SA apartheid government. As you may know, there was no truth to this rumor. We had no reliable source within the Movement at the time. Although several low-key attempts to acquire one was made, the CIA did not regard it as a high priority, due to the intelligence available through Eastern bloc entities at the time, and the view that the ANC/SACP did not constitute a threat to the USA or NATO.

However, when a code name had to be assigned after the 1996 recruitment, the subject suggested "Inkululeko" and pointed out the potential disinformation value thereof, as she had no Zulu ties whatsoever, being of European extraction.

The importance of this source multiplied wonderfully in 2000 when she was approached and recruited for the position of operations chief of staff for a newly created governmental agency, the PIU, or Presidential Intelligence Agency.

We believe the PIU was set up in an effort to counter the never-ending infighting, the legacy of jealousy and politics of the other three arms of the SA intelligence community, the National Intelligence Agency, the Secret Service, and Military Intelligence. All PIU staff were drawn from nonintelligence sources, with the sole exception of the director, an ANC and Umkhonto veteran.

2. ORIGIN OF OPERATION SAFEGUARD

In March of this year, a known member of a Cape-based militant Muslim splinter group with suspected ties to al Qaeda and Iranian strongman Ismail Khan was arrested by the SAPS on charges of the illegal possession of firearms.

During interrogation, the suspect, one Ismail Mohammed, indicated that he had information that could be of use to the SA intelligence community, and intended to use this information as plea-bargain leverage.

As luck would have it, a member of the PIU conducted an interview with the suspect. The information regarded the identity of Inkululeko.

Her heart was full when she walked out into the sun and the southeaster. Pakamile was inside, being clucked over by two black ladies from the day care who had taken him to their bosom. The child psychologist, a short dapper white man in his thirties with put-on caring and an inflated idea of his importance, was waiting for his five minutes of fame. The Welfare people with their forms and files knew their place in the hierarchy of bureaucracy and so sat outside on a wooden bench.

Allison Healy walked with her male colleagues down the steps and over the street as Van Heerden once more invaded her thoughts. She said, "You go ahead," because she wanted to turn on her cell phone, maybe there was a message. She dawdled as the wind plucked at her dress, punching in her PIN number and waiting for the phone to pick up a signal.

She saw the woman in the gray suit leave the building with the small hunchbacked man.

She looked down at the phone again. YOU HAVE TWO MESSAGES. PLEASE DIAL 121.

Thank goodness. She keyed in the numbers and waited, her brown eyes following the man and woman up Wale Street.

"Hullo, Allison, it's Rassie. Good articles this morning, well done. Phone me, there are some interesting things. Bye."

To save this message, press nine. To delete it, press seven. To return a call, press three. To save it . . .

She hurriedly pressed seven.

Next message:

"Allison, Nic here. I just want to . . . I want to see you, Allison. I don't want to wait till the weekend. Please. I . . . miss you. Phone me, please. I know I'm a pain. I talk too much. I'm available tonight. Oh, good work in the paper today. Phone me."

To save this message . . .

Irritated, she pressed seven.

End of new messages. To listen to your . . .

Why didn't Van Heerden call?

The white woman and the black man were disappearing up the street, and on impulse she followed them. It was something to occupy her mind. She walked fast, the wind at her back. She pushed the cell phone into her handbag and tried to catch up, her eyes searching until she saw the woman turn in at a building. Someone called her name. It was the Somali at the cigarette stand. "Hi, Allison, not buying today?"

"Not today," she said.

"Don't work too hard."

"I won't."

She walked fast to the place where the woman had turned in, eventually looking up at the name above the big double doors.

WALE STREET CHAMBERS.

Just a simple call. *Hi, Allison, how's it going?* How much would that take? Was that too much to ask?

Some of the information from the interview with Ismail Mohammed was surprisingly accurate. He stated that:

i.   Inkululeko was a more recent source than generally believed.

ii. There was no evidence that Inkululeko had a direct Zulu connection and that the contrary should be explored.

iii. Inkululeko was not a member of Parliament or the ANC leadership (which the constant rumors had indicated over the years).

iv. Inkululeko was most definitely part of the current SA intelligence setup and held a senior position within the intelligence community.

v.   The Muslim structures (unspecified) were getting closer to identifying Inkululeko, and it was only a matter of time before full identification would be made.

It is significant to note that Mohammed referred to Inkululeko as "he" and "him" during several interviews, indicating the level of true knowledge, despite the accuracy of the above statements.

The major question, of course, is how the SA Muslim structures acquired this knowledge.

According to Mohammed, they have been feeding disinformation regarding international Muslim activities, operations, and networks into the SA governmental and intelligence systems through a deliberate and well-planned process, with checks and balances on the other side to try and determine which chunks of disinformation got through to the CIA.

One such instance that we know of is the warning this office passed on to Langley in July of 2001 of a pending attack on the U.S. embassy in Lagos, Nigeria. The tip-off was received from Inkululeko, and additional U.S. Marines were deployed in and around the Lagos embassy at the time. As you know, the attack never materialized, but the intensified security measures should have been easy to monitor by Muslim extremists in Nigeria.

Fortunately for us, Inkululeko received the report on the Mohammed interview directly and was understandably disturbed by the contents. After giving the matter some thought, she put a proposal to this office.

41.

On the road between Francistown and Nata a strange thing happened.

He seemed to withdraw into a cocoon, the pain melted away, the overpowering heat in him and around him dissipated, he seemed to leave the discomfort of his body behind and float above the motorbike, distanced from reality, and though he could not understand how it had happened, he was awed by the wonder of it.

He was still aware of Africa around him, the grass shoulder to shoulder in khaki green and red-brown columns marching across the open plains beside the black ribbon of tarmac. Here and there acacias hunched in scrums and rucks and mauls. The sky was a dome of azure without limits, and the birds accompanied him, hornbills shooting across his field of vision, swallows diving and dodging, a bateleur tumbling out of the heavens, vultures riding the thermals far to the west in a spiral endlessly reaching upward. For a moment he was with them, one of them, his wings spanned tight, as wires registered every shuddering turbulence, and then he was back down there, and all the time the sun shone, hot and yellow and angry, as if it would sterilize the landscape, as if it could burn clean the evil sores of the continent with steadfast light and searing fire.

Why was the heat no longer in him, why did the shiver of intense cold run through his body like the frontal gusts of a storm?

It freed thoughts, like the chunks of a melting ice sheet, mixed up, jumbled, floating in his heart, things he had forgotten, wanted to forget. And right at the back of his mind a monotonous refrain of whispers.

Gone missing.

His father in the pulpit with pearls of perspiration beading his forehead in the summer heat, one hand stretched out over the congregation, the other palm down, resting on the snow-white pages of the big Bible before him. A tall man in a somber black toga, his voice thundering with disapproval and reproach. "What ye sow shall ye reap. It is in the Book. God's Word. And what do we sow, my brothers and sisters, what do we sow? Envy. Jealousy. And hate. Violence. We sow, every day in the fields of our lives, and then we cannot understand when it comes back to us. We say, Lord, why? As if it was He that poured the bitter cup for us, we are dismayed. So easily we forget. But it is what we have sown."

In Amsterdam the air was heavy and somber as his mood. He wandered through the busy streets, with his thick gray coat wrapped around him, Christmas carols spilling out from the doors along with the heat and eddying over the sidewalk, children in bright colors with red cheeks laughing like bells. He cast a long shadow in all this light. The assassination in Munich lay a week behind him, but he could not shake off the shame of it, it clung to him: this was not war. At a little shop on a corner opposite the canal, he spotted the ostrich eggs first, a heap in a grass basket, fake Bushman paintings on the oval, creamy white orbs; CURIOS FROM AFRICA, cried the display window. He saw wood carvings, the familiar mother and child figures and the tidy row of small carved ivory hippopotamuses and elephants, Africa in a nutshell for the continental drawing room, sanitized and tamed, the dark wound bound up with a white capitalistic bandage, peoples and tongues and cultures packaged in a few wooden masks with horrible expressions and tiny white ivory figurines.

Then he spotted the assegai and the oxhide shield, dusty and half forgotten, and he pushed open the door and went in. The bell tinkled. He picked up the weapon, turning it in his hands. The wooden shaft was smooth, the metal tip very long. He tested the shiny blade that was speckled with flecks of rust.

It was expensive, but he bought it and carried it off, an awkward parcel gift-wrapped in colorful ethnic paper.

He had sawed off the shaft in the shower of his hotel room, and the smell of the wood crept up his nose and the sawdust powdered the white tiles like snow and he remembered. He and his uncle Senzeni on the undulating Eastern Cape hill, the town down below in the hollow of the land as if God's hand were folded protectively over it. "This is exactly where Nxele stood." He laid out the history of his forefathers, broadly painted the battle of Grahamstown: this was where the soldiers had broken off the shafts of the long assegais, where the stabbing spear was born, not in Shaka's land, that was a European myth, just another way to rob the Xhosa. Even our history was plundered, Thobela.

That was the day that Senzeni had said, "You have the blood of Nqoma, Thobela, but you have the soul of Nxele. I see it in you. You must give it life."

He had laid the sawed-off assegai at the feet of his Stasi masters and said from now on this is how he would wage war, he would look his opponents in the eye, he would feel their breath on his face, they could take it or leave it.

"Very well," they agreed with vague amusement behind the understanding frowns, but he did not care. He had made the scabbard himself so that the weapon could lie against his body, behind the great muscles and the spine, so he could feel it where it lay ready for his hand.

Gone missing, sang the male voice choir in his head, and a road sign next to his path said Makgadikgadi and he found the rhythm in the name, the music of syllables.

"The sins of the fathers shall be visited upon the children even unto the third and fourth generation," said his father in the pulpit.

Makgadikgadikgadikgadi, *gone missing, gone missing, gone missing.*

"We are our genes, we are the accidental sum of each of our forefathers, we are the product of the fall of the dice and the double helix. We cannot change that," said Van Heerden with joy, finding excitement in that.

In Chicago he was awed by the unbelievable architecture and the color of the river, by the plenty and the streets that were impossibly clean. He walked self-consciously through the South Side and shook his head at their definition of a slum and wondered how many people of the Transkei would give their lives to let their children grow up here. Once he called out a greeting in Xhosa instinctively, as they were all black as he was, but their throats had ages since outgrown the feel of African sounds and he knew himself a stranger. He waited for the young Czech diplomat below the rumbling of the El, the elevated railway in the deep night shadows of the city. When the man came, he stood before him and said his name and saw only fear in the rodent eyes, a tiny scavenger. When his blade did the work, there was no honor in the blood, and Phalo and Rharhabe and all the other links in his genetic chain drooped their heads in shame.

Gone missing. One day his victims would return, one day the deeds of his past would visit him in the present, the dead would reach out long, cold fingers and touch him, repayment for his cowardice, for the misuse of his heritage, for breaking the code of the warrior, because with the exception of the last, they were all pale plump civil servants, not fighters at all.

He thought the assegai, the direct confrontation, would make a difference. But to press the cold steel in the heart of pen pushers betrayed everything that he was; to hear the last breath of gray, unworthy opponents in your ears was a portent, a self-made prophecy, a definition of your future—somewhere one day, it will come back to you.

Gone missing.

Were the same words used for the people he had killed? Some were fathers, at least somebody's son, although they were men, although they were part of the game, although they were every one a traitor to the conflict. And where was that conflict now, that useless chess game? Where were the ghosts of the Cold War? All that remained were memories and consequences, his personal inheritance.

The emptiness in him had grown; merely the nuances had changed with each city where he found himself, with the nature of the hotel room. The moments of pleasure were on the journey to the next one, when he could search for meaning anew at the next stop, search for something to fill the great hole, something to feed the monster growing inside.

The praise songs of his masters grew more hollow as time passed. At first, it was salve to his soul. The appreciation that rolled so smoothly off their tongues had stroked the shame away. "Look what your people say," and they showed him letters from the ANC in London that praised his service in flowery language. *This is my role,* he told himself. *This is my contribution to the freedom fight,* but he could not escape, not in the moments when he turned off the light and laid down his head and listened to the hiss of the hotel air-conditioning. Then he would hear his uncle Senzeni's voice and he longed to be one of Nxele's warriors who stood shoulder to shoulder, who broke the spear with a crack over his knee.

NATA, read the road sign, but he scarcely saw it. He and the machine were a tiny shadow on the plateau—they were one, grown together on a journey, every kilometer closer to completion, to fulfillment, engine and wind combining to a deep thrumming, a rhythmic swell like the breaking of waves. "Your friend was looking for you early today," the petrol jockey in Francistown had said. He knew, he knew it was Mazibuko, the voice of hate. He had not only heard the hate, he had recognized it, felt the resonance and knew that here was another traveler—this was himself ten or fifteen years ago, empty and searching and hating and frustrated, before the insight had come, before the calm of Miriam and Pakamile.

He was in the hospital, he and Van Heerden, when it happened. When he saw himself for the first time. Afterward, not a day would pass that he did not think of it, that he did not try to unpick the knot of destiny.

He was shuffling down the hospital passage late one evening, his body still broken from the thing that he and Van Heerden had been in. He stood in a doorway to catch his breath, that was all. No deliberate purpose, just a moment of rest, and he glanced into the four-bed ward and there beside the bed of a young white boy a doctor was standing.

A black doctor. A Xhosa as tall as he was. Round about his fortieth year, gray hinting at the temples.

"What are you going to become one day, Thobela?" His father, the same man who Sunday after Sunday hurled God's threats so terrifyingly from the pulpit with a condemning finger and a voice of reproach, was soft and gentle now to chase away the fear of an eight-year-old of the dark.

"A doctor," he had said.

"Why, Thobela?"

"Because I want to make people better."

"That is good, Thobela." That year he had had the fever and the white doctor had driven through from Alice and come into the room with strange smells around him and compassion in his eyes. He had laid cool, hairy hands on the little black body, pressed the stethoscope here and there, had shaken out the thermometer. *You are a very sick boy, Thobela,* speaking Xhosa to him, *but we will make you better.* The miracle had happened, that night he broke through the white-hot wall of fever into the cool, clear pool on the other side where his world was still familiar and normal, and that's when he knew what he wanted to be, a healer, a maker of miracles.

Where he stood watching the white boy and the black doctor in the doorway, he relived the scene, heard his own words to his father, and felt his knees weaken at the years that had been lost in the quicksand. He saw his life from another angle, saw the possibilities of other choices. He sagged slowly down against the wall, the weight too much to bear, all the brokenness, all the hatred, the violence and death, and the consuming deep craving to be free of it swallowed him up. Oh Lord, to be born again without it; he sank to his knees and stayed like that, head on his chest and deep, dry sobs tearing through his chest, opening up more memories until everything lay open before him, everything.

He had felt the black doctor's hand on his shoulder and later was conscious that the man was holding him, that he was leaning on the shoulder of the white coat, and slowly he calmed down. The man helped him up, supporting him, laid him down on his bed, and pulled the sheets up to his chin. *You are a very sick boy but we will make you better.*

He had slept and awoken and he had fought again, barefisted, honestly and honorably against the self-justification and rationalization. Out of the bloodied bodies of the dead rose a desire—he would be a farmer, a nurturer. He could not undo what had happened, he could not blot out who he had been, but he could determine where and how he would go from here. It would not be easy, step-by-step, a lifetime task, and that night he had eaten a full plate of food and thought through the night. The next morning before six he went to Van Heerden's room and woke him up and said he was finished, and Van Heerden had looked at him with great wisdom, so he had asked with astonishment at the way he was underestimated: "You don't believe I can change?"

Van Heerden had known. Known what he had discovered last night under a bridge in the Free State.

He was Umzingeli.

Twenty kilometers south of Mpandamatenga, through the fever and hallucinations, he became aware of movement to the left of him. Between the trees and grass he saw three giraffes moving like wraiths against the sun, cantering stately as if to escort him on his journey, heads dipping to the rhythm in his head. And then he was floating alongside them, one of them, and he felt a freedom, an exuberance, and then he was rising higher and looking down on the three magnificent animals thundering on; he surged up higher and turned south and caught the wind in his wings, and it sang. It swept him along, and all was small and unimportant down there, a scrambling after nothing; he flew over borders, rolling kopjes and bright rivers and deep valleys that cut the continent, and far off he saw the ocean, and the song of the wind became the crash of the breakers where he stood looking out from the rocky point. Sets of seven, always sets of seven. He folded his wings and waited for the oasis of calm between the thunder, the moment of perfect silence that waited for him.

42.

By quarter past two, sleep began to overcome Tiger Mazibuko, so he put the machine pistol under the rubber mat at his feet and climbed out of the car for the umpteenth time. Where was the fucker, why wasn't he here yet?

He stretched and yawned and walked around the car, once, twice, three times, and sat on the edge of the hood, wiping the sweat from his face with a sleeve, folded his arms, and stared down the road. He did the calculations again. Maybe Mpayipheli had stopped for lunch or to have his wounds tended to by a quack in Francistown. He looked again at his wristwatch—any minute now things should start happening. He wondered if the dog was riding with his headlight on, as bikers do. Probably not.

Sweat ran down his back.

He did not pay the Land Rover Discovery much heed, as other luxury four-wheel-drive vehicles had passed. This was tourist country, Chobe and Okavango to the west, Makgadikgadi south, Hwange and

Vic Falls to the east. The Germans and Americans and the Boers came to do their Livingstone thing here with air-conditioned 4x4s and khaki outfits and safari hats, and they thought the suspect drinking water and a few malaria mosquitoes were a hang of an adventure and went home to show their videos—look, we saw the big five, look how clever, look how brave.

It approached from the direction of Kazungula, and he tried to stare past it to keep watch on the road. Only when it pulled off the road opposite him did he look, half angry because he did not want to be distracted. Two whites in the front of the green vehicle, the thick arm of the passenger hanging over the open window. They looked at him.

"Fuck off," he called across the road.

The small eyes of the passenger were on him, the face expressionless on the thick neck. He could not see the driver.

"What the fuck are you staring at?" he called again, but they did not answer.

Jissis, he thought, *what the fuck?* And he raised himself from the hood and looked left and right before he began to cross. He would quickly find out what their story was, but then the vehicle began to move, the big fellow's eyes still on Mazibuko, and they pulled away and he stood in the middle of the road watching them drive away. What the fuck?

3. THE NATURE OF OPERATION SAFEGUARD

The plan devised by Inkululeko was essentially a disinformation initiative, primarily aimed at directing suspicion away from her.

Although the transcript of the Mohammed interview was in her sole possession, Inkululeko knew suppression thereof would be potentially dangerous and incriminating, due to the fact that both the police (to a lesser extent) and interviewer had some degree of knowledge, which was bound to surface at some time or other.

She approached this office with suggestions that were developed into Safeguard in conjunction with us. The core of the operation plan was to "hunt down" Inkululeko, to "flush him out."

Our source recruited the services of a retired intelligence officer from the former military arm of the ANC, Umkhonto we Sizwe (MK), one Jonathan ("Johnny") Kleintjes. This was a particularly brilliant move, for the following reasons:

i. Kleintjes was in charge of MK/ANC intelligence computer systems during the so-called Struggle in the period before 1992.
ii. He was the leader of the project to integrate those systems of the former apartheid government's intelligence agencies almost a decade ago.
iii. He was suspected of having secured sensitive and valuable information during the process. Like so

many of these intelligence rumors, there were different versions. The most persistent was that Kleintjes had found evidence within the mass of electronic information that both the ANC/SACP alliance and the apartheid government had been up to some dirty tricks in the eighties. In addition, a very surprising list of double agents and traitors on both sides, some of them very prominent people, was contained in the data.

iv. Kleintjes had apparently deleted these files, but only after making backups and securing it somewhere for possible future use and reference.

Inkululeko's aim was to use Kleintjes as a credible operative (both from a South African and U.S. perspective) for the disinformation project to protect her cover and win his trust at the same time, the latter pertinent to acquiring the missing data at a later stage.

The operation plan was fairly simple: Under her orders, Kleintjes would prepare a hard drive with fabricated intelligence about the "true identity of Inkululeko." He would then approach the U.S. embassy directly and ask to speak to someone from the CIA about "valuable information."

We, in turn, would act predictably and tell him never to come to the embassy again but to leave his contact details, as we would be in touch.

A meeting would be set up in Lusaka, Zambia, away from prying eyes, during which the data could be examined by the CIA and, if credible, be bought for the price of $50,000 (about R575,000).

Obviously, our side of the bargain was to accept the data as the real thing, thereby casting suspicion on the persons mentioned therein and drawing away any possible attention to her as a candidate for the identity of Inkululeko.

She would then write a full report on the operation and present it to the minister of intelligence for further action, bypassing her immediate superior, a man of Zulu extraction whose name would be among the strongest "candidates" for the identity of Inkululeko.

Again, this was a shrewd move, as she was next in line for his position, and the minister would have little choice but to suspend him from duties until the matter had been resolved. Which would have placed her in the top echelon: the National Intelligence Coordinating Committee, chaired by an intelligence coordinator, which brings together the heads of the different services and reports to the cabinet or president.

Unfortunately, Operation Safeguard did not go as planned.

The Ops Room was almost empty.

Janina Mentz sat at the big table and watched one of Rajkumar's assistants disconnect the last computer and carry it off piece by piece. The television monitors were off, the radio and telephone equipment's red and white lights were out, the soul of the place was dead.

A fax lay in front of her, but she had not yet read it.

She thought back over the past two days, trying hard to see the positive in the whole mess, trying to identify the moment when it all went wrong.

KAATHIEB.

The team leader in Lusaka had sent digital photos via e-mail. The letters in Johnny Kleintjes's chest were carved in deep red cuts, as if by a raging devil.

LIAR.

"It's Arabic," said Rajkumar, once he had completed his search.

How?

How had the Muslims known about Kleintjes?

There were possibilities she dared not even think about.

Had Johnny dropped a word to someone, somewhere? Deliberately? The director had his suspicions that Kleintjes had Islamic connections. But why then would they kill him? It made no sense.

Had she been sold out by the Americans?

No.

Mpayipheli?

Had he made a call for help somewhere along the road? Did he have links with the extremists? Had he, like some of his KGB masters since the fall of the USSR, gone in search of Middle Eastern pastures? Had he built up contacts on the Cape Flats while he worked for Orlando Arendse?

But Kleintjes was supposed to be his friend. That didn't fit.

The treachery lay elsewhere.

The treachery lay here. In their midst.

Would it not be ironic to have two traitors in one intelligence unit? But that was the scenario that fitted best.

Luke Powell had said he had lost his two agents yesterday, time of death not yet determined, but if the Muslims had left yesterday evening as the news broke here in the Ops Room, then the timetable fitted well.

She dropped her head into her hands, massaging her temples with her fingertips.

Who?

Vincent? The reluctant Radebe?

Quinn, the colored man with Cape Flats roots? Rajkumar? Or one of their assistants? The variables grew too many, and she sighed and sank back into her chair.

The plan was so good. The operation was so clever, so demonically brilliant, her creation. So many flies with one stroke of genius. She was so self-satisfied that she found secret pleasure in it, but it was born of need and panic.

Lord, how that transcript of Ismail Mohammed had shaken her.

All she could think of was her children.

Williams had called her from the police cells and said he had a bomb; he had better meet her at the office. He had played the tape for her and she had to keep cool because he was sitting opposite her and a part of her wondered if the shock was visible on her face. Could he see the paleness that came over her face? The other part was with her children. How was she going to explain to her girls that their mother was a traitor? How would she ever make them understand? How do you explain to someone that there was no big reason, no great ideological motivation, just an evening of succumbing, that strange night in the American embassy, but it had to be held in the light of a lifetime of disappointment, of disillusion, of fruitless struggle and frustration, decades of pointless aspiration that had prepared her for that moment.

Would anyone believe that she had not planned it? It had just happened like an impulse buy at the supermarket. She and Luke Powell were in conversation among forty or fifty people. He had asked her opinion on weighty matters, politics and economics; he had fucking respected her, deferred to her as if she were more than an invisible gear in the great engine room of government. Because the PIU belonged to the director, despite his promises, despite the initial sales talk to recruit her. She made no difference, she had no real power, she was just another civil servant in just another African intelligence agency.

So, in that moment when Luke Powell made his move, all the flotsam and jetsam of her life pressed on her with unbearable weight and she had thrown it off.

Who would ever understand?

Powell made her a player, gave her significance; for the first time in her life her acts were making a difference. Of course, it became easier, after September 11, nobler, but that did not change the fact that it simply just happened.

When Williams turned off the tape recorder she did not trust her voice, but it came out right, soft and easy just as she wished.

"You had better transcribe that personally," she said to him. Once he had left, she remained sitting in her chair, crushed by the weight, her brain darting this way and that like a cornered rat. Strange how quick the mind was when there was danger, how creative you could be when your existence was threatened. How to draw attention away from yourself? The cells in her brain had dreamed up the Johnny Kleintjes plan out of what had long lain stored away—the rumors that Kleintjes had forbidden data. That had not been a priority with her, just something to store in the files in the back of her head. When the need was greatest, it had come springing out into her consciousness, a germinating seed that would grow diabolically.

So brilliant. Those were Luke Powell's words. *You are brilliant.*

He had appreciated her from the beginning. Sincerely. With each piece of intelligence that she sent to him through the secret channels, the message came back. *You are priceless. You are wonderful. You are brilliant. You are making a real difference.*

And here she sat. Eight months later. Priceless and wonderful and brilliant, with a traitor's identity that was probably secured, but heads would roll and chances were good that one would be hers.

And that could not happen.

There must be a scapegoat. And there was one. Ready to sacrifice.

She was not finished. She was not nearly finished.

She smoothed her hair down and pulled the fax nearer.

This was the story the minister was talking about. The one that had appeared in the *Sowetan.* She did not want to read it. She wanted to move on; in her mind this chapter was closed.

MPAYIPHELI—THE PRINCE FROM THE PAST

By Matthew Mtimkulu, assistant editor
Isn't it strange how much power two words can have? Just two random words, sixteen simple letters, and when I heard them over the radio in my car, it

opened the floodgates of the past, and the memories came rushing back like rippling white water.

Thobela Mpayipheli.

I did not think about the meaning of the words—that came later, as I sat down to write this piece: Thobela means "mannered" or "respectful." Mpayipheli is Xhosa for "one who does not stop fighting"—a warrior, if you will.

My people like to give our children names with a positive meaning, a sort of head start to life, a potential self-fulfilling prophecy. (Our white fellow-citizens attempt the same sort of thing— only opting not for meaning but for sophistication, the exotic or cool to do the job. And my colored brothers seem to choose names that sound as much uncolored as possible.)

What really matters, I suppose, is the meaning the person gives to the name in the course of his life.

So, what I remembered as I negotiated early-morning rush hour was the man. Or the boy, as I knew him, for Thobela and I are children of the Ciskei; we briefly shared one of the most beautiful places on earth: the Kat River valley, described by historian Noël Mostert in his heartbreaking book *Frontiers* as "a narrow, beautiful stream that descended from the mountainous heights of the Great Escarpment and flowed through a broad, fertile valley towards the Fish river."

We were teenagers and it was the blackest decade of the century, the tumultuous seventies: Soweto was burning, and the heat of the flames could be felt in our little hidden hamlet, our forgotten valley. There was something in the air in the spring of 1976, an anticipation of change, of things to come.

Thobela Mpayipheli, like me, was fourteen. A natural athlete, the son of the Muruti of the Dutch Reformed Mission Church, and it was well known that his father was a descendant of Phalo along the Maqoma lineage. Xhosa royalty, if you will.

And there was something princely about him, perhaps in his bearing, most definitely in the fact that he was a bit of a loner, a brooding, handsome outsider of a boy.

One day in late September, I was witness to a rare event. I saw Mpayipheli beat Mtetwa, a huge, mean, scowling kid two years his senior. It was a long time coming between the two of them, and when it happened, it was a thing of beauty. On a sliver of river sand in a bend of the Kat, Thobela was a matador, calm and cool and elegant and quick. He took some shuddering punches, because Mtetwa was no slouch, but Thobela absorbed it and kept on coming. The thing that fascinated me most was not his awesome deftness, his speed or agility, but his detachment. As if he were measuring himself. As if he had to know if he was ready, confirmation of some inner belief.

Just three years later he was gone, and the whispers up and down the valley said he had joined the Struggle, he had left for the front, he was to be a soldier, a carrier of the Spear of the Nation.

And here his name was on the radio, a man on a motorcycle, a fugitive, a common laborer, and I wondered what had happened in the past twenty years. What had gone wrong? The prince should have been a king—of industry, or the military, perhaps a member of Parliament, although, for all his presence, he lacked the gift of the gab, the oily slickness of a politician.

So I called his mother. It took some time to track them down, a retired couple in a town called Alice.

She didn't know. She had not seen her son in more than two decades. His journey was as much a mystery to her as it was to me. She cried, of course. For all that was lost—the expectations, the possibilities, the potential. The longing, the void in a mother's heart.

But she also cried for our country and our history that so cruelly conspired to reduce the prince to a pauper.

43.

The late afternoon brought a turning point.

With every hour his frustration and impatience grew. He no longer wished to wait there; he wanted to know where the dog was, how far off, how long to wait. His eyes were tired from staring down the road, his body stiff from sitting and standing and leaning against the car. His head was dulled by continually running through his calculations, from speculation and guesswork.

But above all it was the anger that exhausted him; the stoking of the raging flames consumed his energy.

Eventually when the shadows began to lengthen, Captain Tiger Mazibuko leaped from the Golf and picked up a rock and hurled it at the thorn trees where the finches were chittering irritably and he roared something unintelligible and turned and kicked the wheel of the car, threw another stone at the tree, another and another and another, until he was out of breath. He blew down with a hiss of air through his teeth and calm returned.

Mpayipheli was not coming.

He had taken another road. Or the wounds perhaps . . . No, he was not going to start speculating
again—it was irrelevant; his plan had failed and he
accepted it. Sometimes you took a chance and you
won, and sometimes you lost. He made a decision, he
would wait till sunset, relax, watch the day fade to twilight and the twilight to dark, and then he was done.

When he climbed back in the car they came for
him.

Three police vehicles full of officials in uniform. He
saw the three vehicles approaching, but it registered
only when they stopped. He realized what was going
on only when they poured out of the doors. He sat
tight, hands on the steering wheel, until one shouted
at him to get out with his hands behind his head.

He did that slowly and methodically, to prevent
misunderstandings.

What the hell?

He stood by the Golf, and a pair of them ducked
into the car. One emerged triumphant with the Heckler & Koch. Another searched him with busy hands,
pulled his hands behind his back, and clamped the
handcuffs around his wrists.

Sold out. He knew it. But how? And by whom?

4. THE EXECUTION OF OPERATION SAFEGUARD
    After Johnny Kleintjes had visited the U.S. embassy,
    we set up contact with him and agreed to meet him
    in Lusaka.

Inkululeko kept her side of the bargain by duly recording the embassy visit, as well as starting a surveillance program of Kleintjes.

The operation went perfectly according to plan.

Because of the controlled nature of Safeguard, this office did not deem it necessary to allocate more than two people for the Zambia leg. And agents Len Fortenso and Peter Blum from the Nairobi office were drafted for the Lusaka "sale" of the data.

I acted as supervisor from Cape Town and take full responsibility for subsequent events.

Fortenso and Blum confirmed their arrival in Lusaka after a chartered flight from Nairobi. That was the last contact we had with them. Their bodies were found on the outskirts of Lusaka two days later. The cause of death was gunshot wounds to the back of the head.

Allison Healy wrote the lead article with great difficulty. Her concentration was divided between anger at Van Heerden and sadness for the lot of Pakamile.

She had cried when she left him behind, she had hugged him tight, and the ironic part that broke her heart was the way the child had comforted her.

"Don't be sad. Thobela is coming back tomorrow."

For the sake of the child, she had called every contact and informant who might possibly know something.

"It depends who you believe," Rassie had said from Laingsburg. "One rumor says he's wounded. The other says they have shot him dead in Botswana, but I don't believe either of them."

"Shot dead, you say?"

"It's a lie, Allison. If the Botswana police had shot him, it would have been headline news."

"And what about the wounding story?"

"Also a load of rubbish. They say a chopper pilot shot him but not with the chopper, you know what I mean. With this kind of thing rumors run wild. All I know is that the RU have gone home, and the whole operation in the Northern Cape has been called off."

"That is not good news."

"How do you mean?"

"It could mean that it's all over. That he is dead."

"Or that he is over the border."

"That's true. Thanks, Rassie. Phone me if you hear something."

And that was the sum total of information. The other sources knew or said even less, so at last she began with the story, building it paragraph by paragraph, without enthusiasm and with Van Heerden's betrayal hanging over her like a shadow.

A member of the Presidential Intelligence Unit's operational staff is under house arrest and awaiting an internal disciplinary hearing after the tragic accidental death of Mrs. Miriam Nzululwazi last night.

The rest was more of a review than anything else because they had laid down guidelines for the report, she and the news editor and the editor. The final agreement with the minister was that they would break this news exclusively but sympathetically, sensitive to the nuances of national interest and covert operations. When she was finished she went outside to smoke in the St. George's Mall and watched the rest of the world on their way home. Streams of people so determined, so serious, so stern, going home just to journey back tomorrow morning, a never-ending cycle to keep body and soul together until the Reaper came. This useless, meaningless life went on with gray efficiency, pitiless: tomorrow there would be other news, the day after, another scandal, another matter dished up to the people in big black sans serif lettering.

Damn Van Heerden. Damn him for being like all other men, damn him for a shoplifter, a swindler.

Damn Thobela Mpayipheli, for deserting a woman and child for a pointless chase across this bloody country. All it would leave was yellowing front pages in newspaper archives. Didn't he know that next month, next year, no one would even remember except Pakamile Nzululwazi living somewhere in a bloody orphanage, staring out the window every evening, hoping, until that too, like other hopes, faded irrevocably and left nothing but the vicious cycle of waking up and going to sleep.

She crushed the cigarette under her heel.

Fuck them all.

And she knew how to do it.

5. MUSLIM EXTREMIST INVOLVEMENT

Johnny Kleintjes was found executed in a room in the Republican Hotel in Lusaka, the word "KAA-THIEB" slashed with a sharp pointed object into his chest—Arabic for "liar."

This obviously indicates Muslim extremist involvement, and the big question is how local or foreign groups gained knowledge of the operation. The most likely explanation is a leak within the Presidential Intelligence Unit itself—and there are several facts that substantiate this suspicion:

i. The operation was infiltrated at an early stage—the Muslims were in Lusaka, waiting for Kleintjes and the CIA operatives. The PIU was the only agency with knowledge of Kleintjes's involvement.

ii. After eliminating Fortenso and Blum, the unknown operatives blackmailed Kleintjes's daughter in Cape Town to bring a specific hard drive to Lusaka. (She asked one Thobela Mpayipheli, a former friend and colleague of Kleintjes Senior, to do this on her behalf, as she is physically challenged—see below.) The suspected Muslim group, I believe, was not after the fabricated Kleintjes data but the information he had allegedly secreted during the 1994 integration process.

iii. From this follows the obvious: the extremists have a mole within the PIU and suspected the mole's identity was going to be compromised by the data.

iv. Kleintjes himself was known for his Middle Eastern sympathies and could have been protecting the Muslim mole.

v. Furthermore, the PIU member arrested by Botswana police was waiting in ambush to intercept Mpayipheli and the hard drive, close to the Zambian border. We believe the Botswana authorities were tipped off to stop the drive (containing the information about the Muslim mole) from falling into the hands of the PIU. The only people who knew he was waiting in Botswana are part of a small, exclusive group within the PIU.

The only remaining question, in my opinion, is not if Islamic extremists have an operative within the SA Presidential Intelligence Unit, but who it is. From this, it naturally follows that the original data might shed some light on the Muslim mole within the South African intelligence community.

At this time, the hard drive is still missing.

6. THE MATTER OF UMZINGELI

In 1984 a top CIA field agent and a decorated, much valued veteran, Marion Dorffling, was eliminated in Paris. The modus operandi of the assassin was similar to at least eleven (11) similar executions of U.S. assets and operatives.

The CIA had enough intelligence from Russian and Eastern European sources to conclude, or at least strongly suspect, that one Thobela Mpayipheli, code name Umzingeli (a Xhosa word for "hunter") was responsible for the murder. According to available information, Mpayipheli was an MK soldier on loan from the ANC/SACP alliance to the KGB and Stasi as a wet work specialist.

Coincidently, I was a rookie member of the CIA team in Paris at the time.

When Mpayipheli's involvement in Operation Safeguard became public knowledge, I filed a request to the field office in Berlin for possible documentation from former Stasi files to confirm the 1984 suspicions. Our colleagues in Germany obliged within hours (for which I can only commend them).

The Stasi records confirmed that Mpayipheli/Umzingeli was Marion Dorffling's assassin.

I notified Langley, and the response from deputy director's level was that the Firm was still very much interested in leveling the score. Two specialized field agents from the London office were dispatched to deal with the matter.

Allison Healy's fingers danced lightly but intensely across the keyboard. Her passion appeared in the words on the screen.

Fugitive motorcyclist Thobela Mpayipheli was
a ruthless assassin for the KGB during the Cold
War, responsible for the deaths of at least fifteen
people.

According to his longtime friend and former
policeman, Dr. Zatopek van Heerden, Mpayipheli
was recruited by the Soviets during MK training
in what was then the USSR. Van Heerden is currently a staff member of the UCT Department of
Psychology.

She scanned it quickly before continuing, suppressing with difficulty the impulse to write, "his
longtime friend, the world-class asshole Dr. Zatopek
van Heerden."

In an exclusive and frank interview, Dr. Van
Heerden disclosed that . . .

The phone rang and she grabbed it up angrily
and said, "Allison Healy," and Van Heerden asked,
"Have you got a passport?" and she said, "What?"

"Have you got a passport?"

"You asshole," she said.

"What?"

"You are a total, complete, utter asshole," she
said before realizing her voice was so loud that her
colleagues could hear. She took the cell phone and
walked toward the bathrooms, speaking in a whisper

now, "You think you can fuck me and run off like a . . . like a . . ."

"Are you cross because I didn't leave a message?"

"You could have phoned, you bastard. What would it have taken to make one call? What would it have cost to say thank you and good-bye, it was good, but it's over. You men are all the same, too fucking cowardly—"

"Allison—"

"But not last night, oh no, last night you couldn't talk enough, all the things that you said, and today not a bloody word. Couldn't you lift a finger to press a telephone button?"

"Allison, are you interested in—"

"I am interested in nothing to do with you."

"Would you like to meet Thobela Mpayipheli?"

The words were queuing up behind her tongue, but she swallowed them down. He had taken the wind from her sails.

"Thobela?"

"If you have a passport, you can come along."

"Where to?"

"Botswana. We are leaving in . . . er . . . seventy minutes."

"We?"

"Do you want to come, or not?"

44.

He had to give her the last directions over the cell phone, as it was an obscure route at the Cape Town International Airport behind hangars and office buildings and between small single-propeller airplanes that looked like children's toys left around in loose rows. Eventually she found the Beechcraft King Air ambulance with its Pratt & Whitney engines already running.

Van Heerden was standing in the door of the plane, waving to her, and she grabbed the overnight bag from the backseat, locked the car, and ran.

He stood aside so she could climb the steps and then he pulled the door shut behind her, signaling to the pilot. The Beechcraft began to move.

He took her bag and showed her where to sit—on one of the three seats at the back. After making sure her seat belt was fastened, he sat down beside her with a sigh. He leaned over and kissed her full on the lips before she could pull away, and then he grinned at her like a naughty schoolboy.

"I should—," she began seriously, but he stopped her with a hand.

"May I explain first?" His voice was loud, to be heard over the engine noise.

"It's not about us. It's about Miriam Nzululwazi."

"Miriam," he said with grim foreboding.

"She's dead, Zatopek. Last night."

"How?"

"All they say is that it was an accident. She fell. Five stories down."

"Good Lord," he said, and let his head drop back against the cushion of the seat. He sat like that for a long time, staring ahead, and she wondered what his thoughts were. Then just before the Beechcraft sped down the runway, he said something she couldn't hear and shook his head.

"You have a terrible temper," he said as the roar of the engines quieted at cruising altitude and he loosened his safety belt. "Do you want some coffee?"

"And you are a bastard," she said without conviction.

"I was in conference all day."

"Without tea or lunch breaks?"

"I meant to phone you in the afternoon, when it was more quiet."

"And so?"

"Then I had a call from a Dr. Pillay of Kasane, who said he had found my telephone number in the pocket of a badly injured black man who had fallen off his motorbike in northern Botswana."

"Oh."

"Coffee?"

She nodded, watching him as he made the same offer to the doctor and pilot in the cockpit. She thought how close she had come to putting the article into the system. She had been at the door of the editorial office when she turned and ran back to delete it. She had a temper. That was true.

"What is his condition?" she asked Van Heerden when he came back.

"Serious but stable. The doctor said he has lost a lot of blood. They gave him transfusions, but he is going to need more and blood is in short supply up there."

"What happened to him?"

"Nobody knows. He has two bullet wounds in the hip, and his left shoulder was badly bruised in the fall. Some locals found him beside the road near the Mpandamatenga turnoff. By the grace of God, no one phoned the authorities; they just loaded him on a bakkie and took him to Kasane."

She absorbed the news, and another question arose. "Why are you doing this?"

"He is my friend." Before she could respond, he added, "My only friend, to be honest," and she wondered about him, who he was and what made him this way.

"And this"—she indicated the medical equipment—"what is all this going to cost?"

"I don't know. Ten or twenty thousand."

"Who is going to pay?"

He shrugged. "I will. Or Thobela."

"Just like that?"

He grinned but without humor.

"What?"

"Perception and reality," he said. "I find it very interesting."

"Oh?"

"Your perception is that he is black—and a laborer, from Guguletu. Therefore, he must be poor. That is the logical view, a reasonable conclusion. But things are not always what we expect."

"So he has money? Is that from the drugs or the assassinations?"

"A valid question. But the answer is 'not from either of those.'"

He saw her shake her head dubiously, and he said, "I had better tell you the whole story. About me and Orlando and Thobela and more American dollars than most people see in a lifetime. It was two years ago. I was moonlighting as a private investigator, probing a murder case the cops couldn't crack. In a nutshell, it came out that the victim was involved in a clandestine army operation, weapons transactions for UNITA in Angola, diamonds and dollars. . . ."

He finished the story by the time they landed in Johannesburg to refuel. When they took off again, she pushed up the armrest between them and leaned against him.

"Am I still a bastard?" he asked.

"Yes. But you are my bastard," and she pressed her face in his neck and inhaled his smell with her eyes shut.

That afternoon she had thought she had lost him.

Before they flew over the N1 somewhere east of Warmbad, she was asleep.

She stayed in the plane, looking out the oval window of the Beechcraft. The air coming in the open door was hot and rich in exotic scents. Outside the night was lit up by car lights, the moving people casting long deep shadows, and then four appeared from behind a vehicle with a stretcher between them, and she wondered what he looked like, this assassin, drug soldier, the man for whom Miriam Nzululwazi had wept in her arms, the man who had dodged the entire country's law enforcers for two thousand kilometers to do a friend a favor. What did he look like? Were there marks, recognizable features on his face that would reveal his character?

They struggled up the steps with the weighty burden. She went to sit at the back, out of the way, her eyes searching, but he was hidden by the bearers, Van Heerden, the doctor who had flown with them, Dr. Pillay, and one other. They shifted him carefully onto the bed in the aircraft. The white doctor connected a tube to the thick black arm, the Indian said something softly into the patient's ear, pressing the big hand that lay still, and then they went out and someone pulled the door up and the pilot started the engines.

She stood up to see his face. The eyes caught hers, like a searchlight finding a buck, black-brown and frighteningly intense, so that she could see nothing else, and she felt a thrill of fear and enormous relief. Fear for what he could do, and relief that he would not do it to her.

The black man slept and Van Heerden sat with her again and she asked, "Have you told him?"

"It was the first thing he wanted to know when he saw me."

"You told him?"

He nodded.

She looked at the still figure, the dark brown skin of his chest and arms against the white bedding, the undulations of caged power.

William Blake, she thought.

What immortal hand or eye
Could frame thy fearful symmetry?

"What did he say?" she asked.

"He hasn't said a word since."

Now she understood the intensity of those eyes.

In what distant deeps or skies
Burnt the fire of thine eyes?

"Do you think he will . . ."

She looked at Van Heerden and for the first time saw the worry.

"How else?" he said in frustration.

On what wings dare he aspire?
What the hand dare seize the fire?

"But you can help him. There must be a legal—"

"It is not he who will need help."

That's when she grasped what Van Heerden was afraid of, and she looked at Mpayipheli and shivered.

When the stars threw down their spears,
And water'd heaven with their tears,
Did he smile his work to see?
Did he who made the Lamb make thee?

On the last leg to Cape Town she woke with a heavy body and a stiff neck and she saw Van Heerden sitting next to Mpayipheli, his white hand holding the Xhosa's, and she heard the deep bass voice, soft, the words nearly inaudible to her above the engines, and she closed her eyes again and listened.

". . . go away, Van Heerden? Is that part of our genetic makeup, too? Is that what makes us men?

Always off somewhere?" He spoke in slow, measured tones.

"Why was it that I could not say no? She knew, from the beginning. She said men go away. She said that is our nature, and I argued with her, but she was right. We are like that. I am like that."

"Thobela, you can't—"

"Do you know what life is? It is a process of disillusionment. It frees you of your illusions about people. You start out trusting everyone, you find your role models and strive to be like them and then you are disappointed by one after the other and it hurts, Van Heerden, it is a painful road to walk and I never understood why it must be so, but now I do. It is because every time the hope in you dies a little, with every disillusion, each disappointment in others becomes a disappointment in yourself. If others are weak, that weakness lies in you. It is like death: when you see others die, you know it lies in wait for you. I am so tired of it, Van Heerden, I am so tired of being disillusioned, of seeing all these things in people and in myself, the weakness, the pain, the evil."

"It's—"

"You were right. I am what I am. I can deny it, I can suppress it . . . and hide it, but not forever. Life does as it will, it throws you around. Yesterday there was a moment I realized I was living again. For the first time in . . . a long time. That I was doing something meaningful. With satisfaction. That I was vibrating inside and outside, in time, in rhythm. And do you know what was my first reaction? To feel guilty, as if that canceled out the meaning of Miriam and Pakamile. But I have had time to think, Van Heerden. I understand it better. It is not what I am that is wrong. It is what I use it for. Or let it be used for. That was my mistake. I allowed other people to decide. But no more. No more."

"You have to rest."

"I will."

"I left money with the doctor for the motorbike. They will send it down with a transport carrier in a week or so."

"Thank you, Van Heerden."

"We land in twenty minutes," said the pilot.

NOVEMBER

45.

On her lunch hour, Allison Healy drove out to Morningside with the long parcel and takeout on the backseat. Mpayipheli sat on the veranda in the sun, his bare torso showing the bright white bandage around his waist. She walked toward him with the parcel in her hand.

"I hope this is what you wanted."

He pulled off the gaudy gift-wrapping with its multicolored African motif.

"They insisted on wrapping it," she apologized.

He held the assegai in his hands, tested the strength of the steel, drew a finger down the edge of the blade.

"Thank you very much," he said quietly.

"Is it . . . good enough?"

"It is perfect," he said. He would have to shorten it, saw off more than half of the shaft, but he would not spoil her effort with details.

She put the bowls of curry and plastic cutlery on the table. "Would you prefer a proper knife and fork?"

"No, thank you." He leaned the assegai against the table and took his food.

"How are you feeling?" she asked.

"Much better."

"I'm glad."

"I want to start on Monday, Allison."

"Monday? Are you sure?"

"I can't wait any longer."

"You're right," she said. "I will show you."

Quinn phoned her from the airport.

"The name is false and they paid in cash, ma'am, but the pilot's flight plan was submitted according to regulations. There is not much we can do."

"What does he say?"

"They landed in Chobe, ma'am. That's almost on the Zambian border. The patient was a big black man with two gunshot wounds in the hip. His condition was stable. They gave him about two liters of blood. The other two were white, a man and a woman. The woman had red hair, plump and light-skinned. The man was dark and lean, of average height. He and the black man spoke in Afrikaans, he and the woman spoke English. When they arrived they transferred the patient to a station wagon or a four-wheel drive, he's not sure. They did not take the plate number."

"Thank you, Quinn."

"What shall I do with the pilot?"

"Just thank him and come back."

TRANSCRIPT: Commission of Inquiry into the death of Mrs. Miriam Nzululwazi (38). 7 November.

PRESENT: Chairman: Adv. B. O. Ndlovu. Assessors: Adv. P. du T. Mostert, Mr. K. J. Maponyane. For the PIU: Ms. J. M. Mentz. Witnesses: No witnesses were called.

CHAIRMAN: Mr. Radebe, according to article 16 of the Intelligence Services Act of 1994, as amended, you have the right to representation during these proceedings. Have you waived this right?

RADEBE: I have, Mr. Chairman.

CHAIRMAN: Do you understand the nature of the inquiry and the charge of misconduct against you?

RADEBE: I understand it.

CHAIRMAN: According to article 16(c), you are entitled to representation by a person in your department, and if no such person is available or suitable, by someone outside your department, are you aware of this right?

RADEBE: I am, Mr. Chairman.

CHAIRMAN: Do you waive your right to representation?

RADEBE: Yes.

CHAIRMAN: According to article 15(1), you are required to prepare a written admission or rejection of the charge against you. Has this document, as submitted by you, been composed of your own free will?

RADEBE: It has, Mr. Chairman.

CHAIRMAN: Would you read it to this committee, please?

RADEBE: I, Vincent Radebe, admit that my conduct and actions hindered and complicated an official operation of the Presidential Intelligence Unit.

I admit that through gross negligence I was responsible for the death of Mrs. Miriam Nzululwazi on 26 October of this year. I neglected to lock the door of the interview room, which resulted directly in Mrs. Nzululwazi's leaving the room without escort and in a disturbed state of mind. Her fatal fall from the fire escape of the building was a direct result of my conduct.

I admit, further, that on the same day I unlawfully and without official sanction abducted the six-year-old son of Mrs. Nzululwazi and kept him at my abode overnight. I admit that on 27 October I handed over the boy, Pakamile, to personnel of the *Cape Times* and thereby undermined an official operation of the Presidential Intelligence Unit.

I declare that I acted alone in both instances and wish to blame or involve no other person.

I wish to plead the following mitigating factors, Mr. Chairman: When I made my career choice on completion of my studies at the University of the Witwatersrand, it was my genuine desire to make a positive contribution to this country. Like so many of my compatriots, I was inspired by the forgiving and positive vision of Mr. Nelson Mandela. I also wished to dedicate my life to the building of the rainbow nation. The Presidential Intelligence Unit, in my opinion, presented me that opportunity.

But sometimes passion and dedication are not enough. Sometimes zeal blinds us to our own faults and shortcomings.

I understand that the protection of the state and the democracy sometimes demands difficult decisions and actions from its office bearers, actions whereby ordinary and innocent civilians are sometimes directly and negatively affected.

I know now that I am not suited to this career—and never was. The incidents of 26, 27, and 28 October were extremely traumatic for me. I was deeply disturbed by the manner in which, in my opinion, the basic human rights of, first, Mr. Thobela Mpayipheli and later Mrs. Miriam Nzululwazi were infringed upon. Even now, as I read this document, I am unable to grasp how the purpose of the operation, however important or vital to national security it might have been, justified the means.

My mistake, Mr. Chairman, was to allow my dismay to affect my good judgment. I was negligent when I should have been diligent. I regret deeply my part in Mrs. Nzululwazi's death and particularly that I did not make a stronger stand or protest more vigorously through official channels. My greatest weakness was to doubt my own judgment of right and wrong. This country and its people deserve better than that, but I can assure you that that will never happen again.

That is all, Mr. Chairman.

CHAIRMAN: Thank you, Mr. Radebe. Do you agree that this document be recorded as written admission of the charge against you?

RADEBE: I agree.

CHAIRMAN: Have you any questions, Mrs. Mentz?

MENTZ: I have, Mr. Chairman.

CHAIRMAN: Proceed.

MENTZ: Vincent, do you believe that part of, as you would call it, the building of the rainbow nation is to supply classified information to the intelligence services of other nations?

RADEBE: No, ma'am.

MENTZ: Then why did you?

RADEBE: I did no such thing.

MENTZ: Do you deny that during the operation you supplied information to Muslim extremist groups?

RADEBE: I deny that emphatically.

CHAIRMAN: Mrs. Mentz, do you have proof of these allegations?

MENTZ: Mr. Chairman, we have tangible evidence that key information was leaked to an international network of Muslim extremists. We cannot directly link Vincent with this process, but his undermining behavior speaks for itself.

CHAIRMAN: I have two problems here, Mrs. Mentz.

First, Mr. Radebe has not been charged with high treason but with negligence. Second, your allegations rest on circumstantial evidence, which I cannot allow.

MENTZ: With respect, Mr. Chairman, I do not believe that leaving the interview room door unlocked was negligence. I believe it was deliberate.

CHAIRMAN: Your allegations must be proved, Mrs. Mentz.

MENTZ: The truth will come out.

CHAIRMAN: Do you wish to submit evidence, Mrs. Mentz?

MENTZ: No.

CHAIRMAN: Do you have any further questions?

MENTZ: No.

CHAIRMAN: Do you wish to introduce evidence regarding further questions, Mr. Radebe?

RADEBE: No, Mr. Chairman.

CHAIRMAN: Mr. Radebe, this commission of inquiry has no choice but to find you guilty of misconduct as noted. We take note of your presentation of mitigating circumstances. This commission is adjourned until 14:00, when we will consider actions to be taken against you.

As the woman drove out of the parking garage at Wale Street Chambers, Allison Healy followed her with her heart in her throat. Mpayipheli lay flat on the rear seat. They drove through the city, always four of five car lengths behind, down the Heerengracht, onto the N1, and then east toward the northern suburbs.

"Please don't lose her," came the deep voice from the back.

It was Williams, who had begun the thing, who nearly ended it.

Williams who knew everyone, but no one knew him. Williams whom she had plucked out of the SAPS, an affirmative action appointee wasting his time behind a desk somewhere in the regional commissioner's office. The rumors had spread over the Western Cape in fragments: twenty-eight years in the police and never took a bribe. If you want to know something, ask Williams. If you need someone you can trust, get Williams. A colored man from the heart of the Flats, joined the force without finishing high school and climbed the ladder like a phantom, without powerful friends or powerful enemies, without fanfare, the invisible man. Just what she wanted, and it was so easy to get him. Merely the sincere promise that he would never again be chained to a desk did the trick.

"Janina," he said. He had called her that from the beginning. "Do you want his address?" His tone of voice was somewhere between irony and seriousness.

"Go for it," she said, and picked up a pen.

"I expect that you will find him at the house of a Dr. Zatopek van Heerden, plot seventeen, Morning Star."

"A medical doctor?"

"That I cannot say."

"How, Williams?"

"They brought the motorbike in through the Martin's Drift border post, ma'am. On a three-tonner, without papers, and the story that it belongs to a South African who had an accident somewhere in northern Botswana."

"And they let him in?"

"Money changed hands."

"And?"

"The driver had an address with him that was copied down."

"How did you . . . ?"

"Oh, I hear things."

46.

The Stasi records confirmed that Mpayipheli/
Umzingeli was Marion Dorffling's assassin.

I notified Langley, and the response from deputy
director's level was that the Firm was still very much
interested in leveling the score. Two specialized field
agents from the London office were dispatched to
deal with the matter.

After the tip-off from Inkululeko, the agents flew
to northern Botswana, acquired a vehicle, and made
visual contact with the PIU Reaction Unit member
who was waiting in ambush for Mpayipheli. They
witnessed the arrest of the Reaction Unit member
by Botswana authorities but, despite waiting at the
roadside through the night, could not intercept
Mpayipheli or the hard drive.

They returned to Cape Town and were about to
leave for London when the urgent contact signal
was received from Inkululeko (she leaves her car's
indicator on in her home driveway). When contact
was established, Inkululeko supplied the address
where Mpayipheli was apparently recuperating

from wounds sustained during his cross-country flight. She granted us three hours before the PIU Reaction Unit would reach the same address.

The image that remained with Allison Healy afterward was the one of blood—the carotid artery that kept pumping spouts of the liquid, first against the wall and later onto the floor, powerful jets in an impossibly high arc that gradually lessened until the fountain of life dried up with repulsive finality.

In long discussions afterward with Van Heerden she would try to purge it from her mind by reconstructing the events over and over again. Try to analyze her emotions from where they had stood as they ate their meal through to the end of it all one day later.

They sat at the table in Van Heerden's kitchen. At Mpayipheli's request, he had made coq au vin in the traditional Provençal manner. The serving dish stood in the middle of the table, steaming a heavenly aroma, golden couscous in a dish alongside. Three people in a happy domestic scene, the Xhosa man's hunger practically visible on his face, the way he eyed the food, eager posture, hands ready, impatient for her to finish serving.

It was a pleasant occasion, a convivial gathering, a mental photograph frozen in time to take out and remember with satisfaction later. *Don Giovanni* playing in the sitting room, a baritone aria that she was unfamiliar with but that fell with melodious machismo on her ear, the man she was beginning to love beside her, who continually surprised her with his cooking skill, his fanatical love of Mozart, his deep friendship with the black man, his ongoing teasing of the both of them. And Thobela, who carried his grief for Miriam Nzululwazi with so much grace—how her perception of him had changed. A week ago on the plane he and his past had filled her with fear, but now tenderness grew in her out of the conversations on the veranda when he related his life to her. There were moments when he described how he had met Miriam and how their love and companionship had blossomed that she had to fight back the tears. Here they sat now on the eve of his attempt to claim Pakamile, the future full of promise for everyone and the world, a wonderful moment framed in the dark reflection of a red wine glass.

She would never be sure if she had heard the sound. Perhaps, but even if she had, her untrained ear could never have distinguished it from others, nor her consciousness read danger in it.

Mpayipheli had moved with purpose, one moment in the chair beside her, the next a mass of kinetic energy moving in the direction of the sitting room, and then everything happened at once. Chaos and noise that she could only sort chronologically with great difficulty after the fact. First the dull thud of human bodies colliding with great force, then the apologetic reports of a silenced firearm, a short staccato of four-five-six shots followed by the crack of the coffee table breaking, shouts of men like bellowing animals, and she found herself in the doorway of the living room, the only light shining over her shoulder, and all she could see was rolling shadows and half-light.

Mpayipheli and a man were on the ground, writhing and grunting for life or death, the silver flash of a steel blade in between, and another man, tall and athletic on the other side of the room with a gun in his hand, the long snout of a silencer searching out a target on the floor, but calm and calculating, unhurried by the frenetic motion of the two figures.

And then Van Heerden. She had not seen him leave the kitchen, was unaware that he had gone out the other door into the passage. Only when the tall man placed his gun on the floor did she realize that Van Heerden was holding the double-barreled shotgun to the man's head, and he called to her, "Allison, go into the kitchen, close the door," but she was frozen. Why couldn't she move? Why couldn't she react? she would ask herself and Van Heerden over and over in the weeks afterward.

Mpayipheli and the other one stood up against each other; his opponent, the one with the knife, had small eyes close together and a thick neck on massive shoulders.

"Tiny," Van Heerden called, and threw something across the room that the Xhosa deftly caught.

Tiny. Everything regressed, everything rolled back to an ancient time, and the one with the neck said, "Amsingelly," with his head lowered and his broad-bladed knife weaving in front of him.

"Umzingeli." Thobela's voice was a deep growl and then softer, much softer: "Mayibuye."

"What fucking language is that, nigger?"

"Xhosa." And she would never forget the look on Mpayipheli's face, the light from the kitchen slanting onto it, and there was something indescribable there, a strange illumination, and then she saw the object he had plucked out of the air—it was the assegai, the one she had bought for him in the curio shop on Long Street.

> This office has been unable to re-establish contact with the two agents and can only assume that the mission was not a success.
>
> Inkululeko has been unable to supply any information as to what transpired at the house that belongs to a member of a local university's department of psychology.
>
> We will continue to pursue the matter but regret to inform you that we have to presume the worst.

"He's not here, ma'am," screamed Captain Tiger Mazibuko over the phone with a raging frustration that made her shudder.

"Tiger . . ."

"The doctor is here and he says if we don't leave within fifteen minutes, we will never see the hard drive again. And a redhead who says she is from the press. Something happened here, there's blood on the walls and the furniture is fucked, but the dog is not here and these fucking people won't cooperate. . . ."

"Tiger." Her voice was stern and sharp, but he ignored her, he was out of his mind. "No," he said. "I am finished. Totally fucking finished. I've already made a cunt of myself, I am finished. I didn't sit for two fucking days in a cell in Botswana for this. I didn't sign up for this. I will not expose my people to this. Enough, it's fucking enough."

She tried calm. "Tiger, slow down. . . ."

"Christ, jissis," he said, and he sounded as if he would cry.

"Tiger, let me speak to the doctor."

"I'm finished," he said.

"Tiger, please."

High on the slopes of the Tygerberg in the heart of a white neighborhood, he climbed out of Van Heerden's car. He was one block away from his destination, because there could be eyes, possibly two sets in a vehicle in front of the door and one or two bodyguards inside.

He moved purposefully to the dark patches on the sidewalk, because a black man here in the small hours was out of place. On the street corner he stopped.

The Cape night opened up for him, a fairy tale of a thousand flickering lights as far as the eye could see, from Milnerton in the west the coastline swept down to the lit carbuncle of the mountain. The city lay there like a slowly beating heart, the arteries curling away to Groote Schuur and Observatory and Rosebank and Newlands, and from there the Flats made a curve east, through Khayalitsha and Guguletu to Kraaifontein and Stellenbosch and Somerset West. Rich and poor, shoulder to shoulder, sleeping now, a resting giant.

He stood, hands by his side. He looked.

Because tomorrow would be his last day here.

Somewhere between three and four in the morning a part of Janina Mentz's consciousness dragged her from a deep sleep. A sense that all was not right—a panicky, suffocating feeling. She opened her eyes with a jerk of her body, and the big black hand was over her mouth and she smelled him, the sweat, saw the blood on the torn clothes, saw the short assegai in his hand, and she made a sound of terror, her body instinctively shrinking away from him.

"My name," he said, "is Thobela Mpayipheli."

He pressed the blade to her throat and said, "We don't want to wake the children."

She moved her head up and down, pulling the sheets instinctively up over her chest where her heart leaped around like a wild animal.

"I am going to take my hand off your mouth. I want only two things from you, and then I will leave. Do you understand?"

Again she nodded.

He lifted his hand, shifting the blade away from her, but still he was too close to her, his eyes watchful.

"Where is Pakamile?"

Her voice would not function, it came hoarsely through her dry mouth that failed to form words. She had to start over. "He is safe."

"Where?"

"I don't know the exact place."

"You lie." And the blade came nearer.

" No . . . Welfare, they took him."

"You will find out."

"I will. I . . . there isn't . . . Tomorrow I'll have to . . ."

"You will find out tomorrow." And her head worked frantically up and down in confirmation, her heart had slowed a fraction.

"Tomorrow morning at eleven you will have Pakamile at the underground parking lot of the waterfront. If he is not there, I will send a copy of the hard drive to every newspaper in the country, understand?"

"Yes." Grateful that her voice flowed more easily now.

"Eleven o'clock. Do not be late."

"I won't."

"I know where you live," he said, and stood up. And then he was gone, the room empty, and she took a deep breath before slowly getting out of bed and going to the bathroom to throw up.

47.

Bodenstein saw the GS stop in the street just before opening, and he knew he knew the rider but recognized him only when Mpayipheli removed the helmet.

"Fuck," said Bodenstein, and went out, amazed.

"Thobela," he said.

"I came to pay you."

"Look at the bloody bike."

"A few scrapes. It's fine."

"A few scrapes?"

"I've come to buy it, Bodenstein."

"You what?"

"And I need another helmet. One of those System Fours that we only have in small sizes left. There are still a couple in the storeroom behind those boxes the exhausts came in."

It was just Van Heerden and him in the parking garage. He stood by the motorbike; Van Heerden sat in his car with the CIA agent's silenced machine pistol.

Allison had chosen not to come.

At one minute to eleven a black man came walking toward him from the shopping center entrance with a long, confident stride, and he knew instinctively that it was Mazibuko—he matched the voice and the rage to the physical before him.

"I will get you, dog," said Mazibuko.

"Where is Pakamile?"

"I'm telling you I will get you. One day when this data is not important anymore, I will find you and I will kill you, as God is my witness, I am going to kill you."

They faced each other and he felt the hate radiating from the man, and the temptation was strong, the fighting blood welled up in him.

"The question you must ask, Mazibuko, is whether there is more in you than just the anger you feel. What is left if that is gone?"

"Fuck you, Xhosa." Spittle sprayed.

"Are they using you? Are they using the rage that is eating you?"

"Shut up, you dog. Come, take me now, you fucking coward." Tiger's body leaned forward, but an invisible thread held him back.

"Ask yourself: how long until it's no longer useful, before things change. A new administration or a new system or a new era. They are using you, Mazibuko. Like a piece of equipment."

Captain Tiger Mazibuko cracked at that moment, his hand went to the bulky bulge under his jacket and it was only the sharp voice of Janina Mentz that made him waver a moment, an authoritarian cry of his nickname, and he stood, torn between two alternatives, his eyes wild, his body a hair trigger, his fingers on the butt of the gun, and then Mpayipheli said quietly: "I am not alone, Tiger. You are dead before you can point that thing."

"Tiger," Janina called again.

Like a man on high wire, he struggled with balance.

"Don't let them use you," said Mpayipheli again.

Tiger dropped his hand, speechless.

"Where is the hard drive?" he heard Mentz's voice from somewhere between the cars.

"Safe," he said. "Where is Pakamile?"

"In the car back here. If you want the child, you will have to give it to Tiger."

"You don't understand your alternatives."

"That is what you don't understand. The child for the hard drive. Non-negotiable."

"Watch me carefully. I am going to take a cell phone out of my pocket. And then I am going to phone a reporter from the *Cape Times*. . . ."

Mazibuko stood before him, watching his every move, but his eyes had changed. The wildness had gone, and there was something else growing.

He took out the cell phone, held it in front of him, and keyed in the number.

"It's ringing," he said.

"Wait!" screamed Mentz.

"I have waited enough," he said.

"I will get the boy."

"Please hold on," he said over the phone, and then to Mentz: "I am waiting."

He saw Mazibuko turn away from him.

"You stay here," he said, but Mazibuko did not hear. He was walking toward the exit, and Thobela saw something in the set of the shoulders that he understood.

"You have two choices in life," he said so only he could hear it. "You can be a victim. Or not."

Then he saw Pakamile and the child saw him, and the moment threatened to overcome him completely.

The white Mercedes-Benz stopped at the traffic lights and one of the street hawkers with packs of white plastic clothes hangers and sunshades for cars and little brown teddy bears knocked on the window and the driver let it slide down electronically.

"The hard drive is safe," said the driver, not in his native Zulu tongue but in English. "Not in our possession, but I believe it is absolutely secure."

"I will pass it on," said the hawker.

"Allah Akhbar," said the small man, his delicate fingers relaxed on the steering wheel, and then the light changed to green up ahead and he put the car in gear.

"Allah Akhbar," said the hawker, "God is great," and watched the car drive away.

The driver switched on the radio as the announcer said, "And here is the new one from David Kramer, singing with his new find, Koos Kok, 'The Ballad of the Lonely Motorbike Rider' . . ."

He smiled and ran a finger under the snow-white shirt collar to relieve the pressure a fraction against the small hump.

Reverend Lawrence Mpayipheli was busy searching for the ripest tomatoes and snipping them loose with the pruning shears, the scent of the cut stems full in his nose, the plump firmness of the red fruit under his fingers, when he heard the engine before the door and stood up stiffly from behind the high green bushes.

There were two of them on the motorbike, a big man and a little boy, and he thought, *It can't be,* and he prayed just a short *Lord, please,* aloud, there in the middle of the vegetable garden. He waited for them to take off the hard hats so he could be sure, so he could call his wife in the clear voice that could reverberate across the backyards of Alice like the ringing of a church bell.

ACKNOWLEDGMENTS

As usual, I am indebted to so many people and sources who contributed to this book. I can never thank you enough.

The Afrikaans Language and Culture Society's grant made it possible to take the GS on most of the routes described in the book and do a motorcycle tour of the Kat River valley and research in Grahamstown.

Lisa Ncetani and the long, long list of Xhosa, Zulu, Tswana, Sotho, and Ndebele co-passengers on business flights between Cape Town and Johannesburg, shop attendants, shoeshine men, taxi drivers, and porters: thank you for answering my questions so patiently and helping a white Afrikaner understand a little better.

One of the more unsettling discoveries during the research was how little material is available about the more recent Xhosa lifestyle, culture, and history—especially on the Internet. But Timothy Stapleton's *Maqoma—Xhosa Resistance to Colonial Advance* (Jonathan Ball, 1994) and Noël Mostert's excellent *Frontiers* (Pimlico, 1992) were two indispensable sources.

Dr. Julia C. Wells, historian at the University of Grahamstown, provided insightful information and comments on the history and development of the short stabbing spear, or *assegai*. Muneer Manie helped with the Arabic, and Ronnie Kasrils's book *Armed & Dangerous* (Mayibuye, 1993, 1998) was a similarly rich source of information on Umkhonto we Sizwe and the role of the East Germans and Soviet Russia during the Struggle.

Intriguing and stimulating conversations with the late Reverend Harwood Dixon, who was a missionary in the Eastern Cape for many years, and the enigmatic Professor Dap Louw from the University of the Free State's Psychology Department had a great influence on the characters in the book. Similarly, I am indebted to Stephen Pinker's *How the Mind Works* (W. W. Norton & Company, 1997), John L. Casti's *Paradigms Regained* (Abacus, 2000), Richard Dawkins's *River Out of Eden* (Phoenix, 2001), Desmond Morris's *The Naked Eye* (Ebury Press, 2000), Brian Masters's ever re-readable *The Evil That Men Do* (Black Swan, 1996), and Geoffrey Miller's excellent *The Mating Mind* (Vintage, 2001).

I constantly made use of the Internet archives of *Die Burger, Beeld,* and *Die Volksblad*. Other websites that provided essential information were Kalshnikov (www.kalashnikov.guns.ru), Valery Shilin's Gun Club (www.club.guns.ru), the U.S. Marines (www. hqmc.usmc.mil), Denel (www.denel.co.za),

Heckler & Koch (www.heckler-koch.de), Frikkie Potgieter's rich source on the SADF and SANDF (http://members.tripod.com/samagte/index. html), Frans Nel's Griekwa Afrikaans (www.ugie.co.za), the Intelligence Resource Program (FAS) (www.fas.org), and the Central Intelligence Agency (www.cia.gov).

To my agent in London, Isobel Dixon: thank you for not giving up on finding a U.S. publisher. To my American editor, Judy Clain: thank you for believing and for this incredible opportunity.

And to the world's best copyeditor, Stephen H. Lamont: thank you for that magic blue pencil.

Finally, to my wife, Anita: without your love, support, and faith, this would not have happened.

Deon Meyer
Melkbosstrand
March 2004

ABOUT THE AUTHOR

Deon Meyer is a freelance strategic consultant in Cape Town, South Africa. He started his career as a newspaper reporter and worked at the University of the Free State, in advertising and Internet strategy, before starting his own company in 2000. He lives in Melkbosstrand with his wife, Anita, and their four children. His Afrikaans novels have been translated into English, French, German, Dutch, Italian, Czech, and Bulgarian. He has won the ATKV literary prize twice, the French Le Grand Prix de Littérature Policière in 2003, and has been shortlisted for the Sunday Times Fiction Award and M-Net Literary Award. He is passionate about Mozart, cooking, Free State and Springbok rugby, and BMW motorcycles.

Read on for the first pages of
Deon Meyer's
Blood Safari

"Set mainly in the game preserves of South Africa, Meyer's stellar thriller delivers muscular prose with a hero to match. . . . Lemmer is a true original. . . . Once again, Meyer shows he's a writer not to be missed." —*Publishers Weekly* (starred review)

"The action is as exciting as any reader of thrillers has a right to demand. . . . As Meyer writes, money and poverty and greed do not lie well together. But they make a hell of a thriller."

—*The Guardian* (UK)

PART ONE

I

I swung the sledgehammer in a lazy rhythm. It was Tuesday, 25 December, just past noon. The wall was thick and stubbornly hard. After each dull thump, shards of brick and cement broke off and shot across the plank floor like shrapnel. I felt sweat tracking through the dust on my face and torso. It was an oven in there, despite the open windows.

Between hammer blows I heard the phone ring. I was reluctant to break the rhythm. In this heat it would be hard to get the machine going again. Slowly, I put the long handle down and went through to the sitting room, feeling the shards under my bare feet. The phone's little screen displayed JEANETTE. I wiped a grimy hand on my shorts and picked it up.

'*Jis.*'

'Merry Christmas.' Jeanette Louw's gravelly voice was loaded with inexplicable irony. As ever.

'Thanks. Same to you.'

'Must be good and hot out there . . .'

'Thirty-eight outside.'

In winter she would say, 'Must be nice and cold out there,' with undisguised regret about my choice of residence. 'Loxton,' she said now, as if it were a faux pas. 'You'll just have to sweat it out, then. What do you do for Christmas in those parts?'

'Demolish the wall between the kitchen and the bathroom.'

'You did say the kitchen and the bathroom?'

'That's how they built them in the old days.'

'And that's how you celebrate Christmas. Old rural tradition, huh?' and she barked out a single, loud 'Ha!'

I knew she hadn't phoned to wish me Happy Christmas. 'You've got a job for me.'

'Uh-huh.'

'Tourist?'

'No. Woman from the Cape, actually. She says she was attacked yesterday. She wants you for a week or so, paid the deposit already.'

I thought about the money, which I needed. 'Oh?'

'She's in Hermanus. I'll SMS the address and cell phone number. I'll tell her you're on your way. Call me if you have any problems.'

I met Emma le Roux for the first time in a beach house overlooking the Old Harbour of Hermanus. The house was impressive, three new Tuscan storeys of rich man's playground with a hand-carved wooden front door and a door knocker in the shape of a lion's head.

At a quarter to seven on Christmas night a young man with long curly hair and steel-rimmed spectacles opened the door. He introduced himself as Henk and said they were expecting me. I could see he was curious, though he hid it well. He invited me in and asked me to wait in the sitting room while he called 'Miss le Roux'. A formal man. There were noises from deep in the house—classical music, conversation. The smell of cooking.

He disappeared. I didn't sit down. After six hours' drive through the Karoo in my Isuzu, I preferred to stand. There was a Christmas tree in the room, a big artificial one with plastic pine needles and mock snow. Multicoloured lights blinked. At the top of the tree was an angel with long, blonde hair, wings spread wide like a bird of prey. Behind her the curtains of the big windows were open. The bay was lovely in the late afternoon, the sea calm and still. I stared out at it.

'Mr Lemmer?'

I turned.

She was tiny and slim. Her black hair was cut very short, almost like a man's. Her eyes were large and dark, the tips of her ears slightly pointed. She looked like a nymph from a children's story. She stood for a moment to take me in, the involuntary up-and-down look to measure me against her expectations.

She hid her disappointment well. They usually expect someone bigger, more imposing—not this general average of height and appearance.

She came up to me and put out her hand. 'I'm Emma le Roux.' Her hand was warm.

'Hello.'

'Please sit down.' She gestured at the suite in the sitting room. 'Can I get you something to drink?' Her voice had an unexpected timbre, as if it belonged to a larger woman.

'No thanks.'

I sat down. The movement of her petite body was fluid, as though she were completely comfortable inside it. She sat down opposite me. Tucked up her legs, at home here. I wondered whether it was her place, where the money came from.

'I, ah . . .' She waved a hand. 'This is a first for me, having a bodyguard . . .'

I wasn't sure how to respond. The lights of the Christmas tree flicked their colours over her with monotonous regularity.

'Maybe you could explain how it works,' Emma said without embarrassment. 'In practice, I mean.'

I wanted to say that if you order this service, you ought know how it works. There is no reference manual.

'It's simple really. To protect you I need to know what your movements are every day . . .'

'Of course.'

'And the nature of the threat.'

She nodded. 'Well . . . I'm not exactly sure what the threat is. Some odd things have happened . . . Carel convinced me . . . You'll meet him in a moment; he's used your service before. I . . . there was an attack, yesterday morning . . .'

'On you?'

'Yes. Well, sort of . . . They broke down the door of my house and came in.'

'They?'

'Three men.'

'Were they armed?'

'No. Yes. They, um . . . It happened so fast . . . I . . . I hardly saw them.'

I suppressed the urge to raise my eyebrows.

'I know it sounds . . . peculiar,' she said.

I said nothing.

'It was . . . strange, Mr Lemmer. Sort of . . . surreal.'

I nodded, encouraging her.

She looked at me intently for a moment and then leaned over to switch on a table lamp beside her.

'I have a house in Oranjezicht,' she said.

'So this is not your permanent home?'

'No . . . this is Carel's place. I'm just visiting. For Christmas.'

'I see.'

'Yesterday morning . . . I wanted to finish my work before packing for the weekend . . . My office

. . . I work from home, you see. About half past nine I took a shower . . .'

Her story did not flow at first. She seemed reluctant to relive it. Her sentences were incomplete, hands quiet, her voice a polite, indifferent monotone. She gave more detail than the situation warranted. Perhaps she felt it lent credibility.

After her shower, she said she was dressing in her bedroom, one leg in her jeans, precariously balanced. She heard the garden gate open and through the lace curtain she saw three men move quickly and purposefully through the front garden. Before they disappeared from her field of vision on the way to the front door, she had registered that they were wearing balaclavas. They had blunt objects in their hands.

She was a modern single woman. Aware. She had often considered the possibility of being the victim of a crime and what her emergency response could be if the worst happened. Therefore, she stepped into the other leg of her jeans and hastily pulled them up over her hips. She was half dressed in only underwear and jeans, but the priority was to get to the panic button and be ready to sound the alarm. But not to press it yet, there was still the security gate and the burglar bars. She didn't want the embarrassment of crying wolf.

Her bare feet moved swiftly across the carpet to the panic button on her bedroom wall. She lifted her finger and waited. Her heart thumped in her

throat, but still she was in control. She heard the
squeal of metal stubbornly bending and breaking.
The security door was no longer secure. She pressed
the alarm. It wailed out from the ceiling above and
with the sound came a wave of panic.

Her narration seemed to draw her in and her
hands began to communicate. Her voice developed
a musical tone, the pitch rising.

Emma le Roux ran down the passage to the
kitchen. She was fleetingly aware that burglars and
thieves did not use this method. It fuelled her terror.
In her haste she collided with the wooden back door
with a dull thud. Her hands shook as she pulled back
both bolts and turned the key in the lock. The second
she jerked open the door she heard splintering in the
hall, glass shattering. The front door was breached.
They were in her house.

She took one step outside and stopped. Then
turned back into the kitchen to grab a drying cloth
from the sink. She wanted it to cover herself. Later
she would scold herself for such an irrational act,
but it was instinctive. Another fraction of a second
she hesitated. Should she grab a weapon, a carving
knife? She suppressed that impulse.

She ran into the bright sunlight with the drying
cloth pressed to her breast. The neatly paved backyard
was very small.

She looked at the high concrete wall that was
meant to protect her, keep the world out. It was

now keeping her in. For the first time she screamed 'Help me!' A distress call to neighbours she did not know—this was urban Cape Town, where you kept your distance, pulled up the drawbridge every night, kept yourself to yourself. She could hear them in the house behind her. One shouted something. Her eye caught the black rubbish bin against the concrete wall—a step to safety.

'Help!' she called between the undulating wails of the alarm.

Emma didn't remember how she made it over the wall. But she did, in one or two adrenalin-fuelled movements. The drying cloth stayed behind in the process, so that she landed in her neighbour's yard without it. Her left knee scraped against something. She felt no pain; only later would she notice the little rip in the denim.

'Help me.' Her voice was shrill and desperate. She crossed her arms across her bosom to preserve her decency and ran to the neighbour's back door. 'Help me!'

She heard the dustbin overturn and knew they were close behind. The door opened in front of her and a grizzled man in a red dressing gown with white dots came out. He had a rifle in his hand. Above his eyes the silver eyebrows grew long and dense, making wings across his forehead.

'Help me,' she said with relief in her voice.

The neighbour rested his eyes on her for a second, a grown woman with a boyish figure. Then he raised his eyebrows and his gaze to the wall behind her. He brought the rifle up to his shoulder and pointed it at the wall. She had almost reached him now and looked back. A balaclava appeared for an instant above the concrete.

The neighbour fired. The shot reverberated against the multiple walls around them and the bullet slammed into her house with a clapping sound. For three or four minutes after that she could not hear a thing. She stood close to her neighbour, trembling. He did not look at her. He worked the bolt of his rifle. A casing clinked to the cement, noiselessly to her deafened ears. The neighbour scanned the wall.

'Bastards,' he said as he aimed along the barrel. He swung the rifle horizontally to cover the whole front.

She didn't know how long they stood there. The attackers had gone. Her hearing returned with a rushing sound, then she heard the alarm again. Eventually he slowly lowered the rifle and asked her in a voice full of concern and eastern Europe, 'Are you all right, my darlink?'

She began to cry.